About the Author

Tracy lives with her partner Simon in Surrey and works part-time for her local citizen's advice bureau. Tracy has been writing for a number of years and has had a few short stories published in *My Weekly* magazine. As well as belonging to a local writing group, she enjoys amateur dramatics and can regularly be found dressing up in strange costumes and prancing about the stage pretending to be all manner of odd characters. *The Summer Theatre by the Sea* is Tracy's second novel.

Also by Tracy Corbett:

The Forget-Me-Not Flower Shop

Tracy Corbett

THE SUMMER THEATRE BY THE SEA

avon.

A division of HarperCollins*Publishers*
www.harpercollins.co.uk

Published by AVON
A Division of HarperCollins*Publishers* Ltd
1 London Bridge Street
London SE1 9GF

www.harpercollins.co.uk

First published in Great Britain by
HarperCollins*Publishers* 2018

2

A catalogue copy of this book is available
from the British Library.

ISBN: 978-0-00-829068-9

This novel is entirely a work of fiction. The names,
characters and incidents portrayed in it are the work of the
author's imagination. Any resemblance to actual persons,
living or dead, events or localities is entirely coincidental.

Typeset in Birka by Palimpsest Book Production Limited,
Falkirk, Stirlingshire

Acknowledgements

A few years ago, I auditioned for my local drama group's production of *A Midsummer Night's Dream*. I envisioned myself playing one of the glamourous female leads, like Hermia or Helena. Instead, I was cast as Puck! I was forced to ride a bicycle, perform cartwheels and wear shorts (something I hadn't done since leaving school). As disgruntled as I was, I ended up loving the role, and as such, an idea formed for a story.

Life hasn't always been straightforward, there have been a few bumps along the road, but being involved in amateur dramatics has been a gift, a great stress-reliever, and an amazing way to make wonderful and lifelong friends. So, I'd like to say a huge thank you to everyone involved in The Quince Players Amateur Dramatics Society, your support and friendship mean the world to me.

My family, as always, continue to cheer me on from the side-lines, enjoying seeing my writing career develop and watching my dreams come to fruition. My parents, in particular, proofread my stories and offer unconditional love and encouragement no matter what. I am very grateful, and very lucky to have them.

To my lovely partner, Simon, who constantly checks chart

positions and sends me screenshots throughout the day with captions like 'wow, you're next to Stephen King!' (even though it's a book he wrote ten years ago!).

I'd also like to thank Rosanna Ley for being a fab mentor, friend, and for the skill and wisdom she imparts during our writing holidays in Spain. I can highly recommend them!

To my amazing agent, Tina Betts, for supporting me in my writing journey, and to the wonderful team at Avon, including Rachel, Victoria and Ellie, who are all so encouraging, professional, and just downright lovely people.

Finally, I feel it would be remiss of me not to thank all the volunteers who work tirelessly for the RNLI, putting their lives at risk to save others, and rescuing us mere mortals from peril.

For my other family,
The Quince Players

The Isolde Players present
A Midsummer Night's Dream
by
William Shakespeare

The characters in the play:
Hippolyta (Queen of the Amazons) – Glenda Graham

Hermia (in love with Lysander)
and Peaseblossom – Lauren Saunders

Lysander (loved by Hermia), Philostrate
and Pyramus – Daniel Austin

Demetrius (suitor of Hermia) and Thisbe – Nate Jones

Helena (in love with Demetrius), Snout
and Wall – Paul Naylor

Oberon (King of the Fairies), Egeus
and Snug – Barney Hubble

Titania (Queen of the Fairies) – Sylvia Johns

Puck (servant to Oberon) – Kayleigh Wilson

Nick Bottom (a weaver), Theseus
and Mustardseed – Tony Saunders

Moth and Cobweb (fairies) – Freddie
and Florence Saunders

Directed by Jonathan Myers
Backstage crew – Quentin and Vincent Graham

Chapter 1

Thursday, 5 May

With a certain amount of apprehension, Charlotte Saunders watched her boss adjust the front of his pale-pink tie, his matching silk handkerchief folded into the pocket of his pinstriped suit jacket.

'He said you assaulted him.'

Charlotte felt her indignation rise another notch. 'I did no such thing.' Why was she getting the third degree? It should be Dodgy Roger in here getting it in the neck, not her.

Lawrence raised a knowing eyebrow. It was a trait she'd become familiar with. It usually preceded a right royal bollocking. Fortunately for her, she'd rarely been on the receiving end of one of his rants. She was his protégé; the grad student he'd spotted at an exhibition and taken a chance on. She couldn't believe her luck when he'd offered her a position with his high-flying design company – a position most designers twice her age would kill for – and now it was under threat, all thanks to Dodgy Roger.

'It was hardly assault, Lawrence.' She felt her cheeks colour. 'I tapped him on the forehead with my notebook. He was asleep on the job.' As she'd already told him.

Lawrence reacted with a disappointed tut. 'He also said you called him a moron.'

She cringed. Not exactly her finest moment.

'A poor choice of words, I admit, but I was upset.' Charlotte straightened in her chair, wishing she'd stopped off to buy painkillers on her way over. The pounding in her head was getting worse. She wasn't sure whether it was the same headache as yesterday, or a new one.

When it came to using CAD, SketchUp or Photoshop, she was an expert – all those late nights studying and unpaid internships had culminated in a first-class honours degree in Interior Design. But nowhere amongst space planning and selecting soft furnishings had it covered dealing with Neanderthal workmen who knew they could get away with murder because the boss was family and the young designer they'd been assigned to work with was still trying to prove herself in a highly competitive industry.

Lawrence's other eyebrow joined the one already raised. 'And stupid.'

Well, he was. Who else would paint emulsion over acrylic? 'I may have been a little harsh, but Roger blatantly ignored my instructions. The radiator pipes weren't sunk into the plasterboard and he failed to replace the cracked ceramic Verona basin.'

Lawrence sighed. He got up from behind his large leather-topped desk, flicking away the tiniest smidgeon of dust from the lapel of his jacket. 'That's as may be, but we need to work as a team here at Quality Interiors. Power through such negativity and stop spilling each other's beers.'

She failed to understand his meaning.

He perched on the corner of his desk. 'Bottom line, we can't afford to lose this client or risk damaging the company's reputation by engaging in a lawsuit. The negative publicity would ruin us. And there's no popularity in poverty.'

Was he misquoting *The Wolf of Wall Street*? He must spend his evenings reading *101 Greatest Ever Sales Quotes*. Glancing down, she spotted the button on her suit jacket was undone and quickly fastened it. 'I agree.'

'The client has complained and it's a legitimate complaint. The job doesn't meet the spec. It's over budget and it's late. I need to be seen taking action.' He smiled, the white of his teeth jarring with his sun-baked, all-year-round tan.

Thank goodness, they were on the same page… Crikey, he had her using clichés now. 'Quite rightly.'

'I'm glad you see it that way, Charlie.' He rested his hands in his lap.

She hated it when he shortened her name… although right at that moment she certainly felt like a right 'charlie'.

Noticing her reflection in the glass cabinet, she tucked a wayward dark curl behind her ear, her natural waves defying the straighteners yet again. Not helpful when trying to present a polished exterior. Why was she worrying about her appearance? Focus, woman.

'A company is known by the people it keeps.' He walked over to the cabinet housing his many accolades. 'Short-term pain, long-term gain, as they say. A sacrifice for the good of the firm.' He picked up one of his industry awards and rubbed away a mark before placing it back on the shelf. 'It's not what I want to do, believe me, but my hand has been forced.'

And about time too. Lawrence Falk ran a hugely successful and profitable firm. They had a six-month waiting list for sales visits alone and their work regularly featured in all the top design magazines, so why he allowed such an incompetent man to damage that prestigious reputation, she didn't know. Surely family ties weren't worth that much? They certainly weren't in *her* family. But then she rarely saw her family, so that might be why. Their move to Cornwall seven years earlier, coupled with her long working hours and demanding job, had hampered any attempts to maintain a close relationship. It was something that never ceased to sadden her. But she couldn't think about that right now, she had more important things to worry about. 'I appreciate it's a difficult situation, but I'm sure your sister will understand... eventually.'

Lawrence turned to her. 'What's my sister got to do with this?'

Charlotte mirrored his frown. 'I imagine she won't take kindly to you firing her husband.'

Lawrence held her gaze, his voice as smooth as his perfectly styled hair. 'Who said I was firing Roger?'

A chill of foreboding crept into her shoulders, tightening the muscles around the base of her neck. God, her head hurt. 'Well, you did... didn't you? Someone has to be accountable and all that. I assumed we were talking about Roger?'

Lawrence gave her an insincere smile. 'You know, Charlie, when you assume, you make an "ass" out of "u" and "me".'

She tried to see past the latest cliché and comprehend his meaning. Her fingers fiddled with the button on her jacket. 'Wh... what are you saying?'

He opened his hands, another perfected 'trust me, I'm about to fleece you' gesture. 'This pains me more than it does you, Charlie ...'

She doubted that.

'... but I have to let you go. You're an amazing designer, but this client is too influential to ignore.'

Ringing in her ears delayed the meaning of his words filtering through to her brain. For a moment, she just sat there, stunned. 'But... but why? It wasn't me who messed up. There was nothing wrong with my designs or my surveyor's measurements. This was down to poor workmanship, nothing else.' The walls seemed to be closing in on her. Her dream job was slipping from her clasp.

'You took your eye off the ball.'

She crossed her legs, then uncrossed them, trying to keep her composure. 'I was juggling three jobs, Lawrence. I couldn't be there every second to babysit. And I shouldn't have to.'

He gave a half-hearted nod. 'But at the end of the day, it's your responsibility to ensure the job is delivered on time and to brief. It's your client, your job, your head on the block when it goes tits-up.' Removing a ruler from his drawer, he measured the gaps between his trophies, adjusting any that didn't meet his exacting standards. Standards she'd been drawn to, feeling they matched her own desire for perfection. 'I'm sorry, love, but it's a dog-eat-dog world out there.'

She stood up, no longer able to contain her frustration. 'So, Roger gets away with yet another piss-poor job? No matter what he costs the firm, you let him off... again.' The urge to topple over his trophies was overwhelming, but her brain alerted her to the fact that trashing the boss's office would not strengthen her defence.

Lawrence shrugged. 'Don't be a sore loser, honey. Victory goes to the player who makes the next-to-last mistake. You know that.'

What on earth was he on about? 'Sorry, I don't follow?'

He pointed at her with the ruler. 'You vandalised the shower screen.'

'Hardly *vandalised...*'

'The entire ceiling needs replastering. That was you, right, not Roger?' He asked the question in such a way that it was obvious he already knew the answer.

Technically, it was true: she had slammed the shower-screen door so hard it had shattered, but only because Roger had drilled through a water pipe and then tried to cover it up with gaffer tape. When she'd peeled away the protective covering, water had spurted from the wall, soaking her jacket and skirt. Squealing from the shock of cold water hitting her midriff, she'd slipped backwards, her legs had parted company and the small slit in the back of her skirt had ripped all the way up to her bottom. She'd had to negotiate the Tube journey home with her jacket tied around her middle, trying not to flash her knickers to the other commuters. Talk about humiliating.

Lawrence sighed. 'Look, take some time off. Lie low for a while. Maybe we can look at rehiring you in a few months' time. But for now, I have to let you go. The company can't afford to fight this.' He dropped the ruler in the drawer, closing it with an 'I'm done' thud.

Tears threatened to surface. 'So that's it? You're firing me?' Her voice caught. 'This is so unfair.'

Lawrence opened his office door. 'Life is unfair, honey.'

She had no recollection of driving home. Her head thumped with a rhythm that made it hard to form coherent thoughts. She'd been fired? Sacked? Thrown under the bus so Lawrence could protect his family? It wasn't fair. This wasn't her fault... well, not entirely. Surely Dodgy Roger should be held accountable too? Why should he be allowed to get away with such ineptitude whilst she lost her career, something she'd fought for and worked so hard for all these years, giving up spending time with her friends, her family, just so she could achieve her dream of becoming a designer? What had it all been for?

By the time she'd parked up in the underground car park and made her way to the lift, indignation had switched to fury. She jabbed at the lift button. Lawrence couldn't do this to her. It amounted to unfair dismissal. Ethan would agree with her, he'd support her. Together they would raise a grievance, challenge her dismissal...

So it was something of a shock to walk into the plush apartment in Kingston upon Thames that she shared with her boyfriend of four years to discover him packing a suitcase.

Confusion was the first emotion to hit. Why was Ethan at home on a Thursday? It wasn't even lunchtime. Did he have a business trip planned? But then why wasn't it logged on their shared calendar? Their iPads were synchronized for real-time updates, so even if it was a last-minute booking, she'd know about it.

The look on Ethan's face gave further cause for alarm. 'What are you doing home?' His tone was surprisingly accusatory.

Part of her wondered if she'd caught him having an affair. Was she about to discover a woman hiding in the wardrobe? No, that wasn't possible... mostly because the wardrobes were disturbingly empty.

Ethan was holding a suit-carrier bag. He threw it onto the bed, as if ridding himself of an incriminating weapon. 'I wasn't expecting you.'

She hadn't been expecting him either.

Her brain was still trying to compute what her eyes were

telling her. Clothes lying on the bed. Wardrobe doors open. Empty hanging rails. Two large suitcases sitting on the floor, their wheels denting the thick pile beneath. If Ethan didn't move them soon, they'd permanently mark the carpet. Her brain was deflecting again.

'I've been fired.' Saying the words aloud made the reality of her situation even more painful. She'd lost her job. No, not lost. It had been *stolen*. She'd been unfairly cut loose, the sacrificial lamb, tossed onto the scrapheap as though she didn't matter. But if she expected Ethan to be as upset as she was, she was woefully disappointed. He looked annoyed. Although, somehow, she sensed this wasn't due to injustice on her behalf. 'Fired?... Why?'

Ignoring his question, she focused on what was happening in the bedroom that she'd shared with her partner for nearly two years, a room with subtle lighting, a king-sized bed and designer fitted wardrobes... which were currently empty.

She looked at Ethan. He wasn't dressed in his usual work suit with Tom Ford shirt and tie, he was wearing jeans and a polo shirt. His dark-blond hair had been cut since this morning – another appointment not recorded on their calendar.

The pounding in her head increased. 'Why are you packing? What's going on here?'

He stepped forward as if about to speak, but something flickered across his face. Irritation? Guilt? Panic?

She waited, but no explanation was forthcoming. 'Ethan...?'

He drew his shoulders back, showing off the full extent of his six-foot height. Even in heels, she didn't reach his chin. He swallowed awkwardly. 'Okay, there's no easy way to say this.'

She took off her suit jacket, suddenly feeling hot. He still hadn't spoken. 'Ethan?'

He folded his arms across his chest. 'I've accepted a job in Paris.'

The words tumbled out in such a rush that she wasn't sure she'd heard him correctly. 'Paris ...?' Nope, her brain still wasn't catching on. Nothing he was saying made any sense. 'I don't understand. What job in Paris?'

He shrugged. 'It all came about quite suddenly.'

'What, since this morning?' It was no good, she had to move the suitcase before it ruined the carpet. Slipping off her Carvela courts, she tilted the suitcase against the bed. Blimey, how much stuff was he taking with him? 'We ate breakfast together. We discussed our plans for the day. You didn't think to mention you were off to Paris?'

Scooping up the clothes on the bed, he dumped them in the second suitcase and zipped it shut. 'I thought it was easier this way.' His tone bordered on belligerent.

'I don't understand.' She smoothed away a crease in her grey skirt. 'How long is this job for? A week? A month?'

He hesitated. 'It's permanent.'

It took a moment before the penny dropped. 'Are... are you leaving me?'

If she expected instant denial and assurances that she was mistaken, followed by a plausible explanation as to why he was taking a job in another country, it didn't come.

His eyes dropped to the floor. Silence descended. It was a good while before he nodded, confirming her fears.

The heat she'd felt just moments before turned to an icy chill. Her skin contracted, sending shivers racing up her arms. 'But... why?'

He rubbed his forehead. 'You can't be that surprised, Charlotte. Things haven't been good for a while.' He rammed the suit-carrier bag into the suitcase.

Hadn't they? This was news to her. 'Things are fine... aren't they?' She walked towards him. He'd crease his suit if he carried on shoving it like that. Why was she thinking about his suit at a time like this? But she knew why. When faced with adversity, her default setting was to try and erase the problem. She cleaned, she straightened, she dusted and scrubbed, anything to maintain the polished exterior and disguise the mess lying beneath. 'I don't understand what you're saying.'

He wheeled one of the cases from the bedroom, refusing to make eye contact. 'I'm not happy.'

She followed him into the open-plan lounge. 'What's not to be happy about?' She gestured to the space around them, the pale dove-grey walls and glass French doors leading onto a balcony overlooking the Thames. 'We've created a beautiful home together. We have good jobs... or at least we did until an hour ago.' She shook her head, still trying to come to terms with her new unemployed status. 'We eat at fancy restaurants. We're planning to visit interesting destinations. We lead the perfect life ...'

'And that's the problem, Charlotte. Everything has to be perfect.' He picked up one of the mauve-silk cushions, strategically placed in the middle of the corner sofa. 'There's no room for spontaneity. Everything has to be planned and logged on that bloody calendar of yours.' He threw the cushion against the wall. 'We've never even visited any of the places on that damned list.'

She flinched. The soft furnishings hadn't come cheap.

Instinctively, she padded across the wooden flooring in her bare feet and picked up the cushion. 'But we lead such busy lives...'

He threw his hands in the air. 'I know, but it's like my whole existence is mapped out for me. I can't take it anymore, you're too exacting, too uptight. Look at you, even *now* you're tidying up.'

She glanced down at the cushion. He had a point. 'I like a tidy house. I thought you did too?'

He shook his head. 'But you take it to the extreme. You won't even let me make you a cup of tea because I don't make it to your specific requirements.'

She hugged the cushion, trying to stem the onset of tears. 'That's hardly a reason to break up.'

He walked towards her, his gait animated. 'The other night you said no to sex on the couch.'

Why on earth was he bringing that up? 'Well, of course I did. It's brand new.'

He ripped the cushion from her hand, making her flinch. 'It's a couch! Who cares?'

The sight of her carefully chosen accessory being tossed away as if it were a used tissue triggered a surge of indignation. She was tired of being blamed for all that was amiss in the world. 'I thought you appreciated having a nice home? I've spent the last two years creating a beautiful living space for us to enjoy as a couple, and now you're saying it's not what you want?'

'It's too ...'

'What, Ethan?' She rounded on him, hurt fuelling her anger. 'Because I don't understand. What is it that's so bad you feel the need to up sticks and leave for Paris?'

He seemed to search for the appropriate word. 'Suffocating.'

The word landed like a blow. Hard. Fast. Zapping the air from her lungs.

Suffocating …?

Ethan looked at her, defiance in his stance. 'There, I said it. I didn't want to, but you forced my hand.' He turned and marched back into the bedroom to fetch the second suitcase. 'Look, I'm sorry, I didn't want it to be like this.'

She followed him. 'I'm sure you didn't, which is why you were planning to sneak out without even telling me. What were you going to do, text me when you arrived in Paris?' She had to jump out of the way when he wheeled the suitcase past, perilously close to her toes. 'I deserve better. At least say it to my face.'

He turned abruptly, causing her to nearly bump into him. 'Fine. I'm leaving you, Charlotte. I don't want to be with you anymore. I've accepted a cash offer on the flat. The buyers will be renting it furnished for three months first. They move in at the end of May.'

She couldn't believe what she was hearing. 'That's only three weeks away.'

For the first time since she'd arrived home he looked contrite, but only fleetingly. 'Sorry, it was too good an opportunity to pass up.'

That was it? 'But surely you can't do that without my consent?'

'Actually, I can.' He went into the hallway and unhooked his jacket from the stand. 'I've owned the place for seven years. The mortgage is in my name. You've lived here for less than two. That doesn't entitle you to claim a beneficial interest. I've checked.'

Her head throbbed, each pulsating thump as painful as the impact of his words. Who was this man? She barely recognised him. They'd shared a life together, a bed, a five-year plan, and all he could say was that she had no legal right to anything? 'But you could've told me you were selling up. You didn't have to spring it on me last minute. Didn't I at least deserve that?'

He slipped his jacket on. 'Probably. I'm being selfish, I know.'

She folded her arms, in an effort to stop herself from shaking. 'You said it.'

For a moment, he looked like he was about to retaliate, but then sighed. 'I thought that's how we worked. We've never been overly mushy or sentimental. Our relationship has been pragmatic and mutually beneficial. I bought the place, you did it up. An agreeable business arrangement.'

'A business arrangement?' Was that really how he saw it? How could he be so cold, so unfeeling?

He shrugged. 'Of sorts, yes.' He placed his hand on her shoulder, the weight of it unwelcome and invasive. 'Come on, you have to admit it was never going to go the distance.' He held her gaze. 'It's better this way.'

Tears were beginning to surface. 'How is it better, Ethan? I've just lost my job and now you're telling me that in three weeks' time I'm going to be homeless.'

He kissed her cheek. 'Think of it as a new start. You'll bounce back, you're made of tough stuff. It's one of the things I've always admired about you.'

Stung, she stepped away from him. 'Wow, just what every girl longs to hear. How much she's *admired*. Lucky me.'

He opened the door. 'Take care, Charlotte. Good luck.' And

with that he was gone, wheeling both suitcases towards the lift.

She'd need more than good luck. In the space of one morning, she'd lost everything. Her career, her boyfriend, her home. She had nothing left.

Slamming the door behind him, she sagged against it, fury giving way to heartbreak as she slumped to the floor. Angry tears ran down her face. She hated crying, it always made her feel so out of control, so untethered, but she couldn't stop the onset. She was hurt, mad, shocked. Her perfect life was gone. Shattered. Wiped out.

What the hell was she going to do?

Chapter 2

Tuesday, 17 May – 14 weeks till curtain-up

Barney Hubble leant against the iron railings and drew in a breath of salty air as he watched a fishing boat drag its nets from the water. There was nothing remarkable about this particular Tuesday evening in May, and yet the sight of the water sparkling under the fading daylight and the rush of waves ebbing and flowing over the sandy beach below, was strangely hypnotic. How different his life was now compared to back in London.

For a start, he walked everywhere. He'd never walked anywhere in London, other than endlessly marching up and down hospital corridors. And he swam most days, relishing the battle of challenging riptides and the exhilaration of diving into freezing-cold water, feeling his skin contract beneath his wetsuit. He was also able to indulge in his passion for music. He didn't earn much from his gigs, but he enjoyed it and it made him feel alive... unlike when he'd worked on the hospital wards and he'd felt permanently dead.

As a kid, he'd learnt both guitar and piano at school before progressing to singing in bands. He'd never ventured into acting before, but last summer his housemates had coerced him into joining the local amateur dramatics group. Despite his initial reluctance, he'd discovered that it was a great way to make new friends and ingrain himself into the local community. Something he hadn't even known he'd wanted, and certainly something he'd never experienced in London.

His parents had never been big fans of hobbies. It was all work, work, work, for Henry and Alexa Hubble. A philosophy they'd tried to instil into their son. Not that he was against hard work, he just wanted more from life. Maybe it was selfish, but specialising was his parents' dream, not his. He'd given med school his all, but nothing had prepared him for the relentless onslaught of being a junior doctor.

So, he'd taken a gap year. But the year was now up and his parents wanted to know when he was returning to his studies. It was a reasonable enough request. Trouble was, he wasn't ready to leave Cornwall. He was still working out what he wanted out of life. He loved living by the sea, he was rediscovering his passion for music, and he was trying out new experiences... like playing Oberon in *A Midsummer Night's Dream*.

The sound of voices rose above the crash of waves below. He turned and watched his mates Nate and Paul cross the quayside to join him.

'I can't believe I'm being forced to wear a dress again.' Nate slung his worn leather jacket over his shoulder. He'd never forgiven the last director for casting him as an ugly sister in Cinderella. For everyone else, the sight of a tattooed, bearded twenty-five-year-old dressed to look like Amy Winehouse was hysterical. Nate had never enjoyed the joke. 'I mean, seriously, which part of me screams love-struck damsel in distress?' He held out his tattooed arms. His biker T-shirt was stained with grease, and his normally spiky brown hair flattened from wearing his crash helmet.

Paul shrugged. 'Comic irony? No one would ever mistake you for a girl, even in a dress. Ergo, visual humour.'

Nate didn't look convinced.

'And anyway, men have often played female roles in the theatre,' Paul said, heading up the hill towards the hall, looking dapper in his blue Ben Sherman suit, complete with narrow tie and pointed shoes. 'Where do you think the word "drag" comes from?'

Nate looked blank.

Paul gave him a questioning look. 'It stands for "dressed as girl". It began during Victorian times to denote a male actor playing the part of a female for comic effect.'

Nate shrugged. 'I never knew that.'

Paul raised an eyebrow. 'Unsurprisingly, I did.'

Unlike his mates, Barney didn't feel as though he had a specific style. He favoured jeans and T-shirts, wore leather flip-flops in the summer, and owned a few Fat Face shirts. Not exactly the height of fashion. He'd often been told he was a dead ringer for Elvis Presley, but he couldn't see it himself. It was probably his Hawaiian heritage on his mother's side. Whatever the reason, he imagined the three of them made an unusual sight when they went out together, especially when Dusty joined in the fun.

'At least I get to play Demetrius as well as Thisbe,' Nate said, as they reached Bridge Street Hall. 'But I'm still not happy about playing a girl.'

Paul patted his shoulder. 'That's life, I'm afraid. Others don't always see us the way we see ourselves.'

Barney picked up on the sombre note in Paul's voice. 'I

thought you were pleased to be offered the part of Helena?'

Paul smiled. 'I'm delighted, dear boy.' But his response lacked conviction.

Barney was prevented from questioning him further by the noise coming from the hall. As they pushed through the wooden doors, they were greeted by the distinctive odour of stale sweat and smelly feet, a constant no matter how thoroughly the place was cleaned.

Most of the village got involved in the productions, even if it was just selling programmes or helping backstage, but getting enough people to audition was always the tricky part, hence the multiple roles. The summer production was performed at the Corineus Theatre, a beautiful outdoor amphitheatre cut into the Cornish coastline. With its stone walls and clifftop views, and a backdrop of crashing waves and swirling winds, it was a stunning location. Performing there was magical.

Barney didn't need to be told that Lauren Saunders had also arrived at the hall. He could tell from Nate's body language: his eyes homed in on her like an FBI tracking device. There was nothing subtle about the way Nate gazed longingly at her. And there was no way Lauren was as oblivious to his interest as she made out. Whether she felt the same remained a mystery. Sometimes Barney sensed she did, other times not so much.

Tonight, she was wearing a grey tunic dress over leggings, her long hair tied loosely at the base of her neck. 'Freddie! Stop pulling Florence's hair!' she yelled, her expression softening as her twin eight-year-olds ran across the hall, their startling red hair and freckles a contrast to their mother's pale skin and dark hair. Both kids were eagerly talking and laughing. They each drew in a big breath, then simultaneously told their mum they'd been cast as fairies in the play.

Unlike Nate, Freddie seemed delighted to be wearing a dress. 'It'll have a skirt made of petals and everything,' he gushed.

Paul ruffled his hair. 'Good for you, mate.'

They were joined by Lauren's dad, who was followed into the hall by his two lady admirers, Sylvia Johns and Glenda Graham. No one could work out whether Tony Saunders was genuinely clueless that both women were into him, or whether he was just stringing them along, enjoying the attention. Either way, it was amusing to watch.

Barney nodded a greeting. 'I'm assuming you got cast in the show, Tony?'

Tony grinned. 'I'm playing Bottom.' His flash of white teeth evoked an audible sigh from both women. At sixty-two, the man would shame most men half his age. His reddish-blond hair hadn't greyed; his stomach hadn't inflated, and his tanned skin hadn't suffered from hours spent at sea. 'Including two other parts. That's a lot of lines for someone my age. You youngsters have it easy.'

Nate didn't look like he agreed.

Despite being a decent actor, Nate wasn't a confident reader, so often tripped up over the text. Unfortunately, the show's director didn't possess the art of tact, and if someone messed up, he wouldn't hesitate to humiliate them in front of the whole room – as Nate had discovered at the audition, when he'd mispronounced his line, 'Tarry, rash *won ton*!' causing the director to bellow, '*Wanton*, not won ton! You are not ordering Chinese food, Mr Jones!'

Jonathan Myers was a typical theatrical type, who wore

glasses on a chain around his neck and sported a terrible comb-over. Appearing at the front of the stage, he asked everyone to take a seat. 'As you all know, my name is Jonathan Myers. I'm a professional, RADA-trained actor' – as he liked to remind everyone on a regular basis – 'and the director of this year's summer extravaganza, William Shakespeare's *A Midsummer Night's Dream*. I think you will agree, this will be the Isolde Players' most adventurous production to date.' He started clapping, encouraging everyone to join in, always eager to receive a round of applause. 'We shall begin this evening with an improvisation, something to warm up our bodies and focus the mind. The single most important attribute an actor should possess is...?' He cupped his ear, encouraging a response.

The group mumbled, 'Focus', only to be met with a shaking of Jonathan's head and an exasperated, 'Louder!' to which everyone dutifully yelled, 'FOCUS!' – except Nate, who yelled, 'Louder!' and then cringed when everyone laughed.

Jonathan waited for calm. 'Thank you. Now, I would like you all to pair up and prepare a short mime entitled "A Fool in the Forest".' Before he'd even added, 'You have ten minutes', Kayleigh Wilson had sprinted the length of the hall and 'bagsied' Barney as her partner, ever hopeful that their brief spell dating would turn into something more meaningful. But there was no spark – not on his side at any rate. She was a nice enough girl, but he wasn't interested in getting serious with her. Trouble was, she had other ideas.

Nate didn't fare much better. He lost out on partnering Lauren to seasoned actor Daniel Austin.

A despondent Nate was stuck with Paul, who, never one to take offence, said, 'It's just as well we're mates,' and slung an arm around his shoulder. 'Your enthusiasm for working with me is quite touching.'

Ignoring Paul's sarcasm, Nate shoved his hands inside his jeans pockets, staring daggers at Daniel. 'He does it to wind me up.'

Paul sighed. 'Then don't let him see it affects you, or he'll keep doing it.'

In contrast, Kayleigh was beaming like she'd won an Oscar, sparkling like the diamanté lettering adorning the backside of her pink velour tracksuit. Kayleigh had big eyes and waist-length brown hair, making her an official 'babe', as Nate would say. But she wasn't Barney's type. Too girly, too annoyingly bouncy, and far too young aged just twenty. He was only twenty-seven himself, but five years studying for a medical degree, followed by two years completing his foundation programme, had induced a level of maturity that defied his age... not that his parents agreed. 'Immature' and 'irresponsible' were accusations regularly thrown in his direction.

Someone's phoned beeped, making Barney flinch.

It'd been over a year since he'd left Queen Mary's Hospital and yet the sound of the dreaded doctor's bleeper still brought him out in a cold sweat. It was every junior doctor's nightmare. Day or night, whether you were sleeping, eating or on the loo, the damned thing would go off and panic would set in. You never knew what awaited you at the other end, and no matter how junior you were, you were expected to know the answer, incurring the wrath of the nurses if you didn't. People often had a preconceived idea that being a doctor was somehow heroic. They wanted to hear stories about saving lives, but would they want the reality? The daily horrors, the tiredness, the uncertainty; being sworn at, spat on and shat on? Feeling so crushed by responsibility that all you wanted to do was curl up in a ball and cry? Probably not. Was it any wonder he was resisting a return?

'I would be grateful if phones could be turned off,' Jonathan said, looking around for the culprit. 'Distractions are not welcome in the sanctuary of creative space.' He gave a theatrical bow. 'Much obliged.'

Barney switched his phone to silent, noticing another text from his mother. The frequency of 'call me' messages was increasing. The topic of conversation never varied. When was he coming home? When would he be resuming his medical training? If the questions never changed, neither would his answers.

Once all the mimes had been critiqued by the director, who'd frowned the whole way through Barney and Kayleigh's very un-Shakespearean offering of a 'pair of clowns camping', he signalled for quiet. 'Please join me now in a vocal warm-up.' He puffed out his chest and walked around the room. 'Breathe in for the count of four...'

There was something surreal about standing in a circle, breathing in unison. Tony looked relaxed, Nate looked focused, Paul's efforts were half-hearted, and Daniel sounded like he was doing yoga, letting out a low hum with each breath – whilst Kayleigh sounded like she was having an orgasm, panting like Meg Ryan in *When Harry Met Sally*.

Jonathan stopped behind Glenda and placed his arms around her middle. 'Feel your diaphragm expand... two... three... and contract... two... three...'

Glenda started giggling. 'Jonathan, I didn't know you had it in you. Naughty man.' She wiggled her bottom and winked at Tony, who was standing opposite her in the circle. Her dirty laughter resulted in a disgruntled look from Sylvia, who pursed her coral-pink lips – the colour as stark as her salmon trousers.

If Glenda favoured the natural look, her neutral linen clothes creased and loose-fitting, Sylvia's style could only be described as an homage to Dolly Parton.

'What's her problem?' Glenda said, pretending she didn't know that Sylvia had the hots for Tony. Tormenting Sylvia seemed to be one of Glenda's favourite pastimes. She was a nice enough woman, who helped out in the community and undertook lollipop-lady duties at the primary school, but there was something hard about her too. Barney couldn't put his finger on what, but he wouldn't want to cross her, put it that way.

'Excellent.' Jonathan clapped his hands, encouraging everyone to breathe normally. 'Now, I'd like everyone to sing the note of C.'

Before he could twang his tuning fork, Kayleigh, Glenda and Sylvia had let rip, their collective sound on a par with a cat Barney had once helped escape from a drain.

Thankfully, Kayleigh ran out of breath and the sound improved. As the seconds ticked by, it became clear that an unspoken competition was taking place between the two rival women. Each getting louder, trying to outdo the other, as their note reached its crescendo.

Sylvia's face grew redder.

Glenda began to physically shake.

Freddie and Florence started laughing, which set Barney off. It was childish, but he couldn't help it. He felt a momentary pang of remorse when Lauren told her kids off for being rude. But he felt better when he heard Paul snort and Tony start chortling.

Finally, Sylvia broke off, almost collapsing from a lack of oxygen. Glenda whooped and punched the air, only curtailing her celebrations when Jonathan glared at her. 'If you two ladies have finished?' He struck his tuning fork against the table.

As with the breathing exercise, some people found it embarrassing, some hard to pitch, others like Freddie and Florence sang out as though they didn't have a care in the world, just as eight-year-olds should do. Florence began twirling on the spot. Freddie followed suit. Barney thought 'what the heck' and joined in, followed by Tony, and then a smiling Lauren. It wasn't long before everyone was twirling, singing horribly off-key and letting go of their inhibitions. Even Paul looked better by the time Florence had made herself so dizzy she'd fallen over and everyone had run over to check she was okay. That was the thing about community. Everyone cared.

Barney glanced at Glenda. Or if they didn't, they at least pretended to.

Jonathan gave up on the warm-up. 'My ears can stand no more.' He minced over to the front of the stage. 'Let us begin reading through the script. But first, I would like to share with you my vision for the show.'

Barney sat down next to Paul, who was busy checking his phone. 'Everything okay, mate? You seem distracted?'

Paul switched his phone to silent. 'My brother's getting married.'

As Jonathan spouted on about 'blue-filtered lighting for the forest scenes', Barney lowered his voice. 'That's a good thing, isn't it? I thought you got on well with Will?'

Paul shrugged. 'I do, of sorts.'

'Then what's the problem?' Barney ignored Jonathan's complicated explanation of swivelling set changes.

Paul chewed on his lower lip. 'Dusty's not invited.' He waited until the director had moved on to the topic of rehearsal schedules. 'Apparently, his fiancée is unwilling to have a drag queen ruin her special day. If I don't agree, then I'm not invited to the wedding either.'

Barney frowned. 'That's a bit harsh. When's the wedding?'

'September.'

'Then you have four months to make them see sense. No way should you miss your brother's wedding over something so narrow-minded.'

'Have you finished, gentlemen?' Barney realised that Jonathan was looking at them. 'I hate to interrupt such an in-depth conversation, but I am trying to direct a masterpiece here.'

Barney squirmed. 'Sorry.'

Jonathan nodded curtly, rubbing a smudge away from his glasses. 'Now, let us start with our lovers plotting to run away together. It will give everyone an opportunity to see how Shakespeare should be done.' He gestured to where Daniel was sitting. 'If you would oblige?'

Never one to turn down a chance to show off, Daniel sprung from his seat, followed by a reluctant-looking Nate, who was also in the scene in his role as Demetrius.

Ignoring Daniel's yoga hums, and attempting to 'focus', Nate addressed Lauren. '"Relent, sweet Hermia; and, Lysander, yield thy crazed title to my certain right."' Nate turned to look at the director. 'I have no idea what any of this bollocks means.'

Daniel smirked. 'That much is obvious.'

Jonathan removed his glasses, pinning Nate with a glare.

'Then I suggest you make full use of the notes section at the back of your script.' He smiled at Daniel. 'As you were.'

Daniel obliged. '"You have her father's love, Demetrius – let me have Hermia's."'

Jonathan lifted his hand. 'Wonderful diction, Daniel.'

Daniel gave a theatrical bow. 'Why thank you, kind sir.' He glanced at Nate. 'One tries.'

Nate mumbled, 'Knob,' under his breath.

Daniel approached Lauren. '"My love is more than his."' He pointed to Nate. '"My fortunes every way as fairly ranked. I am beloved of beauteous Hermia."' He sneered at Nate, who was now looking really pissed off. '"Why is your cheek so pale, my love? How chance the roses there do fade so fast?"' Taking Lauren's hand, he kissed her on the cheek. '"The course of true love never did run smooth."'

His dramatic delivery was met with a round of applause, accompanied by the sound of a phone buzzing.

Nate turned to Barney and mouthed, 'Smug git.'

Barney's laughter faded when he realised that Paul was looking sheepish. 'Sorry, I thought it was my phone vibrating, and I answered it.' As if passing over an explosive device, he handed Barney his mobile. 'It's your mum.'

Bollocks.

As he took the phone and headed outside to face the music, Barney heard Lauren deliver her next line. '"By all the vows that ever men have broke…"'

Oh, the irony… as Paul would say.

Chapter 3

Tuesday, 24 May

Lauren Saunders nudged the wok further onto the gas stove before it toppled off and sent fajita mix flying across the kitchen. The fat hissed, spitting oil over the bank statement she'd received that morning. Perhaps trying to sort out her finances whilst cooking wasn't the most sensible idea, but when else was she supposed to do it? What with school runs, rehearsals, and her shifts at Piskies café, it didn't leave much time for anything else.

There was a loud crash from the lounge. Keeping one eye on the spitting wok, she turned to see what mischief her children were up to. Living in such cramped conditions was an annoyance, but the open-plan living area at least allowed her to supervise while cooking.

Freddie was crouched behind an upturned dining chair ready to ambush his unsuspecting sister. Both children were wearing the ninja outfits Sylvia Johns had bought them for their birthday last month: black jumpsuits trimmed with red piping, and a large belt, complete with silver buckle and plastic sword.

'Mind what you're doing with that thing,' Lauren warned

Freddie, even though her son probably couldn't hear above the blaring TV. The flimsy weapon might bend on impact, but it could still take an eye out.

Her daughter was crawling along the floor like an SAS operative, outwitting her brother, whose focus remained fixed on the bedroom door. When his twin prodded him in the back with her sword, Freddie let out a cry of indignation, and gave chase.

Lauren turned back to the stove. She didn't mind the mayhem. In fact, she loved it. As a kid, she'd constantly been told to calm down and be quiet. She didn't begrudge her parents preferring a peaceful house, but the experience had shaped her views on child-rearing. Rightly or wrongly, her kids were encouraged to be noisy and playful.

Lauren placed the tortillas in the ancient microwave. She noticed a splodge of oil had stained the bottom of the bank statement. That was one way to deal with a minus balance – obscure it from view so she couldn't be reminded that it was another week before payday.

Wafting away the steam rising from the wok, she opened the window above the sink, thumping the frame with her palm to get it to shift. Like everything else in the local-authority flat, the windows were in desperate need of replacing.

On the street below, she spotted a post-office van pull up outside the Co-op. She found herself hesitating in case Nate Jones appeared, allowing herself a moment's wishful thinking. She'd met the local postie soon after moving to Penmullion seven years ago. He'd proved to be a good friend, who frequently looked after the kids for her. They'd regularly hung out when performing in plays together or drinking at Smugglers Inn, but when it became clear he wanted more than she could offer, she backed off. It wasn't as though she could allow anything to happen between them, so why torture herself fantasising? Life might be challenging as a single parent, but adding another adult into the equation would only upset the balance and confuse the children. So, until they were older, relationships were off the table... no matter how tempted she might be.

Moving to Cornwall had been the right decision. The kids loved living by the seaside, and so did she. The local school wasn't overpopulated, and the teachers often took the children outside for lessons. It was a wonderful education for them. The town of Penmullion was quaint and full of history. There was a relaxed sense of well-being about the place, as well as a tight community spirit. They enjoyed early-morning walks along the beach, picnics in the summer, and fresh air all year around. It made an ideal setting to raise a family.

Removing the guacamole and salsa from the fridge, she sniffed the contents. Both were past their sell-by date, and consequently half price, but there were no signs of mould, so hopefully they were safe to consume.

Moving down from London had been good for her too. She'd made friends, joined a drama group, and enjoyed lots of free time with her kids. Penmullion was beautiful, and her dad was on hand to help, so there were lots of positives. There were a few negatives too. Lack of money being one of them.

She hid the bank statement on top of the fridge. Out of sight, out of mind... Who was she trying to kid?

With no professional skills, and a lack of available jobs in Cornwall, money was tight. She loved working at the beach café, but the hours were part-time and the salary was minimum wage. She received a top-up of welfare benefits, but it didn't cover all her rent and household expenses. As a result, over the last year, she'd managed to run up a debt. She was sticking to the repayments, but it was hard going. She didn't mind denying herself stuff, but she hated the thought of Freddie and Florence going without.

Returning to the wok, she gave it a shake, smiling as the kids practised their kung-fu kicks. The sight of them, collapsed in a fit of giggles, rolling around the floor, made every sacrifice worthwhile. They were happy, and they were loved, that was all that mattered.

But it still pained her that she couldn't afford to buy them the new bicycles they so desperately wanted. Maybe one day. But not yet, and certainly not until she'd repaid Glenda Graham the five hundred quid she owed her.

She'd borrowed the money late last year to buy Freddie and Florence their Christmas presents, pay the winter gas bill, and clear the balance on this year's school trip to the Isle of Wight. As per the loan agreement, she'd been dutifully paying Glenda back twenty-five pounds per week. With only a couple more weeks to go, she'd soon be debt-free. Maybe then she could save up for the bikes. In the meantime, it was discounted food, home haircuts, and a pay-as-you-go mobile... which at that moment started to ring.

Lauren couldn't have been more surprised when her sister's name appeared on the display. Calls from Charlotte were a rarity.

Stirring the fajita mix, she pressed 'call accept'. 'Hey there, sis. Everything okay?' Covering the phone with her hand, Lauren shouted through to the lounge, 'Telly off, please. Wash your hands and sit up at the table. Tea's ready.'

'Have I called at a bad time?' Her sister sounded a tad shaky.

Charlotte was normally the epitome of control. She worked for a fancy London design company, earned megabucks, and lived in an apartment with a lift. Who had a lift? Certainly not Lauren. Her flat had a rickety iron staircase that usually reeked of stale wee.

'Not at all,' she lied. 'I'm just dishing up the kids' dinner. How are you? It's been a while.'

Her sister's reply wasn't immediate. 'Things aren't... great.'

Lauren pressed the start button on the microwave. She couldn't remember Charlotte's life being anything other than 'great'... Well, apart from when their mum died, but other than that, Charlotte lived the 'perfect life', as her sister referred to it. Lauren had given up striving for perfection a long time ago. Not that she didn't have a perfect life, it was just very different to her sister's.

She heard Charlotte sniff. 'I'm just going to come out and say it... would it be okay if I came and stayed for a while?'

Lauren removed cutlery from the drawer. Had she heard correctly? In the seven years she'd lived in Cornwall, Charlotte had never once visited. Her sister was always too busy with work, her career as an interior designer taking up all her time, even weekends. Consequently, it'd been up to Lauren and their dad to retain contact, visiting Charlotte in London whenever they could, which wasn't often.

Freddie and Florence came charging into the kitchen, the hoods of their outfits pushed away from their faces. They climbed onto the plastic chairs, making them squeak. 'Please can I have some water?' Florence rubbed her nose with her hand.

Lauren poured water into their plastic *Toy Story* beakers, which were too young for them, but she couldn't afford to replace. 'Use a tissue, please, Florence.' She handed her daughter a roll of kitchen towels, which doubled as napkins in the Saunders house.

Balancing the phone between her shoulder and ear, Lauren dished up the fajita mix, her focus returning to her sister. 'What's brought this on?' She moved Freddie's hand before she burnt him with the wok. 'Don't get me wrong, I'm not complaining. It's just unexpected. Have you finally taken some holiday from work?'

Her sister made an odd sound. 'I wish.' Another pause. 'I've been fired.'

Lauren stopped serving dinner. '*Fired?*'

The sound of her raised voice had both children reverting to ninjas, making gun shapes with their hands and shouting, 'Fired!'

Lauren shushed them. 'Eat your tea, please.' Their grinning faces made her laugh. She'd never make a stern parent. 'Sorry, Charlotte. It's mayhem here. You were saying?'

Her sister sighed. 'I've lost my job... and Ethan and I have broken up.' There was a catch in her voice.

Wow, another shock announcement. Not that Lauren had ever really liked Ethan, even though they'd only met a couple of times, but that was beside the point. 'What happened?'

'One of my commissions went tits-up, and Ethan's accepted a job in Paris.' Charlotte's words came out in a rush. 'I've tried to get temporary work, but my heart's not in it. I think maybe I need some time out to clear my head and work out what to do next. So... can you put me up, please? Just till I get back on my feet.'

Lauren was conflicted. She'd love to see Charlotte, so would the kids, but how would her sister react to life in Penmullion? It was a far cry from London, with its trendy bars, city traders and cutting-edge fashion.

Sensing Lauren's hesitation, Charlotte added, 'I wouldn't ask if I had anywhere else to go, but Ethan's selling the flat.'

Lauren tucked Freddie's chair under the table. 'You're dropping filling down your front,' she told her son. 'Lean forwards so it lands on the plate.' She ruffled his hair.

He gave her a big smile, guacamole stuck in the gap where a front tooth should be.

Lauren wandered through to the lounge and sat down on the worn sofa. As a kid, she'd looked up to Charlotte: she was the sister with aptitude, strength and organisational skills; she'd coped with adversity, solved problems, and looked after them all when their mum had died. But now, as an adult, she was worried that Charlotte would find fault with her choices, and the life she'd made for herself and her kids.

She didn't voice these concerns. Instead, she said, 'Of course you can stay.' Charlotte had never asked Lauren for anything in her entire life. Her sister was a self-made, self-sufficient individual, who relied on no one. Things must be dire if she was asking for help.

Her sister sighed. 'Thanks, Lauren. I really appreciate it. Would Friday be okay?'

Friday? Three days to clean the flat, buy food – which she couldn't afford – and make up a spare bed. It wasn't long enough. 'You'll have to sleep in the lounge, I'm afraid. We don't have a spare room.'

Silence hung in the air. 'That's... fine.' It clearly wasn't. 'Thanks, Lauren. I'll text you when I'm leaving.' Charlotte hung up.

Lauren leant back against the sofa. She could feel a lump beneath her that she hadn't noticed before. A spring was working its way through the fabric. Another annoyance to add to the list.

Gathering her thoughts, she got up and went into the kitchen. 'Finished?'

Her kids nodded in unison. 'Yuu-mm-yy.' Florence licked her fingers.

'Good girl. Here, use this, please.' Lauren handed her a fresh kitchen towel. 'Satsumas or yoghurt for pudding?'

Freddie pulled a face. 'Can't we have ice cream?'

Florence scowled at her brother. 'We can't afford ice cream.'

Shock hit Lauren. 'Why on earth would you think that, Florence?'

''Cause we don't have any money in the bank.' Her daughter looked like a typical eight-year-old, swinging her legs, rubbing her tiny hands on the kitchen towel, but her words made her sound a lot older. 'I saw the thingy.' She pointed to the top of the fridge where the bank statement poked out from under the treat jar – a jar that was currently devoid of sweets.

'Oh, darling. Of course we can afford ice cream,' Lauren lied, wishing for once that her daughter wasn't quite so advanced for her age. 'I just forgot to buy some this week.' She bent down and kissed Flo's cheek. 'Now, I don't want you to worry about what a silly bank statement says. They've probably added it up wrong.'

Florence frowned. 'Like Freddie does in maths class?'

'I do not!' Freddie looked indignant. 'You do.'

'Do not.'

'Do too…'

'Hey, no bickering. Be nice to each other, please. I'll get some ice cream at the weekend.' *When I have some money*. 'Now, what would you like?'

They settled on yoghurt. Lauren busied herself clearing the table and picking at the leftovers, trying to stem the surge of shame. She'd tried so hard to keep her money worries from her kids. In future, she'd ensure paperwork was filed away. But that was the least of her concerns. With her sister visiting, and another mouth to feed, her finances weren't going to improve. And if Charlotte had lost her job, then money would be an issue for her too. Somehow Lauren was going to have to make her income stretch even further.

The kids finished their dessert and ran into the lounge.

'No jumping about until your dinners have gone down,' she called after them.

'Yes, Mummy!' Their sing-song reply made her laugh. Thank God for her kids.

Unlike Charlotte, Lauren had never really known what she wanted to be when she grew up. She'd done okay at school, but she hadn't wanted to continue studying. She was too excited by what the world had to offer... and then their mum had died and the world no longer seemed like such a wonderful place. But she'd never been lazy and, after leaving school, had tried numerous jobs in the hope of finding her calling. She'd worked in a bar, trained as a nursery assistant, and worked as an usher at the local theatre. She'd always loved drama at school, and getting to watch plays for free every night was the best job ever.

At nineteen, she'd met a boy called Joe and thought she was in love. When she fell pregnant, Joe broke things off, making her realise that she wasn't in love, and neither was he. His interest steadily decreased as her belly size increased. Six months after she gave birth, he disappeared from their lives completely. She grew tired of chasing him for child-maintenance payments. His refusal to have any contact with the kids led her to accepting her dad's offer to move to Cornwall with him. She'd hoped that an idyllic setting, and help from her dad, would make life a little easier. And, for the most part, it had.

Lauren ran the hot tap, swishing it around the washing-up liquid bottle, trying to make the meagre contents stretch a bit further.

Moving to Penmullion had definitely been the right decision. She was happy; so were her kids. And even though her dad didn't help out as much as she'd hoped he would, it was still good to be together as a family.

A loud crack from the lounge was followed by a squeal. Lauren dropped the wok into the sink, splashing suds everywhere, and ran into the living-room area. Florence was sitting on the floor, rubbing her arm. Freddie was patting her head, his red cheeks clashing with his hair. 'Sorry, Florence. Didn't mean it.'

Next to them, the ancient carpet-sweeper was bent at an angle, missing its handle.

Brilliant. Her pedantic sister was coming to stay, and Lauren couldn't even vacuum.

Florence looked up, her blue eyes tearful. 'Are you mad, Mummy?'

Lauren shook her head. 'Of course not, sweetie. Accidents happen.'

She sat down next to her daughter.

Freddie jumped onto the sofa and resumed waving his sword about.

Yep, moving to Cornwall had been the right thing to do... even if it did still have its challenges.

Chapter 4

Friday, 27 May

Charlotte battled her way out of the loos and queued up for a hot drink, needing something to calm her agitation. It was only ten a.m., but the motorway service station at Leigh Delamere East was full of people heading down to the coast for the May bank holiday weekend. She hadn't realised quite how busy the roads would be. She'd been driving for three hours, and still had another hundred and twenty miles to go. At this rate, it would be dark before she reached her destination.

Collecting her takeaway cup from the counter, she headed outside, trying to remember what her GP had said about focusing on the positives of her situation, instead of dwelling on the negatives – which wasn't easy. The grief she'd felt at leaving her old life behind was indescribable. But, much to her surprise, her visit to the GP had been extremely helpful. Far from dismissing her tearful ramblings, he'd listened patiently and had diagnosed a mild anxiety disorder. At first, she'd been reluctant to accept any failing in her mental health, but as he'd spoken about the impact of stress, and its ability to exacerbate physical pain, she'd realised that denying her condition was foolhardy. He'd said battling to keep things 'just so' was like clinging hold of a stick under water, the effort of not dropping it was so exhausting that, in the end, you'd drown trying to keep afloat. Sometimes you just had to let the stick sink to the bottom and trust that, eventually, it would float back up to the surface and continue its journey down the river. A nice analogy.

Ethan's decision to leave was out of her control, he'd said. As was losing her job. The best thing she could do was stop beating herself up for not being able to control everything, try to relax, and take the opportunity of an impromptu holiday.

The spring weather had been steadily improving all week, so a spell at the seaside might improve her spirits. It would be good to spend some time with her family, and it'd been over a year since she'd seen her niece and nephew, so really, this trip was a blessing... even if it had been forced upon her.

She sipped her latte. It didn't taste great, but it was warm and sweet and gave her energy levels a boost. She managed another few mouthfuls before binning it.

It was hard to believe that, up until a few weeks ago, her life had been going to plan. Her career was flying high, her finances were stable, and the five-year plan for achieving the 'perfect life', which she'd drawn up with Ethan, was on schedule. They'd planned that, within the next two years, they'd move to a town house with a good resale value, and they'd up their pension pots with additional contributions. It wasn't the most dynamic of plans, and perhaps, on reflection, it lacked a certain sense of romance, but it was pragmatic and considered, and it'd been what they'd both wanted. Or at least, what she'd thought they'd both wanted.

Unbuttoning her purple suede jacket, she climbed into her car, gearing herself up for rejoining the M4.

It felt a lot longer than three weeks since Ethan had dropped his bombshell. The initial shock had subsided, but the confusion hadn't. Why hadn't she seen it coming? There must have been signs, clues to suggest Ethan wasn't happy, and yet she'd been oblivious. While she'd been working long hours, carrying out the renovations on the apartment, adhering to their five-year plan, he'd been plotting his relocation to bloody Paris.

How had she got things so wrong?

His words still haunted her, how he'd described their relationship as a 'business arrangement'. What a cruel thing to say, and unfair too. Not everyone was mushy when it came to romance. It didn't mean she wasn't invested, or that she didn't have feelings. Their relationship was built on the merits of a shared life. It was uncomplicated, straightforward, and if she was honest, a little boring at times, but that was only to be expected after four years... right?

She moved into the fast lane, taking the opportunity of a gap in the traffic to put her foot down, blinking away the latest onslaught of tears threatening to surface.

It wasn't just breaking up; she was still smarting over losing her job, and struggling to come to terms with how quickly everything had unravelled. One minute she was employee of the month, the next she was being handed her P45. The only chink of light had come when she'd contacted the government's arbitration service and they'd advised her that she might have a case for unfair dismissal. Determined not to go down without a fight, she'd lodged a claim with the employment tribunal. But until her case was heard, she needed a place to lick her wounds and regroup. And Cornwall was the ideal setting to wait it out.

Previously, the idea of swapping her city life for fish and

chips, and endless caravan sites, hadn't overly appealed. But Cornwall was one of England's finest tourist attractions, unspoilt and breathtakingly rugged, which was why her sister had moved there, along with their father, when the twins were babies. They'd become disillusioned by the frantic pace and congestion of London, and needed to 'step off the treadmill'. Whatever the reason, it was still hard not to feel abandoned. Her entire family had relocated four hundred miles away, leaving her behind. And it'd left a wound. A wound aggravated by the strain of a five-hour drive that hampered her ability to visit. But Lauren and her dad couldn't see that.

Thankfully, for the next forty minutes, the traffic kept moving and she made good progress. Bristol docks came into view, with its vast car park of new vehicles waiting to be shipped abroad, closely followed by the impressive Brunel bridge.

The switch from city to countryside wasn't immediate, despite the enormous 'Welcome to Cornwall' sign. The roads narrowed, the houses shrunk, the air became salty and moist. The earlier mist had burnt away, leaving some semblance of spring-like weather in its wake.

She shifted position, trying to get comfortable and ease the tension in her upper back. She should have removed her jacket when she'd stopped for a comfort break. She twisted her head from side to side, trying to ease the stiffness.

It wasn't long before the road became a single lane. Her satnav – or rather 'Posh Joanna' as she'd named her, due to the fact she sounded uncannily like Joanna Lumley – directed her through numerous towns and villages, each one decreasing in size and signs of civilisation. Posh Joanna estimated her arrival time was still another twenty-nine minutes away. Lauren and her dad really had moved to the sticks.

The narrow road led her through a small market town with a large clock centred in the main square. As she queued at the traffic lights, she studied the sights. The words 'quaint' and 'old-fashioned' sprung to mind. Interior design jobs in London usually involved wealthy clients spending a fortune recreating the period look. Here, they achieved shabby-chic without even trying.

According to her sister's directions, they lived in the next town. 'Ignore your satnav,' Lauren had said. 'Or you'll end up face down in the ford.' Useful to know, but difficult to adhere to, when simultaneously driving and reading scribbled instructions lying on the passenger seat.

Posh Joanna instructed her to 'turn around when possible' – quickly followed by 'turn left and then immediately left'. This latest direction resulted in her coming face-to-face with a tractor. With no space to pass, she turned sharply onto an unmade lane, vaguely aware of the tractor driver waving in her rear-view mirror as she bumped down the track.

Several things gave cause for alarm. There was nowhere to turn around, the hedgerow either side encroached onto the lane and, ahead of her, the road was submerged under water.

'Stay on this road for the next mile,' Posh Joanna said.

'Oh, don't be so daft. How can I stay on this road for a mile? Look at it.' Vaguely aware that Posh Joanna wasn't able to respond, she slowed to a stop.

Killing the engine, she climbed out of the car, mulling over whether this was in fact just a large puddle, and not the ford her sister had warned her about.

'If you're thinking about driving through it, I wouldn't.' The sound of a man's voice was so unexpected that she physically jolted.

The feeling enhanced when she turned around and saw the rather unusual sight of a glamorous woman hugging a tree. Her sparkly dress and blonde beehive hairdo were at odds with her rustic surroundings. She clearly wasn't the owner of the voice... and then Charlotte looked again. The woman wasn't hugging the tree – she was handcuffed to it!

'You couldn't pass me the key, could you, love?'

Okay, not a woman. A man dressed as a woman. Not surreal at all.

Charlotte looked again. Man or woman, she was stunning: her skin luminescent, even beneath make-up; her eyes a startling shade of blue. Her nails were manicured and painted gold, and her figure was lithe and delicate. She was better turned out than Charlotte, who'd always prided herself in maintaining a well-kept exterior.

The woman smiled, her pink lips parting to reveal pearly-white teeth. 'The key?'

Right. The key. Charlotte followed her eyeline. 'Where did you last see it?'

The woman nodded downwards. 'It landed somewhere over there.'

Charlotte looked around. True enough, lying on the edge of the dirt track was a tiny key. She was about to pick it up when her brain alerted her to the potential safety issues of releasing someone in restraints. 'Are you a criminal?'

The woman raised an eyebrow. 'Hardly.'

Charlotte folded her arms across her chest. 'You're handcuffed to a tree.'

'I'm well aware of that.'

'For my own safety, I'd like to know why before releasing you.'

The woman let out a sigh. 'Let's just say, things got a little wild last night. I'm sure you don't want to hear all the intimate details.'

Charlotte picked up the key. 'You're right, I don't.' She made her way over to her. 'Would the person who did this have returned at some point?'

The woman seemed to consider this. 'Difficult to tell. Maybe.' She lifted her hands so Charlotte could access the lock. 'I'm Dusty, by the way.'

Charlotte deliberated whether to engage. 'Dusty' was hardly regular. But she didn't radiate aggression, only vulnerability. 'Charlotte.'

Dusty smiled. 'Nice to meet you. Pardon me for saying, but you have cheekbones to die for.' When Charlotte stopped unlocking, Dusty must have sensed her alarm, because she added, 'No need to panic. I bat for the other team, if you get my drift.'

Charlotte laughed. Satisfied she wasn't about to be attacked, she removed the handcuffs.

'Free at last.' Dusty rubbed her wrists. 'How can I ever thank you?'

'Well, you could direct me to Penmullion. I'm a bit lost.'

'That I can do.' Released from the tree, Dusty circled her arms. 'Reverse back up this lane. When you reach the crossroads, go straight over. You'll see a sign for the town at the bottom of the hill.'

'Thanks.' Charlotte was about to walk away when she added, 'Can I give you a lift somewhere?'

Dusty smiled. 'Kind of you, sweetie, but I'm good.' She kissed her cheek. 'Thank you for rescuing me. You're an angel. Now, if you'll excuse me, I'm in desperate need of a pee.' She disappeared into the hedgerow.

Cornwall was an odd place, Charlotte decided. If it weren't for the silver handcuffs lying on the ground, she might have thought she'd hallucinated the whole thing.

Thirty minutes later, having scraped her car trying to reverse back up the narrow lane, she found the town of Penmullion. The view coming over the hill was delightful. In the distance, she could see the sea, the tops of the white cliffs merging into the clouds above. The sharp descent into the town made driving conditions precarious, so she decided to leave sight-seeing for another time and focus on arriving in one piece.

Posh Joanna sprang back into life, directing her through the town to where her sister lived, announcing excitedly, 'You have reached your destination.' Except there didn't appear to be any houses along Dobbs Road, only shops.

She pulled over and checked the address. She was definitely in the right place. She got out of the car and rolled her shoulders, trying to shift the ache in her back.

According to the sign hanging above the entrance, number fifteen wasn't a residential property but the Co-op supermarket. Lauren must live in the flat above. Not exactly what she'd expected.

It took a while to find the entrance. The door was concealed within a set of giant gates leading to the loading area behind. Things became more surreal when she spotted a sign with an arrow directing her up a wrought-iron staircase. Experiencing an instant flood of panic, she walked around to the back of the building, hoping to see a lift. No such luck. She was going to have to climb the staircase, wasn't she?

The tremors in her legs began long before she took her first step. Her breathing grew shallow, and the dizziness caused black spots to appear in her peripheral vision. The gaps between the steps meant that there was daylight between her and the concrete below. If she'd known where Lauren lived, she might have reconsidered coming to stay. But then she remembered that she had nowhere else to go, and kept climbing, willing herself not to look down, hoping this holiday would prove to be a cure for acrophobia as well as anxiety.

By the time she reached the top, she was shaking. There was a gate, followed by two further steps down onto the rooftop. She looked around. There were large pots filled with flowers, and a table and chairs set up by a swing set. Ahead of her, a green door had the number 15a attached to the front. Trying to slow her breathing, she walked across and knocked on the door. Loud music emanated from inside. After a few minutes of knocking, she gave up and tried phoning Lauren, only to get her voicemail. Her sister probably couldn't hear above the noise.

She tried the door handle, surprised to find it unlocked. When the door swung open, the music hit her with force, exacerbating the throbbing in her head. She stepped inside the small, dark flat. The hallway opened into the lounge-cum-diner. The walls were covered in mock-wooden cladding, the carpet brown and threadbare. A single bulb hung from the ceiling, shining a dim light on the orange and burgundy sofa. It looked like a set from a 1970s sitcom. But it wasn't. It was where her sister lived.

She'd imagined Lauren's life as being like something from *Escape to the Country*, where people moved to chocolate-box cottages with fishponds and surrounding fields... not dirty dishes in the sink, laundry scattered about the place, and a broken blind hanging from its hinges.

And then she heard voices. The sound of running, screaming

and laughter. Her niece appeared first, wearing an electric-blue polyester dress, her long red hair plaited into bunches. Behind her, Freddie danced into the room wearing an equally cheap metallic outfit, his red hair disguised beneath a long white wig. They appeared to be dressed as characters from *Frozen*. Charlotte wasn't sure which was more disturbing: their lack of fire-retardant clothing, or witnessing her nephew dressed as Elsa. Maybe cross-dressing was a requisite of living in Cornwall?

When the music cut off, she was about to alert them to her presence when a man wearing a white sheet jumped out from behind the sofa, making her scream. With her heart thumping erratically in her chest, she rounded on the man. At least, she assumed it was a man. 'Who the hell are you?'

He removed the sheet from his head, revealing a shock of jet-black hair. Definitely a man. He couldn't be more than late twenties. He was also extremely good-looking. But that was beside the point. He'd frightened the life out of her. 'I could ask you the same question.'

She was saved from answering when both kids ran at her. 'Auntie Charlie!'

Amongst hugs and kisses and jumping up and down, she was dragged further into the room. 'Okay, okay, calm down. I'm pleased to see you too.'

The man ran a hand through his static-ridden hair, easing it back into shape. He looked like a big kid: his blue T-shirt tired and worn, his jeans ripped and low-slung.

She forced her gaze away from his shapely arms. 'Where's my sister?' she asked, her tone pricklier than she'd intended, but she was still reeling from being startled.

His face was flushed, no doubt from the exertion of

running. 'She's working at the café. I'm keeping the kids occupied until her shift finishes.'

Florence enveloped Charlotte in a hug, her tiny arms gripping her aunt's waist. 'Do you want to play *Frozen* with us, Auntie Charlie?'

Charlotte patted her niece's head. 'Not just now, Florence. Maybe later.'

The man extended his hand. 'I'm Olaf,' he said, making both kids squeal with laughter.

Charlotte looked at him quizzically. 'Are you trying to be funny?'

He rolled his eyes. 'And failing, obviously.' His hand was still outstretched. 'Barney.'

She accepted his offer of an introduction, ignoring the warmth in his grip. 'Thank you for minding the children, but I'll take it from here.'

He raised an eyebrow. 'I'd prefer to wait until Lauren gets back.'

She felt herself frown. 'And I'd prefer it if you left.' Again, she sounded rude, but she didn't appreciate the way he was checking her out... at least, she was pretty certain she didn't.

He let out a low whistle. 'Are you sure you're Lauren's sister?'

Ignoring what she suspected was an insult, she removed herself from Florence's grasp and unzipped her handbag. 'How much?'

Barney, or whatever his name was, looked puzzled. 'I'm sorry?'

She opened her purse. 'I don't know what the going rate is for childminding.'

He laughed, but it wasn't a humorous sound. 'Are you kidding me?'

Charlotte rubbed her temple. God, her head hurt. She should have stopped off to buy more painkillers. 'Do I look like someone who kids?'

He shoved his bare feet into a pair of flip-flops. 'Nope, can't say that you do.'

She caught a glimpse of Calvin Klein boxers when he hoisted up his jeans.

He beckoned the kids over and gave them a hug. 'See you soon, trouble-twins.'

'Not if we see you first, Hubble-trouble,' the children chorused in unison.

Charlotte couldn't follow what they were saying. Were they speaking Cornish?

Amongst laughter and play-fighting, the children waved him off, his popularity evident. Hers, she suspected, was still in doubt.

When he was gone, she moved to unbutton her jacket... only to discover it was already unbuttoned. When had she done that?

Straightening her shoulders, she mentally ticked off all the jobs that needed doing in the flat. 'Good, well, now he's gone, why don't we tidy up ready for when Mummy gets home?'

Both children swivelled to look at her, their mouths open, their foreheads creasing into frowns like something from *The Exorcist*.

What had she said...?

Chapter 5

Monday, 30 May

Days like today reminded Barney why he was resisting a return to London. Penmullion beach was busy with visitors enjoying the spring bank holiday. The sun had been growing steadily hotter all day, not scorching, but warm enough to encourage holidaymakers onto the beach. A few brave souls were in the water. Some walked their dogs. Others hired out boats. Most were gathered near Piskies café at the far end of the cove, enjoying the view.

When the last of the fish surfboards were returned to the rental kiosk, he closed up for the afternoon, hoping to enjoy one last surf before the tide turned. Attaching his leg rope, he picked up his longboard and jogged down to the water. The wind had picked up, swirling gusts across the water, creating top waves. Ideal conditions for a battle with nature.

Despite spending most of the day in the water, the sting of the cold still shocked his skin as it seeped under his wetsuit. Positioning himself on his board, he paddled out to sea. This was why he loved Cornwall. With the wind whipping against his face, and the splash of the water licking his feet, he could forget his troubles and just feel.

Not that he had many troubles. For the most part, he was happy, satisfied to live each day as it came, in control of his destiny... well, almost. There was still the issue of his career, which was currently on pause, but other than that, he enjoyed a carefree existence.

Barney angled his board towards the beach, waiting for the next wave. From this distance, he could see the RNLI boat station next to the surf kiosk, and Piskies café. Across the other side of the cove, the cliffs rose upwards past Smugglers Inn to where Morholt Castle and the Corineus Theatre jutted out against the skyline. He never grew tired of the view.

As a wave approached, he pushed up using his hands, and then leapt to a standing position. Bending his knees, he lifted his arms, trying to maintain his balance as he rode the wave. It was exhilarating.

He'd fallen in love with surfing aged seven, whilst holidaying in Hawaii and visiting his mother's family. But it was only when he'd moved to Cornwall that he'd been able to master the art.

Surfing wasn't possible in East Dulwich where he'd grown up, but thanks to Grandma Maggie, he'd enjoyed many other hobbies. He was naturally good at studying, so, for the most part, he'd met his parents' high academic expectations, which allowed them to ignore his other more creative desires such as music. His parents hadn't always approved of his gran's preference for fun rather than study, but they also knew that without her help they would have had to pay for childcare, so they indulged her more relaxed style of co-parenting.

His upbringing hadn't been unhappy by any means. His parents adored him – a little too much at times – but spending his days on the beach felt far more rewarding than stitching up a head wound ever had... which didn't bode well for a future in medicine.

The wave died beneath him, tossing him into the sea. The familiar rushing sound of water filled his ears as he was dragged under. He gave in to the momentum, waiting until the wave fizzled out so he could kick his way back up to the surface.

Satisfied that he'd caught the last of the decent breaks, he paddled back to shore and carried his board up the beach to the kiosk. The best of the day's sunshine had faded, but there were still a few patrons outside the café, enjoying the late-afternoon glow. Among them was Lauren's sister, sitting on a small section of beach, staring out to sea. Talk about a fish out of water. As he neared, he could see she was wearing dark, tailored jeans, a white shirt and a tan-coloured leather jacket. Her handbag was tucked next to her as though she feared someone might nick it. She looked as stiff as his surfboard.

She was quite a contrast to Lauren, who appeared from the café at that moment, carrying a tray of drinks, her hoodie tied around her middle, her sunglasses pushed onto her head. The sisters had the same slight frame, the same brown eyes and the same dark hair, but whereas Lauren wore hers long, Charlotte's barely touched her shoulders. She kept tucking it behind her ears as if trying to keep it neat. No chance: the wind was too unruly. Her curls danced about her face as if taunting her. If Lauren was carefree, enjoyed a beer and a laugh, and loved life by the sea, then her sister was the polar opposite. All buttoned-up and rigid. Still, he shouldn't judge. She might be allergic to sand, or something.

Their brief encounter last Friday hadn't gone well, but it wasn't fair to judge a person based on one prickly exchange.

After all, he'd taken her by surprise. Jumped out on her. No wonder she'd reacted badly. He needed to try again. He'd head over there and properly introduce himself.

As he struggled out of his wetsuit, changed into cut-off jeans, and shook the sand from his 'I love a Hawaiian honey' T-shirt, his phoned pinged. Kayleigh. She wanted to hook up. Christ, she really wasn't taking the hint, was she? Since going on a few dates with her earlier in the year, he'd been struggling to shake her off, and it was now May. He'd tried being polite, mentioning their 'friendship' whenever he could, in the hope she'd get the message, but it hadn't deterred her. He wanted to ignore her, but that didn't seem very gentlemanly, so he sent a '*sorry can't, I'm busy*' reply in the hope she'd take the hint and leave him alone. It wasn't the best plan, but he was at a loss as to what else to try.

Bending forwards, he shook the wet from his hair.

History had shown he wasn't very good when it came to ending things with women. He'd had a couple of relationships while at university, but differing life goals and a lack of free time meant pursuing them was pointless. He'd been accused of being 'commitment-phobic' and 'immature' on both occasions. He hadn't disagreed. Was it such a crime to want something casual and relaxed? Medicine had been depressing enough. He hadn't needed the drama of girlfriends wanting to know 'where the relationship was going' all the time. He'd just wanted a bit of fun.

But since moving to Cornwall, his aversion to relationships had been softening. His previous life had been all about work, and his social life – well, what he'd had of one – had been spent playing at being a 'grown-up'. He was an only child, so his experience of hanging out with 'little people' was limited.

But as the surf kiosk was situated next to Piskies café, he often kept an eye on Lauren's kids after school. At first, he'd done it out of friendship – he liked Lauren, she was a good mate – but then he found himself anticipating their arrival, checking how long it would be before school broke up and they'd run onto the beach and jump on him. It'd taken a while to realise what he was feeling. When he did, he couldn't have been more shocked. He wanted a family. And no one could have been more surprised than him.

Shoving his flip-flops into his backpack, he jogged across the sand to the café.

Spotting him approach, Lauren waved, her smile welcoming. They'd initially met via the drama group, but their friendship had developed when he'd started working at the kiosk. She was a good laugh, easy to get along with, popular with the customers. Hopefully her sister would turn out to be just as affable.

But things didn't get off to the best start when he inadvertently kicked sand over her handbag. She brushed frantically at the leather, trying to clean it. Anyone would think he'd set fire to it. He waited until she looked up.

'Hi. Charlie, isn't it? We met at Lauren's last Friday. I was the one under the sheet.' He hoped his laughter might break the ice.

It didn't.

She stopped shaking her bag. 'My name is Charlotte.' The bite in her words matched the venom in her glare. 'I don't like my name being shortened.'

Okay, strike two. He tried again. 'Well, it's nice to meet you, Charlotte.' Her lack of warmth failed to detract from the appeal of her beautiful chocolate-coloured eyes. 'I'm Barney.'

She glanced away, as though looking at him caused her discomfort. 'I remember who you are.'

Christ, this was going well. 'Lauren tells me you've come to stay for the summer?'

Shielding her eyes from the sun, she blinked up at him. 'I'm planning to return to London as soon as possible.'

Another snub. He was running out of pleasantries, but decided to give it one last shot. Not that he was swayed by her good looks, or anything. 'Lauren says you've lost your job. Bummer.'

She stiffened even more, if that was possible, her glare switching to where her sister was currently serving ice creams to a family of hikers across the other side of the café. 'Did she now?'

'She didn't go into details,' he added, worrying he'd just unwittingly dropped his friend in the shit.

'Yes, well, it's a temporary situation. I'm sure it'll be sorted soon.'

For a moment, he thought he caught her checking him out. He felt stupidly flattered when her eyes dipped to his chest, a faint hint of colour forming on her cheeks. Things might be looking up – and then he realised he'd forgotten to put his T-shirt on. *Shit*. He was standing in front of her bare-chested. No wonder she was staring. She probably thought he was a right poser.

'And what do you do for a living, Mr...?'

He dragged his T-shirt over his head. 'Hubble.'

Her expression switched to confusion. 'Your surname is Hubble?'

He nodded, flattening down his T-shirt. 'Yep.'

'Your name is Barney Hubble?' A frown formed on her

perfectly smooth forehead. 'Are you deliberately toying with me?'

He sighed. 'No, that is actually my name.' He shrugged, used to disbelieving looks and piss-taking about his name. 'What can I say? My parents never watched *The Flintstones*.'

She smiled, which might have eroded all her other flaws if he wasn't the subject of her mirth. So, she found his name funny, huh? She hadn't found it so amusing when he'd called her Charlie, had she? Talk about double standards.

Making no effort to hide her amusement, she brushed a speck of sand from her pristine jeans. 'You were about to tell me what you do for a living?'

His enthusiasm for winning her over was starting to wane; he really didn't like being laughed at. Not by a woman. Not by a hot woman. 'A bit of this and a bit of that.'

He needn't have worried. His answer killed her smile quicker than if he'd said, 'I eat people for a living,' which told him everything he needed to know about her. Who the hell was she to criticise what he did for a living? She might be beautiful, but looks didn't count for much if she was a judgemental snob.

If Lauren hadn't appeared next to him at that moment, he might have walked off.

'I see you've met my sister.' Lauren gave him a hug, and then turned to Charlotte. 'Barney's a really good friend of mine. He's an amazing singer. You'll have to come and watch his gig tonight at Smugglers Inn.'

Charlotte didn't look impressed. 'I have plans. Maybe another time.'

Lauren gave her sister a pointed look. 'Surely nothing that can't wait. It'll be good for you to meet a few of the locals.'

Charlotte looked as if that was the last thing she wanted to do. 'I need to do some research. If my claim for unfair dismissal is unsuccessful, then I'll need alternative employment. And I can't expect to find a proper job if I sit around socialising all the time.'

Her emphasis on the word 'proper' sent flares of annoyance shooting up his spine. Sod her. He didn't need another person in his life telling him to grow up and get a proper job. He had enough of that from his parents.

It was time to leave before he said something he'd regret. 'Well, this has been fun.' He made no attempt to hide the sarcasm in his voice. 'I hope you enjoy your holiday. Good luck with the job hunting.'

Poor Lauren squirmed next to him, making him feel a tad guilty. It wasn't her fault that her sister was colder than ice. He blew her a kiss. 'See you later, Lauren.'

Leaving the beach, he fought against the shame battling inside him. It wasn't important. Charlotte Saunders was of no consequence to him. He shouldn't feel so rattled by her blatant dismissal of him. Everyone else in Penmullion thought he was a cool guy. Someone who'd got life sorted. They envied him. It shouldn't bother him that one highly strung, opinionated, gorgeous woman looked down her nose at him... but it did... and it really pissed him off.

Chapter 6

Thursday, 2 June

Charlotte had only been in Cornwall for six days, but she was already tearing her hair out – literally, the moisture in the air making it curl, no matter how often she straightened it. Her headaches weren't easing, and she was fidgety and restless. She guessed her body had become acclimatised to working long stressful days and was unaccustomed to lazing about doing nothing.

The employment tribunal had advised that there was a backlog of claims, so it might be a few weeks before a date was set. She had planned to look for another job while she was here, but then realised that the likelihood of being offered another position, when she'd been fired from the previous one, was remote. She was better off waiting until the outcome of her claim was decided before contemplating her next move. Until then, she needed to find something to occupy her time.

Her attempts to keep busy by helping Lauren around the flat hadn't worked out either. When her offer to contribute to the rent had been refused, she'd figured that she needed to earn her keep by doing chores instead. It didn't take a genius to work out that Lauren was struggling financially, but her sister was determined to manage on her own and didn't want to be seen as a 'charity case'. Charlotte hadn't meant to cause offence, so by way of an apology, she'd blitzed the flat from top to bottom, scrubbing the bathroom until her arms ached and removing all the mould from the discoloured grout. She'd mended the blind, sorted the children's books into alphabetical order, and boxed up their toys to avoid any unnecessary accidents. But far from appreciating her efforts, Lauren had seemed more annoyed than grateful. It was all very confusing. Especially as it was obvious that Lauren could do with the help.

For the past seven years, Charlotte had foolishly believed that her sister lived an idyllic lifestyle, but she'd discovered the reality was quite different. Lauren worked part-time in a café, relied on benefits, and left her kids with all manner of childminders. But Lauren seemed to like her life, claiming to be happy existing at a slower, less material pace, placing value on free time, socialising with friends, and partaking in hobbies such as amateur dramatics.

Their dad was the same. Charlotte had imagined an emotional reunion, whereby Tony Saunders enveloped his eldest daughter in a bear hug, told her he'd missed her and everything would revert to how things had been before her mum had died. Instead, she'd spent one brief evening with him before he'd had to rush off, something about a fishing boat caught on the nearby rocks. It was all highly depressing. All she'd been able to glean from Lauren was that he lived on a narrowboat, worked for a local fisherman, and spent his free time manning the local RNLI boat station.

The only people that were pleased to see her were Freddie and Florence. She'd quite enjoyed reading them bedtime stories, picking them up from school, and teaching them to bake cupcakes. They were surprisingly good company.

She checked her watch. It wasn't even lunchtime. Lauren was working at the café, and the kids were at school. What was there to do on a Thursday in Penmullion?

She guessed there was only one way to find out.

It wasn't the warmest of days, so she slipped on her navy rain mac over her silk shirt and white pencil skirt. She considered changing her footwear, but decided she wasn't going far, so stuck with her nude courts. It took a lot for her to ditch the heels.

Dobbs Road wasn't in the desirable part of town, so she had to walk down to the main quayside if she wanted anything other than pound shops and budget supermarkets.

The road was extremely steep; the houses either side were cut into the rock face, their driveways at acute angles to the road. Her slow walk turned into a speedy trot as her momentum increased on the downhill slope. Thankfully, the road levelled out before she reached the water's edge, preventing her from landing head first in the sea. Quite apart from the embarrassment that would have caused, her shirt was dry-clean only.

In order to reach the other side of the quay, where most of the boats were moored, she needed to cross the narrow footbridge. Determined not to be defeated by the drop below, she focused on the view ahead, and tried to slow her breathing, as she negotiated the unstable walkway. It wasn't the sturdiest of bridges, with lengths of rope supporting the wooden slats. She tried not to look down, ignoring the sound of splashing water beneath, which evoked memories of falling into a weir when she was a child and nearly drowning.

The sound of a cockerel startled her. She turned to see a huge bird waddling across the bridge. It was making the most godawful noise. Was it normal for random animals to be wandering about? Keen to avoid any contact with the bird, she hurried to the other side.

Her father's boat was moored somewhere along this side of the quay. She hadn't consciously decided to visit, but now she was here, it seemed appropriate to call in and say hello. If nothing else, it would show a willingness to 'bond'. Besides, she was curious to see where he lived.

A long line of narrowboats were moored along the water's edge. She instinctively knew which boat belonged to her dad. The sight of *The Lady Iris* brought a lump to her throat. He'd named his boat after their mum? Emotion rooted her to the spot. She took in the teal paintwork and abundance of potted flowers adorning the upper deck. The side of the boat was decorated with painted, purple irises, her mum's favourite flower. The image allowed her mind to drift back to a happier time before their family had been ripped apart.

She'd enjoyed a happy childhood, with a kind, doting mother, a relaxed, chilled father, and a congenial younger sister. She'd worked hard at school, had a few close friends, and spent her time listening to music and drawing pictures of grand houses with swimming pools and vast landscaped gardens. She hadn't been a big socialiser, but she'd started to come out of her shell at university, loving her design course and finding a few kindred spirits. A few months into the course, her mother was diagnosed with breast cancer. Iris Saunders died before Charlotte had finished her first year.

Her mother's death affected them all differently. Lauren became rebellious, dropping out of school, entangling herself with a boy who ditched her the moment she fell pregnant. Her father sank into a deep depression, gave up work, and lost any desire for life. It'd been left to Charlotte to hold the family together, picking up responsibility for paying the bills, buying food, and keeping Lauren on the straight and narrow. She'd encouraged her father to seek counselling, and urged him to take the medication he'd been prescribed. Unable to deal with her own grief, she'd focused on her career, knowing it was the only way to provide security and structure for her family. She'd thrown herself into study, spending long hours training, trying to impress in a tough industry. She lost touch with friends and rarely had any free time, but it was necessary if she was to help them all recover from the loss of their mother... and then Lauren and her dad had moved away. After all she'd done, all the sacrifices she'd made, they left without even a thank you for having looked after them.

She dug out a tissue. She hated crying.

Over the years, she'd tried to make peace with her feelings. Her dad had been so consumed by grief that he wasn't in any fit state to realise what his daughter had given up. It wasn't his fault. Depression was a crippling illness, she understood that. And Lauren was barely sixteen when their mum had died, she couldn't be expected to realise the impact it had had on her older sister.

But life had moved on. Her dad had recovered, and he and Lauren had built a life for themselves in Cornwall... A life that didn't include her.

Recovering from the shock of seeing the boat's name, she made her way onto the gangplank, or whatever it was called. It certainly felt like she was walking to her doom. *Don't look down*, her brain instructed – which was challenging when the wood beneath creaked, threatening to tip her into the murky water.

A woman appeared from inside the cabin, her bright-orange jumper and yellow capri-style trousers blending with the hanging baskets tied to the rigging. 'Well, hello there,' she called, sounding surprised, but not unfriendly. 'No prizes for guessing who you are. You're the spitting image of your sister.' She offered Charlotte her hand. 'Mind the step, there you go. Much as I admire your shoes, I'm not sure they're suitable for wearing on a boat.'

Charlotte stepped onto the deck, relieved to be on solid footing. 'You may have a point.'

The woman's big laugh drew attention from passers-by. 'I'm Sylvia Johns, a friend of Tony's. And you must be Charlotte. Your dad's told me so much about you. Goodness me, he's proud of you.'

A lump formed in Charlotte's throat. Her dad was proud of her?

'Fancy that, a fashion designer in London. How thrilling! He follows your career, you know. Always keen to know who you're working for.'

Her good feeling disappeared. 'Interior designer, not fashion.' So much for her dad following her career. 'And unfortunately, I've recently been fired.'

The woman stilled. 'Oh, dear.' She quickly rallied. 'A blip, I'm sure. Now come inside, let's make you feel welcome. *Tony!*'

Her dad appeared, his expression affable and relaxed. He'd aged a bit. He wasn't quite as jovial as he used to be, but other than that, he hadn't changed. He was wearing galoshes, a knitted hat, wellington boots and a yellow jacket. She recoiled when he hugged her, the stench radiating off him was toxic. 'Dad, you stink.'

He laughed. 'I've been working on the fishing vessels.'

She pushed him away. 'I don't want that stench on my clothes. This shirt cost a fortune.'

'Relax, it's only fish.' His laughter faded, but he released her. 'It's good to see you.'

She swallowed awkwardly, aware she was being prickly again. 'I thought I'd come and check out where you lived.'

'That's nice.' He shrugged off his jacket.

'Make yourself comfortable, lovey. I'll put the kettle on.' Sylvia gestured to a chair. 'Your dad loves having visitors, don't you, Tony?' She didn't wait for a reply. 'Lauren and the kids are often over here. They adore going out on little trips, sleeping in the bunkers, isn't that right, Tony?'

Her dad kicked off his wellington boots and pulled up a wicker chair. 'How are you enjoying Cornwall?' he asked Charlotte, seemingly unfazed by Sylvia's incessant chatter.

'It's okay.' Charlotte didn't feel it was appropriate to tell him she was struggling to unwind, she was getting on her sister's nerves, or that she'd recently been diagnosed with stress-related anxiety. 'Penmullion is beautiful.'

Sylvia appeared from the galley with a tea tray. 'Isn't it just? I know they say Kent is the garden of England, but I think it should be Cornwall.'

Charlotte watched Sylvia trying to balance the tray. Was this woman her dad's girlfriend? If she was, she was very different to their mum.

Sylvia handed her a cup of weak tea in a floral china cup.

'Thank you.' Charlotte managed one sip before looking around for somewhere to put it down. The cabin was small, the padded bench seats along either side took up most of the room.

When Sylvia's back was turned, her dad leant across and took her cup, discreetly pouring the contents into the plant pot sitting on the floor. 'Lovely woman. Makes a terrible cup of tea,' he whispered, making her smile for what felt like the first time in ages. God, she'd missed her dad.

Her smile soon faded when Sylvia turned and saw her empty cup. 'Goodness me, you were thirsty. You're just like your dad, he knocks them back in no time too.'

The sound of her dad chuckling made up for the trauma of being forced to drink another cup of Sylvia's tea. But as she watched her cup being refilled, the sound of an alarm went off, making her jump.

Her dad was up before she knew what was happening. 'Sorry, love. Got to go.' He gave her shoulder a quick squeeze. 'We'll catch up soon.' He was out the door before she could find her voice.

Charlotte watched him sprint down the jetty. 'What's going on?'

Sylvia picked up the discarded hat he'd thrown to the floor. 'Your dad volunteers for the RNLI. When the alarm goes off, he has to respond. He's the senior helm, you know.'

No, she didn't know. All she knew was that he volunteered there. She'd assumed he had a desk role; he'd always worked in an office when he'd lived in London. She was starting to realise she knew very little about her family's new lives in Cornwall.

'Only the other night he rescued a Polish family whose boat had sunk. None of the family could swim, and they weren't wearing life jackets. It was on the local news and everything.'

Her dad running off to save lives was another surprising development. 'Will he be gone long?'

'Could be hours. Looks like it's just you and me.' Sylvia offered her a custard cream. 'Now, tell me all about yourself, and don't leave anything out. I want to hear all the details.'

As much as Charlotte didn't want to spill her life story, an excuse to refuse didn't surface quick enough. Resigning herself to the inevitable, she spent the next twenty minutes engaged in polite chit-chat before she could make her excuses and leave.

Extricating herself from Sylvia's tight hug, she thanked the woman for her hospitality and made her escape, almost running across the footbridge to the safety of the quayside.

It was strange, but talking about Ethan hadn't upset her anywhere near as much as it should. Why was that? she wondered. After all, he'd been a big part of her life for a long time. She should miss him. She should be crying herself to sleep every night, wishing he would call, raging at the way he'd treated her, but she wasn't. She just felt a low level of annoyance at the way her life had been upended. Realising she hadn't been as invested in the relationship as she'd imagined, was both alarming and depressing. How had she got things so wrong?

Not wanting to return to the flat just yet, she decided to explore Penmullion.

Her feet were sore from walking on cobbled stones in heels, but the views across the cove made up for it. The sand below was pale gold, a contrast to the white cliffs and deep blue of the sea. To her right, she could see the café where her sister worked, and the RNLI boat station. Shielding her eyes, she looked across the water, wondering if she'd spot her dad rescuing whoever it was who'd got into trouble, but she couldn't see anything.

As she followed the line of the horizon, the cliff incline rose sharply. There appeared to be some kind of castle in the distance, the stone pillars jutting out from the rock face. A wave crashed below, sending spray up and over the railing. She moved away, unwilling to ruin her mac with salt water.

Behind her, a row of tiny shops lined the quayside, from art galleries advertising works by local artists, to cafés specialising in Cornish pasties. They were quaint and inviting, painted in a series of pastel colours. She walked past the Coddy Shack fish and chip shop, and Candy Cravers sweet shop, admiring the window displays.

She came across a delightful little shop, painted sunflower yellow, with a white bay window. The sign above the overhang said, 'Dusty's Boutique'. The mannequin in the window was dressed in a red wrap dress, the hem cut at an angle, the layered two-tone fabric striking and unusual. The door was open, inviting her to browse, so she decided to venture inside.

The interior looked like something from Carnaby Street rather than a picturesque town in Cornwall. There were photos on the walls of 1960s singers dressed in Mod outfits and Mary Quant monochrome mini dresses. The items on display were colour-coordinated and arranged to show them at their best. It was a real gem. She'd just unhooked an A-line skirt from the rail when a man appeared from the rear of the shop.

'Good afternoon. Welcome to Dusty's. Please feel free to browse.' He was a good-looking man with almost white-blond hair and startling blue eyes. He reminded her of someone, but she couldn't think who. Probably one of her clients back in London. He was dressed in a narrow, fitted grey suit with a thin paisley tie and winkle-picker shoes.

She smiled, appreciating his sense of style. 'It's a beautiful shop. I adore the design.'

'Well, aren't you a love. Coming from someone with such sophisticated dress sense, I'll take that as a real compliment. Is that Karen Millen you're wearing?' He touched the fabric of her mac.

She nodded. 'The skirt is Ted Baker.' Realising one of her shirt buttons was undone, she quickly fastened it.

He pushed the rim of his thick black glasses up his nose. 'Paul Naylor. This is my boutique,' he said, extending his hand. 'Delighted to make your acquaintance.'

'Charlotte Saunders.' She shook his hand, thinking how nice it was to meet a smart, intelligent, well-mannered man. A man who also had the added bonus of being in proper employment. Not like Barney Rubble or Hubble, whatever his name was. Laziness and a lack of focus were not attractive qualities. She wouldn't be entertaining *his* company anytime soon... no matter how good-looking he was. And boy, was he handsome. But he knew it. Only a cocky man would introduce himself shirtless, flaunting his hairless chest, tanned skin and defined muscles like he was some kind of exotic male dancer. Talk about brazen.

The owner of the boutique was studying her. 'Are you here on holiday?'

She dragged her thoughts away from unsuitable men. 'Kind of. I'm visiting family.'

'I'm guessing you're related to Tony and Lauren Saunders?'

She nodded. 'Father and sister.'

He smiled. 'Delightful people. Love them to bits.'

Charlotte wondered if anyone ever referred to her as delightful? Probably not, which was quite depressing, really. Still, it wasn't like she didn't know that she could be uptight. It was nice that someone thought so highly of her family, though. 'Do you know them well?'

He nodded. 'We're part of the same drama group. I'm rehearsing a play with them at the moment.' He gestured to a poster on the wall. 'If you're still in Penmullion in August, you'll have to come along and watch. I'm playing the part of Helena.'

Charlotte had studied the play for A-Level English, so knew a tall gangly female was needed for the part. He fitted the bill perfectly.

She glanced at the poster. 'I might just do that.'

'If you're really keen, you could always help out with the production. They're looking for a set designer.'

Intrigued, she went over and read the poster for the Isolde Players' production of *A Midsummer Night's Dream*. The play was a favourite of hers.

Paul joined her by the poster. 'Tempted?'

Was she? She'd never designed for the stage before. It might prove fun. 'Perhaps. I'm an interior designer.'

He looked impressed. 'Then it's a match made in heaven. I think you'd fit rather nicely with our little group.'

She wasn't sure she agreed with him. She'd never found social interaction that easy, but it was nice of him to say so. Perhaps she should offer her services. It would be good to try a new activity, and it might give her something to focus on whilst she awaited the outcome of her ET application.

It wasn't like she had much else to do in Penmullion.

Chapter 7

Wednesday, 8 June

Barney buried his head under the duvet, praying the pounding would stop. Why had he drunk so much last night? He hadn't meant to. He'd been to rehearsal, as he normally did on a Tuesday evening, and then a group of them had gone to Smugglers Inn to enjoy a quick pint. His last recollection was of playing a few songs on his guitar, Nate and Dusty performing 'Islands in the Stream', and avoiding Kayleigh Wilson, who'd wanted to duet with him on 'Empire State of Mind'. He didn't remember much about getting home. He was just grateful he wasn't on an early shift at the kiosk; his head hurt too much to be of use to anyone.

The pounding grew louder, an incessant banging that rattled through his fragile skull. Someone please make it stop. He vaguely became aware of Nate's voice, muffled through the fog of a hangover, standing over the bed shaking his shoulder, saying something about 'the door' and needing to 'throw up'.

A few seconds later, he heard the unmistakable sound of retching coming from the bathroom. As he shifted position, trying to get comfortable, he realised the banging wasn't in his head, it was coming from the front door.

Cursing whoever it was, he rolled out of bed, wearing only his boxers, and padded down the hallway. He remembered at the last moment to dip his head so he didn't smack into the beam above. Concussion wouldn't ease the pounding in his head.

Sliding back the heavy bolt, he opened the wooden door, ready to let rip at whoever it was for waking him up. The sight of his parents standing on the walkway outside rendered him speechless. He had a sudden urge to shut the door and return to bed. He didn't, of course. Mainly because they'd only resume banging.

'We've been standing here for fifteen minutes,' his mother said, looking surprisingly awake considering the early hour. Her black hair showed no sign of grey roots and she was wearing a patterned red shirt that made his eyes ache. She looked annoyed. Nothing unusual about that. 'Why didn't you answer the door? And why aren't you dressed?'

He rubbed his face, unable to cope with so many questions. 'Because it's still early,' he said, trying to force his brain to function.

'It's eleven fifteen.' His mother's irritation increased a notch. 'Are you going to invite us in, or leave us standing out here all day?'

He stood back to allow them in. 'Hi, Dad. Nice jacket.'

Henry Hubble peered over the top of his half-moon spectacles. His grey-white beard was neatly trimmed, and his blue shirt and stone-coloured chinos looked freshly pressed. 'Good morning, son. Late night?'

Barney nodded, and then wished he hadn't. He needed painkillers. 'Something like that. Make yourselves at home. I'll put some clothes on.'

'Good idea.' His mother searched for somewhere to sit down.

Unfortunately, Dusty's glittery dress from the previous night was sprawled across the sofa, along with her blonde beehive wig and patent leather boots.

'Not mine,' he said, in case his parents thought he'd developed an inclination for cross-dressing or, more likely, had pulled last night.

His mother tutted.

He tried to view the place through their eyes. On paper, The Mousehole was a charming fisherman's cottage built in the eighteen-hundreds, with an open fire and period features. The owners had converted the tall building into a rental property boasting three double bedrooms and a modern, open-plan kitchen-diner. It was quaint, tastefully restored, and perfectly located within a stone's throw of the beach. Normally, the place looked quite inviting. Paul was a neat-freak who regularly tidied up after his three less-disciplined housemates who didn't share his obsession for clean living. Typically, his parents had chosen to visit on the one day the place was a mess. Discarded takeaway cartons and beer cans decorated the floor and kitchen table.

He found a pair of crumpled jeans hanging over the back of a chair. Shaking out the creases, he pulled them on. 'Did I know you were coming?' He wasn't entirely sure whether he was expecting them or not. Maybe he'd forgotten, although that was unlikely. He wouldn't have got legless last night if he'd known his parents were coming to visit.

'We decided to surprise you.' His mother frowned. 'Your trousers are inside out.'

He glanced down. She was right. It might explain why he'd

been struggling to do up the zip. 'Unusual for you to take time off work.'

His mother fixed him with one of her looks. 'You didn't give us much alternative. You don't return our calls or texts. What else were we supposed to do?'

Respect my decision to choose my own life, he wanted to say, but his head wasn't up to an argument. He opted for keeping things civil. 'Can I get you a cup of tea?'

His mother surveyed the dirty kitchen and unwashed crockery balancing on the side. 'I think not.' She removed a pair of fishnet tights from the armchair, but still didn't sit down.

His dad was studying a painting on the wall, his hands clasped behind his back as if the sight of a fishing boat caught in a storm was an interesting medical conundrum.

The sound of Nate chucking up floated down the stairs.

Feeling a little nauseous himself, Barney went over to the sink and poured a glass of water.

A creak on the stairs alerted them to the arrival of Paul. He was as pale as paper, his bloodshot eyes half-closed, his fitted blue sweater and black jeans as conservative as his mood. 'Good morning, Mr and Mrs Hubble. An unexpected pleasure.' He shook hands with Barney's dad. 'You're looking well, Henry.'

Unsure how to respond to such polite familiarity, Henry Hubble nodded. 'Er... likewise. Paul, isn't it?'

'That's right.' Paul joined Alexa by the fireplace and kissed her cheek. 'You're looking dazzling as always, Mrs Hubble.'

Barney's mother's gaze travelled to the discarded female attire lying on the sofa. 'Thank you, young man.' She tutted when she spotted a spill of beer on the coffee table.

Paul picked up the pile of clothes and headed back upstairs. 'I'll leave you to it. Nice seeing you both.' As he passed Barney in the kitchen, he leant closer so he could whisper in his ear, 'Hang in there. My parents don't approve of my lifestyle either.'

Barney nodded, grateful for his friend's show of solidarity.

His mother waited until Paul was out of sight. 'Is there somewhere private we can talk? Your father and I have something we need to discuss with you.'

No prizes for guessing what that might be.

Barney thought he could do with some fresh air, especially as Nate was still throwing up. 'We'll go out. Give me five minutes to get dressed. They serve a decent brunch at Smugglers Inn, if you're hungry.'

'We'll wait outside.' His mother was clearly eager to leave The Mousehole, with its filthy inhabitants, messy interior, and sounds of amplified retching.

Ten minutes later, having taken two paracetamol and drunk another pint of water, he joined them on the cobbled walkway. 'This way,' he said, leading them past the white-stone cottages down towards the quayside. 'There's an impressive view across the bay.' He knew it wouldn't be enough to persuade them that staying in Cornwall was a good idea, but he hoped it might soften their resistance a little.

His parents thrived on hard work, long hours and the buzz of a stressful environment. Packed commuter trains, crowded streets and constant noise combined to form a drug, fuelling their determination to achieve in their high-flying careers. Noise pollution did nothing for Barney. It didn't inspire him, it depressed him. Life in Penmullion was much kinder on the soul.

Over the last few weeks, he'd been busy rehearsing for *A*

Midsummer Night's Dream, he'd taken on extra shifts at the surf kiosk, and added more gigs to his schedule, eager to prove he wasn't a layabout or afraid of hard work. But no matter how much he crammed into his new life in Cornwall, he knew it would never be enough for his parents.

'See where the cliffs meet the sea?' He pointed to the horizon. 'You can just make out *HMS Isolde*, a three-hundred-year-old battleship anchored near the disused naval port.' The morning mist was lifting, the breeze dragging the damp air away from the bay. 'It's worth a visit, if you're planning on staying for a while.' God, he hoped they weren't staying.

'We're only here for the day.' His mother made no attempt to search out the ship.

No one could say he didn't try.

As well as increasing his workload, he'd been partying hard too. He didn't need a shrink to tell him he was drowning his brain in alcohol to avoid thinking about his future. He loved life in Penmullion, it was everything he'd ever wanted, but it still lacked something. Whether he admitted it or not, there was a gaping career-shaped hole in his life. And he had no idea how to fill it.

Smugglers Inn wasn't busy. One of the regular bar staff laughed when he walked in, confirming his suspicions that he'd made a fool of himself last night. He went over to the bar and ordered three coffees, not wanting to tempt fate by putting food in his stomach. They opted to sit outside. Fresh air and a pleasant view might ease the trauma of the lecture he felt was coming his way.

He selected a table near the grassy bank. The bushes and trees rose upwards to where the posh hotels overlooked the sea, giving a nice contrast to the crashing waves ahead of them. The tide ebbed and flowed, inviting him to come in and play. It was tempting, but even he wasn't up for a surf today.

They'd barely sat down when his mother said, 'Your father and I would like to know when you will be returning to your studies?' There was never any preamble with Alexa Hubble, she always cut to the chase.

He couldn't blame her. The first either of them had known of his quitting medicine was after he'd purchased a one-way ticket to Cornwall. It was cowardly and unfair of him, and they had every right to be angry. After all they'd done for him, all the sacrifices they'd made, paying his living expenses, providing a monthly allowance, ensuring his time spent studying was as easy as possible, he'd left without a proper explanation. He'd hurt them, confused them, and left them severely out of pocket. He was a rotten son.

He took a long breath, hoping the cool June air might ease his headache. For nearly a year, he'd avoided answering questions about his return. He'd given excuses, employed all kinds of delaying tactics, hoping time would enable him to reach an answer, but he was no nearer resolving the issue of what to do about his career than when he'd left London.

It was time to stop fudging and answer honestly. 'I'm not sure I want to return.'

His mother stilled. 'I beg your pardon?'

He sighed. 'I know it's not what you want to hear. I'd hoped time out would clarify things for me, but it hasn't. I'm more confused than ever.'

His mother looked at him like he was speaking a foreign language.

His dad frowned. 'What's there to be confused about? You've

successfully completed your medical degree and the two-year foundation programme. The hard part is done. All you need to do is select a specialism.' He made it sound so simple.

'But that's just it, I don't want to specialise.'

'Nonsense.' His mother dismissed his words with a wave of her hand. 'Of course you want to specialise. If you can't decide which direction to take, then we'll help you. We have openings on the postgraduate medical diploma at Hammersmith, but you'll need to commit soon if you want to secure a place this coming autumn.'

'I can get you onto the cardiology or orthopaedic programmes at St. George's,' his dad added, looking hopeful. 'Just give me the nod and it's done.'

Barney felt the weight of expectation crushing him. His parents had supported him, encouraged him, used their influence to secure him decent placements, and how had he repaid them? He'd thrown in the towel. 'I appreciate your efforts, really I do—'

'Even if you choose general practice,' his dad said, cutting him off. 'It's not what your mother and I had hoped for, but we'd support you becoming a GP, if that's what you wanted.'

'But it isn't what I want.'

His mother rubbed her temples. 'Then what do you want, Barnabas, because quite frankly you're testing our patience.' She paused when the coffees arrived, waiting until the bar manager had disappeared inside before continuing. 'We didn't object when you announced you were taking a gap year, did we? Neither of us felt it was ideal, but we supported you. Well, you've had a break, it's time to get back to work.'

He looked at his mother. 'I already work. I'm not sitting around twiddling my thumbs.'

'Singing in a pub and teaching tourists to surf is not proper work, and you know it.'

On the word 'proper', Barney recalled Charlotte Saunders' dismissal of his employment status with equal derision. She hadn't been impressed by his lack of a suitable career either. 'Do you know how insulting that is? A lot of people in this area work in the tourist industry. It's a perfectly legitimate way to earn a living.'

Alexa Hubble showed no signs of remorse. 'I agree, for someone who hasn't spent seven years using public resources training to be a doctor.'

He couldn't argue with that. 'I get that you're disappointed. I am too. I stuck with the programme because I didn't want to quit. I knew I'd be letting a lot of people down, but I can't help how I feel.'

His dad placed a hand on his wife's arm, preventing her responding. 'So how *do* you feel, son?' He was no doubt trying to be sensitive, even though he probably wanted nothing more than to shake some sense into his only child.

Barney shrugged. 'I'm not sure medicine is for me. The stress, the long hours—'

'Long hours?' His mother cut him off. 'Your generation has it easy. When your father and I trained, we worked a hundred-hour week.' She stopped talking when her husband squeezed her arm, silently conveying that she wasn't helping.

Henry nodded for Barney to continue. 'Go on.'

What was the point? They wouldn't understand; they were made differently to him. When confronted with a patient, they saw a medical problem that needed solving. It was science, factual, they were able to remain emotionally detached. When faced with the same scenario, Barney just wanted to scream, cry, and run away. These were not traits that would make him a good doctor.

He had a sudden flashback from his early days on the wards. It was late one evening and his shift was due to finish. When his bleeper went off, he'd briefly considered ignoring it, letting whoever was on next pick it up. But his morals wouldn't let him do that, so he'd headed off to the ward. On arrival, he'd heard the nurse say to the patient, 'It's okay, the doctor's here now,' which had only increased his panic. The patient was Mrs White, a seventy-seven-year-old woman with terminal cancer. Her body was a bag of bones, her skin sallow and bruised. She was in severe pain, the agony of dying etched on her face. 'Please,' she'd said as he'd neared. 'Please help me.'

He'd been frozen to the spot. The nurse had looked at him expectantly, willing him to ease the woman's suffering. But how could he? Medical training covered disease, medication, and fixing broken bones. It didn't tell you how to respond to a dying patient who just wanted the torment to end. Helping people had been the motivation for becoming a doctor. He liked the idea of fixing problems, but he'd quickly discovered that there wasn't always a cure. No one had covered that on his course.

'How much longer?' Mrs White had asked him. 'Why doesn't the Lord take me? I'm ready to go.' Tears had filled her eyes, mixed with desperation and pleading.

When the nurse had leant across and whispered to Barney, 'Shall I call the palliative care team?' he'd grasped the suggestion like being tossed a life jacket at sea. Help was on its way, but then Mrs White had said, 'Will you stay with me, Doctor? I don't have anyone else.'

He'd sat with her for several hours, holding her hand, even

though she'd slipped into a morphine-induced coma. When Mrs White died later that day, Barney had twenty-nine minutes left before the start of his next shift.

The sound of his mother dragged him back to the present. 'We're still waiting for an answer.'

Failing to find the right words, he reverted to avoidance. 'I need a bit more time.'

'No more time, Barney. We've been patient enough.' His mother dropped a cube of sugar in her black coffee. 'You need to stop prevaricating and focus on your career. We haven't spent thousands of pounds supporting your education to see it go to waste.'

He bristled. 'If it's about the money, then I'll pay you back—'

'It's not about money,' his dad interjected. 'It's about wanting you to succeed in life.'

'And what about being happy, Dad? Doesn't that count for anything?'

'Happiness is overrated,' his mother said, and then caught the look on her husband's face and stopped stirring her coffee. 'What I mean is, happiness will come later. You need to put in the hard work first, build your career. Once you're established, you can meet a nice girl, settle down and have a family, content in the knowledge that you can provide for them. Trust me, we know.' She forced a smile at Henry, who smiled back... once he realised what was required of him.

The idea of meeting a nice girl conjured up another image of Charlotte Saunders. Why, he wasn't sure. 'Nice' wasn't a word that immediately sprang to mind when thinking about her. And why was he thinking about her? 'I wish more than anything I shared your commitment to medicine, really I do. But I don't think it's for me.'

'Then work harder,' his mother barked. 'You don't just give up on seven years of medical training.' She lowered her voice when she realised people were looking. 'I blame your mother,' she said, directing her comment at Henry. 'I knew encouraging him to play around with non-academic interests was a bad idea. But would you listen? Now look where it's led!' She pointed at her son. 'A wasted talent. Letting everybody down.'

A mist of red fog descended. He knew his mother didn't mean it. She was just worried he'd go off the rails like his cousin had done, ending up unemployed and alcohol dependent. But he wasn't about to make the same mistake. They just needed to get off his case. He was twenty-seven, for fuck's sake. He could make his own decisions. 'I'm sorry I'm such a disappointment to you,' he said, getting to his feet. 'You don't need to tell me I'm letting you down, I see it on your faces every time I look at you.'

'Your mother doesn't mean—'

'Yes, she does. She means every bloody word, and she's right. I am a let-down. But you couldn't be more disappointed in me than I am in myself.' He dug out ten quid from his wallet and threw it on the table. 'Now, if you'll excuse me, my shift starts in half an hour. Have a safe journey back to London. I'm sorry you didn't get the outcome you were hoping for.'

He stormed off, ignoring his parents' protests and curious glances from the other punters. He didn't need anyone telling him he was inadequate. Not some snooty designer from London, or his mum and dad. He was perfectly aware he was a screw-up.

Chapter 8

Thursday, 16 June

Lauren glanced at the kitchen clock, wishing time would slow down this morning. She'd yet to brush her hair, or put the bins out – and it was recycling day.

The toaster popped, sending a burnt slice of bread flying into the air like a clay pigeon being released from an automated trap. She tried to catch it, but it bounced off the fridge, landing on the disgusting linoleum flooring. Thankfully, her housework-obsessed sister had mopped the floor yesterday, so she felt safe in applying the 'five-second rule' and picked it up.

Blowing on it, she dropped it onto the breadboard, making a mental note to add 'new toaster' to the list of things to buy once her loan had been cleared later on today. She'd circled the date on the calendar, the last instalment. It was the only thing keeping her sane this morning.

'Breakfast is ready!' She used the last of the cheap margarine on the toast, relishing the prospect of buying proper butter next week, when she'd be twenty-five quid better off.

'How far away is Looe?' Her sister looked up from the newspaper.

Lauren wiped her hands on a tea towel. 'It's on the other

side of the coast.' Her children had yet to appear from their bedrooms. 'Freddie! Florence! Breakfast is getting cold.'

Charlotte tucked her straightened hair behind her ears – a lack of grooming time in the mornings clearly wasn't an issue for her. 'Too far to commute?'

Lauren plated up the toast, catching sight of her reflection in the fridge. Next to her perfectly presented sister, she looked like she'd slept rough. 'Sorry, what?'

'Looe? Could you get there for work?' Charlotte had been studying the jobs section in the *Penmullion Gazette*, highlighting the positions she felt Lauren should apply for to 'better her situation'.

Her sister meant well, but Lauren wasn't interested in working in a building society, a call centre, or trying to sell social media space to online retailers – she could barely understand the apps on her phone. 'No, Charlotte, I could not get to Looe for work. Apart from the fact that I have school-age children, I'm not looking to change jobs. I'm happy working at the café.' As she'd told her sister on countless occasions. 'Kids! I'm not going to ask again!'

Florence appeared in the kitchen wearing her Princess Fiona nightie.

'Sweetie, why aren't you dressed?' Lauren glanced at the clock. 'It's twenty past eight. We need to leave in ten minutes, and you haven't eaten breakfast.'

'I've got tummy ache.' Florence rubbed her stomach, emphasising the point.

Charlotte wasn't done with her career advice. 'I know you say you're happy working at the café, but do you really want to spend the rest of your days serving stewed tea and limp sandwiches?'

'What sort of tummy ache?' Lauren knelt down, assessing whether her daughter had a genuine ailment, or whether it was a lame excuse to stay home and watch TV. 'Where does it hurt?'

Florence pulled her sad face. 'All over, Mummy.'

Charlotte picked up the kitchen scissors. 'I'm sure we can find something much more fulfilling. I'm cutting out the jobs I think are suitable.'

Lauren felt her daughter's forehead. 'You don't have a temperature.'

'I'm very hot,' Flo said, in a slightly dramatic fashion. 'And cold too.'

Lauren kissed her daughter's cheek, which showed no evidence of being too hot or too cold. 'You might feel better once you've had something to eat.' She eased her onto a kitchen chair. 'Eat a slice of toast, and then we'll reassess.' She marched over to Freddie's bedroom door. 'How many times do I have to call you for breakfast?'

He was sitting on the floor playing with his Lego. At least he was dressed for school. Well, of sorts. His shirt was buttoned up wrong. It would have to do. She didn't have time to correct it.

'Kitchen, now, please.' She folded her arms, a feeble attempt at being stern.

Grinning, he got up from the floor and went into the kitchen, carrying his partially built truck. 'Can I stay home with Florence today?'

'No, and Florence isn't staying home, she's going to school.' Lauren ushered him onto a chair. 'Please put the truck down. We haven't got time to mess about this morning.'

Before Lauren had even collected his toast from the counter,

Charlotte was unbuttoning his shirt. 'We can't have you going to school looking scruffy, can we?'

Lauren supressed a sigh. Normally, she'd count to ten in a bid to calm her agitation but, with the clock rapidly ticking down, she didn't even have time for that this morning.

Charlotte realigned the buttons. 'Is this shirt ironed?'

Lauren loved her sister, really, she did. But right at that moment, she had an overwhelming urge to pour Charlotte's specially selected, loose-leaf, two-minute-brewed English breakfast tea over her head. 'No, Charlotte, it's not. Funnily enough, I don't have time to iron school shirts, which last a day before being covered in mud and require washing again.'

Lauren was subjected to a slow shake of the head. Her sister was not impressed.

Well, tough. She didn't have the time or inclination to pander to Charlotte's obsessiveness. She didn't mind her sister staying; she was glad to help out, and the kids loved having Auntie Charlie around – even if she did make them tidy up constantly – but it was challenging, to say the least.

'Eat your toast, please, Freddie.' Lauren picked up a discarded hair clip from the windowsill, tidying her appearance before her sister offered to plait her hair for her, like she'd done when they were kids. Well, they weren't kids anymore. Charlotte needed to realise she was no longer the boss of her younger sibling. So what if she wasn't organised, successful or driven? She muddled along as best she could, trying to provide a happy and stable upbringing for her kids. Charlotte had no idea what it was like to be a single parent. If she did, she might be a bit more understanding.

Someone knocked on the door. Great. That was all she needed.

'Keep eating, please.' Lauren checked her watch. 'We'll be leaving for school in five minutes.'

Ignoring Charlotte's comments about the merits of laundry-delivery services in London, Florence moaning about her tummy ache, and Freddie not wiping his hands before smearing margarine over his Lego truck, she answered the door.

It was a shock to find Glenda Graham standing on her doorstep. The woman didn't normally come to her home. No one else knew about the loan, and she wanted to keep it that way. Even more alarming was the sight of her two bulky sons hovering in the background. Vincent and Quentin often helped out backstage with the plays, but they never said much, and didn't exactly radiate friendliness, so she'd always kept her distance. She'd certainly never invited them to visit her home.

'Hello, Lauren, love. How are you this fine morning?'

As much as she didn't appreciate Glenda's intrusion, knowing this would be their last interaction stopped her from making a fuss. The sooner she paid the last instalment, the quicker she'd be debt-free. 'I'm well, thank you, Glenda. A little rushed, we're running late for school.'

'Then I won't keep you. I know how it is trying to juggle the demands of family.' Her smile was sincere. Lauren felt a little bad for never having warmed to the woman. It was probably down to owing her money. '*Never a borrower nor a lender be*,' her dad would constantly tell them growing up. It was an admirable sentiment, and one she didn't disagree with, but asking a utility company to wait for their money while she saved up wasn't feasible or realistic.

She withdrew the folded notes from her back pocket. 'It's

all there, but please check it.' She handed Glenda the money.

Glenda's mass of grey corkscrew curls sat on top of her head like a large hat, wild and frizzy. 'No need, I trust you.'

'Thank you.' Maybe dealing with Glenda hadn't been so bad after all. She'd trusted her to pay up each week, and respected her wish for discretion... well, until today at least. 'I really appreciate you helping me out.'

'My pleasure, love.' Glenda counted the notes, despite having just said she trusted her. She handed the money to Vincent, who repeated the count before pocketing the cash.

It wasn't worth getting upset about. The debt had been repaid. Lauren could finally move on with her life.

She was about to close the door, eager to get her kids to school, when Glenda said, 'Same payment, same time next week.'

Lauren wondered if she'd heard correctly. 'But that was the last payment, Glenda. Twenty weeks at twenty-five pounds per week. I've been keeping track. I can show you the payment dates in my diary if you want to check?'

'No need. But the debt is far from paid. You still owe interest.' Glenda removed a small black book from her oversized leather handbag.

'Interest?' Lauren's heart rate began to increase. 'But... but I didn't realise there'd be interest?'

Glenda smiled. 'Oh, love, all loans are subject to interest. You're a smart girl, surely you knew that?'

'Well... yes, if I was borrowing from a bank, but we're friends... aren't we?'

Glenda squeezed her hand. 'We are indeed, good friends. Which is why you get mates' rates.'

Lauren's head was spinning. 'Mates' rates?'

'That's right.' Glenda's slow smile revealed a discoloured front tooth. 'If you can't help out your friends when they're in trouble, it'd be a pretty bleak world, wouldn't it?'

Lauren nodded, but she was on autopilot.

'Which is why I only charge two hundred and fifty per cent.'

A rush of cold raced up Lauren's spine. 'But that's extortionate!'

Vincent and Quentin took a step closer to their mother, their arms folded across their wide chests.

Glenda's voice became consoling, as if it wasn't her causing Lauren's grief, but someone else. 'No, no, love. It's a fraction of what the payday loan companies charge. And then there's my overheads. I don't have the security of the big banks, you see, so I can't compete with their lower rates. But I offer something the banks don't, credit for people like yourself who can't get a loan elsewhere.' She sighed, as if weighed down by the responsibilities of her situation. 'Nothing gives me greater pleasure than helping out a friend in need, but I can only do that if I charge interest. There needs to be money in the pot for the next person, you see?'

All Lauren could do was nod. 'How... how much is still owing?'

'Now that's a good question.' Glenda opened the little black book, flicking through the pages. 'Where are you... ah, here you are.' She scribbled something down, made a point of checking the figures. 'One thousand, two hundred and fifty pounds on the nose.'

For a moment, the world stopped. All sound ceased. Even Lauren's heart seemed to stutter to a halt, stunned by the words coming out of Glenda's mouth. 'But... but I only borrowed five hundred pounds.'

Glenda sighed. 'I know, love. It's hard to hear, I get that. But it's a difficult financial market out there.'

'But... that's not fair, Glenda. You can't just add interest without informing me. We had an agreement.'

'We did indeed, love.' Vincent handed his mother a scrappy piece of notepaper. 'And the terms of our agreement state that I can add interest and vary the frequency and repayment amounts as I see fit.' Glenda held out the crumpled piece of paper for her to see. 'There's your signature, right at the bottom. See?' She pointed to Lauren's name. 'You accepted the terms and conditions. This is a valid and legal contract.'

Tears blurred Lauren's vision as she tried to read the scribbled words in front of her. She had a vague recollection of signing something, but she'd naively assumed it was just confirmation that she'd borrowed the money. She hadn't even asked for a copy. God, she was stupid.

Glenda's arm snaked around Lauren's shoulder, all empathy and kindness. 'You know me well enough to know I don't want to see you suffer, so we'll keep our weekly arrangement of twenty-five pounds. I think that's reasonable, don't you?'

Lauren couldn't think straight. 'It'll take me years to pay that off.'

Glenda released her. 'I'm sure you'll manage.'

Whatever she was about to say next, she was interrupted by Charlotte, who appeared by her side. 'The kids have finished their breakfast. Florence is still complaining of a tummy ache. Shall I call the doctor?'

Lauren wanted to shut the door, but Glenda had wedged her foot in the gap. 'You must be Charlotte. Lauren's told me so much about you. Welcome to Penmullion.' It was like the previous conversation had never happened. 'I'm Glenda, a friend of the family.'

Charlotte smiled. 'Nice to meet you, Glenda.'

'And these are my boys.' Glenda gestured to Vincent and Quentin's retreating backs as they disappeared across the rooftop, their task of 'backing up Mummy' concluded. 'I'm sorry to hear Florence is poorly. Would you like me to take Freddie to school for you?'

Lauren's 'No,' was overridden by Charlotte's, 'If it's no trouble?'

Glenda's expression turned saintly, her acting attributes coming to the fore. 'No trouble at all, that's what friends are for.'

Fighting her emotions, Lauren shook her head. 'I'll take Freddie to school myself, thank you. I have to go.' She closed the door, not caring if she banged Glenda's foot. The woman should have moved it.

Charlotte looked stunned. 'That was a bit rude. She was only offering to help.'

'I don't need her help.' Lauren marched into the kitchen. 'Why aren't you ready for school?' Both kids jumped at the sound of their mother's raised voice. 'Freddie, stop playing around. Put your shoes on now!'

Florence continued to rub her stomach. 'But I don't feel well.'

'You'll feel better once you're at school with your friends.' The word 'friends' caused bile to rise in Lauren's throat. She'd thought Glenda was a friend. How wrong she'd been. 'Come on, I haven't got all day. Will you please get dressed, you're trying my patience this morning.'

Florence started to snivel. 'But my tummy hurts.'

'Then go back to bed,' she snapped, ushering her daughter out of the kitchen. 'I'll come and check on you in a minute.'

A dejected Florence disappeared into her bedroom.

Charlotte cleared away the breakfast things. 'Glenda seemed like a nice woman to me.'

Lauren supressed the anger building within her. 'Appearances can be deceptive.'

'I don't get it.' Charlotte wiped the table. 'You trust your kids with that layabout Barney Hubble, but you won't let a nice middle-aged woman like Glenda take Freddie to school.'

Lauren rounded on her sister. 'When I want parenting advice, Charlotte, I'll ask for it, okay? Or any other kind of advice, for that matter. I can find my own jobs and clean my own home.' She snatched the cloth away from her sister. 'I was coping fine until you showed up.'

Charlotte flinched. 'Well, excuse me for trying to help.'

'If you want to help, Charlotte, stop interfering and take Freddie to school so I can work out what the hell is wrong with Florence.'

Her sister's cheeks flushed, but she walked off without another word.

Lauren didn't know what to do with herself. Part of her wanted to thump something, the other part of her wanted to scream at the unfairness of it all. It felt like the walls were closing in on her, suffocating and unrelenting. She scrubbed the sink, even though Charlotte had cleaned it yesterday. She didn't care, she needed to vent.

It wasn't until the front door slammed that she allowed her emotions to surface. Collapsing onto a kitchen chair, she slumped forwards, dropping her head onto the table. She had no idea how long she stayed there crying, but once she started she couldn't stop. How had she been so naive? Glenda wasn't a friend; she was a wolf in sheep's clothing. Someone who pretended to be kind and caring, but underneath was conniving and mean. Never once had Glenda mentioned adding interest to the loan, whatever the stupid contract said. Not once. And now she had to find over twelve hundred quid when she couldn't even afford sodding butter!

'Why are you crying, Mummy?' The sound of Florence's voice startled her.

Mortified, she sat up and wiped her eyes.

Florence appeared by her side, putting her tiny hands on Lauren's cheeks. 'Do you have a tummy ache too, Mummy?'

Lauren couldn't prevent the tears resurfacing. 'Yes, my love. I'm afraid I do.'

Chapter 9

Friday, 24 June

Charlotte was stiff from sitting for so long. The wooden bench seat wasn't the most comfortable. She rolled her shoulders, trying to loosen her joints, taking a moment to enjoy the view. It was a beautiful summer's day. Penmullion beach was almost empty. The pale sky above was peppered with wispy clouds dancing across the face of the sun, creating tiny sparkling crystals on the water's surface. It was perfect. Well, almost... if you ignored wasps and flies buzzing about, sand blowing everywhere, and the glare of the sun reflecting off the white paper as she tried to draw.

It'd been two weeks since she'd met with the director of the Isolde Players to discuss their upcoming production of *A Midsummer Night's Dream*. She'd been eager to show him her creative mood-board, anticipating his instant delight at having her on the production team. Presentations had always been her forte at Quality Interiors, so she'd been brimming with confidence when she'd arrived at the director's home, only to discover Jonathan Myers was far from impressed. He'd dismissed her mood board with its story narrative, fabric samples, and impressive graphics, with little more than a cursory glance. Instead, he'd wanted to know where the floor plans were? The scaled models? The props and furniture list? How the scene changes worked? None of which she had an answer for.

It was one of the most challenging design meetings she'd ever experienced, and that was saying something. He gave her two weeks to come up with a better plan, or he'd need to look elsewhere for a designer. Talk about humiliating. Unable to bear the idea of being sacked twice in short succession, she'd assured him of her commitment, and left with her tail between her legs.

Feeling somewhat despondent, she'd called in to see Paul at his boutique, hoping someone with his artistic flair would understand her disappointment. He'd loved her mood board, adored the shades of blue she'd used to create ethereal moonlight, and assured her she was on the right track. She just needed to invert her design concept, so that the space worked from the inside out, rather than from the outside in, which had been surprisingly insightful. Feeling in better spirits, she'd thanked him and headed off to the library to research stage design.

Consequently, she'd spent the last two weeks studying the fundamentals of theatre production. In truth, she'd been glad of the distraction. Having a project to focus on gave her an excuse to avoid her sister.

Lauren appeared from the café at that moment, looking tired, her black top and jeans draining the colour from her face. She smiled, joking with an elderly couple enjoying afternoon tea, but her smile faded when no one was looking.

She came over, carrying a tray of beverages. 'I probably haven't made it right, but I thought you might be thirsty.'

Lauren placed a mug of tea on the table, careful to avoid the pile of drawings and textbooks.

There was a good chance that the tea wouldn't be great, but Charlotte was touched by her sister's thoughtfulness. 'Thank you,' she said, but Lauren had already walked off, her half-hearted, 'You're welcome,' almost lost in the breeze.

Charlotte didn't mean to be difficult, but she knew it came across that way. She placed the mug on top of her pile of completed drawings, using it as a paperweight. She'd empty the contents later when no one was watching.

She'd been in Penmullion for nearly a month now, and things were no less strained with Lauren than before she'd come to stay. She knew her sister was upset with her, but she didn't know why. As a house guest, she'd tried to be useful and help with chores and errands, but everything she did seemed to cause annoyance. And the more she tried, the more she seemed to get it wrong. It never used to be this hard.

As kids, they'd been a close-knit family. Although, it was sometimes difficult to remember what life had been like before their mum had died. Like living two separate existences, pre- and post-cancer. One minute she was studying for her degree, the next she was parenting her sixteen-year-old sister and dealing with her father's depression.

But the pre-cancer memories lurked somewhere deep inside, tiny chinks of light amongst the greying fog of sadness. Like the time her mum had suggested a family camping trip. No one had taken Iris Saunders seriously, mainly because she liked her creature comforts too much. Whether it was using expensive face cream, or the way their small kitchen always smelt of disinfectant, there was nothing to suggest her mum would enjoy 'slumming it'.

Reacting to snorts of laughter and teasing from her husband and younger daughter, Iris's response was to immediately book the trip, and off they went to the New Forest.

It was the summer of '97. Blair had just been elected Prime Minister, Lauren wanted to be a Spice Girl, and her dad pretended he didn't have a thing for Pamela Anderson, even though he always mysteriously appeared whenever *Baywatch* started. Her mum watched sophisticated shows like *Ally McBeal*, loved Bon Jovi, and never wore trainers. The only time she'd ever seen her mum's polished veneer slip was when she attended a fancy-dress party as Madonna, complete with coned-corset bra and black suspenders. The sight of her mum appearing in the lounge caused her dad to drop his red wine over the new beige carpet, delaying them heading off, as her mum insisted on cleaning up first.

For Charlotte, that year had been about watching *Neighbours*, being in love with Marti Pellow, and asking for a 'Rachel' haircut for her tenth birthday. A hairstyle that hadn't lasted long once they'd reached the muddy campsite. Like her mum, she'd favoured cleanliness, pretty things, and wasn't keen on the idea of camping al fresco with sheep in the next field and no running water. And she'd been right to be worried. The campsite had been boggy, the toilet block smelt of urine, and her dad hadn't been able to work out how to erect their new Millets tent.

Leaving her mum and dad arguing over badly inserted tent pegs, and promising not to dirty her new plimsolls, she'd taken Lauren exploring. Being the sensible older sibling, when they reached a weir, she'd suggested walking down to the bridge to cross it. Ignoring her sister's advice, Lauren had jumped across. Charlotte had two options, walk to the bridge and risk the wrath of her parents for not keeping an eye on Lauren, or jump too. The gap had been maybe four feet. Unfortunately, she hadn't factored in slippery ground, or her sister screaming as she'd launched herself from the safety of the bank and landed with a bruising splash in the freezing, fast-running water. As the current dragged her under, sweeping her away from Lauren's frantic yelling, all she could think of was how much trouble she'd be in for ruining her new plimsolls.

Instinct had taken over. She'd reached upwards and grabbed hold of a rusty pipe protruding from the concrete wall. As water whipped against her face, filling her mouth, preventing her from crying out for help, she'd heard muffled voices above. Her dad's hands had gripped hold of hers and she was pulled to safety.

She hadn't cared that she'd scraped her knee, or had a discarded crisp packet stuck to her face, she was just relieved to be on dry land. As her dad checked her over, her mum stood at a safe distance, grimacing from the smell, happy her daughter hadn't drowned, but already planning a trip to the laundrette.

It was at this point that a large mud ball had landed on the front of her mother's pristine white blouse, causing Iris Saunders to gasp. All eyes had turned to look at the eight-year-old culprit. A grinning Lauren had stood defiantly, holding another mud ball, ready to launch.

'Don't you dare,' her mum had said, pointing her finger to emphasise the seriousness of her command. 'Put that down, right now.'

But Lauren had launched the mud ball anyway. It missed, mostly because Iris Saunders had charged at her youngest daughter and rugby-tackled her to the ground. Charlotte and her dad had exchanged a worried glance, until they'd realised it was laughter emanating from the pair, and not a serious wrestling bout. The next thing Charlotte knew, her dad had joined in, half-heartedly trying to split them up, but getting a face-full of mud for his efforts. He'd retaliated by smearing mud over them both. There was nothing to do other than join in.

This brief encounter with the world of camping became known as 'Muddy Sunday' in the Saunders household. Unsurprisingly, the following year they went to Magaluf.

Charlotte looked over at her sister now, no longer an eight-year-old scamp, but a mother herself, all grown up and responsible. She didn't like the idea of causing Lauren grief. Maybe she should go back to London? But she had no job or income. Her employment tribunal case had been listed for the fifth of September, so she needed to stay in Cornwall for another couple of months. Would that be enough time to make amends with her sister? She hoped so. The question was, how?

Her attention was drawn to the sight of Barney Hubble emerging from the sea, carrying a surfboard. His wetsuit was pulled down low and hung off his hips, his black hair was slicked back from his face. Thankfully, she was wearing sunglasses, so she could enjoy the view without appearing to stare. It was bad manners to ogle.

Physically, she couldn't deny an attraction – something she'd never experienced with Ethan, which was something of a puzzle. Ethan was a good-looking man. Tall, angular, well proportioned. She'd certainly appreciated his appearance, even if looking at him hadn't caused a physical stirring – which in truth, had been part of the appeal. It was easier to remain in control if you weren't blinded by superficial distractions that befuddled your brain and made you say crazy things like, 'I love you'.

She didn't need a shrink to tell her this wasn't healthy. Falling in love shouldn't be something to be afraid of. So why was she? Was it a fear of losing the person, as she'd had with her mum? Or maybe it was about losing control, and not wanting her emotions to derail her from logical thinking. Or maybe it was simply that she hadn't met 'the one'.

Tilting her head sideways, she watched Barney's chest muscles move beneath his tanned skin as he jogged across the sand. It was no different to looking at a fine painting, she reasoned. She was a designer, after all; beauty was her business. There was no need to feel light-headed, or wonder how it would feel to touch his skin, feel the warmth of his...

Aware of a sudden blush creeping into her cheeks, she refocused on researching how to build a fly rig. Her slight dizziness was probably due to her aversion to heights, caused by imagining the character of Puck flying across the stage, rather than the sight of Barney Hubble with his top off.

In fairness, her first assessment of the man may have been a little judgemental. He had some attributes. He could surf, he was clearly good with children, and it turned out he was an extremely reliable childminder. But it wasn't enough to tempt her into striking up a liaison with him. In her book, renting out surfboards wasn't a proper career.

His sudden grin led her to the conclusion that he knew she was eyeing him up, and he was enjoying the attention. And just when she was reassessing her opinion of him.

He gestured to her top button.

Glancing down at her white shirt, she expected to find a button undone. Puzzled, she looked up, trying to ignore the sight of water sliding down his torso.

'It looks better undone,' he said, reaching the table.

Not this again. 'Not everyone likes to flaunt, Mr Hubble.' She dragged her eyes away from his chest.

'I'm not flaunting.' There was laughter in his voice. 'I'm swimming. It's a warm day.' He nodded to her shirt. 'Aren't you hot, all buttoned up?'

Sighing, she removed her sunglasses. 'If I was hot, then I would do something about it, wouldn't I?' She didn't want to admit that, actually, she was a bit warm. No way was she giving him the satisfaction of being right. 'Funnily enough, I'm capable of regulating my temperature, thank you very much.'

'I'm just saying; your cheeks are red.'

'I'm sitting in full sun,' she said... although this wasn't the only reason. 'Undoing my top button won't make a difference.' She fiddled with the button, trying not to stare at his bare chest.

'How do you know until you try?' His disarming smile was filled with mischief.

Flustered, she returned to her fly-rig design. He was a distraction she could do without. 'Thank you for the fashion advice. I have work to do.'

His laughter drifted away on the breeze as he jogged back to the surf kiosk.

She only realised she'd been fixated on his retreating bottom when Sylvia Johns said, 'You look busy, love.'

Startled, she looked up, guilt flaming the heat in her cheeks.

Sylvia was wearing a sky-blue dress and big straw hat.

'Goodness me, you girls are pretty.' Her smile was warm and friendly. 'Tony's a lucky man. And you're both so talented and resourceful. Only the other day I was telling him to invite you over for dinner so we could hear more about your design work. It must be such a fascinating industry to work in.'

As much as Sylvia's overenthusiasm encroached on her personal space, Charlotte couldn't deny that the woman meant well. She also showed more interest in her career than her dad ever had.

'What are you working on?' Slipping on a pair of purple-rimmed glasses, Sylvia looked at her drawings. 'Are these for the play? Tony said you'd offered to help. What a lovely thing to do. Community is everything, I always say.' She picked up a drawing, not realising it was tucked under the pile of drawings held down by the mug of tea.

Charlotte watched in horror as the mug overturned and the contents splashed across the table, landing on her white jeans.

'Oh, love, I'm sorry!' Sylvia's hat flew off, causing another cry of distress, as a gust of wind sprayed sand across the table.

The wind changed direction, sending her drawings spiralling towards the sea.

Ignoring Sylvia's cries of, 'I'll fetch a cloth!' – which seemed a little pointless in the circumstances – Charlotte kicked off her shoes and ran onto the beach, trying to retrieve the scattered drawings.

As she ran, jumped and chased, attempting to catch them as they taunted her, staying just out of arm's reach, a sense of panic enveloped her. It wasn't just the potential loss of two weeks' hard work; it was the unfairness of it all. She wanted to be in control and she wasn't.

And then she became aware of Barney racing past. With no hesitation, he ran into the sea and carefully lifted two drawings from the water. 'Grab that one!' His yell directed her to another drawing hovering above the waves.

Holding on to the pictures she'd managed to rescue, she ran over to the rocks. The sketch of the full staging, complete with lighting rig, thrust stage and elaborate tree house, was pinned against the rock face. It'd taken her hours. The moment the gust let up, it would slip into the sea.

Getting wet was unavoidable. There was no time to roll up her jeans, so she ran into the water, yelping as the cold hit her legs. She reached the rocks and slapped her hand against the picture, holding it in place.

It was a flawed plan. With the other drawings in her left hand, she couldn't move, and her weight was off balance. A wave crashed against her legs, causing more instability. She was about to topple into the sea, taking the pictures with her, when something scooped her up like she weighed nine pounds, not nine stone. 'I've got you.'

Alarmingly, she found herself in the arms of Barney Hubble. Inappropriate as it was, she couldn't deny the gratitude she felt, even if it did feel like a scene from *An Officer and a Gentleman*.

He carefully negotiated his way onto the beach.

Wet had seeped through her shirt, she could see the outline of her bra forming through the material. Talk about embarrassing. But this was nothing compared to the feel of his hot skin next to hers, and the strain of his arm muscles as he transported her to safety.

'The drawings should dry out,' he said, as though carrying a woman caveman-style was a normal Friday-afternoon activity. 'Take photos of the drawings just in case they fade. At least that way you'll have a copy.' He lowered her onto the sand, next to where he'd secured the rest of her drawings under a stone. 'I'm assuming these are for the show?'

She nodded, intense shivering overriding her ability to speak.

He added the pages she was holding to the pile under the stone. 'These are good,' he said, gently shaking droplets of water from the main picture. 'This'll look amazing at the theatre. Lauren said you were talented. She was right.' His eyes dipped to her chest. 'Well, that's cooled you down.'

She followed his eyeline to where her white shirt clung to her breasts, the outline leaving nothing to the imagination – even with the top button still done up. Her hair was plastered to her head, she was covered in sand, and her white jeans were stained with tea. It was her idea of hell. And yet she found herself laughing – albeit a little hysterically. It was 'Muddy Sunday' all over again.

Barney looked momentarily dazed when she started giggling, and then his face eased into a grin. 'You okay?'

She shook her head. 'No.' And then she started laughing harder, her legs giving way until she sank down onto the sand. Why was she laughing? What was wrong with her?

Her mirth faded when Sylvia appeared, kicking sand everywhere as she thundered to a stop. 'I'm so sorry, Charlotte! What a klutz. I'll never forgive myself for ruining your drawings.'

'It's fine, really. Barney rescued most of them.' She accepted his hand, letting him pull her to her feet.

'What a hero!' Sylvia hugged Barney and then began wiping the drawings with the cloth she had in her hand.

Oh, God. 'No, don't wipe them!' Charlotte dived for her pictures. 'Just let them dry out.'

Sylvia stopped. 'Oh, okay, sorry love. You know best.' She looked a little hurt.

Feeling bad, Charlotte touched her arm. 'Honestly, they'll be fine. No harm done.'

Not to the pictures, anyhow. Her appearance, on the other hand, had taken a battering. She collected the drawings, ready to return to Lauren's flat, where she could assess the damage, and dry them out with a hairdryer.

Barney's suggestion of taking photos was a good one. She turned around to thank him, but he was back at the kiosk, talking to a young boy who'd arrived for a lesson. She allowed herself a moment's appreciation of his smooth back and angular shoulder blades. There was no doubt about it, Barney Hubble might not be her type, but he certainly had his good points.

Unfortunately, she was now indebted to him... and she wasn't entirely sure she was happy about that.

Chapter 10

Thursday, 30 June – 8 weeks till curtain-up

Barney sat down on one of the hall's wonky plastic chairs, resigning himself to a long wait. The Isolde Players had been rehearsing twice weekly for nearly two months, and they'd reached that messy stage of a production when the actors were no longer allowed to use scripts. Some of the actors were already line-perfect, like arse-lick Daniel Austin. Others left it to the last minute and then panicked when they realised how little time was left before curtain-up. And then there were people like Nate, who, despite spending hours studying the script, couldn't make the words stick.

Unfortunately, this didn't prevent the director screaming abuse at him when he messed up. Jonathan Myers was a bit of a dick, in Barney's opinion. He suspected the man was jealous of Nate's natural ability, and publicly humiliating him probably boosted his fragile ego, but it did little to encourage his poor friend.

Thankfully, the rehearsal had temporarily halted so Kayleigh could take photos for the programme. She wasn't a professional photographer, but as a keen amateur, she'd been assigned the task.

Jonathan clapped his hands. 'Can I suggest everyone takes the opportunity of a lull in proceedings to review their lines.' He frowned at Nate, who looked away, eyes cast downwards. 'Please listen out for your name when called.' He gestured to where Kayleigh was erecting a lighting umbrella. 'Who do you want first?'

Kayleigh bent the umbrella into shape. 'Daniel and Lauren.'

Daniel darted over, responding like the obedient puppy he was. Lauren joined him a few moments later, when she'd finished wiping chocolate smudges from Freddie's hands.

Nate sat down next to Barney, looking fed up. 'I had no problems remembering my lines last night. How come when I get down here, they go out of my head? I've got a brain like a friggin' sieve.' His frustration increased when Daniel placed his hand on Lauren's shoulder and whispered something in her ear, making her laugh.

Dusty, who was sitting on the other side of Nate, glanced up from filing a split red nail. 'Don't fret. Lauren's not interested in Daniel.' Her blue silk dress slipped off her knees as she crossed her legs, revealing a flash of sheer stocking.

Barney could still remember the first time he'd met Dusty. He'd just finished a gig at Smugglers Inn, when a stunning six-foot blonde had walked into the bar, wearing a sequinned catsuit, and kissed him full on the lips. His shock at being accosted by a beautiful woman had only increased when she'd opened her mouth and, in a deep voice, said, 'Get us a beer, will you, love.' But he'd got to know her over the last year, and now considered her an equally good mate to both Nate and Paul.

Nate folded his arms across his chest. 'She wouldn't react like that if I touched her.'

Dusty checked her nail for smoothness. 'That's because she likes you. She doesn't like Daniel. Not in that way, at least.'

Nate frowned. 'That doesn't make sense.'

'Of course it doesn't. The behaviour of the female of the species rarely does. Tell him, will you?' She tapped Barney on the knee.

'Jesus, don't ask me about women. I'm as clueless as he is.' A point emphasised when Kayleigh waved at him from across the hall. 'I think what Dusty means is, Lauren doesn't fancy Daniel.'

A burst of laughter drew their eyes to the couple as they posed for a photo.

Nate's frown deepened. 'Then why's she laughing?'

Barney shrugged. 'She's being polite?'

He didn't think for a second that Lauren was into Daniel. The guy was creepy as hell. He was deathly pale, and wore square glasses that swamped his bony face. Looks aside, Daniel was spiteful. And that wasn't a trait Barney admired. Lauren might not fancy Daniel, but as for how she felt about Nate, he wasn't sure. There was definitely an attraction, but sometimes that wasn't enough. After all, he fancied Charlotte Saunders, but nothing was going to happen between them. So that just proved his point.

When Charlotte had arrived at the hall earlier and headed down to the cellar to start set painting, she'd virtually blanked him. There'd been no repeat of the connection they'd shared when he'd rescued her drawings from the sea last Friday. Stupidly, he thought they'd made a breakthrough. Covered in sand, sea, and spilt tea, he'd seen a glimpse of the woman beneath the frosty exterior, and he'd liked what he'd seen. But it was like that moment had never happened. She was back to being all buttoned-up, and ignoring him. And a woman blowing hot and cold was another trait he wasn't attracted to.

His thoughts were interrupted by Kayleigh asking Sylvia, Freddie and Florence to come up for their photos. Sylvia looked every inch the surrogate grandmother as the kids climbed onto her lap. When she tickled them, they laughed, creating a great photographic opportunity.

Barney felt a pull in his chest. Christ, he was getting broody. He thought only women suffered from that?

Kayleigh checked her list of names. 'Lauren and Nate, please.'

Dusty caught Nate's arm. 'This is a golden opportunity to usurp that dweeb Daniel. Use those admirable attributes of yours to charm her.'

Nate pulled a face. 'What attributes?'

Dusty gave him a disgruntled look. 'Oh, please. You own a mirror, try looking in it.' She squeezed Nate's bicep. 'And if all else fails, flex the guns. Women love that.'

Nate shrugged her off. 'People are watching.'

'Oh, stop worrying. You're not my type.'

'Glad to hear it.' Nate headed over to Kayleigh, who instructed him to stand behind Lauren. She was perched on a stool, looking unusually rigid. For the first time since meeting Charlotte, Barney spotted a family resemblance. She was a dead ringer for her sister.

Kayleigh peered over the top of her camera. 'Rest your chin on Lauren's head.'

After a moment's hesitation, Nate did as he was asked. The pair looked like frightened rabbits.

Standing on the sidelines, watching, was a very smug-looking Daniel.

When he sniggered, Barney felt Dusty's hackles rise.

'Someone needs to wipe that smile off his face... both of them.' She leant closer, lowering her voice. 'Did you know, I overheard him say to Jonathan that he's not happy Paul and I are sharing the role of Helena, and that he'd rather act opposite a *real* woman?'

Barney flinched. 'I hope you challenged him?'

'Of course I did.' She smiled. 'I told him I would rather act opposite a *real* man, but we can't always get what we want.'

Barney's sudden laughter caused heads to turn.

But Dusty's smile faded. 'It's bad enough that my family give me grief. I don't need it from the likes of him.' She pointed her nail file in Daniel's direction. 'Nasty little man.'

Barney watched Nate clumsily place his hand on Lauren's shoulder. 'Talking of family, has anything more happened about Will's wedding?'

Dusty resumed filing. 'An invitation arrived in the post this morning. It was addressed to Mr Paul Naylor in bold typeface, followed by the words "and only him" in brackets. Not exactly subtle.'

Across the room, Lauren glanced up at Nate, a fleeting look of longing passing across her petite features. It was gone in a nanosecond, but it was definitely there. Shame his mate hadn't seen it; he was too preoccupied trying not to look at her. 'Have you decided what you're going to do?'

Dusty shook her head, making her wig sway. 'Part of me thinks I shouldn't rock the boat, and should just stay away. But the other part of me thinks, why should I? If the Naylor family love Paul, then they should embrace me as well, but they don't. They're too afraid of upsetting the bridal entourage. Anyone would think I was a mass murderer.'

Barney could empathise with the trials of trying to appease family. 'It seems a shame to miss Will's wedding.'

'I agree. But if Paul and I don't make a stand now, then they'll know they can bully us and we'll never be allowed to attend any future family gatherings. And I don't think that's fair.'

Lauren and Nate moved away from the camera, both turning in the same direction and bumping into each other. This was followed by embarrassed apologies, shy smiles, and hurrying away from each other.

Nate returned to his seat, reprimanding himself for behaving like a 'complete tool'.

Barney was about to assure him it wasn't that bad, when Jonathan yelled, 'Lauren! Kayleigh needs a shot of you with Glenda.'

Barney was sure he saw Lauren grimace as she returned to Kayleigh, and not just because the director had bellowed at her.

His feeling was compounded when Nate said, 'Something's going on there.' Nate nodded to where Glenda stood behind Lauren. She was smiling into the camera, her hands squeezing Lauren's shoulders like a bird of prey gripping its victim. 'I don't think Lauren's ever been a fan of Glenda, but now it's like she can't even look at her.'

Barney was inclined to agree. There was definitely tension between the two women. Glenda chatted away with nothing to indicate anything was amiss but, far from engaging with her, Lauren's expression remained blank. She closed her eyes, as if trying to shut the older woman out.

'You don't think she's borrowed money from her, do you?' Nate looked worried.

Barney shook his head. 'Unlikely. She must've heard about Glenda's reputation.'

Dusty checked her reflection in a compact mirror. 'She's not known as Glenda-the-Lender for nothing.' She wiped a smudge of lipstick from her front tooth. 'Lauren's smarter than that.'

Nate didn't look convinced. 'But people in desperate situations make bad decisions.' He checked to make sure no one could overhear. 'I get the impression money's a bit tight.'

Dusty dropped the compact into her white Louis Vuitton handbag. 'Of course it is, she's a single mother. Lauren is also very proud. If I were you, I wouldn't broach the subject. Not unless you want to kill off any chance of a romance.'

Barney nudged Nate, alerting him to Tony Saunders, who'd joined the women for the next photo. 'It also might cause trouble elsewhere.'

Glenda smiled up at Tony, while Lauren stared straight ahead, her expression frozen. It was an awkward shot.

The crestfallen look on Nate's face matched the one on Sylvia's. They both watched the scene unfold, mourning for something they both wanted but didn't think they could have.

Jonathan bellowed from the other side of the hall. 'It would be good to get something done tonight, other than a few snaps, Kayleigh, dear. Time is pressing on.'

'Only a couple more to go!'

'Glad to hear it.' Jonathan gave her a dismissive wave.

Barney opened his script, intending to practise his lines, but Dusty nudged him in the ribs. 'No luck deterring your admirer, I see.'

He followed Dusty's gaze to where Kayleigh was waving

coyly at him. 'Christ knows why. I couldn't make it more obvious I'm not interested.'

Dusty raised an eyebrow. 'Then perhaps kissing her face off at the Smugglers Inn Valentine's party wasn't such a good idea.'

Barney flinched. 'I was drunk.'

Dusty grinned. 'Ah, the folly of many a downfallen man.'

Barney's laughter was cut short by an irate Jonathan. 'No more chatting, people!' He stamped his foot. 'Act Two, Scene Two.'

Amongst the frantic flicking through of scripts, everyone checked to see if they were needed.

Dusty pulled a face. 'Oh, joy. It's my scene with Daniel the irritating spaniel.' She stood up, flattened down the front of her shiny blue dress and joined Daniel on stage, who was already curled up in a sleeping position, ready to start.

'It's good to know some of my cast are professional.' Jonathan shot Nate a disappointed glare.

Nate looked affronted. 'What did I do?'

'It's what you didn't do, Mr Jones.' Jonathan wagged a finger. 'Rehearsals cannot progress when actors fail to learn their lines.'

'I bloody have learnt them,' Nate mumbled. 'So friggin' unfair.'

'Teamwork, people. We don't want anyone letting the side down.' Jonathan looked around the hall, his ruddy complexion reminding Barney of a constipated patient he'd once treated.

Barney's idea of teamwork clearly differed from the director's. Not that he wanted to swap places with Jonathan – he was a follower not a leader. But still, he wasn't sure that crushing a person's confidence demonstrated appropriate people-management skills. 'Ignore him, he's an asshole,' he assured Nate, speaking low enough that Jonathan wouldn't hear. He wasn't about to put himself in the firing line.

As the actors prepared for the scene, Tony strolled over. 'Thanks for your help last night, Nate. I'm sorry it was a late one, but I've had word from the crew, and they've rejoined the race.'

'Not that they deserve it.' Nate's eyes followed Lauren as she returned to her seat. 'People just don't respect the sea. And then they expect us to rescue them.'

'To be fair, they couldn't have predicted an engine failure.'

Nate ran his hand through his hair. 'They should've been better prepared before they set off.'

On stage, Jonathan pointed to where he wanted Dusty to lie. She looked quite disgruntled as she lowered herself to the grubby floor, avoiding discarded bits of chewing gum and splinters of wood.

Barney felt for her; Dusty wasn't dressed for rolling around the floor. He turned to Nate. 'Are you talking about last night's shout?'

Tony nodded. 'A yacht got into trouble taking part in a round-the-world race.'

Barney was full of admiration for the RNLI. Nate would often get called out, usually in the middle of the night, returning with bizarre rescue stories... unless they were too traumatic to talk about, and then he would shut himself in his room. Barney could empathise with this better than most. He'd been the same during his days as a junior doctor. 'Was anyone hurt?'

Nate dragged his eyes away from Lauren. 'No casualties. Just a busted engine.'

Their attention was diverted to the stage, where things were getting somewhat testy.

Daniel had run towards Dusty and dropped to his knees. He was now clasping hold of her legs, preventing her from getting up. '"And run through fire I will for thy sweet sake!"'

Dusty slapped Daniel's hand, trying to make him let go. '"I thought you lord of more true gentleness."' There was an audible ripping sound. 'You're tearing my dress!'

Daniel fell backwards. 'And you're ruining the scene!'

Jonathan ran on stage. 'People, please!' He placed his arm around Daniel's shoulder, but Daniel wasn't appeased.

'I can't work like this! *He* doesn't know his lines,' Daniel said, pointing at Nate, 'and *he's* a freak!' He jabbed a finger in Dusty's direction.

Dusty flipped him the bird. '*She*, you ignorant bastard!'

Barney was just deliberating whether Dusty needed an ally in her corner, when someone tapped him on the shoulder. He turned to find Kayleigh pouting at him like a Kardashian posing for a selfie. 'I need to take your photo, lover boy.' She hooked her finger into his T-shirt and led him over to the camera set-up. 'Time to get cosy.'

Oh, hell. He'd rather eat his own socks... not that he was wearing any.

And to think he'd been feeling sorry for Nate and Dusty. At that moment, he'd have traded places with either of them.

Chapter 11

... Later that evening

Charlotte couldn't describe the elation she'd felt when the director finally approved her designs. There was no logic to her reaction. It was amateur theatre, she wasn't getting paid, and the conditions she was expected to work in could rival those of a Victorian poorhouse, and yet elated she remained. Maybe it was the challenge of turning her creative ideas into reality. Or the satisfaction of winning over the director's initial negative response. Whatever the reason, his approval had evoked a genuine sense of enthusiasm she hadn't experienced in a long time. So, despite not having the right tools or environment to work in, she was relishing the opportunity to create something amazing and ensure her stay in Cornwall wasn't a complete washout.

Working in a cramped, cold cellar beneath a village hall wasn't exactly ideal. It was dingy, with poor lighting and thick stone walls that dripped with water. Ducking under the piping, she tried to find a decent paintbrush amongst the array of moth-eaten offerings stored in an old wooden bucket. There wasn't much floor space, and the pipes running along the ceiling rattled every time someone flushed the loo. It was a far cry from the conditions she was used to working in as an interior designer. Strangely, she didn't mind, which was a puzzle in itself.

She found the size of brush she needed, but the bristles were matted together. She tried to locate some white spirit amongst the ancient tins of paint stacked in a tiny cubbyhole. Above her, she could hear the muffled voices of the actors rehearsing their lines. She spotted a tin of paint stripper that'd seen better days. The lid wouldn't budge. Wrapping the top in a piece of cloth, she twisted it, forcing the lid off. She poured the rancid-smelling liquid into an old mug and put the paint-brush in to soak.

The other reason for getting involved with the Isolde Players was that it was an excuse to spend time with her family. When she'd told her dad and sister about her involvement, her announcement had been met with a mixed response. Her dad had raised an amused eyebrow and said, 'You know it's not The Globe?' as though the idea of her volunteering for a community project was on a par with the Queen running the dog show at a local fete. And Lauren had visibly flinched, clearly unhappy about her sister encroaching on her hobby. Maybe Lauren thought she'd try and take over, or criticise her acting talent. Neither of which she had any intention of doing. The plan to return to her old life in London was still her priority. But she didn't want to leave Cornwall without building bridges first.

Swirling the paintbrush in the stripper, she tested it to see if it had softened. It wasn't great, but there was some bend in the bristles. She wiped the excess on the cloth and returned to the large canvas hanging from the rafters. The backdrop was twelve feet by ten, so scaling up from an A3 drawing was testing her design skills. With no CAD programme to assist her, she was having to paint freehand, something she hadn't done since college. She began marking up the canvas using a grid as a guide. She then painted in the midnight-blue background, followed by the tree trunks, building layers and shadows so the woodland came to life. She outlined the moon, which dominated the middle of the backdrop. Her aim was to give the illusion of a magical land where fairies truly existed.

Using a combination of silver and pale-blue paint, she mixed up a test colour and tried it on the canvas. It worked surprisingly well. The moon now glowed.

The door creaked above. A pause followed, before she heard the sound of Barney's voice. 'Okay to come down?'

'There's not much room,' she said, her warning pointless as he appeared anyway.

He ducked under the water pipes. 'I thought you might like a cuppa. It's cold down here.'

Suppressing an inward sigh, she took the mug. 'Thanks.' Politeness forced her to take a sip before she could put it down, but much to her surprise it didn't taste too bad. In fact, it was pretty good. She took another sip, just to be certain.

Barney grinned. 'It's not laced with strychnine.'

She felt herself frown. 'Pardon me?'

'The expression on your face. It's just tea, I promise.' He was wearing a fitted T-shirt and knee-length cargo shorts, showing off his tanned legs.

She took another sip. 'Sorry, I wasn't expecting it to be quite so nice.'

He laughed. 'Blimey, you really do have a low opinion of me.'

'It's not that. I'm just a bit fussy when it comes to tea.'

He raised an eyebrow. 'You, a bit fussy?' Stepping over the roller trays on the floor, he studied the backdrop, taking in the intricate leaves and branches sprouting from the tree trunks like wizened hands reaching up to touch the sky. 'You are one conundrum.'

Unsure of his meaning, she went over and stood next to him. 'Explain, please?'

His eyes didn't leave the backdrop. 'For someone who's so tightly coiled, you sure unravel when you paint.'

She paused, the mug halfway to her lips. 'Is that a compliment or an insult?'

He turned to look at her. 'It's a compliment. This is stunning.'

'Oh.' She swallowed awkwardly. 'Thank you.'

'You have paint on your cheek.' He reached out, but she ducked before he could wipe it away. No way was she letting him touch her.

'It's only emulsion. It'll come off.' She drank another mouthful of tea and placed the mug on a large dice, a prop from a previous show. 'How's the rehearsal going?'

He let out a small laugh. 'Eventful. So far there's been two tantrums, one fight and three people crying.' He shrugged. 'A typical rehearsal.'

She couldn't work out whether he was being serious.

'I'm not needed at the moment. I thought I'd come down and see if you wanted a hand.'

She stopped loading up the brush with paint. 'You want to help?'

'Don't look so surprised.' He handed her a cloth so she could wipe the handle. 'Am-dram is about teamwork. It doesn't matter whether you like people or not. If they need help you offer it.'

She turned back to the canvas, fighting the urge to ask why he didn't like her. Although, if she was honest, it didn't take a genius to work out why. She could be difficult at times. Her striving for perfection sometimes rubbed people up the wrong way. Especially if the person didn't share her desire for a neat, orderly life.

'Not that I don't like you,' he said, as if reading her thoughts.

She glanced over. 'Sure about that?'

He shrugged. 'Let's just say, the jury's still out.' And then he grinned.

She handed him the paintbrush, unsure of how she felt about being teased. 'Cover this middle section, please. And don't paint over the lines.'

'Wouldn't dream of it.' He took the brush. 'So, how do you like Penmullion?'

She watched him, checking he could be trusted not to ruin her design, before replying. Satisfied he was sticking to the brief, she went in search of pale-green paint to highlight the edges of the leaves. 'It's okay. A little quaint for my taste.'

He frowned at her. 'Quaint? I've never heard it called that before. You must see it differently to me.'

There was no pale-green paint. The best she could find was khaki. 'What am I missing then?' She used a screwdriver to prize open the rusty lid. The contents had all but dried up.

'Well, for a start, there's a beach on my doorstep,' he said, as though this was enough of a reason to love Penmullion.

When nothing more was forthcoming, she said, 'That's it?'

'Isn't that enough?' He blew out his cheeks. 'Okay...' His expression turned ponderous. 'I wake up every morning to the sound of herring gulls.' He resumed painting. 'The town is filled with independent shops run by people I know by name. I can swim and surf every day. I eat fish that's been caught that morning. When I play a gig, people clap and talk to me afterwards, they don't ignore me like they sometimes did in London. And when I lie in bed at night, I drift off to sleep listening to the sound of the waves crashing against the cliffs.'

He conjured up an attractive picture.

'You moved here from London?' Charlotte asked.

'That's all you got from that?' He turned back to the canvas. 'Must be losing my poetic touch.'

She spotted a small tin of dark-green paint. It wasn't perfect, but it might do if she could find some white. 'I admit it sounds... nice.' She ignored his laughter. 'I just meant, why would you leave a vibrant city like London for, you know, a backwater existence?'

He shrugged. 'I've nothing against London, it just didn't suit me. I wanted something different.'

She lifted paint pots, searching for white. There didn't appear to be any. 'But London is filled with such opportunity.' Could she use beige?

'Maybe.' He shrugged. 'What is it about London you love so much?' His strokes slowed as he reached her pencil line. At least he was adhering to her instructions.

She tried to open the beige paint tin with the screwdriver. 'So many things. The variety of restaurants, theatres on your doorstep, the ease of getting around town...' Even though using the Tube made her claustrophobic, but that was beside the point. She wrestled with the lid, it was rusted shut. Placing the tin on the floor, she knelt on it so she could get better leverage. 'Not to mention career opportunities' – despite work currently being a sore subject – 'museums, art galleries, exhibitions' – that she never actually went to, but fully intended to when she had enough time.

'Didn't you find it stressful?'

She pushed down on the screwdriver. 'Well, yes, sometimes. But that's what being a grown-up is all about. No one said life was easy.' The lid creaked. 'We can't all sit around on the beach listening to the waves and smoking weed.' The lid bent upwards, ripping the screwdriver from her hands. 'Ouch!' She jumped up, the pain in her hand almost causing her to swear.

He appeared next to her and took hold of her hand. 'Let me see.'

'It's just a scratch.' She tugged, but he wouldn't let go. 'Can I have my hand back, please?'

'No.' He dragged her over to the light. 'Not until I'm satisfied you haven't done anything major.'

'I can do that myself.' She tried to retrieve her hand, but he wasn't letting go.

'I can do it better.' He lifted her hand to the light. 'When was your last tetanus jab?'

'No idea. Within the last ten years.' She made a noise of protest as he manoeuvred her over to the sink. He ran her hand under freezing-cold water. 'And what makes you better equipped to tend to a graze than me, eh, Mr Surfer Dude?'

'I'm a doctor.' He tore off a wodge of paper towels and dabbed the wound, wiping away excess blood.

'Oh, please. You are not.' Being pressed against his body was making it hard to keep her composure. She could smell remnants of aftershave and fabric conditioner. There was no call for him to invade her personal space in such a way.

He looked closer at the wound. 'It needs cleaning and dressing. Sit down, I'll fetch the first-aid box.'

The relief she felt when he let go of her hand was superseded by indignation when he physically plonked her onto a rickety wooden throne. If he thought she was going to sit still and...

'Don't move,' he said, disappearing up the narrow stairway.

'I am not a dog,' she called after him. 'I do not respond to commands.' But when she stood up, she came over a little dizzy, so sat back down again. It was probably just the sight of blood, and the throbbing in her hand. She stayed seated, not because he'd told her to, but because it was the prudent thing to do. Once the dizziness had passed, she would tend to the wound herself. A doctor, indeed. Did he think she was born yesterday?

He reappeared with a first-aid box. 'Not feeling faint, are you?' He placed his hand on her forehead. She batted him away. 'Good to see there's nothing wrong with your reactions.' He opened the box and tore open a small white packet. 'This might sting.'

'I'm more than capable of... *ouch*!'

'Hold still and it'll be over quicker.' He carefully wiped around the wound.

'I never asked for your help.' She sounded grumpy, but she didn't care.

'You like being in control, I get that. This will be a new experience for you.' He crouched down on his haunches. 'Think of it as character-building.'

She tried to ignore the weight of his arms resting on her thighs. 'My character is just fine, thanks.'

'Would it kill you to accept help for once?' His face was a picture of concentration as he cleaned the graze. 'Particularly from someone who knows what they're doing.'

She glared at him, even though he wasn't looking at her. 'Right, because you're a doctor. Pull the other one.'

He looked up. 'This may come as a shock, but I wasn't lying.'

She raised her eyebrows. 'You're a doctor?'

He inspected the wound. 'Technically, I'm on a sabbatical, but I think I'm qualified to treat a graze.'

'A doctor?' She couldn't believe it. 'Who sounds like a cartoon character?'

He opened a packet of plasters. 'That's my parents' fault. I was named after the eminent surgeon Barnabas Winston. I think they hoped it might inspire me to become a medical pioneer.'

'And has it?'

He shook his head. 'Not in the slightest.'

'They must be disappointed.'

He gave her a rueful smile. 'You have no idea. Any allergies?'

She frowned. 'Pardon me?'

He held up the plasters.

'Not to my knowledge.'

'Plus, they never watched TV so their blunder didn't become apparent until I started school.' He folded a small piece of gauze in half and covered the wound. 'You can imagine the ribbing I got.'

She could. She still wasn't sure she believed him, though. 'Where did you train?'

'Queen Mary's, University of London.' He answered without any hesitation.

Thinking up a university wasn't difficult; she needed more proof. 'What's the medical definition of paracetamol?'

He smiled. 'Analgesic antipyretic derivative of acetanilide.'

Okay, that was slightly more impressive. 'What's it used for?'

'It's a common analgesic with mild anti-inflammatory properties.' He peeled the backing away from a plaster. 'Anything else?'

This new development was puzzling. Her brain was struggling to compute. 'So, if you're a trained doctor, why are you dossing about in Cornwall on the beach all day?'

He secured one end of the gauze. 'I do not doss. I have two jobs. I work hard.'

'You know what I mean. Renting out surfboards isn't exactly a proper job.'

He pinned her with a glare. 'Did my parents hire you?'

What on earth was he on about? 'No, why would they?'

'Let's just say they share your view of my current employment status.'

'I'm not surprised.' She assessed his first-aid skills. He'd done a reasonable job. 'Whether you work hard or not, it's still not the same as being a doctor. I don't get it.'

'People rarely do.' He ripped off the backing of a second plaster, but dropped it before he could secure it.

Seeing him fumble was somehow a comfort. She didn't like having to adjust her opinion of him. 'You're clearly not the most competent medic on the planet.'

'Why do you think I left?' He selected another plaster.

She'd meant it as a joke, but realised she'd hit a nerve. His shoulders slumped a little. 'Sorry, that was crass of me.'

He carefully attached the plaster to her skin. 'It's not your fault I was a crap doctor.' When he looked up, something shifted within her.

It was like standing up too quickly, when the world lurches to the right before settling back in place. He smiled, but it didn't reach his eyes. He looked... troubled. She knew better than most how devastating it was when your career went down the toilet. It was clear he wasn't as blasé about the situation as he made out. Maybe she needed to show a little more compassion.

'And for the record, I don't smoke weed.' His dark-blue eyes were speckled with flecks of copper, she noticed.

'Sorry?' He still had hold of her hand.

'You accused me of sitting on the beach all day smoking pot.' His thumb skimmed over the pulse in her wrist. The throb in her hand seemed to increase. 'Inhaling marijuana speeds up the heart rate, expands the blood vessels in the eyes, and reduces the body's ability to carry oxygen.' His tone was seductive, as though he was offering her words from a sonnet, not a medical dictionary. 'It also increases the risk of cardiovascular disease, and lung hyperinflation.'

She should remove her hand from his. Her dizziness had passed... hadn't it?

His hand slid up her arm. 'The effects can often leave a person feeling relaxed and light-headed.'

Someone shouted down from above, breaking the moment. 'Barney, you're needed upstairs!'

He stood up. 'I'd better get back to rehearsal. Keep the wound covered for twenty-four hours. If the skin gets hot or you feel unwell, go to A&E immediately.'

'Thank you.' She struggled to regain her composure. That was twice he'd come to her aid. And she really wasn't happy about it.

He stopped by the bottom of the stairs. 'Oh, and by the

way.' He waited until she looked at him. 'You look much better slightly unravelled.' And with that he disappeared, any hint of insecurity gone.

She glanced down. The top three buttons of her denim shirt were unbuttoned.

How the hell had that happened?

Chapter 12

Wednesday, 6 July

As the bus came to a stop outside the junior school, Lauren checked her watch, wondering if she had enough time to pop home and change her outfit. After-school club finished at four-thirty, and it was now twenty past, so no, there wasn't enough time. She'd just have to deflect questions about why she was wearing one of Auntie Charlie's fancy suits. Even her hair was neat, twisted into an updo. All part of her efforts to improve her financial situation.

The doors on the bus hissed open. Clinging hold of the handrail, she tried to negotiate the gap between the step and the pavement in a too-tight skirt and heeled courts.

It'd been a pointless exercise. There was no way the building society would offer her the position of cashier. Apart from the fact that she didn't have any banking qualifications or office experience, company policy dictated that anyone with debts was automatically excluded from handling customer finances. Funny that.

She crossed the street and headed for the school gates, ignoring the surprised look on the caretaker's face when he spotted her hobbling down the road in shoes that were too big for her.

Lauren didn't know whether Glenda had formally registered the debt with any of the credit-reference agencies, but she wouldn't put it past her. So, when the interviewer had asked whether she had any unsecured debt, she'd answered honestly. Shame had burned in her cheeks as he'd noted down her response. It'd been almost as humiliating as when she'd approached her dad last week and asked him for a loan. She hadn't divulged why she'd needed the money, but his response had been crushing, if not unexpected. She'd received the usual lecture about needing to 'stand on her own two feet' and how she needed to 'budget better' and not succumb to the 'buy-now-pay-later culture' he felt was 'ruining the country'. She wished she'd never asked, but desperation had forced her hand.

Ahead, she could see the lollipop lady guiding children across the road. She didn't need to see the woman's face to know it was Glenda Graham. Her shock of silver hair gave her away.

She didn't want to deal with Glenda today, she was feeling fragile enough as it was, but at least it would enable her to give her this week's twenty-five quid and get the transaction over and done with.

The idea of being indebted to Glenda for months to come had been the driving force behind applying for the cashier's job. Maybe Charlotte had been right. Perhaps putting fun and quality time with her kids ahead of earning a decent salary was irresponsible. But getting a 'proper' job, as Charlotte encouraged, was easier said than done. She was a single parent, with no decent qualifications, who worked part-time in a café. Her CV wasn't exactly impressive. Something that had become apparent during the excruciating thirty-minute interview with the recruitment agency.

As she waited by the crossing, her plan was to slide the

money into Glenda's pocket and keep walking, but Glenda wasn't about to make life easy for her.

'Hello there, my lovely. How are you on this glorious, sunny afternoon?' The lollipop swivelled around to the STOP side.

Unable to pass, Lauren forced a smile. 'I'm well, thank you, Glenda.'

'You're looking very fancy today.' Glenda reached out and felt the quality of the designer fabric. 'Expensive clobber. Come into some money, have you?'

Lauren didn't like the inference. Her finances were none of Glenda's business. 'Here's your money.' She handed over the folded notes.

'Cheers, my dear.' Glenda pocketed the money but, instead of allowing Lauren to cross, stood firm. 'You're a good girl. Reliable. I like that. It makes my life easier. Enables me to help others. Know what I mean?'

Lauren sidestepped, trying to move past Glenda, but the woman wasn't budging.

'So, I'm going to do you a favour. Help you out, so to speak.'

Maybe Glenda was about to relent on the amount of interest she was charging?

'As from this week, I'm increasing your weekly payments to fifty quid.'

For a moment, Lauren wondered if she'd heard correctly. 'Fifty...? But why? I... I can't afford that much.'

Glenda tried for a consoling look. 'It makes sense when you think about it. This way, you'll be able to clear the debt quicker so you can spoil those lovely kids of yours and buy more fancy clothes.' Her hand gripped the jacket material. 'Wouldn't that be nice, eh?"

Lauren shook her head. 'There's no way I can afford fifty

pounds a week, Glenda. So, thanks for the offer, but I'll stick with the current amount.' She needed to stand firm.

Glenda sighed. 'Well, now that's not going to work for me.' She leant closer. 'See Amanda over there?'

Lauren looked over to where another mother was greeting her young child at the school gates, using a walking stick to balance her weight.

'Amanda has multiple sclerosis. Her loser husband left her when she got the diagnosis. Ran off with a younger woman.'

'That's terrible.'

'Isn't it?' Glenda's grip tightened. 'Amanda's kid needs a new school uniform and shoes – the old ones let in water. But she's got no spare cash.'

Lauren swallowed.

'Like I told you before, I'm no high-street bank. I can't lend money if I don't have money. So, if you won't increase your payments, then I can't lend anything to poor Amanda. And you wouldn't want that, would you?'

Lauren shook her head, a sense of numbness creeping into her limbs. She was already struggling to pay twenty-five pounds a week; how on earth would she cope with an increase? She couldn't. It was as simple as that. 'It's not reasonable to expect me to find fifty pounds a week, Glenda.'

The woman's expression narrowed. 'Our contract states that I can vary the terms as I see fit. Remember?'

How could she forget? Charlotte's suit suddenly became very constricting. The waistband seemed to shrink, cutting off the blood supply to her lungs.

Glenda hadn't let go of her arm, which was starting to ache. 'You don't want to end up like poor Amanda, do you? Trying to convince Social Services you're not an unfit mother.'

Lauren's skin began to burn. What was Glenda implying?

Glenda nodded to where Amanda was hobbling down the road. 'Someone reported her to the local authority. Told them they were worried about her kids not being properly looked after.'

Lauren might be struggling financially, but she wasn't about to let Glenda accuse her of being a bad mother. 'I look after my kids.'

'I know you do, lovey. You do a fine job.' Glenda paused. 'Most of the time.'

'What's that supposed to mean?'

'Hey, don't shoot the messenger.' Glenda's nails dug into her arm. 'I'm not judging. But the other mothers talk. You hear stuff when you do this job.'

'What stuff?'

'Like today for instance. Class 4B have been on an excursion down at the beach. But so far no one's picked up your kids and it finished an hour ago.'

Lauren froze, her head trying to compute what Glenda was saying. Oh, God. She'd forgotten Freddie and Flo's school trip. How had that happened?

She tried to move, but Glenda wasn't letting go of her arm. 'Some might say that was irresponsible. You've put your kids at risk. I'm not saying anyone would report you for that, but you need to think about how it all adds up. Before you know it, your kids are in foster care and you're battling with the courts. You don't want that, do you?' Glenda pulled her closer. 'You're a smart girl, you know what I'm saying.'

Lauren did. But she had more pressing things to worry about. 'I'm sorry, Glenda. I've got to go.'

'So, we have an agreement, yes?' Glenda wasn't relenting.

'Don't worry about settling up today. I'm not unreasonable. Bring me another twenty-five quid by Friday and we'll be straight for this week.' Finally, she let go of her arm. 'Good girl.'

Lauren stumbled backwards, rubbing her sore arm.

Glenda marched into the road and held up the STOP sign. 'Let me know if I can be of any help,' she called out, waving her across.

The irony wasn't lost on Lauren, even in her heightened state of panic. Glenda could bloody well help by not screwing her over and threatening to report her for being an unfit mother – which, right at that moment, she was. Oh, God. She'd screwed up.

Fighting off the tightness in her chest, she ran down the road towards the beach. Well, she tried to run, but Charlotte's skirt was too tight. When she reached the quayside, she raced down the stone steps. The sand sank beneath her feet, making progress hard, so she kicked off her shoes. The rocks loomed in the distance, jutting up from the sea, their grey shapes a contrast to the blue sky behind. The sun was out. Bodies filled the beach, making it hard for her to pick out her kids. Where were they?

And then she spotted them, dancing about in the sand, their red hair a contrast to their green uniforms. They were with Nate. He was tossing a Frisbee into the air for them to catch. She stopped running and tried to catch her breath. Nothing bad had happened. Her kids were safe. She could stop panicking.

Shrugging off Charlotte's suit jacket, she headed over to where they were currently fighting over the Frisbee. Nate was distracting them from their squabble by holding the toy out of arm's reach. Her kids jumped up like playful puppies, squealing with laughter. She wasn't sure whether she should be grateful that her kids had Nate to look out for them, or concerned they were becoming too attached. It was probably too late to be worrying about that.

When her kids spotted her, they ran over, talking animatedly about their day.

'We collected seashells and hermit crabs and seaweed.' Freddie's words came out in a tumble.

'And a broken oar from a fishing boat swept out to sea,' Flo added, excitedly.

Lauren smiled. They weren't exactly traumatised by her absence, were they? 'It sounds like you had a fun day. Sorry I wasn't here to collect you. I was running an errand and got delayed.' Feeble. Pathetic. Definitely an unfit mother.

'That's okay. Nate looked after us. Did you know he rescued a cow?' Freddie's face glowed with wonder. 'How cool is that?'

'Very cool.' It was like her kids hadn't even noticed she'd messed up... unlike Glenda.

As they continued regaling her with their exciting day, Nate ambled over, a smile on his tanned face. The sleeves of his white T-shirt were rolled up to show off his tattoos, and his cut-off jeans hugged his thighs. 'Hey, Lauren. I've been trying to call you.' His eyes travelled over her unusual attire and flustered appearance. 'Everything okay?'

'I switched my phone off temporarily and forgot to switch it back on.' She wasn't about to admit that she had no credit. 'I'm so sorry.'

He smiled. 'No harm done. I was on the beach anyway. Figured you'd be here soon enough.' If he thought she was a bad mother, he was too polite to say so.

'Thank you for looking after them.' And thank God she had him listed as a childminder with the school.

'No worries.' The kindness in his eyes made her skin tingle.

She looked away, focusing on her children. 'Say thank you to Nate, please.'

Freddie gave him a high five. Flo hugged him. 'Love you, Nate!'

Nate laughed. 'Love you too, munchkin.'

So much for them not getting too attached.

Her kids ran off, eager to continue their game. 'Don't go far,' she yelled after them.

When she looked back at Nate, he was watching her, his head tilted to one side. 'What's with the suit?'

She didn't want to see his expression, so ambled down the beach. 'I went for a job interview.'

He fell into step beside her. 'I didn't know you were job hunting. I thought you liked working at the café?' It was too much to hope he wouldn't question her.

'I do, but there's no harm in seeing what else is out there, is there?' It sounded feeble, even to her own ears. But how else was she supposed to improve her finances?

He nodded slowly. 'Guess not. It's just, you always struck me as having the right balance between working and looking after your kids. You do an amazing job.'

If only he knew. What with Charlotte pushing her to 'better herself' and Glenda accusing her of being an unfit mother, she fell woefully short of 'amazing'.

Her sigh must have been audible, because he touched her arm. 'You can talk to me, you know. About anything.'

She looked at his concerned expression, full of warmth and affection. It would be so easy to fall into his arms and rest her head on his shoulder. Maybe then she wouldn't have to worry so much about balancing everything. But that would just play into Glenda's hands and confirm she wasn't up to looking after her kids by herself. 'I'm fine,' she said, looking away. She didn't want to see the pity in his eyes.

'I'm here for you. You know that, right? If you need anything, like help with the kids, or chores around the flat, just say the word.'

'You do more than enough already. Thanks again for looking after them today.'

'I like hanging out with them.' And then he cleared his throat, as if gearing himself up to say something. 'The offer extends to... um, money... if you need it.'

She stopped walking. 'Why would you say that? What have you heard?'

'Nothing.' He held up his hands. 'Nothing, I promise. It's just, I figure it must be tough bringing up two kids on your own.'

'I don't need any help, thank you.' Her face burned with humiliation.

'Okay, whatever you say. I just wanted to throw it out there. Sorry.'

Any further response was cut off by the sound of Freddie shouting. 'Mum! Mum!'

She turned quickly to see him sprinting across the sand. He almost fell into her. 'Okay, calm down. What's happened?'

'Flo's fallen. I tried to pull her out, but she's stuck.'

Lauren looked over to where he was pointing. A wave crashed against the rock face spraying up whitewash. For the second time that day, she found herself running.

Nate charged ahead, reaching the rocks in seconds. He

climbed up, jumping across the gaps in the rocks, calling Flo's name.

Lauren's body wouldn't move fast enough. If felt like forever before she reached the rocks. 'Wait here, Freddie, I don't want you falling as well. And don't run off.' She kissed his cheek and climbed onto the rocks, the slippery surface making it hard to keep her balance in a tight skirt.

As she reached Nate, she heard him say, 'It's okay, sweetheart, Mummy's here.' He'd found her. Thank, God.

Lauren knelt down, positioning herself over the gap in the rocks. It took a while for her eyes to adjust to the darkness. And then she saw her daughter's freckled face looking up at her.

'I'm a bit stuck,' Flo said, her bottom lip wobbling.

Lauren frowned. 'You are, aren't you, sweetie? How have you managed that?'

'I was hiding from Freddie.'

She lowered her hand, gesturing for Flo to take hold. 'Are you hurt?'

Flo shook her head. 'My welly boot's stuck under the rock.'

'Can you pull it out?' She squeezed her daughter's hand. 'Give it a big tug for me?'

Flo squealed in pain. 'Ow!'

'Okay, darling. Don't worry. We'll try something else.' She realised her skirt was wet from lying on the rock face. Not that it mattered. She turned towards Nate, hoping he might have an idea, only to discover he'd stripped down to his underpants. The shock of seeing his near-naked body in such close proximity momentarily distracted her from what was happening.

Before she knew it, he was lowering himself into the gap

next to her daughter. 'Hey there, squirt,' he said, as he eased himself down. 'Room for two down here?'

Flo half-smiled, her hand reaching out to him. Lauren's heart pinched.

'I'm going to crawl under you and release your boot, okay?'

She nodded.

Lauren reached down and stroked her daughter's head. 'Not long now.'

Florence looked distressed. 'Am I in trouble, Mummy?'

'No, my darling. You're not in trouble.'

For the next few minutes, while Nate silently worked out of sight, all she could think of was how this was another black mark against her as a parent. She obviously hadn't been paying attention. She'd been too busy musing over her feelings for Nate, imagining what it would be like to touch him, to have him in her life...

A wave crashed over the rocks, snapping her from her reverie. Good. There was no time for wishful thinking.

When she heard Nate call out, 'Okay, she's free!' a swell of relief consumed her.

His face reappeared above the rocks, wet and covered in debris. He pulled himself onto the rock face and took hold of Flo's hands, handling her daughter like she was precious cargo – which she was, of course. He eased her free and then carried her down to where Freddie was waiting.

Nate climbed back onto the rocks to help Lauren down, his expression one of concern. 'You okay?'

'Thanks to you, yes.' She hugged him, which was a bad idea. His skin was warm and smooth and smelt of seawater.

When he whispered, 'Anything for you,' she had to force herself to let him go, the impact of his words making her shiver.

Trying desperately to hold it together, she climbed down off the rock face and sunk to her knees, enveloping her daughter in a hug. 'Well, that was a bit of an adventure, wasn't it?'

Freddie patted his sister on the head and then turned to Nate. 'Is that how you rescued the cow?' he asked, as only an eight-year-old could.

Nate laughed, causing another swell inside Lauren's chest. 'Similar. Lucky for me, Flo's only got two legs.' He jumped back onto the rock face to retrieve his clothing.

Lauren tried very hard not to stare at his body.

Instead, she looked at her daughter, checking for signs of injury. She appeared to be okay, although her expression was troubled. 'What's wrong, sweetie? Are you okay?'

Flo wrinkled her brow, her beautiful face smeared in seaweed and dirt. 'I was just thinking how Auntie Charlie's not going to be very happy about her suit.'

It was such a daft thing to say that Lauren started laughing. 'No, my love, she isn't.'

Florence frowned. 'Can I stay at Granddad's while you tell her?'

Lauren's laughter increased.

And at that moment, all her money worries paled into insignificance. So what if she had a debt? Or that her flat was cramped and shabby, and she didn't have a high-flying career? All that mattered was her family. Spending time with them was more important than paying off Glenda, or getting a better paid job. She wasn't going to compromise on that. Because without them, life just wasn't worth a jot.

Chapter 13

Thursday, 14 July – 6 weeks till curtain-up

The view from Titania's grove was impressive, even in the fading daylight. The scaffolding had yet to be covered in foliage, but the elevated platform meant that Charlotte could look out across the sea and take in the full impact of the location. The Corineus Theatre was stunning. She'd designed for palatial mansions before, even a grand stately home, but she'd never worked in an amphitheatre. The seating was cut into the rock face, and the stage jutted out over the sea, as if suspended in thin air. Below her, the waves collided with the rocks, sending up lively sprays of water. Not that she was looking, it was too far down, but she could hear the surf slapping against the shoreline.

It'd been a productive week. She'd spent most days at the theatre building the set, turning her ideas into reality, assisted by her dad. She couldn't remember the last time she'd spent a week in his company. They'd worked in companionable silence, constructing the treehouse for Oberon and Puck to hide in, only stopping to chat during tea-breaks and lunch. But their fleeting interludes had given her an insight into the man he'd become, and she was startled by what she'd discovered.

For eleven years, she'd convinced herself that grieving for the loss of a significant family member was normal, healthy, and only to be expected. So she'd never questioned as to why she continued to feel sad, and assumed the rest of her family felt the same. But her dad wasn't sad anymore. He loved his life by the sea. He worked on the fishing boats, which he said gave him an adequate income. He took part in hobbies, which gave him a social life, and he volunteered for the RNLI, which made him feel useful. He was content, no longer weighed down by grief and sadness. This became even more evident when he began whistling, something she hadn't heard him do since childhood.

Sylvia had also turned up a couple of times to 'help'. Unfortunately, she was more of a hindrance, even when it came to completing a simple task, like varnishing the wooden toadstools. Three times she'd knocked over the pot, spilling liquid everywhere and treading it across the stage. The time it'd taken to clear up, Charlotte might as well have done the job herself. But as Sylvia regularly made her dad smile, she could forgive her less practical attributes.

Despite the trials of dealing with Sylvia, she was amazed to find herself looking forward to waking up each day and starting work on the set. She'd almost go as far as to say she was enjoying herself. Her headaches had gone, and although the stiffness in her shoulders remained, she certainly felt more relaxed. This morning, she'd actually left the flat without feeling the need to tidy up first, a real breakthrough. She wouldn't go so far as to say she'd 'dropped the stick', but she'd certainly loosened her grip.

Being involved with amateur dramatics was surprisingly fun – if you ignored the chaos, disorganisation and bizarreness of people pretending to be other people. They were a nice group, particularly Paul from the boutique. He'd joined her on a trip to the neighbouring town last Monday to source a lantern for the show, and they'd ended up having lunch followed by an afternoon shopping. He was funny and quick-witted and had excellent taste in clothes. She hoped they might stay in contact when she returned to London.

The only person she wasn't keen on was Daniel Austin. When she'd been introduced to him, he'd lifted his chin as if he was somehow superior and had offered her a limp, sweaty hand. For a moment, she'd wondered if he wanted her to kiss it. Thankfully, he didn't. But his greeting of, 'Good to have some new blood in the society,' didn't endear her to him and made him sound like a creepy vampire.

She moved away from the edge of the raised platform, gripping the handrail as she descended the four steps. The ties on the front of her nude-coloured blouse flapped in the breeze. She wanted to reach up and ensure the knot hadn't come undone, but clinging hold of the handrail was more important. The platform wasn't that high up, but the sheer drop behind was enough to turn her legs to jelly. The tree house she'd built was even higher. How the actors would cope up there, she didn't know. She was just grateful her dad had been on hand to lay the flooring so she was spared from working six feet off the ground.

It was unusual for the rehearsal not to have started by now, especially as it was gone eight o'clock, but there was a distinct lack of play-related activity. The director was talking animatedly on his phone, the children were running around the stage, and her dad was helping Barney and Nate carry costumes down from Glenda's car.

Her gaze lingered on Barney's backside as he reversed down the myriad stone steps leading from the car park to the theatre. She looked away, scolding herself for ogling, and focused on Lauren instead, who was sitting on the bottom row of the seating, her body language dejected. There were no formal chairs at the theatre, only rows of seating cut into the earth circling the stage, topped with wooden planks.

Her sister's good humour had been dented by a heated conversation with Glenda earlier, which had left her quiet and moody. Charlotte had asked what was wrong, but her sister wasn't forthcoming. Progress with her dad might be good, but she was getting nowhere with Lauren.

Glenda arrived with the material for the fairy grove, her hair blowing behind her like chain mail. 'Looks quite cosy up there,' she said, handing over a heavy bin-liner. 'It's almost better than my caravan.' Her laugh was jolly. 'I've left gaps in the hems for you to feed the fairy lights into, so you can hide the wires.'

Charlotte looked inside the bag, excited to see the midnight-blue panels ready to hang. 'I can't tell you how much I appreciate your help, Glenda. Sewing isn't one of my strengths.'

'Happy to help, love. Now, where's that handsome dad of yours? I've got some breeches for him to try on.' She wandered off, leaving Charlotte wondering how her dad felt about having two women vying for his affections. It was surreal, to say the least.

Charlotte's attention was drawn to the sight of a tall woman descending the stone steps wearing the red wrap dress she'd seen on display in Paul's boutique. She was wearing astonishingly high stilettos, with a diamanté-encrusted red bow pinned to the front of her blonde beehive hairdo. It was only as the woman neared that Charlotte realised it was the transvestite she'd discovered handcuffed to a tree on her first day in Cornwall. What on earth was she doing here?

Charlotte was about to approach the woman, when the director shouted, 'Charlotte!' making her jump. 'Kayleigh Wilson is indisposed this evening. Be a dear and read in for Puck, will you?'

Charlotte froze. *What did he just say?* 'Sorry, Jonathan, for a moment I thought you asked if I could read in for Puck.'

'I did.' He walked over and handed her a script. 'Be a love.'

'But... I can't act.' She tried to catch his arm, but he was already walking away.

He dismissed her concerns with a wave. 'You don't need to act, just read the lines.'

Her heart rate sped up. Everyone was looking at her. 'Seriously, I'm not the right person to do this. I've never even been on stage before,' she said – even though she was standing in the middle of the stage at that moment.

'Actually, you have.' Lauren's voice cut through the panic filling her head. 'You played the grandma in *Ernie's Incredible Illucinations* at school.'

She looked over at her sister. *Not helpful*. 'I was nine. I hardly think that counts.'

'Places, please.' Jonathan clapped his hands. 'Act Two, Scene One. We'll pick up where we ended on Tuesday.'

She wanted to run and hide, but there was nowhere to go. It would take at least fifteen minutes to climb the steps up to the car park – she knew this, as she'd been doing it all week, and behind her the sea cut off her escape. This was not what she'd signed up for.

The stiffness in her shoulders tightened. 'Isn't there someone else that could do it?' She looked at the transvestite, wondering if she could read the lines instead? She certainly hadn't come over as timid when they'd met back in May. But Jonathan was no longer listening.

Barney appeared next to her, looking relaxed and cheerful. 'Hey, there, Puck.'

She glared at him. 'Not funny.'

He laughed. 'I wasn't trying to be.' He took her script and flicked through the pages. 'Here you go. Page sixty-three. Don't panic, you don't have much to say.'

This was of no comfort. And then he put his arm around her. Bloody cheek. If he thought...

'"My gentle Puck, come hither."'

Oh, he was acting. Right. Well, she'd forgive him... on this occasion.

He led her to the front of the stage. '"Thou rememberest, since I sat upon a promontory and heard a mermaid on a dolphin's back uttering such dulcet and harmonious breath that the rude sea grew civil at her song?"'

His voice resonated right through her. She was quite mesmerised, especially as he was looking at her in such a way that made her skin tingle.

'It's your line,' he whispered.

'What?... Oh, God, sorry.' She looked at the script. '"I remember."' *Was that it?*

He moved away, directing his speech to where the audience would sit. '"That very time I saw, flying between the cold moon and the earth, Cupid all armed. A certain aim he took and loosed his love-shaft smartly from his bow."'

The director jumped up when someone snorted. 'It wasn't

funny the first time, people! And it's certainly not funny now. Concentrate, please!'

She looked at Barney, who mouthed the word 'love-shaft' at her, letting her in on the joke. The director was right, it was very childish. So why was she laughing?

Barney reverted to his character. '"The bolt of Cupid fell upon a little western flower. The juice of it on sleeping eyelids laid, will make man or woman madly dote upon the next living creature that it sees. Fetch me that flower and be thou here again."'

His delivery was so hypnotic, she felt as though someone had put a potion on *her*. Not that she was about to fall madly in love with him. No way. He was playing a part. He was supposed to sound seductive. He was just very good at it, that was all.

She checked her script. '"I'll put a girdle round the earth in forty minutes."'

'Well done,' he whispered. 'Now we exit into the tree house.'

'Oh, right.' And then her brain caught up with his words. 'We do *what*?'

He ushered her across the stage, moving her out of the way of Nate, who was running across the stage, pursued by the transvestite, who abruptly stopped and gave Nate a blank look.

Not a strange sight at all.

'"You draw me, you hard-hearted Adam Ant,"' prompted Nate.

'*Adamant*, Mr Jones. You are not an eighties pop singer!' Jonathan's hands went to his head. 'Lord, preserve me.'

Barney was up the makeshift ladder before Charlotte had even reached the first rung. Part of her wanted to stay at the bottom – after all, no one would expect her to act out the moves as well as read the words, right? Plus, she was wearing skinny jeans and heels, she hadn't come suitably dressed for tree climbing. But then, how would it look if the person who'd built the tree house wasn't prepared to risk going up it? As a designer, she needed to road-test her construction. It was only fair. However much it pained her.

Nate addressed the transvestite. Charlotte really needed to stop calling her that, but she couldn't remember her name. Randy? Sandy? '"Get thee gone, and follow me no more."'

Barney's face poked out from the tree house. 'You okay?'

No, she was not okay. 'Yes, I'm fine.' Except her nerves kicked in the moment her foot connected with the first rung. Trying to secure her footing in heels as she climbed up with script in hand wasn't easy. The ladder was concealed beneath dense camouflage netting that she'd managed to procure from the British Army store.

As if sensing her anxiety, Barney held out his hands and pulled her up the ladder. It was a sudden movement, one which meant she landed with her upper body balancing in the tree house, her arse balancing precariously out of it. She lifted her head. 'I'm stuck.'

He grinned. 'I can see that.' He grabbed the belt loops at the back of her jeans and hoisted her into the tree house.

The momentum of hauling her up caused the construction to shift. She reached out for something to grab. Oh, God, they were about to die. She closed her eyes, waiting for the sound of creaking as they tumbled to the ground...

'You can open your eyes now.' There was definite amusement in his voice. He thought it was funny, did he?

Peeking out of one eye, she could see the tree house was

still standing. It also alerted her to the fact that she was gripping hold of his thigh. Flustered, she let go.

He patted the back of her hand. 'Not a fan of heights, huh?'

She was tempted to remark, *you think?* But as her body was shaking and her hands were white from clinging on, she felt it wasn't the time for sarcasm. 'You could say that.'

He smiled. 'Do you want to try and sit up?'

'No!' Her reaction made him laugh. 'I mean, no thank you. I'm fine lying down.' She couldn't move if she wanted to. Sitting up would involve a lot of shuffling, instability, rocking the platform and, most significantly, touching Barney, something her nerves couldn't cope with.

Directly below, she could faintly hear Nate delivering his lines. '"Do I not in plainest truth tell you I do not, nor I cannot, love you?"'

She felt the same way about the man she was squashed into a tree house with.

On paper, Barney Hubble was a catch; a handsome doctor who'd come to her rescue on two separate occasions. But, in reality, he was having a mid-life crisis – twenty years too early – and constantly invaded her personal space. He made her feel out of control, and that wasn't something she appreciated.

He removed a bent packet of cigarettes from his jeans pocket. 'Fancy a smoke?'

'I don't smoke. And it's not safe.' She pointed to the wood surrounding them. 'Or healthy. As a doctor, you should know better.'

He grinned. 'I do. These are Paul's. He left them in the pub last night.'

'Oh. Well, I'm glad to hear it.' For some reason, she was

relieved he didn't smoke. 'Talking of Paul, I noticed he isn't here tonight.'

The sound of Nate's next line prevented Barney responding. '"Tempt not too much the hatred of my spirit. For I am sick when I do look on thee."'

Barney looked amused, for some reason. 'You're right, he's not.'

'The woman who's reading in for him. What's her name?'

Barney glanced down at the actors below. 'Dusty.'

'Dusty, that's it.' She snapped her fingers.

He raised an eyebrow. 'You know her?'

'Not really, I met her once. She seems like an interesting character.' Her arms were starting to ache, she needed to roll over onto her back.

'That's one way to describe her.' He watched Charlotte's pathetic attempts to move, before offering his services. 'Need a hand?'

'No, thanks.' In trying to turn over, the tie around the neck of her blouse got caught underneath her. 'I didn't realise Dusty was a member of the group. Does she have a part in the play?'

Barney hooked his finger in the knot and loosened the tie, enabling her to move. The sensation of silk sliding across her skin made her shiver. 'She's playing Helena.'

Charlotte frowned. 'But I thought Paul was playing Helena?'

His expression turned rueful. 'They're kind of sharing it.'

Am-dram was very strange, she decided. She shifted onto her side. 'I don't suppose you have any chocolate, do you?' A sugar rush might ease the shaking.

He squeezed his hand into his jeans pocket, sliding out the contents. 'Murray mint, ten-pound note, keys, or a condom. Take your pick.'

'You carry a condom?' Her jerky movement landed her on her back. Well, that was one way of doing it.

'Don't get too excited, I think it's expired.' He lifted the packet to the light, trying to make out the use-by date.

She felt herself blush, which was a stupid response. He was a modern man; why wouldn't he carry protection? It was just the intimacy of their close physical proximity that was causing the heat in her face to increase, no other reason.

She needed a distraction. 'So, what makes you think you're a bad doctor?' She moved her head, trying to escape a wayward twig digging into her scalp. 'You didn't kill someone, did you?'

He looked affronted. 'Of course not.' And then grinned. 'Well, never intentionally.'

She realised he used humour to deflect awkward questions. 'I won't judge, I promise. I'm genuinely curious.'

She waited for him to make a smart comment about her inability not to judge, but instead he just shrugged and said, 'Lots of little things.'

Her hair was still caught on the twig. 'Give me an example.'

'Lift your head.' He freed her from the clutches of the branch. 'My first week on the ward, I was asked to insert a catheter into a female patient.'

She stopped ruffling her hair. 'Go on.'

'I couldn't do it. The more I tried, the more flustered I became. Eventually, the consultant appeared and politely enquired as to why I'd spent twenty minutes trying to insert a catheter into the woman's clitoris.'

Charlotte nearly choked on her laughter. 'You did not!'

Barney was laughing too. 'I swear to God, I did.'

'But... but how could you not know? Surely you're familiar with the female form?'

His laughter faded into a seductive gaze. 'Intimately.'

Well, she'd walked right into that one.

'In my defence, there's only one obvious place a pipe can be inserted into a man. Things aren't quite so apparent on a woman.'

She giggled. 'I imagine you must've been quite embarrassed.'

'Mortified would be a better description.'

'Well, you did a good job patching me up.' She showed him her hand.

He inspected the fading wound. 'It's healing well.'

'See? You're not completely inept.' She laughed again, mostly to cover the tingles creeping up her arm from his warm touch.

'You know, you're beautiful when you let go.' The intimacy of his remark killed her laughter quicker than if he'd said, 'Shall we jump from the clifftops into the sea?' Her hand instinctively went to the tie around her neck, but he stopped her. 'Leave it,' he said, sliding his hand into hers. 'You can retie it later.'

Nate's voice below echoed into the rafters. '"Yet you, the murderer, look as bright, as clear, as yonder Venus in her glimmering sphere."'

Barney lowered his face to hers, the weight of his body pressing against her. His slow grin caused a bolt of something liquid to race up her spine. He was invading her personal space again. She should push him away. So, why didn't she?

His smile was laced with intent. 'Now, Charlie, you can't tell me you're not having fun?'

Charlie?

And then he kissed her.

Chapter 14

Sunday, 17 July

It was a busy Sunday afternoon on Penmullion beach, and Lauren had the afternoon off from the café. It was lovely to kick back and savour the warmth of the July sun, and watch the wispy clouds floating across the sky. She drew in a long breath, loving the feel of the sand beneath her bare feet, and the movement of her tie-dye tunic soft against her skin. The sounds of summer ebbed and flowed: the wind kicking up and dying away, herring gulls squawking, the waves slapping against the sand, and the sound of her children laughing.

Freddie and Florence were building sandcastles, their freckled faces happy and worry-free as they ran across the beach, filling their buckets, puzzling as to why the water kept draining away from the moat.

It was bliss. No stressing about loans or debts, only the pleasure of spending a lazy day on the beach with her family.

The only fly in the ointment was her sister.

It'd been something of a surprise when Charlotte had agreed to join them for a picnic. Her aversion to sand, seawater and anything unsanitary, was evident for all to see. But she'd accepted the invitation and even offered to make the sandwiches.

Her sister had also accepted the loan of a pair of shorts, which might have been seen as progress, if she hadn't teamed them with an olive-green silk shirt and black court shoes, instead of casual T-shirt and flip-flops. Charlotte was sitting bolt upright on the picnic blanket, hugging her knees to her chest, flinching every time the kids accidentally splashed water over her.

Lauren adjusted her large straw hat, protecting her eyes from the sun. 'Why don't you lie down? You don't look comfortable.'

Charlotte's attention was fixed on the kids in the water. 'One of us needs to keep an eye on Freddie and Florence.'

Lauren closed her eyes. 'They'll be fine. Just relax.'

'Have you forgotten what happened less than two weeks ago?'

Lauren didn't need to see Charlotte to know she was being subjected to one of her sister's disapproving looks.

'Flo could've drowned.'

Her sister was being a little overdramatic. 'Hardly.' Thanks to Nate, anyway. 'And besides, you can't wrap kids in cotton wool, however much you want to. If I spent all my time worrying about what might happen to them, I'd be a nervous wreck.'

'I don't understand how you can be so blasé.'

Lauren sighed. 'I'm not blasé, I'm realistic. I have enough things to stress about, I don't need to add anything extra.'

There was a brief pause. 'What things?'

Trust her sister to pick up on that.

'Just normal stuff. Being a single parent isn't always easy.'

Thankfully, her expression was hidden behind sunglasses. 'And before you start, can we please not have the lecture about how it's my fault for not getting a better job and improving my situation.'

'I wasn't going to.' Charlotte sounded put out.

'Good. Because I'm happy with my lot. Flo's accident reminded me there's nothing more important than family and spending time with my kids.'

'I agree.'

For a second, Lauren wondered if she'd heard correctly. She shuffled onto her elbows. 'You do?'

Charlotte scowled. 'Don't look so surprised. I didn't appreciate how hard you worked, and how much you have to juggle, before I came to stay. I made a judgement. I was wrong. I apologise.'

Lauren was speechless.

'I just wish you'd let me help you on occasion.' Her sister returned to looking at the kids.

Was she serious? 'I do let you help.'

'Actually, you don't.' Charlotte glanced over her shoulder. 'When I clean the flat, you get annoyed because you can't find where I've put things. When I iron the children's uniforms, I get told I'm wasting time on something that doesn't need doing. Even the ham I bought for the sandwiches was wrong. Although I've no idea why – Freddie and Flo enjoyed their lunches...'

How could Lauren admit that she didn't want her kids getting a taste for posh ham from the butchers when she could only afford the cheap stuff from the convenience store.

'... and when I tried to pay the phone bill you went ballistic.'

On that point, Lauren sat up. 'Because it's not your responsibility, it's mine. I have to stand on my own two feet. Budget better. Not rely on others to bail me out.'

Charlotte brushed sand away from her shorts. 'You don't want my help? Fine. But try and see it from my point of view. I've been staying with you for nearly two months, and you won't let me contribute anything towards the bills.'

'You're unemployed.'

'I have savings.' Charlotte got to her feet, shaking sand away from the picnic blanket before placing it back down. 'I'm living with you rent-free, for which I am very grateful. At least let me buy a few treats on occasion.'

The awkward silence that followed was filled with Freddie and Florence charging up the beach with their buckets. Having deposited more water into the moat, and scattering sand over the blanket, they ran back to the sea.

Lauren might have laughed if she didn't feel so conflicted. Accepting financial help from her sister would make life so much easier. But as her dad had pointed out, she needed to be financially independent. Charlotte would be back in London soon, so what was the point of becoming reliant on extra money if it was just going to dry up again. She'd be back to square one. She'd be better off trying to manage on her own and feel the benefit of one less mouth to feed when her sister returned to London. That was the theory, anyway. It was a long shot, but what else could she do?

Still, a bit of posh food now and again wouldn't do any harm, would it? And her sister was right, the kids had loved their sandwiches. 'Okay, but only on one condition.'

Charlotte looked exasperated. 'Why does there have to be a condition?'

'Because you're asking me to make a compromise. I think it's only fair you agree to change something too.'

Her sister's expression turned cautious. 'What is it you want me to do?'

Aware her request might cause another disagreement, Lauren braced herself. 'I want you to let go a bit.'

Charlotte looked puzzled. 'Let go? Let go of what?' On hearing Freddie yelp, she jumped to her feet, not settling until she could see he was just messing around with his sister.

Lauren hadn't stirred, she knew the difference between a playful yelp and when her kids were in trouble. 'Your emotions.'

Charlotte swung around to look at her. 'My emotions?'

'Do you remember, as kids, we joined the Mickey Mouse Birthday Club? Each year we'd go up to The Palladium with hundreds of other kids and watch a film and sing that song about Mickey being better than Donald Duck?'

Charlotte lifted her hands to the sky, looking uncannily like their mother. 'What on earth made you think of that?'

'One year, we were on opposite teams and we tried to outsing each other. You must've been about ten.'

Charlotte frowned. 'Was that the year we ended up having a food fight?'

'That's the one. The organisers couldn't stop the two teams from singing, no matter how hard they tried. And then a boy threw his piece of cake and all hell broke loose. Crisps and sausage rolls flying about, kids laughing and screaming.' The vision of her sister covered in cake would be forever imprinted on her mind. 'I laughed so hard, I wet myself.'

Charlotte smiled. 'Oh, God, you did, didn't you?'

'And you poured orange juice over that awful boy's head because he made fun of me.'

Her sister fiddled with the button on her shirt. 'I'm not sure I understand where this is going?'

'When was the last time you let go like that?'

Charlotte raised an eyebrow. 'Excuse me? Have you forgotten Muddy Sunday?'

'Apart from then?'

Another pause. 'I can't remember.'

'My point exactly.'

Charlotte looked flustered. 'It would hardly be appropriate to act like that now. I'm an adult.'

'But you never laugh anymore, not properly. You're always so controlled and serious.' She crossed her legs. 'Maybe it's being with us in Cornwall that depresses you. Perhaps in London you had more fun?'

Charlotte transferred her weight from one foot to the other. 'Not really.'

'Not even with Ethan?'

Charlotte looked down at the sand. 'He wasn't the fun type. But then, I'm not sure I am either.'

There was a pause before Lauren spoke. 'You used to be, before Mum died.'

Charlotte sat back down on the blanket. 'People change.'

'Or they get stuck.'

Lauren was subjected to a frown. 'What do you mean?'

'I'm no expert, but I'm not sure you've ever properly grieved. You were so busy taking care of me and Dad, keeping strong for us, that you forgot to look after yourself. I never once saw you cry after the funeral. You were always so practical, so... together.'

'But even if that's true, what can I do about it now? This is how I am.'

Lauren did something she hadn't done for years. She reached over and took her sister's hand. 'Just try letting go a bit. Laugh, shout, scream. I don't know, run down the beach, jump into the sea fully clothed, do something to relinquish control. Even if it's letting your hair curl. Do something… reckless.'

Charlotte looked ponderous. 'And you think that'll work?'

'What have you got to lose?'

Whatever Charlotte was about to say next, they were interrupted by the sight of Nate walking across the beach. Her kids ran over to him, splashing him with water. He was wearing his cut-off jeans and a faded Green Day T-shirt. He looked tired. He was also the sexiest thing Lauren had ever seen. His intricate tattoos drew her attention to his forearms. His spiky hair and dark beard made his eyes stand out, and his natural shyness made her want to put her arms around him… which would be a big mistake. She could still recall the feel of his smooth skin and the gentleness of his touch from when she'd hugged him before.

Thankfully, she was wearing dark sunglasses. She dipped her eyes anyway, just in case her expression gave her away. 'Hi, Nate. Late night with the boys?'

He smiled. 'I wish. We had a call-out to one of those party boats. A few bright sparks decided to go swimming and couldn't get back on the boat.'

Flo was hanging on to his hand. 'Did you have to rescue them like you did me and the cow?'

He laughed. 'We did. Your granddad wasn't very happy with them. It's not a good idea to go swimming when you've been drinking alcohol.'

Flo's little face turned serious. 'I'll never do that.'

'Good girl.' The way he smiled at her daughter made Lauren's heart melt.

'Will you play with us?' Freddie offered Nate a bucket.

Lauren jumped in before he felt obliged to join them. 'Nate probably has better things to do with his Sunday.'

'Not really,' he said, and ruffled Freddie's hair. 'How about a game of volleyball. No one's using the net.'

Freddie and Florence ran off to get the ball from the surf kiosk.

Nate looked at Lauren. 'Fancy a game?'

No harm in a game of volleyball, was there? 'Sure.' She got up.

Flo sprinted back over, inadvertently kicking sand over her aunt. 'You too, Auntie Charlie. You can be on my team.'

There was a moment's hesitation on Charlotte's face, a series of conflicted emotions battling it out, before she said, 'Er... okay. I don't know the rules, though.'

'There aren't any.' Flo pulled on her aunt's hands, dragging her to her feet. 'Girls versus boys!'

Lauren smiled at her sister. 'Thank you.'

Charlotte shrugged. 'What have I got to lose, right?'

Lauren threw her hat onto the blanket. 'Come on, shoes off.'

Anyone would think she'd suggested Charlotte cut off her own feet. With some reluctance, she removed her shoes and joined Lauren on the makeshift volleyball court.

Freddie shouted, 'Ready?' and without waiting for a reply punched the ball.

When it didn't make it over the net, Nate picked it up and handed it back to him so he could try again.

Lauren glanced at her sister. 'Can I ask you something? Do you miss Ethan?'

If Charlotte was surprised by the question, she didn't show it. She tucked her hair behind her ears. 'I did at first, but it didn't last long.' She gave Flo a thumbs up when her niece asked if she was ready to receive Freddie's serve. 'He described the relationship as a business arrangement. Maybe he was right. I mean, if I was truly invested, then I'd miss him more, wouldn't I?'

'Do you think it's possible you held yourself back from getting too attached so you didn't get hurt?'

'Maybe. But if I did, it wasn't a conscious decision.' Charlotte squealed when the ball came at her, turning so it smacked her on the bum, making Freddie and Flo laugh. 'What about you, has there been anyone since Joe?' She picked up the ball and threw it over the net.

Lauren shook her head. 'No.'

'You have to punch it, Auntie Charlie,' Flo yelled.

'Oh, sorry, Flo. Next time.' Charlotte shrugged an apology, before switching back to Lauren. 'Why not? Haven't you met anyone you like?'

Lauren risked a glance at Nate. He was stretching up for the ball, his T-shirt riding up, revealing a flash of stomach. 'It's not that. I'm a mum. My kids come first.'

When the ball appeared over the net, Charlotte ducked, leaving it for Lauren. 'I don't understand.'

Lauren punched the ball, sending it flying over the net. 'I can't risk them getting attached to someone who might leave.'

'Good one, Mum!' Flo punched the air. 'A point to us!'

Charlotte looked at her. 'You mean, like Joe did?'

'I have to protect them.' Lauren moved to the back of the court, crouching down, ready for the next serve. 'Maybe one day, when they're older. Until then, it's a no to relationships. No matter how generous and funny and kind that person might be.'

As if reading her mind, Charlotte said, 'Even if that person proves themselves to be reliable and loyal? Maybe even prepared to risk their own safety to rescue one of your kids?'

Distracted, Lauren looked across at Nate, only to be smacked on the side of the head by the ball.

'Oh, Christ!' Nate ran to the net. 'Are you okay, Lauren?'

'Silly Mummy!' Freddie didn't look sorry. He was laughing.

She rubbed the side of her head. 'I'm fine.'

But the sound of Glenda's voice ringing in her ears had her wondering whether she'd suffered concussion. Unfortunately not. Glenda was heading their way. That was all she needed.

'The manager of the café said I'd find you down here.' Glenda waved at the kids, the epitome of friendliness in her baggy shift dress and Scholl sandals.

Why wouldn't the woman leave her alone?

Freddie and Florence continued playing volleyball.

Charlotte waved. 'Hi, Glenda. Fancy a game?'

Glenda laughed. 'Goodness me, no. I wouldn't last five minutes. I've come for a quick word with your sister.'

Lauren moved off the court, keen to keep any conversation private. 'What do you want?'

Glenda looked mildly affronted. 'Bit abrupt, love. I'm being friendly, aren't I?' She held out her hands as though innocent of all crime.

'Sorry, but I don't know why you're here. I've paid you your money this week.'

'You have indeed, love. And I'm grateful. Like I said before, you're a good girl. But something's come up and I need another fifty quid.'

The sight of Glenda's discoloured front tooth momentarily distracted Lauren from registering her words. 'What…? But I can't afford another payment this week.'

Glenda sighed. 'It's Amanda, you see, she's in a tight spot. Her ex still hasn't coughed up his maintenance money. She's short on the rent.'

Panic was starting to grip Lauren. She couldn't believe what she was hearing. 'I'm sorry to hear that, Glenda. But I'm a single mother too.'

'I know, and a fine job you do.' She patted Lauren's arm. 'Let's just hope Social Services feel the same way.'

Lauren recoiled. 'What's that supposed to mean? Have you reported me?'

'Would I do such a thing?' Glenda's attempt at looking outraged fell a little short. 'I'm just saying, if Amanda's evicted, then her kid might get taken into care. You need to think about these things. Make sure you don't put yourself in a similar situation and give the council cause to doubt your ability to provide for them.'

'I'd provide for them a whole lot better if you stopped hounding me for money.' Lauren pulled away. 'I can't find another fifty pounds. I'm sorry, the answer is no.' She needed to stand her ground. This was getting ridiculous.

'Oh well, it was worth asking the question.' Glenda didn't look bothered by her refusal. Surely, though, she wasn't going to leave it there? 'Let's ask that lovely sister of yours instead. She looks like she has a bit of cash to spare.'

Lauren almost fainted. 'Don't you dare! Leave her out of this.'

Nate looked over at the sound of her raised voice. She gave him a little wave, assuring him she was okay.

Glenda wasn't done. 'But, love, what am I supposed to do? You owe me money. And now I need that money back.'

'Glenda, please.' Lauren tried a different tack, hoping that stalling her might derail her ambush. 'Look… even if I wanted to give you the money, I don't have any cash with me.'

Glenda's smile widened. 'No problem, I'll run you to the cashpoint. I don't mind helping you out. It's the least I can do.'

Was she serious? Lauren felt dizzy as well as faint. This couldn't be happening.

'Everything okay over here?' Nate appeared, looking concerned.

Lauren kept her eyes turned away. 'Everything's fine.'

'Anything I can help with, Glenda?' His tone wasn't unfriendly, but there was a definite edge to it.

'Well, aren't you a sweet boy. I don't know. What do you think, Lauren, can he help?'

Panic switched to full-blown terror. The last thing she needed was Nate's help, or worse, his sympathy. He couldn't know about her debt, no one could. She'd be horrified if anyone found out about the mess she'd got herself into. 'Really, it's nothing. We're just discussing costumes for the show.' *Please go away…*

He didn't look convinced. 'Can't it wait until rehearsal on Tuesday, Glenda? Seems a shame to interrupt a family day out.' It was almost as if he knew something. Surely not?

And then Charlotte joined them. 'The kids want an ice cream, Lauren. Are you happy for me to get them one?'

Glenda clapped her hands together in delight. 'Ah, isn't that a nice offer. What a lovely sister you are.'

Charlotte raised an eyebrow, no doubt sensing the tension. 'Is everything okay?'

Lauren nodded. 'It's fine.' Why couldn't everyone just leave her alone.

Glenda took her hand. 'In fact, it's perfect. Lauren just needs to help me run an errand, don't you, love? So, by the time you've got those cheeky kids their ice creams, we'll be back.' She turned to Lauren. 'Unless you'd prefer it if I took Charlotte—'

'No! No, that's okay. I'll do it.' Anything to end the torture. 'Keep an eye on the kids, will you,' she said to her sister. 'I'll be back as soon as I can.' In her eagerness to get away from the look on Nate's face, she almost stumbled.

'You're a good girl, Lauren.' Glenda put her arm around her as she led her away from the beach. 'You always put your family first.'

And wasn't that the truth.

Chapter 15

Saturday, 23 July

Barney had been up since the crack of dawn, helping to set up for the town's annual medieval festival. It was a massive event that drew in visitors from far and wide. The narrow roads leading to the area would be blocked with traffic by mid-morning, so everything had to be delivered first thing, and the car parks cleared, to ensure a successful event. His gig last night at Smugglers Inn had benefited from the increase in visitors, which had boosted his earnings, but the evening had been marred by a call from his mother badgering him to return to medicine in September. He'd ended up drowning his sorrows in beer, and had woken at five a.m. this morning with a raging hangover. Thankfully, he'd been able to go home after setting up for the festival, and had grabbed a couple of hours sleep, showered, eaten a sausage sandwich, and was now heading back there feeling a lot better than he had done earlier.

The morning drizzle had blown away, leaving the promise of another warm July day. Good weather was a huge factor in ensuring the success of the event. Incessant rain would make the grounds around Morholt Castle muddy, and that would keep people away. Income from the event supported the local RNLI, so everyone had prayed for a dry day.

As he strolled past Bridge Street Hall, he noticed the doors were open. He ducked through the doorway, feeling the drop in temperature the moment he set foot inside. 'Anyone here?' His voice echoed up to the rafters.

Charlotte Saunders appeared from the cellar, carrying a roller tray. She startled when she saw him. 'Don't creep up on me like that.'

'I didn't. I called out. What are you up to?'

'Baking a cake. What do you think I'm doing?' She went over to the stage where one of the backdrops hung from the lighting rig.

'Someone's frosty this morning. And there was me thinking our kiss might've thawed you a little.'

She spun around so fast his vision blurred. 'Talking of which...'

'Okay, okay, you don't need to say it.' He held up his hand, to stop the abuse he felt certain was coming his way.

She folded her arms across her chest. 'You don't know what I was going to say.' There was something softer about her appearance today. She was wearing a faded denim skirt, sparkly flip-flops and a white top that had slipped off one shoulder.

He walked over to her. 'I'm guessing it went along the lines of, "You had no right to kiss me, you were very presumptuous, you took advantage of the situation we'd found ourselves in, and under no circumstances ever do it again."' He waited a beat. 'Am I right?'

She held his gaze. 'Well, let's see. Yes... yes... definitely...

and maybe.' She turned her back on him, leaving him to work through his series of statements.

The penny dropped. 'Maybe?'

She handed him a paintbrush. 'Are you here to help?'

'Can't, I'm afraid. I'm on my way out.'

'I wondered why you were looking so smart. Nice shirt.'

'Thanks.' He followed her over to the sink. 'Maybe?... As in, there's a chance of a repeat performance?'

She filled a jar with water.

He decided to chance his luck. 'Personally, I'd be in favour of a continuation.'

She glanced over her shoulder. 'I'm sure you would.'

He moved closer. 'As kisses go, it was pretty hot.'

She stilled.

His mouth was inches from her bare shoulder, inviting him to nuzzle it. If he bent lower...

She slid away, leaving him hanging. 'It was okay. But then I was rather distracted, so it's hard to tell.'

He watched her walk over to the backdrop. Christ, she had a nice arse. 'Any time you'd like a reminder, let me know.'

She tried to hide her smile, which confirmed his theory that there was more to Charlotte Saunders than just a prickly exterior.

In that moment, he made a decision. He went over and took the paint roller from her. 'Tools down. You're coming with me.'

'Excuse me, I need that.' She tried to grab the roller, but he held it out of reach.

'It's a beautiful summer's day. Everyone else is at the Morholt Festival and you're in here painting. Leave this and come and have some fun.'

She looked like she was about to argue, but then something flickered across her face. 'Fun?'

Her hair was wavier than usual, less flat. He liked it. It softened her features. 'Are you familiar with the concept?'

She frowned. 'Of course I am.'

'Good. Then let's go, Charlie.' He took her hand and led her over to the door.

'And that's another thing.' She picked up her handbag. 'My name is Charlotte... Wait!' She tugged on his hand. 'I need to put the roller in to soak.'

He manoeuvred her out the door. 'I'll buy you another one. Live dangerously.'

'I am. I'm spending the day with you, aren't I?'

He laughed. 'You know, there's something very different about you today.' He studied her. 'It's not the hair... which is very nice by the way.' And then it came to him. 'No buttons.'

She ignored him and locked the hall door. 'Where are we going?'

Teasing her was hugely enjoyable, he decided. She was easy to bait. 'Across the quayside and up the hill towards the theatre. Morholt Castle is at the top.'

She removed her hand from his when he took hold of it. 'Is that the ruins you can see from the theatre?'

'Part of it, yeah.' He took her hand again. 'So, no buttons. Are you feeling any withdrawal symptoms? Do I need to arrange therapy?'

She removed her hand again. 'I think I can cope.'

'Then why do your fingers keep twitching? You know, I think it'd help if you held my hand. An aid to breaking the habit.'

She didn't look overly happy, but didn't pull away when he

took her hand again. 'I'm going to regret agreeing to this, aren't I?'

He grinned. 'Now why would you think that?'

He laughed when she gave him an incredulous look.

As they walked along the quayside, he pointed out the boats of interest, enjoying the feel of her hand in his. He couldn't remember the last time he'd held a woman's hand. He'd forgotten how comforting it felt. She listened, looking to where he pointed, asking a few questions as they ambled along. Maybe it was his imagination, but he could almost sense the tension leaving her body. Her hand slowly relaxed, softening so it stopped feeling like he was holding a block of ice. Her stride eased to a stroll and her shoulders lowered a good few inches.

They reached the end of the quay. Her grip tightened as they crossed the bridge. She made a point of not looking down, even when he alerted her to a group of ducks swimming past. When they reached the other side, her hand relaxed again.

The climb up to the castle wasn't overly steep, but it still required a bit of effort, so he stopped talking and saved his breath. The tide was out, making the sea look tranquil. In the distance, two sailing ships sat on the horizon, ready for the festival finale, when they'd sail into shore.

The throng of people grew heavier as they neared the venue, and people were queueing at the ticket gates. Barney bypassed the main entrance and found a side gate.

'Don't we have to pay?' Charlotte looked puzzled.

'Free entry is my payment for helping set up.' He opened the gate for her. 'After you.'

She stopped when the path reached the main area. 'I had no idea it would be so big,' she said, taking in the array of tents and activities taking place. 'Is that a falcon?' She ducked when a large bird swept overhead.

'You can have a go at training them, if you want. Freddie's already signed up.'

'My sister mentioned she was at a festival today. She's doing a stint on one of the stalls this morning. I didn't fancy wandering around on my own.'

'And now you don't have to. You have me as your personal guide. I know what you're thinking. How did you get so lucky?' He led her past the wooden Ferris wheel and Have-A-Go-Catapult tent.

He was subjected to a rueful smile. 'I'm certainly wondering what I did to deserve this.' She shielded her eyes from the sun. 'Where shall we start?'

He pointed to her left. 'Knowing your love of all things orderly, let's stick with tradition and go clockwise.'

'I'm not that bad.' Indignation flashed in her eyes.

He turned. 'Okay, let's go the other way.'

She pulled on his hand. 'No, no, this way's fine.'

Just as he thought. 'How are your archery skills?'

'On a par with my fencing, drag-racing and origami skills.' When he gave her a questioning look, she said, 'Non-existent.'

'For a moment there, I thought you had hidden talents.'

She sighed. 'Nope, what you see is what you get.'

'Now that isn't true at all.' He ignored her puzzled look as they queued for the archery, nudging her when a court jester danced past, the bells on his hat jangling. 'He works in the post office.'

She raised an eyebrow. 'Not dressed like that, I hope.'

The jester played a musical tune on a flute. Behind him, a group of children dressed in medieval clothing followed, mimicking his dance. A little girl trod on the front of her dress and tripped. Barney bent down and picked her up, checking she wasn't hurt before she ran off to catch up with the others.

He realised Charlotte was staring at him, as if trying to make him out.

Good luck with that, he wanted to say.

Her head tilted to one side. 'Why aren't you taking part in the festival?'

He shrugged. 'They needed people to help organise, so I volunteered for that instead.' The queue moved forward. 'I'll take part next year, though. I've always fancied myself as a Knight of the Round Table.'

'Next year?' They reached the front of the queue. 'Won't you be back in London by then, resuming your medical studies?'

He avoided looking at her. 'Maybe. I'm not sure.' He'd had enough discussion about his career; he wasn't up to a repeat performance.

A man and woman led them into a field and gave them a five-minute demonstration on how to shoot an arrow, before retreating to a safe distance.

Charlotte strung her bow, as she'd been shown. 'How can you not be sure?'

He supposed it was too much to hope that she'd let the subject drop. He drew back his bow. 'I told you before, I'm not sure medicine is for me.' He let go, the arrow sailed into the air, wobbled and missed the target.

Charlotte let go of her arrow. 'It seems a shame to waste all that training.' Her arrow formed a perfect arc, hitting the outer circle of the target.

How the hell had she done that? He loaded up another arrow. 'I agree, but no one wants a crap doctor treating them.'

'I don't believe for a second you're that bad. The clitoris story aside,' she said, checking no one was listening. 'And you've already told me you didn't kill anyone. So why do you think you're not a good doctor?' She loaded up her second arrow. 'And give me a specific example. Preferably one that doesn't involve female genitalia.'

He tried to focus on the target, closing one eye so he could zoom in on the central dot. His mind flicked through the many instances of his inadequacy. 'I was on duty in A&E one day. It was manic. Every cubicle was filled. I was dealing with two appendicitises, one pulmonary oedema, two obstructed bowels, and a pancreatitis.'

He paused as he took aim. His arrow swerved into the blue outer circle, hitting the target. Not bad.

'Just as I'd pulled back the curtain of bed eight, a colleague shouted, "*Make sure you've taken an amylase level on the pancreatitis in bed eight*." The woman in bed eight looked at me, and I remember thinking, you're not a blobby pink pancreas.'

Charlotte released her arrow. It hit the inner white circle. Had she done this before?

'Anyway, it made me realise that, as a doctor, you stop seeing patients as people, they become defined by their pathology, stripped of an identity.' He loaded up his final arrow, determined to perform better. 'This particular woman was called Barbara. She lived in Streatham, collected Cliff Richard memorabilia, and had three grown-up kids. None of which played any part in the diagnosis or treatment process.' His arrow wobbled, but had a good flight on it. It landed on the white circle. Not a bullseye, but close enough.

Charlotte pulled back her bow, steadied herself, and released the arrow. It landed with a 'twang' right in the middle of the target.

He turned to her. 'What are you, some kind of archery hustler?'

She shrugged. 'Just lucky, I guess.' She handed the bow back to the woman and joined Barney by the exit. 'So, you think seeing patients as people rather than a condition is a flaw?'

'Hell, yes. My parents frequently tell me it's all part of the coping mechanisms doctors develop to distance themselves from the suffering. Otherwise, they wouldn't survive.'

She followed him onto the path as they headed past the peacock enclosure, towards the drum school. 'I've not worked in that environment, so I don't know if they're right or not. But if a doctor treating me remembered all those intimate details about my life months after treating me, I'd think I had the best doctor in the world, not the worst.'

The sound of the drums increased. 'I think you're romanticising the situation.'

'And I think you're clinging on to the idea that you're a bad doctor so you don't feel so guilty about jacking it in.' She waved at Flo and Freddie as they banged on their drums.

He took a moment to process what she'd said. Is that what he was doing? An awful sinking feeling settled in his stomach. It was the same feeling he got when his parents criticised his decision to leave medicine. He didn't like disappointing anyone, least of all his parents. But every time he tried to make a decision about his future, he just felt more conflicted, not less.

He joined Charlotte by the circle of drummers. She was

talking to Lauren, admiring her Maid Marian costume. Freddie and Flo wore yellow and blue tunics, their red hair concealed under caps with a feather stuck in the top. Barney experienced another pull in his chest as he watched them beat the hell out of their drums. The thought of being a dad was the only thing about his future that he was certain about. It shone like a beacon, giving him a sense of hope. When he imagined himself as a consultant, he didn't feel the same way. Surely that had to count for something?

Charlotte gave up talking to her sister. No one could hear above the noise of the drums. They waved goodbye, signalling they'd catch up later.

Barney and Charlotte walked in companionable silence by the sword school, pottery-making tent, and knight's tavern before the sound of drums faded into the distance, enabling them to hear again. They came across the axe-throwing competition.

Glenda Graham was joyfully taking money from queues of people, stuffing the notes into a leather purse strapped around her middle. A small part of Barney's brain wondered if all the cash would find its way into the RNLI fund. He'd never voice his concerns, as ruining someone's reputation without proof wasn't something he was keen to do. But he did wonder if he should mention Glenda's extracurricular activities to Charlotte. Especially as Nate was convinced that Lauren was indebted to Glenda. There was also the issue of Glenda's two sons, Quentin and Vincent, who sounded like Eton graduates, but looked like a cross between the Krays and the Krankies. Big, dumb, and the muscle behind Glenda-the-Lender's business venture. He wasn't about to get on the wrong side of them. He liked his teeth too much.

He glanced at Charlotte. She'd climbed onto the fence, and

was watching a battle re-enactment in the neighbouring field. People of all shapes and sizes were dressed in suits of armour and chain mail. A canon fired, signalling the first charge. The two sides raced across the field. She laughed when a line of arrows launched into the air and the charging army's general had to duck when a rogue missile nearly landed on his helmet.

Maybe he'd tell her about Glenda another day. He didn't want to ruin her good mood.

When she turned and smiled, he noticed strands of gold highlighting her dark hair. There was a softness in her expression that he hadn't seen before, and he suddenly felt a little light-headed. Must be the hangover. 'Do you want to carry on watching?'

Charlotte shook her head. 'Not really, too much testosterone. What's over there?'

He looked to where she was pointing. 'I'm glad you asked.' He helped her down from the fence. 'Are you feeling brave?'

She looked wary. 'Not in the slightest. Why?'

'How do you feel about a spot of mud wrestling?'

Her wide-eyed expression made him laugh. 'No way. Under no circumstances.' The vehement shake of her head made her hooped earrings swing.

He placed his hand on her shoulder. Her skin was smooth and warm. 'But it's fun. All that rolling around in the mud.'

Her fingers searched for a button on her top. 'Not going to happen.' When he took her hand, she resisted being edged towards the mud pit. 'Think again, pal.'

'Okay, but if it's a no to mud wrestling, then at least say yes to jousting.'

'Jousting? Are you kidding me?' She backed away. 'I'm not getting on a horse!'

He laughed. 'It's not on a horse. This is a static version.' He led a suspicious-looking Charlotte over to where a large circular tube, painted to look like a log, straddled two sturdy ladders. 'Look. You climb into the middle of the log, each armed with an inflatable lance, and try to knock the other person off.' He pointed to the bouncy cushioning below. 'You won't get hurt.'

She didn't look convinced. 'I'm not sure. And I'm wearing a skirt.'

'Are you wearing knickers?'

She glared at him. 'Of course I am.'

Shame. 'Then your dignity will remain intact.' He looked her in the eye. 'Plus, you get to hit me with a stick.'

Her interest grew. 'This is true.'

'And I promise I won't hit you back.'

She chewed on her lip, considering his proposal. Finally, her beautiful face broke into a mischievous grin. 'What are we waiting for?'

He'd fibbed, of course. Once they were on the log and armed with their inflatable lances, he teasingly prodded her, enjoying the look of outrage on her smiling face. She sucked in her breath and clouted him around the head. 'Cheat!'

He retaliated by jabbing her again, making her wobble. She gripped her knees, trying to stay upright – and no doubt trying not to flash her underwear, which was oddly distracting. So much so, that when she whacked him again, he was caught off guard. Her inflatable stick glanced off his head. The blows didn't hurt. The bigger challenge was staying balanced on the log, which became all too apparent when he tried to unseat her with a side blow and ended up falling onto the bouncy cushion below. She'd beaten him twice now.

A few seconds later, she fell too, bouncing a few feet away from him, before landing on his midriff, knocking the wind from his lungs.

'You said you wouldn't hit back.' She tried to climb off him, her laughter and instability sabotaging her efforts.

'I lied.' He poked her in the ribs, making her collapse on top of him again. It was a cheap trick, but he didn't care. He liked seeing her unravel. No other reason, obviously.

She squealed, her body entwined with his like they were playing a bizarre version of Twister. Their close proximity meant that he could savour the full impact of her big brown eyes and soft glossy lips. His arms instinctively tightened around her, setting off a buzz in his blood that immediately travelled south.

And then he was hit by a realisation. Just because he and Charlie Saunders were completely incompatible, there was nothing to stop them enjoying a summer fling, was there? After all, she'd be going back to London in a couple of months and they'd never see each other again. What could possibly go wrong?

Chapter 16

... A few moments later

Charlotte had to admit she was having fun. Even if she was completely shattered. Her eyes were running from laughing so hard, her skirt had ridden up over her thighs and her top was full of creases. She probably looked a complete mess, but who cared. Lauren was right, physical activity was indeed good for releasing tension. Plus, Barney Hubble was looking at her in such a way that it didn't leave much to the imagination. His pupils were dilated, his mouth was slightly open and he was breathing heavily – although that might have been because she was lying on top of him.

'That's twice I've beaten you today.' Her elbow connected with his ribs, making him groan, as she tried to get off him.

'I let you win.' His arms tightened around her waist.

'Oh, really?' She smiled down at him, rather enjoying teasing him for a change. 'Admit it. You lost.'

His grin turned roguish. 'It doesn't feel like I lost.'

She realised he was looking down her top. 'Are you planning on letting me go anytime soon? There are other people waiting to joust.'

He sighed. 'Shame. It's quite comfy down here… when you're not kneeling on my nuts. *Ouch*.'

She rolled off him. 'I was aiming for your head. Easy mix-up.'

He laughed. 'Harsh.'

They crawled to the side of the cushion, the inflatable contraption bouncing beneath them.

It was a relief to get back onto solid ground. The grass had never felt so welcome. She took a moment to straighten her skirt, noticing a smudge of dirt on her top. She gave it a quick rub, but it wouldn't come off.

'Charlotte?'

She rubbed harder. Damn thing. What was it, soil? Chocolate?

'Charlie?'

She looked up.

'I thought that'd get your attention.' He stepped closer, invading her personal space again. Was he going to kiss her? He took her hand. 'Are you having fun?'

She gave a short nod. 'Yes.'

'Good. Then relax and stop worrying about your top.'

'But I…' His finger covered her lips.

'No buts.' He removed his finger. 'The world will not stop turning because of a mark on your top. You look fine. Better than fine. Beautiful, in fact.' His eyes dipped to her mouth. 'Forget about how you look. Focus on how you feel.'

How she felt? Good question. How did she feel?… Warm. Her skin was tingling. It must be the sun. Had she applied sun cream?

'Are you overthinking again?'

She nodded. 'Yes.'

'Let's keep busy. What's next on the schedule?' His hand slipped into hers. 'Shall we check out the real jousting? Nate's taking part.'

'I didn't know he could ride a horse?' She decided it was pointless to keep resisting, and resigned herself to holding hands. It wasn't a huge compromise. The warmth of his fingers threaded into hers was quite comforting. Nonetheless, she didn't want him to get any ideas.

'He doesn't, but he rides a motorbike.'

She frowned. 'I'm not sure that's the same thing.'

'He's one of those people that adapts easily.'

The feel of his shirt brushing against her arm as they strolled along was extremely pleasant. He'd rolled up the sleeves, revealing tanned forearms that she was struggling not to stare at. 'I think he likes my sister.'

Barney laughed. 'I think he does too.'

A big crowd had gathered to watch the jousting. A man's voice came over the tannoy, announcing the contestants.

'Which one is Nate?' She stretched up to see the riders, but they were concealed behind protective armour.

'No idea.'

'Is Paul taking part?'

Barney scratched his head. 'It's not really Paul's thing.'

She looked around. 'Is he here today?'

He looked at her and smiled. 'He'll be along later, when Dusty's boutique closes.'

Of course, it was Saturday. He'd be working.

Her attention was drawn back to the jousting. The rider at the opposite end had lifted his visor and saluted. It was Nate. Everyone cheered. And then the joust began. The riders charged at each other, both missed their targets and rode past. The crowd booed. The second time, Nate made contact, but the other rider didn't. The crowd cheered. On the other side of the course, Freddie and Florence were jumping up and down, rooting for Nate. Lauren was standing behind them, flinching every time the riders met in the middle. When Nate took a blow to the chest, she covered her eyes.

Watching her sister, Charlotte considered how sometimes it was easier to see the obvious when you were looking in from the outside. To anyone else, Lauren and Nate were a good match. They were like magnets, their attraction palpable. It was just a shame her sister couldn't see that.

A cheer went up when Nate's opponent dropped his jousting stick. Nate had won the bout. The announcer introduced the next riders and the crowd began dispersing, moving onto the next spectacle.

'What's going on over there?' Charlotte tried to see past the bobbing heads.

'Mini jousting for kids.'

They made their way over. A smaller course was set up next to the main one, using bicycles instead of real horses. Freddie and Florence were at the front of the queue, obviously encouraged by Nate's performance in the adult competition. Unfortunately, neither child was a particularly gifted bike rider and both lost in the first round. They looked a little upset as Lauren consoled them.

It would probably help if either of them actually owned a bicycle, thought Charlotte, but her offer to buy them both one had been politely declined by Lauren. But at least it was the first time an offer of help hadn't resulted in an argument, so maybe they were finally communicating better. She hoped so.

'Are you hungry?' Barney nodded to a collection of stalls which formed a market area. 'They have everything from pigs on spits, to pottage and venison. The finest in medieval banqueting.'

Charlotte felt herself grimace. 'Sounds disgusting. What are the chances of me finding a sandwich?'

He rolled his eyes. 'Remote.'

There was a bread stall, but it only had loaves, nothing pre-made. Next door was a fruit and veg barrow and a stall selling herbs and spices, behind which, her dad and Sylvia were serving customers.

'Charlotte! Over here, love!' Sylvia nudged her dad, who was measuring out a portion of sandalwood. Her eyes drifted down to Barney's hand holding Charlotte's. 'I think romance is in the air. How exciting.' Her white cloth cap flopped in her eyes.

Charlotte immediately let go. 'No romance, Sylvia. Just friends.'

The woman winked. 'Whatever you say, love.'

Something caught Barney's attention and he wandered off. Great help he was.

Her dad unhooked a large bunch of parsley. 'I wasn't expecting to see you here?'

Charlotte shrugged. 'Barney invited me. Apparently, the festival is a big deal.'

He nodded. 'It is. Probably the biggest event in the calendar. Have you seen your sister?' His purple tunic and baggy white shirt were tied around the middle with a drawstring.

'She was over by the jousting. How are your sales going?'

'Good. This is the last of the stock.' He looked happy, and relaxed too.

Sylvia hung on to his arm. 'It's such a lovely thing to get involved in. Brings people together, isn't that right, Tony?'

'Sure does.' Her dad moved away, his attention switching to a customer. 'Enjoy the rest of your day, sweetheart.'

Sylvia did her best not to flinch when Tony brushed her off, but Charlotte saw the hurt. If her dad wasn't interested, then he shouldn't lead her on. It would be kinder not to give the woman false hope. But then, maybe her dad was like Charlotte herself and kept people at arm's length to avoid getting hurt. Realising she'd done that with Ethan, when Lauren had quizzed her, had been somewhat startling. Another example of how people often didn't see what was right under their nose. Perhaps her dad had created a protective barrier too?

Barney reappeared. 'Right, I've checked the whole area and definitely no sandwiches. But there's a pie stall that looks good.'

'Pie? Won't that be messy to eat?'

He grinned. 'You have two choices. Stay hungry and clean, or enjoy a delicious… tasty… sumptuous pie' – he tickled her midriff – 'filled with delectable ingredients and salty jelly…'

'Get off.' She laughed, wriggling free. 'Show me the pies.'

He raised an eyebrow. 'Isn't that a line from *Jerry Maguire*?'

'No, idiot. That was money.'

'Close enough.' He led her over to where the pie stall was set up. The smells radiating from inside the tent were glorious. 'What do you fancy?'

She wasn't sure her stomach could cope with anything boar-related, so opted for a brie tart and a glass of mead. Barney chose a beef pie and a glass of real ale. The food court was busy, so they moved away from the crowds and found a grassy area by the lake.

Despite encouraging her to 'slum it', Barney produced napkins, paper plates and a sealed wet wipe.

She was impressed. 'Where did you get these?'

'I pinched them from the hotdog van.'

She accepted the offer of a plate. 'Thank you.'

'Yeah, well, I didn't want to risk a meltdown.' He handed her a napkin.

She felt herself blush. 'Am I that bad?'

He left her hanging for a while, no doubt enjoying the look on her face. 'You're all right... when you relax.'

'A glowing endorsement.' She took a bite of tart. It was rich, filled with cream, and probably about a thousand calories. It was heavenly.

He took a swig of beer. 'Have you always been—'

'Highly strung?' She really shouldn't speak with her mouthful. She reached for another napkin.

He smiled. 'I was going to say, a perfectionist?'

'Oh, right.' She swallowed and wiped her mouth. 'Er, I guess so. I think I take after my mum. She was the same.'

'Are your parents divorced? Tony's never mentioned your mum.'

She used the excuse of finishing her mouthful as a way of delaying answering. Saying the words aloud still caused a pinch in her chest. 'She died eleven years ago. Cancer. It hit him pretty hard. Well, it did us all.'

He didn't reply straight away. 'I'm sorry.'

She drank some mead. The warmth of the nectar sliding down her throat was strangely comforting. 'It was a difficult time. Still, you know what they say, what doesn't kill you...'

'Makes you stronger?' He took a bite of pie.

'I was going to say, gives you a lot of unhealthy coping mechanisms and a really dark sense of humour.'

He nearly choked on his pie.

She patted his back, waiting for him to stop coughing. 'I have issues.'

'You think?' He grinned. 'It's not the most uplifting life motto I've heard, that's for sure.' There was no cruelty in his words, and his eyes were twinkling, so she knew he was teasing her. He had nice eyes, she noticed. The same blue as his shirt.

Her fingers were covered in melted brie. No point cleaning them yet, she'd finish her pie first. 'So, what's your life motto?'

He chewed on his pie, seeming to contemplate her question. 'I don't know, really. Something along the lines of: do that shit that makes your heart beat faster and your eyes glow – whether it's painting, acting... sex – do it as often as you can, because that's what life's about. Creating as many passionate, happy moments as possible.' He gave her a knowing look. 'And don't let anyone stop you from doing the things you love, not even yourself.' She hadn't realised that a dollop of brie had landed on her skirt, until he leant across and wiped it away with a napkin. 'Are you going to tell me I'm a dreamer? People usually do. My parents especially.'

She looked down at the mess on her skirt. 'Perhaps it's a little unrealistic.'

'Tell me about it.' He laughed. 'So, what do you want to do now?'

'I don't know.' She tore open the wet wipe and cleaned her hands. 'What haven't we covered yet?'

He checked his watch. 'It's nearly five. We've got a couple of hours before the parade starts. How's your stamina?'

'The mead's helping.'

'Good. Drink up.' He was on his feet, binning the rubbish before she'd stood up.

They continued to explore the festival, ambling along at a leisurely pace, taking in the sights, of which there were many. A mini zoo filled with farm animals. A sculpture workshop. Even a pottery tent, complete with working kiln and oven.

Conversation came easily, she found. Barney Hubble was surprisingly good company. They chatted about the plays he'd acted in, and the enjoyment he got from teaching kids to surf. In turn, she told him about her love of interior design, and how much she was learning from designing for the stage.

Time passed quickly. Before she knew it, it was time for the procession to start and they made their way onto the bleachers. A woman dressed in a long white frock danced in front of the decorated floats, swirling long ribbons in time to the music. A band of drummers followed, noisy and energetic. Next came the jugglers, throwing flame-lit batons into the air, causing the crowd to gasp.

A wagon drove past filled with straw hay bales. The words Buxom Wench were painted in red letters on the side. Sitting on top was a woman wearing a low-cut fancy gown and big wild-west hairdo. She was fanning her face, trying to look coy as she waved and blew kisses at the gentlemen in the crowd.

Charlotte pointed her out to Barney. 'Isn't that...?'

Barney nodded. 'Yep, that's her all right.'

The woman caught Charlotte's eye and blew her a kiss, throwing a handful of rose petals from a wicker basket. Charlotte waved back. Dusty certainly popped up in the strangest of places. And then she stilled... *Dusty*? That was the name of Paul's boutique. What a coincidence. Maybe they were related in some way?

After the parade had finished, Barney suggested they head up to higher ground to watch the evening's music festival. 'We'll get a better view of the fireworks up there,' he said, pointing to the area of the castle above them.

The lights from the festival faded as they climbed higher, away from the throng of visitors and half-cut revellers. The area was cordoned off, but this didn't deter Barney, who lifted the rope and gestured for her to duck underneath.

Never one to break the rules, she hesitated. 'Should we be doing this?'

'I helped organise, remember?' He waited. 'Trust me, it'll be worth it.'

She decided to go with it. What was the worst that could happen? They'd be chucked out for being in a restricted area. Hardly the crime of the century.

The path led to a stone wall covered in vines. At first, she didn't think there was an entrance, but then Barney twisted the ring handle on a wooden door and eased it open. There was something exciting about stepping inside, the contents shrouded in shadows and mystery.

The garden beyond was filled with roses of all kinds, from potted plants to bushes, to climbing plants which were entwined with the vines trailing along the surrounding walls. The sun had almost set, but there was enough moonlight to see the beauty of the flowers.

'Come over here.' Barney led her up a flight of stone steps to the top of a mound. The view was stunning. Directly below, she could see the castle grounds and the festival tents. Music drifted up, mingling with the scent of flowers and the salt of the sea. Penmullion Bay stretched out to the right, the harbour almost empty apart from two tall ships standing proud in the water.

'Are you cold?' He touched her hand, sending a shiver up her arm.

She shook her head. The climb had left her quite warm, aided no doubt by three glasses of mead. The mound was circled by a smaller wall, shielding them from the sea breeze. It was beautiful.

Barney wiped the seat of a wooden bench. 'Come and sit down.' He could be quite the gentleman at times. 'The view's just as good from here.'

She joined him, noticing a plaque screwed to the back of the seat. She peered closer, trying to read the inscription in the dusk. *The legend of Tristan and Isolde is the tragic tale of two lovers fated to share a forbidden yet undying love*. She sat down. 'Is that the same Isolde the drama group are named after?'

'The very same.' His arm snaked around her shoulders.

She contemplated moving, but it was comfy to have something to rest her head against.

'The legend forms the basis for the festival.' He drew her closer, no doubt testing how much he could get away with before she objected.

Strangely, she was in no hurry to move. 'I've heard of the names, but I don't know the story.'

'There've been various versions of the legend throughout the centuries, but the local story is claimed to be the most accurate. Want to hear it?'

'I like a good legend.' She tilted her head so she could watch the stars twinkling above. 'Can you use your acting voice?'

He chuckled. 'How much have you had to drink?'

'Not so much that I won't slosh you if you get fresh.'

His laughter made her head wobble against his arm. 'Okay, settle in, for story time is about to begin.'

'Nice rhyme.'

'Thank you.' He stretched out his legs, crossing his ankles. 'So... Tristan was the nephew of King Mark of Cornwall. Isolde was an Irish princess.' His fingers began playing with her hair. 'After the fall of the Roman Empire, Britain was divided into several clans. Ireland, who had remained untouched by the Roman invasion, grew in power and were able to dominate the weak British tribes. The King of Ireland sent the brutal Morholt to defeat King Mark of Cornwall.'

A loud bang made her jump. 'Jesus, what was that?' She sat up, dislodging his arm from her shoulder.

'The ship's canon.' He nodded at the two ships in the distance. 'It signals their arrival.'

Searchlights circled the water, accompanied by music, which grew in volume – haunting orchestral melodies that swelled up from below.

Barney sat forward, his thigh resting against hers. 'During the bloody battle, Tristan saved his uncle's life by defeating Morholt. But he was injured, and escaped Morholt by boat, which landed on the shores of Ireland.'

The ships' sails began to expand, the sheets of material blowing forward as they caught on the wind. One of the ships had white sails, the other one black. 'Carry on, I'm listening.'

'Tristan was found on the beach by Isolde, and nursed back to health. They fell in love, but she was promised to another.'

The ships began to move in the water, tilting from side to side. 'What happened?'

'When Tristan was about to be discovered by Irish guards, he escaped back to Cornwall to avoid being captured and killed. Isolde vowed to follow him when it was safe, hoping to persuade the king to release her from the promise of an arranged marriage. Tristan requested that the ship carrying her should have white sails to show she was free to marry him, and black sails if not.'

She pointed to the ships. 'Is that why they have black and white sails?'

'It is.' He rested his elbows on his knees. 'Tristan arrived back in Cornwall and helped defeat the Irish, but he was seriously wounded. He took to his sickbed and awaited the arrival of Isolde.'

Charlotte sat back, allowing Barney to resume his previous position, tucking her under his arm. 'I have a feeling this isn't going to end well.'

'Each night he waited for her. Finally, the ship appeared on the horizon, bearing white sails.'

She rolled her head to look at him. 'There has to be a but...?'

'Too sick to sit up, he asked about the colour of the sails. Jealous of his passion for Isolde, and knowing the significance of the colour, his nurse lied and told him they were black.'

Another bang made her jump. A red flare exploded into the sky, followed by a spray of green.

Barney's warm hand found hers. She didn't object. It was nice to be held. 'Tristan fell into despair and died. When Isolde arrived, and learned of his death, she too died from grief.'

A shower of blue and gold shimmered above them. 'That's a horrible story.'

His thumb circled the back of her hand. 'There's a happy ending… of sorts.'

Another firework whizzed into the air. 'I can't see how?'

He got up, dislodging her from the comfort of his embrace, and pulled her to her feet. 'They were buried here in Cornwall.' He manoeuvred her so she was standing in front of the mass of foliage covering the curved wall. 'From Isolde's grave, a rose tree grew, and from Tristan's, came a vine that wrapped itself around the tree. Every time the vine was cut, it grew again – a sign that the two lovers could not be parted, even in death.'

Behind them, the fireworks continued to explode, firing trails of glitter into the night sky to mingle with the stars. Faint music danced on the breeze, heady and hypnotic.

His hand stroked her forearm, stirring her from her thoughts.

'Is this part of some cunning plan to seduce me? Feed me mead, tell me a romantic story and bring me up to this beautiful spot, where we just happen to be alone?'

She felt him smile. He leant closer and whispered in her ear. 'Has it worked?'

The shiver that ran across her skin coincided with another firework exploding. She turned to him, the warmth of his body dragging her mouth towards his. 'Maybe.'

With that one word, he closed the gap and kissed her. If she'd anticipated having any time to formulate her thoughts and decide whether she wanted anything physical to happen or not, it was overridden by an explosion – and not just the fireworks above. With no recollection of how she found herself there, her back was pressed against the wall and she was kissing him with complete abandon. He seemed to take this as encouragement. His hands were everywhere. Under her top. Over her breasts. Unhooking her bra. *Good God.*

Her mind couldn't keep up. Tiny objections kept creeping into her consciousness about the inappropriateness of their location, the unsuitability of their personalities, the differences in their situations, but they were wiped out by feeling, a physical response to what he was doing. It was so powerful she couldn't have stopped if she'd wanted to.

And she didn't want to.

She was starving... craving his touch... his mouth... the weight of him. His hands cupped her bottom and lifted her up, his hips moved between her legs. Her skirt was around her waist. She didn't care. Her hands laced into his hair, gripping hold. His mouth covered hers, hot and insistent and... *Oh, God...*

Let go, her sister had said... *Do something reckless*, her sister had said...

Chapter 17

Tuesday, 26 July – 4 weeks till curtain-up

The weather had been crap all day. So much so, the rehearsal had been moved from the Corineus Theatre to the village hall for the night. Trying to act in an outdoor space whilst being battered by high winds and torrential rain really wasn't much fun. Barney hadn't complained when Jonathan announced that they were changing venue – even if it hadn't helped improve the director's mood. With less than a month till curtain-up, Jonathan was getting increasingly stressed. The situation wasn't helped by the kids messing about, Daniel moaning about the 'authenticity' of his costume, and Sylvia forgetting her moves.

Barney was staying well out of it. He was keeping a low profile, tucked away in the corner of the hall, until he was needed. It also meant he could avoid Kayleigh, who'd taken to sitting next to him whenever she got the opportunity, telling him about her bass lessons and her plans to join him on stage when she could manage a whole song without forgetting the key, which wasn't an appealing prospect. Avoiding her wasn't overly mature, but his subtle hints didn't seem to be working.

The other reason hiding at the back of the hall appealed

was so he could watch Charlotte working on the set without anyone noticing. She was decorating the army netting for the fairy grove with artificial flowers. Dressed in a knee-length skirt and loose-fitting man's shirt covered in paint, she wasn't an obvious object of lust, but in his eyes, she was gorgeous as hell. After all, he knew what lay hidden beneath the conservative exterior. And, boy, had that been a surprise. He was still struggling to convince himself that it had really happened and wasn't just erotic wishful thinking.

She stretched up to attach a flower to the top of the netting. His gaze was drawn to her calves, accentuated by the hint of a tan. She reached higher, her upper body leaning forwards, her backside sticking out, straining against the fabric of her skirt. He seriously hoped last Saturday wasn't a one-off.

As if sensing his need to be cooled off, a shower of cold water sprayed across his face. He turned to see Nate removing his crash helmet, his biker leathers soaked from the rain. 'Everything okay?'

Nate shrugged off his jacket and dumped it over the back of a chair. 'Not really. A man jumped off the cliffs tonight.'

No wonder his mate looked so forlorn. 'Christ, and in this weather, too.'

Nate rubbed his face. 'It took ages to reach to him. We were in danger of being smashed against the rocks.'

As if emphasising the point, the wind outside pelted rain against the windows. 'I assume he died?'

Nate nodded. 'He was alive when we first got to him, but his injuries were too severe. Way beyond my basic first-aid skills. By the time the medics arrived, he was past saving.'

'Suicide?'

Nate unzipped his boots. 'Looks that way.'

It never ceased to shock Barney how much the RNLI had to contend with. Before moving to Cornwall, he'd assumed they only dealt with boating incidents. But over the last year, they'd been called out to rescue numerous swimmers caught in the riptide, hikers falling from the costal path, and even a family trapped in their home when the area was struck by heavy flooding. It was an incredibly demanding job. And they didn't even get paid for doing it. 'Why don't you head home. Give rehearsal a miss.'

'Nah, I'm all right. I need the distraction.' Nate ran his hands through his hair.

Above the mayhem of the kids practising their fairy dance, Jonathan spotted Nate across the room. 'Nice of you to join us, Mr Jones. Can we expect Mr Saunders any time soon?'

Nate didn't rise to the bait. How, Barney didn't know. 'He'll be here soon. He's just finishing up with the police.' It was a much politer response than Jonathan deserved – he clearly didn't appreciate that the RNLI put their lives on the line every time they were called out.

'How very dramatic, if somewhat inconvenient.' Jonathan returned to trying to appease Daniel, who was sulking over the cut of his breeches.

Nate sat down. 'Dickhead.'

Barney tried to ignore Kayleigh smiling at him as she read in for Tony. 'Seriously, mate. Are you sure you want to be here? You look fucked.' It was a look he recognised. That slightly haunted expression, dark-rimmed eye sockets and sickly pallor. 'Stuff Jonathan.'

'I'd rather keep busy.' Nate rubbed his face again. 'Plus, it's not just the call-out.' He lowered his voice. 'I've done something I might regret.'

Barney raised an eyebrow. 'Illegal?'

Nate shook his head. 'But it might land me in hot water.' His eyes drifted to Lauren, who was modelling her costume for an unimpressed Jonathan. 'I saw this poster at the police station about loan sharks. There was a number on it for people to report suspicious activity.'

Barney looked at his friend. 'Tell me you didn't?'

The hall doors crashed open. Tony arrived, accompanied by a gust of wind. The kids squealed. Jonathan's script blew off the table, scattering pages everywhere. Sylvia rushed to close the doors. Daniel hastily retrieved Jonathan's script for him.

Nate shrugged. 'It was a spur of the moment decision.'

Jonathan signalled for Kayleigh to continue reading in while Tony removed his soaked overcoat, assisted by Glenda, much to Sylvia's irritation.

Barney glanced at Lauren, who didn't look like she enjoyed being scrutinised in her shapeless costume, even if Jonathan's attention was only half on her as he bellowed directions at the actors. 'This could end badly. You know that, right?'

Nate's gaze settled on Lauren. 'But look at her? She's lost weight. She hardly ever smiles anymore. I had to do something. So, I called them and gave them Glenda's name.'

Barney considered this. It wasn't the end of the world. After all, Glenda most probably was a loan shark, so maybe sparking an investigation wasn't such a bad thing. 'You didn't give them Lauren's name though, did you?' It was one thing to drop Glenda in it, it was another to implicate Lauren, whose safety might be put at risk. Glenda's sons weren't barred from Smugglers Inn for crimes against knitting. Nate's silence didn't bode well. 'Shit, mate. She won't thank you for interfering.'

Tony appeared on stage and took over from Kayleigh, who skipped down the steps and returned to her seat, waving at Barney as she did so.

Nate's chin dropped. 'But it's not like I stood a chance with her. I'd rather see her happy and hate me, than continue being bullied.'

Sylvia took Tony by the hand and led him across the stage. '"O, how I love thee! How I dote on thee!"' She lay him down and began stroking his imaginary donkey's ears.

Barney slung his arm around Nate's shoulder. 'You're a good bloke, you know that?'

Nate gave him a rueful smile. 'Remind me of that when Lauren finds out what I've done. She's likely to chop my balls off.'

Tony yawned. '"Where's Peaseblossom?"'

'I need a piss.' Nate disappeared into the gents', leaving Barney contemplating the potential fallout of Glenda being reported to the cops.

Lauren joined her dad on stage, treading on the hem of her dress as she did so. '"Ready."'

'Mind my sewing!' Glenda barked, making Lauren flinch.

Nate was right, Glenda wasn't a nice woman. Action was needed. Barney would just have to support his mate when the shit hit the fan. Nate was likely to need it.

Tony nestled closer to Sylvia. '"Where's Monsieur Mustardseed?"' And then he stopped acting and sat up. 'How am I going to do this bit, Jonathan? I'm supposed to be playing Mustardseed as well.'

Jonathan rubbed his left arm, his exasperation unmistakeable. 'I don't want problems, people, I want solutions!' He waved his hand about. 'Lauren, you say it.'

'But I'm Peaseblossom.' Lauren cowered when Jonathan marched onto the stage.

'It doesn't matter! Just say the ruddy line!'

Barney's attention reverted to Charlotte, who was balancing on a set of stepladders as she tried to reach the top of the netting. Much as he wanted to stay put and admire the view, his chances of getting up close and personal again would be severely hampered if she fell off and broke her neck. He shot over and caught the ladder before it toppled over, one hand catching hold of her calf.

Charlotte steadied herself. 'That was a close one.'

He looked up at her. 'Do you have a death wish?' Her hair was wavy, the top button of her shirt was undone, and he had to stop himself sliding his hands up the inside of her skirt.

She raised an eyebrow. 'I've certainly cavorted with the devil of late.'

He smiled. 'And for that, I am truly grateful.' He felt instantly warm when she returned his smile. 'I assume you're referring to me?'

'Who else?' Her cheeks coloured. 'Evil man.'

'Do you need to go to confession?'

'I'd be too embarrassed.' Her fingers fiddled with the button on her shirt.

'Why? It was just sex.'

She wobbled on the ladder. 'Keep your voice down.' Her eyes searched the room, checking no one had overheard. 'And remove your hand, please.'

Barney noticed Kayleigh frowning at him from across the room. He didn't care, but removed his hand anyway. 'You didn't ask me to move it Saturday night.'

Charlotte's blush deepened. 'That's because I was tipsy and hoodwinked by that story of yours.'

'It's not my story, it's legend.'

'And embellished, no doubt, for your own gain.' She looked cute when she was embarrassed.

'Can you blame me? You're gorgeous.' He stroked her arm. 'You had fun, didn't you?'

She chewed on her bottom lip, eventually conceding with a nod.

'Well then, no harm done.' He let his fingers trail over her skin. 'We could even try it again... slower this time.'

Her intake of breath was audible.

A commotion at the front of the stage drew her attention away, much to his annoyance. Jonathan was yelling at the kids; he was unhappy that they'd laughed when Sylvia said, '"I shall seek the squirrel's hoard and fetch thee new nuts."'

'Don't emphasise the word *nuts*, Sylvia! We're not in a school playground. This is a serious piece of theatre.' Jonathan clutched his chest, as if proving the point. His face contorted into a series of odd expressions: distress, anger, pain. When he dropped to his knees, Barney's first thought was that he was being a little overdramatic, even for Jonathan. But the sight of him collapsing face down alerted him to the seriousness of the situation.

Jonathan wasn't acting.

As realisation dawned, the place broke into pandemonium. Screaming, crying, yelling. General confusion and panic ensued.

Lauren appeared next to him. 'Do something! Jonathan's had some sort of seizure.'

It was like being transported straight back to the medical

wards. Everyone was looking for him to step up and save the day. This was why he'd left medicine. He was not equipped to deal with emergencies.

Ensuring Charlotte wasn't about to fall off the ladder, he ran over to where Jonathan lay on the floor. Time seemed to slow. The noise was deafening, heightened by the rain pounding against the roof, making it hard for him to think. All eyes were on him, faces were in various states of panic and upset, and people were mouthing words he couldn't hear above the whirring in his head.

His instincts were slow to kick in. He was out of practice. All his insecurities raced to the surface. The memory of being called to Mrs Kapoor's bedside to find her without a pulse, and being expected to take action ahead of the crash team arriving.

But there was no support. It was just him. *Think*, he told himself.

'What's wrong with him?' Freddie stared down at a motionless Jonathan.

It was a bloody good question. What was wrong with him?

'Okay, can everyone please move away. I need space.' Barney knelt down. 'Take the kids next door, please.' He checked for a pulse. Nothing. He checked Jonathan's neck just to be certain, hoping he was wrong. Still nothing. Breathing? Was the casualty breathing? And then he mentally kicked himself. If there was no pulse then he wouldn't be bloody breathing, would he, you daft sod. Concentrate.

He rolled Jonathan onto his back so he could check his airway. Christ, he was heavy. Barney was used to tending patients lying in hospital beds at convenient heights, not sprawled across the floor. 'Someone call 999. Tell them the casualty is unresponsive.'

Someone wailed. Sylvia, probably.

Tony appeared in front of him. 'What can I do?'

Barney positioned himself over Jonathan's body, ready to start chest compressions. 'I need the defibrillator. It's in the kitchen with the first-aid kit.'

'I'm on it.' Tony ran off.

Barney interlocked his hands. Using all his weight, he pressed down. Just as with Mrs Kapoor, he heard a sickening crack. He'd broken a rib. Bile rose in his throat. He pressed again. Another rib. It felt so brutal, like assaulting someone, not trying to save them. He could feel sweat dripping between his shoulder blades. Another crack. Lauren was on the phone talking to the emergency services. Her words 'there's a doctor in attendance' didn't ease his stress levels.

Tony appeared with the defib and first-aid kit. Thankfully, he knew how to set it up.

Nate crouched down next to him. 'You need me to do the breaths?'

Christ, yes. 'Please, mate.'

Chest compressions were exhausting. No more cracks, which meant all Jonathan's ribs were broken. Barney felt for a pulse. Still nothing. This was not good.

Nate opened the protective polythene and placed the mask over Jonathan's mouth. 'Tell me when.'

Barney stopped pumping. 'Go. Two breaths.'

Nate began administering breaths.

Barney took the pads from Tony and placed one at the top of Jonathan's chest and one at the side. He listened to the woman's voice on the defib giving him instructions. 'Stand back, please.'

Nate and Tony moved away, ensuring everyone kept clear.

The defib wouldn't fire.

'Why isn't it working?' cried Sylvia.

'It won't work if it detects activity in the heart muscle,' Nate said, helpfully fending off questions.

Barney wiped the sweat from his forehead, his eyes were stinging like crazy. He felt sick.

'You okay?' Tony touched his shoulder.

No, he was not okay. 'There's no heartbeat – he's in asystole. He needs adrenaline. How long until the ambulance gets here?'

Tony looked up at Lauren.

'Five minutes,' she said, relaying information from the operator.

By Cornish standards, five minutes was bloody good. But it was still too long. If Jonathan had flatlined, his heart needed restarting, but if the defib was detecting electrical impulses, causing the muscle to quiver but not actually pump blood, then it was a lost cause. Just like Mrs Kapoor. When the crash team had arrived and said, 'No need to continue,' he'd felt like a failure.

Had he made matters worse? Should he have done more? It was history repeating itself.

But he couldn't give up. It was better to do something than nothing, his consultant had said. If you kept going, you gave someone a fighting chance. However slim that chance might be.

Barney resumed chest compressions, ignoring Glenda, who was unhelpfully singing 'Stayin' Alive' next to him, as per the Vinnie Jones advert, trying to aid his rhythm. After thirty compressions, he stopped, waiting for Nate to administer two breaths before continuing. His arms were aching. His hands hurt. Five minutes had never seemed so long.

And then he heard activity by the door. Lauren was shouting to the medics, telling them where Jonathan was. They appeared by his side.

'He needs adrenaline,' was all he could manage.

'I understand you're a doctor?' The female paramedic searched out a vein and inserted a catheter quicker than he'd ever seen anyone do it before.

Barney nodded. 'He needs adrenaline,' he repeated.

'Okay, we've got this. What's his name?' She hooked up a drip.

'Jonathan Myers.'

'Jonathan, can you hear me?' She leant over him.

Why was she doing that? He was gone, wasn't he?

She administered adrenaline and checked again. 'Okay, we have a pulse.' She was on her feet, loading Jonathan onto a trolley. 'Excellent work, doctor. Call ahead, Gavin. Let the primary angioplasty coordinator know we're coming. Let's go.'

And they were off. A flash of green, in and out within minutes.

'I'll go with him.' Daniel ran after the paramedics, his words almost lost amongst the aftermath. People were talking. Praising Barney. Telling him what a good job he'd done.

'You saved his life.' Sylvia hugged him.

Barney didn't feel like he'd done anything. Once again, he'd frozen. His skills had been left wanting. He hadn't been in control. He'd fallen apart.

He realised he was shaking. A mixture of hot and cold ran over his skin. Jonathan would be lucky to survive the journey to A&E.

'There was nothing more you could've done,' Tony said, as if reading his mind, as he peeled Sylvia away from Barney.

Then why did Barney feel as though he'd messed up? Why did he feel so bloody useless and inadequate? His nausea increased. He needed air. He needed a drink.

Fending off the multitude of questions being fired at him, he made his excuses and ducked outside. He started running, and didn't stop until he was sure no one had followed him. On reaching the quayside, he leant over the railing, dragging air into his lungs, trying to catch his breath. He stood in the rain, shivering from the comedown of spent adrenaline and the wet soaking through his T-shirt.

And then he threw up.

Chapter 18

Friday, 29 July

Charlotte flicked through the TV channels just to make sure she hadn't missed anything. She hadn't. God, she was bored. She checked her watch. Ten past nine. The evening was dragging. After a long day on her feet, she'd expected to feel tired. The kids had broken up for the summer holidays and, as Lauren had an early shift at the café today, Charlotte had offered to take Freddie and Florence to the nearby trampoline park. She'd even been persuaded to have a go herself – another attempt to relinquish control and 'drop the stick'. But bouncing around on the springy contraption had been painful and exhausting. It had also served as a reminder of bouncing around with Barney Hubble at the jousting challenge, so she gave up and resigned herself to watching her niece and nephew from the sidelines.

The three of them had enjoyed fish and chips at the Coddy Shack, followed by a walk up to Morholt Castle to tackle the maze. Another mistake. The impressive castle ruins had evoked thoughts of a different kind of 'bouncing'. The memory of which left her feeling slightly stunned. Had she really done that?

Lauren had arrived home from work looking tired, and complaining of a headache. She'd gone to bed early, leaving Charlotte to feed the kids peanut butter sandwiches, and oversee bath time. By seven-fifteen both kids were tucked up in bed, worn out from their day. She'd taken the opportunity of a quiet night to work on her bundle for the upcoming employment tribunal hearing. Even though it had taken her nearly two hours to draft a witness statement and schedule of loss, she'd finished the task. With nothing else to occupy her, she was now feeling somewhat bored. Not the most exciting way to spend a Friday night.

She got up from the lumpy sofa and washed her cup in the sink. The flat was eerily quiet. Last night, she'd been disturbed by the sound of her sister crying. It had felt too intrusive to knock on her door and ask if everything was okay. She couldn't imagine Lauren welcoming an audience, so she'd stayed put, relieved when, in the early hours, the crying had stopped. Lauren had appeared for breakfast wearing dark sunglasses, looking drawn and subdued. Something was very wrong. But Charlotte was at a loss as to how to get her sister to confide.

Drying the cup, she hung it back on its hook. She wasn't ready for bed. She'd finished her latest book, painted her nails and folded her laundry. In London, entertainment was on her doorstep – not that she'd had much time to enjoy it, but that was beside the point, it was there if she'd wanted it. But in Penmullion, unless it was a rehearsal night, there didn't seem to be much else to do. And there'd been no rehearsal last night: it had been cancelled following Jonathan's heart attack. Everyone was still in shock, even though he'd miraculously survived... just.

She noticed an entry scribbled on the calendar pinned to

the fridge. *Friday 29 July – Barney's gig, Smugglers Inn*. She dumped the tea towel on the side, frustrated that her efforts to avoid thinking about him had been thwarted again. She didn't want to dwell on how much fun she'd had with him, or how alive and exhilarated she'd felt at having succumbed to such physical pleasures. It wasn't going to happen again, so what was the point in replaying every touch… every kiss… every stroke of his hand… *Stop it*, she told her traitorous brain, *not helpful*. It'd been a one-off. A moment of weakness. A lapse in concentration. Keeping her distance was the only sure-fire way of ensuring she didn't unravel again… and, boy, had she unravelled. Bloody hell. It'd never been like that with Ethan.

She ran her hands under cold water, trying to dampen the heat building within her.

After a few deep breaths, she was back in control, her mind no longer allowing such inappropriate images to surface. Good.

Back to the matter in hand. Her boredom. Was she going to allow a man to dictate her social life? No, she most certainly was not. If she wanted to enjoy an evening listening to live music, then no one was going to stop her, not even Barney Hubble. And she wouldn't be alone with him, would she? A crowded pub would be perfectly safe.

Before she could change her mind, she swapped her jeans for her favourite brown-satin Ghost dress, freshened up her make-up, and left the flat, convincing herself she was simply alleviating her boredom. There was no other motive.

Smugglers Inn was situated on the other side of the quay. Unfortunately, this meant she was forced to negotiate the footbridge. Frequent visits to her dad's boat hadn't made crossing the construction any less daunting. Wearing wedge heels didn't help either. Her centre of gravity lurched to the left as she tried to walk across. She kept her eyes fixed ahead, resisting the urge to hold on to her dress when a gust of wind rolled in from the sea and exposed more bare thigh than she was happy with.

Safely across, she walked up to where the main collection of restaurants and hotels were situated, overlooking the bay. It was a pretty sight. Lights from the establishments danced happily across the water, inviting the tourists inside. The pubs were busy, the restaurants full, and the neon lights advertising Frenzies nightclub flashed manically.

Smugglers Inn was set on the waterfront. It wasn't a new building, but it had been modernised and looked appealing. She could hear music before she reached the doorway. The venue was a reasonable size, refurbished using natural wood, with a modern twist. The designer in her approved. As she waited for her eyes to adjust to the dim lighting, she looked around. On the right-hand side, a long bar ran the length of the room. Nate was behind it, pulling pints of beer for a group of lads. She hadn't realised he worked here as well as being a postman.

The left side of the pub was scattered with a series of small tables, currently packed with punters enjoying a night out. At the far end was a small stage. Perched on a stool, playing an acoustic guitar, was Barney Hubble. Despite a lack of supporting musicians, she could still hear him above the noise of the pub. She recognised the song: The Arctic Monkeys, 'Baby, I'm Yours'. He had a good voice. He could play too. It was a nice sound. But she didn't want to stand around watching him like some sad little groupie so made her way to the bar.

When Nate finished serving, he came over. 'Hi, Charlotte.' His eyes searched the space behind her, a hopeful expression on his face. 'Lauren not with you?'

She shook her head. 'Just me, I'm afraid. She's having an early night. Bad headache.'

He frowned. 'She's not ill, is she?'

Nate Jones might look like Johnny Depp's bearded younger brother, but underneath the cool exterior was a right softie. How she wished Lauren would let him into her life. 'I don't think so.' Although, it might explain why her sister had been so out of sorts of late. Maybe she'd suggest Lauren visit her GP for a check-up?

Thoughts of doctors drew her attention to Barney. He was lost in his own world, his love of music freeing him from the realities of his situation, no doubt. And then she realised Nate had asked her a question. 'Sorry, what was that?'

'Has Lauren had any strange visitors come to the flat?'

What an odd question. 'Not to my knowledge. Why?'

'No reason.' He rubbed the back of his neck. 'What can I get you to drink?'

She was about to order her usual white wine spritzer, when she remembered her sister's advice to push the boat out a little. 'What can you recommend? A beer, maybe?'

As her first attempt at 'letting go' had resulted in the loss of her knickers, she had resolved to trying something that wouldn't put her at risk of an indecent exposure charge.

'Ginger Tosser or Cornish Knocker.' Nate pointed to the bottles of beer in the cabinet behind. 'They're both produced locally. Quite fruity, but not too heavy.'

'Cornish Knocker, it is.' Words she'd never imagined herself saying.

Nate flipped off the lid. 'Your dad's over there.' He handed her the beer. 'Want a glass?'

'No, thanks.' Drinking straight from a bottle, what a rebel. 'How much?'

'On the house. Have a good night.' He headed off to serve someone else.

Her 'thank you' was lost in the noise.

She went in search of her dad and found him sitting with Sylvia. They were swaying in time to the music, seemingly enjoying themselves. When Barney's song finished, they clapped loudly, along with most of the crowd.

Charlotte spotted Kayleigh, sitting next to the stage, cheering and whistling, giggling with her friends when Barney said, 'This next song is for Nate. It's called, "Fools Like Us".'

Nate acknowledged him with a rueful smile. Poor Nate. She did feel for him.

Her dad saw her approach. 'Hey, love. I didn't know you'd be here tonight. Pull up a chair and join us.'

Before she could respond, Sylvia jumped up and enveloped her in a hug. 'How are you, my lovely? Are you okay?' She touched her cheek. 'Not too traumatised?'

Feeling a tad awkward, Charlotte moved away. 'I'm fine. Why wouldn't I be?' Barney's playing wasn't that bad… in fact, it was extremely good.

'After what happened on Tuesday to poor Jonathan.'

Oh, right. Nothing to do with Barney's singing, then.

'We're all a bit shaken. I keep seeing his purple face every time I close my eyes.'

Her dad placed a hand on Sylvia's shoulder. 'I'm not sure that's overly helpful.'

Charlotte sat down. 'He's going to be okay though, isn't he?'

Her dad nodded. 'Thanks to Barney. It was touch and go for a while, but he's expected to make a full recovery.'

Another attempt to stop thinking about Barney thwarted. This was proving harder than she'd imagined.

'They unblocked his artery and fitted tiny wire mesh tubes called stents to permanently prop open the artery, allowing blood to get through to his heart,' Sylvia said, her pink lipstick almost luminous in the dim lighting. 'It's amazing what they can do these days, the wonders of medicine.'

Charlotte found herself looking at Barney again.

'He'll be in hospital for a while.' Sylvia had to raise her voice to be heard over the music. 'And then he'll need to recuperate. He doesn't have any family, so he's going to a convalescence home for a few weeks, just till he's back on his feet.'

Charlotte tuned back in to the conversation.

'Sylvia's been taking Jonathan home-cooked meals to help him recover,' her dad said, smiling at Sylvia. 'It's over an hour's drive, but she goes in every day.'

'It's no trouble,' Sylvia said. 'And we all know how awful hospital food is. Anyone would do the same.'

Her dad touched Sylvia's hand. 'Not everyone would. You're a very kind woman.'

Sylvia waved away his compliment, but Charlotte could see she appreciated his words.

'Dad's right,' she said, resolved to being nicer to Sylvia. It wasn't her fault she was clumsy. 'It's very thoughtful of you. I'm sure Jonathan appreciates your kindness.'

'Well, bless you. Aren't you a love.' Sylvia took a sip of her drink, something pink with an umbrella. 'Of course, we all want to know who's going to direct the play now? It would be a shame to cancel. We've sold over fifty per cent of the tickets.'

Charlotte agreed it would be a travesty. So many people had put time into making it happen. 'Couldn't you direct it, Dad?'

He shook his head. 'I'm not the right person.' His eyes drifted to Barney on stage. 'I know who'd be perfect for the role.'

It took her a moment to realise what he was suggesting. 'Are you kidding me?'

Sylvia nodded. 'He's such a talent.'

Barney Hubble was also averse to responsibility, spent his days on the beach, and was having a mid-life career crisis – even though he was only twenty-seven. 'I'm not sure he has the right attributes,' she said, not that she knew much about directing plays, but she did know about project planning and leadership. Barney didn't strike her as having either skill. 'Wouldn't it be difficult to balance both acting and directing?'

'He could manage it.' Her dad picked up his beer. 'Don't be fooled by the façade. He's not as carefree as he makes out. I think he'd be perfect.'

Sylvia sided with Tony. 'And I could listen to him sing all night, couldn't you? Perfectly dreamy.'

In an attempt to avoid answering, Charlotte took a mouthful of beer. It was disgusting – it probably wasn't, she just wasn't a beer drinker. Why had she thought otherwise? 'I need a different drink. Anyone need a refill?'

'We're fine, love.' Her dad reverted to watching Barney, leaving her to head to the bar.

Nate was busy, so she perched on one of the chrome bar stools to wait.

Barney was standing at the mic, his stance cocky, as he sang 'I want you, I need you, I love you' and imitated Elvis's famous hip wiggle.

'Looks like him, doesn't he?' Paul said from behind her, his voice instantly recognisable.

'I suppose he does a bit.' When she turned, she almost fell off her stool. '*Jesus!*'

Dusty caught her by the arm. 'Well, I've been called worse. Careful there, honey. How much have you had to drink?'

Not nearly enough, thought Charlotte. 'You're... but I...' She shook her head, trying to reconcile the realisation that Paul and Dusty were the same person. 'You're...?'

There was an amused expression on Dusty's made-up face. Her cheekbones were beautifully contoured, her lips were painted dark red, and her false eyelashes blinked rapidly like car indicators. 'Seriously...? You didn't realise?'

Charlotte shook her head.

And then Dusty beamed, a real kilowatt smile. 'Well, that's the biggest compliment I've had in a while. Bless you, darling.' She kissed Charlotte's cheek, and then laughed, drawing attention from those nearby. 'I can't believe you didn't know. How wonderfully amusing.'

Now the shock was subsiding, Charlotte looked at Dusty again. Other than the voice, there really was no hint of Paul perched on the stool. The blonde wig, psychedelic pink and purple shift dress, white tights and stilettos were a far cry from Paul's tasteful, tailored look. Although, now she thought about it, she recalled the sense of familiarity she'd felt whenever she'd encountered 'Dusty'. 'How did I not see it? I've been hanging out with you all summer.'

Dusty crossed one leg daintily over the other. 'People see

what they're expecting to see, not always what's right in front of them.' She waved at a group of men further down the bar, a playful wiggle of her fingers accompanied by a flutter of long eyelashes. 'I gather I missed quite an eventful rehearsal on Tuesday.'

Charlotte forced herself to stop staring, even if she was still slightly stunned. 'It was pretty grim. My dad says Jonathan's expected to make a full recovery.' *Thanks to Barney*, she added silently, glancing at the stage. He was still there, singing his heart out, channelling Elvis.

'Lucky Barney was there, or else things might've ended very differently.' A beat passed before Dusty added, 'Shame he can't see that.'

'Barney, you mean?' Charlotte kept her eyes focused on the stage, watching as he curled his lip, making Kayleigh scream like one of those teenagers in the black and white footage from the fifties.

'You might've picked up on his lack of confidence where medicine is concerned.' Dusty sighed. 'Stupid sod. Everyone else can see he's a god amongst men.'

For the second time that night, Charlotte nearly fell off her stool. She looked at Dusty in disbelief. 'Hardly.'

Dusty raised a perfectly waxed eyebrow. 'You don't think so? Look at him. Handsome. Talented. A *doctor*. If you can't see it, then you're blind, girlfriend.'

'Did you just call me *girlfriend*?'

Dusty looked sheepish. 'Too much…? It's too much,' she said, answering her own question. 'Barney's always telling me to tone down the diva. I can't help it. It's who Dusty is.'

Charlotte laughed, warming to her friend's alter ego.

'Anyway, back to the subject of my very hunky friend.'

Dusty leant closer, adopting the pose of a woman about to divulge. 'I rather got the impression you liked him. You know, in *that* way.' Charlotte was subjected to a nudge in the ribs.

Denying it would be pointless, mostly because she was sure the heat in her cheeks was visible. 'He's handsome, I grant you, and he has certain attributes, but he's not my type. Besides, I'm only here for the summer. My life is back in London.'

For the first time since arriving in Cornwall, that sentence failed to evoke a sense of elation. It was probably just the build-up to the ET hearing playing on her mind. Uncertainty over her job situation was bound to dampen her enthusiasm for returning to her old life. It was nothing more than that.

'All the more reason to indulge while you have the opportunity. Life's too short. And men like that don't come along every day. Trust me, I know. Besides, the briefer the liaison, the more beguiling the appeal.'

Charlotte raised an eyebrow. 'Does Paul share your opinion?'

Dusty straightened. 'Heavens, no. He's a prude. Never wants to mess up his bed sheets. Dusty, on the other hand? Well, let's just say, she likes to be impulsive.'

'Even if it results in being handcuffed to a tree?'

'Yes, that was rather unfortunate.' And then she smiled. 'But well worth it.'

Charlotte sighed. 'I'm more of a Paul than a Dusty.'

Dusty patted her hand. 'Poor you.'

'And, whereas I can see the appeal of a – fling – and don't get me wrong, I am tempted...' She glanced at Barney, who'd just started singing, 'Just the Way You Are'. 'Getting involved with someone, when I know I'll be leaving in a matter of weeks, doesn't seem very fair. I'd feel like I was using him.'

Dusty's burst of laughter caused heads to turn. 'Oh, darling.

I'm sure he'll survive. If that's the only thing stopping you, go for it.' And then her laughter faded. 'What on earth is *he* doing here?'

Charlotte turned to see who Dusty was referring to. A tall, good-looking man walked towards them. He was dressed in jeans and a suede jacket, his brown hair neatly styled, bordering on conservative. 'Jilted lover?'

Dusty slid off the stool. 'Worse. My brother. Excuse me, will you?'

Charlotte watched Dusty glide towards the man, her gait effortless and elegant. The man seemed pleased to see her, but looked uncomfortable when Dusty kissed him and slid her arm through his. Another family drama, no doubt. It was the same the world over. Everyone was dealing with something.

Charlotte swivelled around, facing the stage again. Barney's rendition of Bruno Mars was good, but his delivery lacked sincerity. He was hiding behind sarcasm, hamming up his performance rather than allowing any feeling behind the words to emerge. But then, acting like a cocky so-and-so was Barney's forte. It was what he did best. Even if she suspected it was a diversion tactic to distract from his insecurities.

And then she remembered his reaction to saving Jonathan. How he'd run from the hall physically shaking, his expression tortured. He'd been exposed as vulnerable, and she guessed that wouldn't sit well with him.

She studied him again, sensing a falseness to his bravado, like he was trying a little too hard to 'perform'. Maybe he wasn't as confident as he made out. It wasn't a valid enough reason to get involved with him, though. Tempting as it would be to enjoy a repeat performance of Saturday night, she'd be a fool to go there. Just like Paul, she wasn't a fan of messy bed sheets.

She climbed off the bar stool, planning to escape before Barney saw her. But when he started singing the Green Day song, 'When It's Time', she couldn't quite make her legs move. Hesitating was her first mistake. Her second was turning back to look at him. His cocky persona had vanished. There was no hint of sarcasm as he sang. His voice was deep and rich, with a hint of gravel – like he needed any help in the sex-appeal department. His voice cracked on the last line, emotion creeping into his words, leaving him visibly upset. When he finished, he thanked the crowd, gave a brief wave and disappeared backstage.

Crap.

If only she'd left before he'd started singing again. As it was, she was torn between going home or checking to see if he was okay. He was a big boy; he didn't need her to look out for him. True. But if he was suffering from the events of Tuesday night, then he might welcome a friendly face. She'd never performed CPR herself. By all accounts, it was a grim experience and often left a person distressed – even if that person was medically trained.

Leaving felt wrong. Staying didn't feel right. Quite a conundrum.

She reasoned that a quick 'hello' wouldn't hurt. Just a friendly enquiry into his mental state. She'd ensure he was okay, and then leave. Good plan.

She made her way through the crowd. The noise had increased, a jukebox was playing a Katy Perry song. Her dad and Sylvia were chatting to a couple on the neighbouring table. Kayleigh had climbed onto a chair and was dancing. One of the barmen shouted at her to get down.

Charlotte reached the door next to the stage area and

knocked. She doubted anyone could hear above the noise. True enough, when no one answered, she tentatively opened it and peered in. A small corridor led to the men's toilets and a store cupboard. She wasn't about to enter the men's loos, so tapped on the store-cupboard door, even though it felt like an odd thing to do.

She was only mildly surprised when it opened. There he stood, his initial frown relaxing into relief when he realised who it was. Up close, she could see that his teal T-shirt had a picture of a guitar on it, emblazoned with the slogan *Electrify the Beat*. His black hair was damp from perspiration. He blinked slowly, his shoulders dropping a notch. He smiled, but it lacked its usual confidence.

Lost for anything profound to say, she was grateful when he stepped back and allowed her inside the cramped space that had once been a cupboard. There was a single dull bulb hanging from the ceiling. A small table leant against the wall. His guitar lay in a case on the floor. Directly behind him was an armchair that had seen better days. It wasn't the most glamourous of dressing rooms.

She wasn't sure what she'd anticipated saying. And strangely, he didn't look like he was waiting for her to speak. He merely stood there, watching her. It was her move.

With no logic or rationale, she placed her hands on his chest and pushed him down onto the armchair. Still he didn't say anything. Good. She reasoned he was smart enough to know that if he uttered anything remotely challenging or teasing she'd be out of there quicker than he'd left the hall on Tuesday.

She dropped her handbag where she stood, took two steps and straddled him on the chair. Her actions had the desired reaction. His pupils dilated, his lips parted, and as she lowered her mouth to his, he rose up to meet her halfway. Just as it had on Saturday, the heat between them exploded like a firework. A spark instantly igniting into a flame. The same frantic rhythm; hands, tongues, an urgency to consume.

There was one difference. She was in the driving seat. The one dictating proceedings. When he tried to take control, she pushed him back against the chair. When his hands laced into her hair she pushed them against the wall, pinning them above his head. He didn't resist. He let her set the pace. And Christ, what a pace. She couldn't believe how quickly she lost all sense of propriety. Dignity and politeness went flying out the window. Once again, she was unravelling, losing control, allowing her body, not her mind, to call the shots. Her knee banged against the arm of the chair. She didn't care. One shoe fell from her foot. She didn't replace it. Her bra strap slipped off one shoulder. She let it go.

As if sensing her need to assert herself, he dutifully sat back and let her indulge, only assisting when she fumbled over his belt buckle, undoing it for her. She dragged his jeans down over his hips, moving against him as though an outside force had taken control of her body. The need to satisfy the itch clawing at her insides surged within her. His low moan sent any remaining restraint tumbling over the cliffs. Her mind was in free fall, her body following suit. When his lips formed the start of her name, she covered his mouth with hers. *Don't speak*, she silently willed him. *Please don't say a word*.

He didn't utter another sound.

Chapter 19

Sunday, 31 July – 3 weeks till curtain-up

Barney felt sick – and that had nothing to do with the amount of beer he'd drunk last night. The sole reason for his rising nausea was listening to his mother's agitated voice. Even the pleasure of looking out across Penmullion Bay on a beautiful sunny afternoon wasn't enough to soothe his irritation. He was standing at the top point of the Corineus Theatre, looking down at the sea, contemplating how to deal with his parents' latest pleadings to 'sort his life out'.

He'd only answered the call because it seemed preferable to getting involved in the discussions currently taking place with regards to the future of the show, now that Jonathan was indisposed. He'd offered no opinion, and had instead climbed onto the cliff edge. It was a steep incline; one false step and he'd tumble onto the rocks… which at that moment didn't seem so unappealing.

'We feel we've been patient enough.' His mother's tone didn't invite debate. 'If you can't decide on a specialism, then let us choose for you.'

And to think, only this morning he'd felt at peace with the

world, following a particularly energising surf. 'I'm more than capable of making my own choices, Mum.'

'Your behaviour would indicate otherwise.'

The sea below sparkled invitingly, the whitewash of the waves lapping against the rocks, tempting him to come in and play. 'I'm not a child anymore.'

'Then start taking responsibility for your future. You have no idea how hard it is for us to sit back and watch you to throw away everything you've worked for.' There was a pause, '... which is why your father and I decided to register you for the postgraduate medical diploma starting in September.'

What? A buzzing sound hummed in his ears.

'You can opt for St Mary's if you don't want to study Internal Medicine at Hammersmith,' she said, no doubt trying to sound reasonable. 'Or even the Deanery hospital in Plymouth, if you're insistent on staying in Cornwall. The choice is yours, but you need to make up your mind, and fast.'

Oh, so *now* he had a choice. Big of her. The buzzing in his head switched to a high-pitched screech. He kicked a loose stone off the clifftop, watching as it bounced off the rock face and plummeted into the sea.

'Are you listening to me, Barnabas?'

He rubbed his face. He didn't want to lose his temper or say anything he'd regret, but it was proving difficult. 'I'm listening.' He kicked another stone, this one bigger. It didn't budge. Pain shot up his foot.

'You've prevaricated long enough. All the courses start in September, so you'll need to relocate in the next couple of weeks if you don't want to miss out. The decision is yours, but your father and I will be very disappointed if you pass up this opportunity to further your career.' She paused. 'Naturally, we'll resume full financial support if you agree to continue with your studies. I know you feel we're being harsh, but we're doing this for your own good.' The line went dead.

Had she hung up on him?

Chucking his phone into the sea was tempting, but he knew he'd quickly regret it, so he shoved it in his pocket and let out a growl, trying to vent his frustrations. He was twenty-seven, for fuck's sake. His parents shouldn't be making decisions on his behalf. But he couldn't really blame them, they wanted what was best for him. It was just a shame they couldn't all agree on what that might be.

His phone beeped. Sighing, he dug it out and checked the message. His mother. *We love you very much*. And didn't he know it, which was why disappointing them caused him so much grief.

He climbed down from the rocks. How did he feel about his parents taking such drastic action? Annoyed? Frustrated? Or simply relieved that his life finally had some direction? All he really knew was that he felt a crippling sinking feeling in his gut.

Below him, the rest of the cast had gathered on stage. The sun's glare bounced off the pale-stone flooring, shrouding them in a hazy glow. Tony and Sylvia stood centre stage, shielding their eyes from the sun as they watched Daniel gesticulating wildly.

Kayleigh was sunbathing, stripped down to a vest top and tiny skirt, the heart tattoo on her stomach visible where she'd rolled up her top.

Lauren and Paul were sitting on the stone steps, their body language giving off very different signals. Paul was relaxed, his legs stretched out in front of him, his face turned up to the sun. In contrast, Lauren hugged her knees to her chest, her large sunglasses swamping her delicate features.

The tension between her and Glenda remained awkward. Glenda sat on a fold-up chair, her demeanour assured and superior, while Lauren shrunk slowly before their eyes, both in terms of weight and cheerfulness. He imagined the dynamics might change once the police paid Glenda a visit. If they ever did.

As he descended the curved steps, he could see Nate carrying a wooden throne down from the car park. Behind him, Charlotte carried a large pair of donkey ears, the wicker material making her nose twitch when it brushed against her. The sight of her eased the sinking feeling in his gut. She was wearing jeans and what looked like one of her sister's tie-dye tops, not a button in sight. Her hair was wavy and soft, and her bum moved gently beneath the stretch of her jeans. And he thought the view across the bay was nice?

He'd discovered there was a lot more to Charlotte Saunders than met the eye. Her outward movements might be careful and deliberate, but beneath the controlled exterior was an incredibly sexy woman. His pulse rate kicked up a notch just thinking about last Friday night. Having had her wicked way with him backstage at Smugglers Inn, she'd left without saying a word. Talk about hot. It was the stuff of fantasises. The fact that she remained cool and aloof whenever other people were around only heightened the sense of anticipation. Engaging in a summer fling was proving enormous fun.

'So, we're all in agreement that the show goes ahead?' Tony's voice came into earshot as Barney reached the stage.

Murmured agreements followed.

Barney walked across the stage, aiming for Charlotte. With any luck, she'd have more props which needed carrying down from the car park and he could assist her. It would be a welcome distraction from thinking about his future.

'Which brings us to the role of director.' Tony blocked Barney's path. 'What do you say, Barney? Will you help us out?'

Momentarily too shocked to speak, he ground to a halt.

Daniel marched over. 'I protest.'

Tony turned to Daniel. 'We took a vote.'

'I didn't vote for him.' Daniel refused to look at Barney.

'But everyone else did,' Sylvia said, giving Daniel a disdainful look.

'And we agreed we'd go with the majority.' Tony turned back to Barney. 'We all think you'd make a fantastic job of directing.'

Daniel's objections were drowned out by a chorus of people telling him to 'shut up!'

Tony looked hopeful. 'What do you say? Will you do it?'

Barney tried not to look at all the expectant faces in front of him. 'Sorry, but I'm with Daniel on this one. I'd make a terrible director.'

'You see?' Daniel looked smug. 'I told you.'

Tony shook his head. 'No, you wouldn't. You understand stagecraft and you're well respected.'

Was he…? 'That's kind of you, but I've only been doing this a year. I don't know much about acting.'

Daniel made a noise. 'My point exactly.'

'You know enough.' Tony gestured to the group, 'And we'd all pitch in and help.'

Everyone except Daniel nodded.

'And the blocking's been done, so everyone knows their moves. It's not like you'd be starting from scratch,' Paul added, unhelpfully.

'Yeah, and the lines are learnt, so that's covered.' Nate nodded in agreement.

Barney glared at his so-called friends. 'Look, I appreciate the offer, but I don't want the responsibility. I'm not a leader.'

Sylvia touched his arm. 'How can you say that? Look at how well you took control when Jonathan collapsed. We all went into a panic, but you were so calm and assured. He would've died if you hadn't taken charge.'

How could he tell them it was all a front? That beneath the surface, he'd sunk into a panic, almost gripped by a fear of messing up. 'Sorry to disappoint you.' He moved away, hating the looks on their faces.

The sinking feeling in his gut returned. And then he stopped mid-stride, realising he was sick of disappointing people. According to his parents, he had no valid reason to stay in Penmullion. But what if he did have a reason? Directing the play would keep him in Cornwall until the end of August. He'd be committed to the project. It would give him a focus, something to occupy his mind and body. It might even help him make a decision about his future.

He turned back to the group, looking from Tony and Sylvia's dismayed expressions to Nate and Paul's hopeful ones. These people had welcomed him into their lives. They'd befriended him when he'd been lost and confused, never judged him, and had supported his music endeavours. He owed them.

'Don't expect any miracles, okay? I'm no Kenneth Branagh.' The words had barely left his mouth before he was ambushed with hugs and kisses.

Over the crowd of heads, he saw Charlotte standing nearby. Her smile let him know that she approved of his decision. The swell in his chest was a completely disproportionate reaction, but he revelled in it anyway.

'Good decision.' Tony slapped him on the back. 'Right, let's get started.'

'Where do you want us?' Sylvia sounded eager.

Eight hopeful faces and one disgruntled one looked at him.

Barney realised they were expecting him to take over immediately. *Oh, crap*.

Lauren came to his rescue. 'We could cover the bit we didn't get to last Tuesday?'

He nodded. 'Good idea. Er... what was that?'

'Act Two, the forest scene. Would you like me to take the kids somewhere quiet and rehearse their dance?'

'That'd be great, Lauren. Thanks.' He touched her arm, shocked to feel how thin she was beneath her loose top. No wonder Nate felt that drastic action was needed.

He took a moment to collect his thoughts, feigning an excuse of needing to check the script before they began. In truth, he was starting to panic. It was just amateur dramatics, he told himself, not heart surgery. No one would die because he didn't make a good job of directing.

He flicked through the script, wishing he'd paid more attention to how Jonathan structured rehearsals. Why everyone thought he was the best person for the job, he didn't know. He turned to the stage, only to find Nate and Paul already in position. He'd thank them later.

Everyone was watching him, waiting to see what he'd do. No going back now. 'Okay, we'll start with the bit where Lysander is trying to stop Helena from leaving.'

Paul nodded and lifted his arms, allowing a reluctant Daniel to hug him. '"When at your hands did I deserve this scorn? Tis not enough that I never deserve a sweet look from Demetrius's eye, but you must flout my insufficiency?"'

Daniel moved as if to kiss her, but stopped. 'Do I seriously need to kiss him?'

Paul growled. '*Her*.'

'You're a *man*,' Daniel snapped back.

'But I'm playing the part of a *girl*. How many times do we have to have this fucking argument?' Paul reverted to character, preventing Daniel from responding. '"I thought you lord of more true gentleness."' He grabbed Daniel by the shoulders. 'Now kiss me, or I'll knee you in the nuts.'

'That's not in the script!' Daniel pushed Paul away. 'And I am not kissing him!'

Barney intervened before a punch-up ensued. 'Okay, we'll stop there.'

'You think I *want* you to kiss me?' Paul jabbed a finger at Daniel. 'I'd rather snog a frog.'

'Take five minutes everyone.' Barney manoeuvred Daniel to one side, out of earshot. 'Look, I know you're not happy—'

'You *think*?'

'But you need to rise above it.' Barney knew flattery would be the only way of placating someone like Daniel Austin. 'Commit to the part. In the original play, they would've kissed, wouldn't they? Act as though Helena is the woman of your dreams, no matter who's playing her, just like a professional actor would do.' He hoped this last bit might hit home.

It had the desired effect. Daniel straightened his shoulders. 'I *am* professional. I have an agent.'

'I know.' As far as anyone knew, Daniel's professional-acting credits included a car-insurance advert and playing a corpse in *Casualty*, but Barney wasn't about to bring that up. 'And anyone watching you can see that. You have quite a stage presence.' Christ, how it pained him to suck up to such an annoying little twerp. But as Daniel was now basking in the praise, Barney knew he was on the right track. 'But if you don't portray Lysander correctly, and show how he's affected by the love potion and smitten with Helena, then you're not going to look very professional, are you?'

After a short period of deliberation, Daniel nodded. 'I'll try, but I make no promises.'

What a drama queen. 'Good man. Have a break and then we'll try the scene again.' He patted Daniel on the back and watched him walk off.

'Nicely played.'

Barney turned at the sound of Charlotte's voice. She was sitting on the ground by the pillars, attaching flowers to the wicker donkey head.

'I didn't realise you were there.' He went over. 'Nice ass.'

She smiled. 'It's amazing what you can make out of papier-mâché.'

'I wasn't talking about the donkey.'

She raised an eyebrow. 'Very amusing.'

He liked that she no longer took offence to his teasing. 'I like to do my bit.'

She attached a bell between the donkey's ears. 'So, promoted to director, huh? I'm impressed.'

He crouched down next to her. 'You are?'

'Of course. I expected you to refuse. You surprised me.'

'I surprised myself.' The sunlight was hitting her in such a way it looked like she was wearing a halo. There'd been nothing angelic about her actions last Friday night. And for that he was truly grateful.

'It was the right thing to do.' She threaded wire around the bell to secure it. 'It would've been a shame to let everyone down.'

He held the bell steady for her. 'I'm still not sure I'm the right man for the job.'

Her expression softened. 'You know, for someone with your skills and confidence, you can be incredibly insecure at times.'

He bent closer so he could whisper in her ear. 'Are you referring to any specific skills?'

'I knew it!' Kayleigh's voice made him startle.

Where the hell had she come from?

She appeared next to him, hands on hips. 'You two are hooking up, aren't you?' Her accusatory gaze switched between him and Charlotte. 'I thought something funny was going on the other night, at rehearsal, and now I'm certain.'

Charlotte's confused look switched to a defensive one. 'No, we're not. Nothing's going on. Why would you think that?'

'Don't bother denying it. I ain't daft.' Kayleigh swung around to face Barney and shoved him in the chest. 'Bastard!'

'What was that for?'

'For messing around behind my back.' Tears pooled in her eyes.

He sighed. 'How many times do I have to say it? We're not together, Kayleigh.'

Kayleigh pouted. 'But we dated. We had fun, didn't we?' She leant into him. 'What about Valentine's Day?'

He tried to peel her hands away when she clutched hold of his T-shirt. 'What about it? It was months ago.'

'I thought it meant something.' Her forehead fell against his chest.

Charlotte was looking at him like he was scum. Great.

'Then I'm really sorry for misleading you.'

Kayleigh's head jerked up, knocking his chin. 'Bastard!'

'So you keep saying.' And she was probably right. It was his fault for not setting her straight before. He only had himself to blame. 'Look, Kayleigh. You're a really nice girl, and we're friends, but that's all. I'm really sorry if you thought it was more than that.'

'Because of her?' Kayleigh jabbed a finger in Charlotte's direction.

Charlotte picked up the donkey head and moved away. Sensible woman.

He wanted to go with her, but he couldn't keep running away from his problems. 'It has nothing to do with Charlotte.' Because it didn't, not really.

'I've seen the way you look at her,' Kayleigh shouted.

'Keep your voice down.' People were watching.

She started to cry. 'If it weren't for her you'd be with me.'

Cruel to be kind, he told himself, and braced himself for the fallout. 'Again, not true, Kayleigh. I'm sorry to be blunt, but you and me were never going to work out.'

Her crying increased.

Okay, a bit too cruel. 'Please don't cry, Kayleigh. I never meant to hurt you. I'm sorry.'

'And so you should be.' She thumped his chest. 'Well, you can find someone else to be in your crappy show, because I'm off.' She pushed him away. 'And don't think you can come crawling back to me when *she's* back in London.' Kayleigh snarled at Charlotte, who hid behind one of the pillars.

'There's no need to quit the show.'

'Yes, there is!' She flipped him the finger. 'We're over!'

He felt it wouldn't be helpful to point out that they were already over. 'Please don't leave. We can sort this out. It's just a misunderstanding.' He tried to follow her as she stormed off. 'Kayleigh!'

But there was no point, she was gone. *Fuck it!* He'd messed up spectacularly. And now there was no one to play Puck. Why had he ever agreed to direct? He was causing more problems than he was solving.

When he turned around, numerous faces looked at him expectantly. No point putting off the inevitable. He went over to the group. 'Kayleigh's quit the show.'

He was met with a chorus of, '*Why?*'

Barney really didn't want to divulge details of his 'thing' with Charlotte, especially as she'd made it abundantly clear that the fewer people that knew about them, the better. 'Personal reasons.'

He should have known that wouldn't suffice.

'What kind of personal reasons?' Glenda was blunt as always.

Paul came to his rescue. 'Kayleigh has a crush on Barney, but he doesn't feel the same way.'

'Tell us something we don't know.' Glenda pulled a face. 'Hardly the news of the century.'

Tony intervened. 'I think what Glenda means is, what happened to make her leave today?'

Barney shrugged. 'She got upset when I set her straight about us not being a couple.' Which was entirely true; no need to mention the bit about him flirting with Charlotte.

As if on cue, Charlotte appeared in his peripheral vision. He really hoped that Kayleigh hadn't blown it for him. He wasn't ready for their fling to be over; things were just heating up.

'I tried to let her down gently, but I failed. Sorry, guys.' He hated to see their disappointed faces. 'Do you want someone else to direct the show?'

Only Daniel nodded. Everyone else assured him he still had their support.

'So, what are we going to do now?' Sylvia looked concerned.

He had no idea.

Paul slapped him on the back. 'Let's forget about Kayleigh and focus on finding a replacement to play Puck.' He squeezed Barney's shoulder. 'Anyone spring to mind?'

Barney shook his head. It was a tall order to learn Shakespeare in three weeks. And who would they ask? Everyone who'd auditioned had been cast in the show.

He realised that the rest of the group were looking at Charlotte. *Why were they…?* And then it dawned on him.

He turned around. Genius idea.

It took a moment for her to realise what they were suggesting. 'No way!'

He moved towards her. 'Just hear me out.'

She backed away. 'No!'

'But you know the show.'

'The answer's still no.'

'You've read in for Puck, so the lines are familiar.'

'I'm not listening.' She sped up, eager to get away.

He ran after her, blocking her path. 'There's no way anyone else will be able to learn the part in three weeks.'

'And neither will I.'

'I'll help you.' He caught her by the arm. 'It'll be fun.'

'Fun?' She swung around. 'Prancing around on stage is not my idea of fun!' She prodded him in the chest. 'Watch my lips. There is nothing you can say that will persuade me to play the part of *Puck*!'

‘Please, Charlie. I wouldn’t ask if there was anyone else.’

‘Too bad.’ She dislodged his hand from her arm. ‘And my name is Charlotte.’

He needed a different approach. ‘What was it you said earlier? About how I’d done the right thing taking on the role of director, as it’d be a shame to let everyone down?’

‘Not the same thing. I’ve never acted before.’ She tried to move past him.

‘And I’ve never directed before. We can evolve together.’ He blocked her escape.

‘Nice try, but no.’ Her fingers searched unsuccessfully for a button to fiddle with on her top.

His hand closed around hers, stilling her movement. ‘Think of how disappointed Freddie and Florence will be if the show gets cancelled.’

That got her. It was a moment before her eyes lifted to his. ‘That’s below the belt.’

‘I know, but I’m desperate.’ He looked at her, beseechingly. ‘Please?’

The steel in her eyes set off warning bells in his head. Through gritted teeth she said, ‘You will pay for this.’

He didn’t doubt it for a second.

Chapter 20

Wednesday, 10 August

Lauren covered her ears with the pillow, trying to block out the noise from the busy street below. It was the height of the tourist season, and the narrow lanes of Penmullion were packed with visitors enjoying a sustained period of good weather. Normally the background noise of children laughing, seagulls squawking, and the tap of horses' hooves on the road was a welcome sound, a reminder of why she'd moved to Cornwall. But that was before she'd got herself into crippling debt. Now she just wanted to block everything out, Penmullion included.

She crawled out of bed and went to close the window. It was stiflingly hot, but the noise prevented her sleeping. Napping at eleven o'clock in the morning wasn't part of her normal routine, but another restless night had left her tired and irritable.

Thankfully, Charlotte had taken Freddie and Florence to the 'first aid for kids' workshop Barney was running at the surf kiosk this morning. An empty flat and a late shift at the café meant she could retreat to her bed without being subjected to any awkward questions.

As she closed the window, noticing another crack in the single pane of glass, she spotted a post-office van parked outside the collection depot. Seconds later, Nate emerged and glanced up at her window. She shut the curtains, not wanting to be seen in her underwear. But curiosity got the better of her, and she parted the curtains a fraction, just enough to see through. He was still looking up, his concerned expression visible even from a distance. It was getting harder to ignore the feelings she had for him. Charlotte was right, he was a good man. Every kind gesture, brave action or show of thoughtfulness weakened her resolve a little bit further. It would be so easy to lower her guard and let him in. But would he like what he found? She was a mess. Physically, financially and emotionally. He was better off staying well clear.

Her phone beeped with a text. She went over to the bedside cabinet and checked the message. It was from Nate. *Everything okay? I want to help. I'm sorry*. She frowned. What did he have to be sorry about?

Without replying, she crawled into bed and buried herself under the duvet. She doubted sleep would come, but she was so tired that she was starting to feel faint. Six hours on her feet, working in a hot, airless kitchen, was taking its toll. Getting through each shift was proving harder and harder. She didn't even have the energy to argue with her sister when Charlotte had replaced the broken toilet seat and bought a new lampshade for the lounge. In fact, if it weren't for Charlotte keeping the fridge stocked with food, they'd be in a worse state than they were.

She wasn't quite sure when the dynamics had changed, but she'd gone from being irritated by her sister's interference, to dreading her leaving. Of course, she'd never admit as much.

Charlotte's life was back in London. The last thing she wanted was for Charlotte to feel pressurised into staying. It wasn't her sister's responsibility to sort out her younger sibling's life, she had her own demons to battle.

Despite Charlotte's continuing efforts to 'fix' everything, Lauren had to admit that her sister was definitely less uptight than when she'd first arrived in Cornwall – as evidenced by her reaction this morning, when Freddie and Florence had appeared wearing matching nurses' uniforms ready for the first-aid workshop. There'd been no shock at seeing her nephew in a dress, and no demands for him to change outfit. She'd simply laughed, removed a loose thread from his hem, and taken them off to the beach.

Lauren suspected that Barney had something to do with her sister's reduced stress levels and improved humour, but Charlotte was keeping her cards close to her chest on that topic, so she refrained from commenting.

A loud knock on the front door rattled the cracked windowpane. Lauren made a mental note to add it to the long list of issues which needed addressing by the landlord.

Lauren buried her head under a pillow, hoping whoever it was would go away.

They didn't. A few moments later there was another knock.

Throwing off the duvet, she climbed out of bed and dragged on a pair of shorts and a vest top. If it was that smarmy salesman again, selling cleaning products, she'd be mightily hacked off.

The knocking increased in volume. 'Okay, I'm coming,' she called, twisting her hair into a knot at the base of her neck.

Only it wasn't the smarmy cleaning salesman standing on her doorstep. It was a tall woman wearing a floral summer dress, red Dr Marten boots, and blue spiky hair. It was a striking combination.

'Goodness me, this place was hard to find,' the woman said, smiling. 'I've been up and down this road five times trying to find flat number 15a.' She thrust out her hand. 'Yvonne Hillier. May I come in?'

Lauren leant against the door frame. She had no intention of letting a stranger into her flat, no matter how friendly they appeared. 'I'm sorry, who are you?'

Yvonne's smile didn't falter. 'Good question, but it's better I explain inside rather than out here. I can assure you it's perfectly safe. I'm here on official business, I have identification, and I'm not the bailiffs.'

The bailiffs? Lauren shuddered. It hadn't occurred to her that the bailiffs might come calling. She'd missed the minimum payment on her catalogue account this month, something she'd never done before. She'd half expected a phone call or stroppy letter, but not a personal visit so soon after defaulting.

Resigned to whatever bad news she was about to hear, she stepped back and allowed Yvonne into the flat. 'Come through.'

'Thank you. What a lovely home you have.' When Lauren raised an eyebrow, the woman smiled. 'Cosy.' Was she blind? 'Is it all right if we sit down?'

Lauren remained standing, but gestured for her guest to sit on the couch. 'Would you like a cup of tea?' It seemed rude not to ask, even though she hoped the woman would refuse. She wanted this to be over with as soon as possible. Whatever 'this' was.

'Maybe later. Let's have a chat first.' Yvonne removed a wallet from her large tote bag. 'As I said, my name's Yvonne and I work for the IMLT.' She handed Lauren an identity badge and business card.

Lauren studied both. 'I'm sorry, I don't know what that is.'

'Most people don't. Why don't you take a seat, and I'll fill you in?'

It felt odd to be taking instruction in her own home, but there was something reassuring about the woman's voice, so she sat down on one of the kitchen chairs.

'That's better.' Yvonne nodded to the card in Lauren's hands. 'IMLT stands for the Illegal Money Lending Team. We're part of National Trading Standards and we work in conjunction with the police and various debt-advice agencies.'

Lauren's hands started to shake. 'The police?' But she'd only missed one payment?

'It's okay, you haven't done anything wrong.' Her smile was back, big and warm and reassuring. 'Our job is to investigate unlicensed lenders. In particular, those lenders who target the vulnerable.'

Lauren couldn't imagine Littlewoods employed unlicensed lenders. 'What does that have to do with me?'

'We're currently looking into the activity of a local woman by the name of Glenda Graham. Do you know her?'

Lauren's hands became instantly clammy. She hesitated before replying. 'Yes, she's a family friend.'

Yvonne nodded. 'And have you borrowed money from this family friend?'

A niggle of annoyance crept up her spine. 'I don't see what business that is of yours.'

The woman's demeanour didn't waver at the rebuke. 'We have reason to believe that Glenda Graham might be a loan shark.'

Lauren almost laughed. 'A loan shark?' A sudden image of the Krays filled her brain. Glenda was hardly a gangland criminal. She was a sixty-year-old grandmother with grey hair who lived in a caravan. 'Of course not. Don't be ridiculous.'

Yvonne waited a beat before responding. 'People often have a false perception of loan sharks. They believe them to be of a certain type, burly men who own pit bulls and baseball bats, but that's not always the case. In fact, most loan sharks look like regular members of the community. They often present themselves as friends, adopting an informal approach, ingraining themselves into a person's life before turning on the pressure.'

Lauren squirmed, fidgeting on the plastic-covered seat.

'Unlike high-street lenders, loan sharks are not regulated and their lending practices are illegal and often unreasonable.'

Lauren shook her head. 'I think you must have the wrong person. Glenda is a lollipop lady at my kids' school. She volunteers at community events and even belongs to the local drama group.'

'I'm sure she does. But that puts her in the perfect position to befriend her victims, most of whom are vulnerable and have been rejected for loans elsewhere.'

Lauren didn't consider herself vulnerable. She certainly wasn't a victim. So it was difficult to see why she was the subject of an investigation.

Yvonne crossed her legs, one booted foot resting on the other. 'Maybe Glenda offered to help you out of a tight spot? Loaned you some money just to tide you over until you got back on your feet?'

The conversation was getting a little too close to home. Lauren wiped her clammy hands on her shorts. 'Like I said, she's a friend of the family. I think I'd know if Glenda was a loan shark. I'm not stupid.' But even as she said it, she knew it was a lie. Maybe she'd always known, but she hadn't wanted to feel like a fool for getting herself mixed up with an illegal moneylender.

Yvonne shook her head. 'I'm not for a moment suggesting you are. But a lot of victims say exactly the same thing. They view the person as a friend, even when that friend charges them interest on the money borrowed.'

Lauren stilled. 'Interest?'

Yvonne nodded. 'A friend wouldn't charge interest on a short-term loan, would they? And certainly not an extortionate rate.'

Lauren wondered whether the thumping in her chest was audible.

'And a friend wouldn't refer to there being a contract in place.'

The garish pattern on the sofa began to blur. Lauren blinked, trying to focus her eyesight.

'A contract whereby the terms keep changing, like the frequency of the repayments or the amount to be repaid.' Yvonne tilted her head to one side. 'And a friend wouldn't become threatening or intimidating if the person owing them money couldn't afford to repay the loan.'

An image of her dad's face loomed large in Lauren's mind. *Never a borrower nor a lender be*. It didn't matter if what the woman was saying was true, she couldn't report Glenda. She was a friend of her dad's. A well-respected member of the community. Her dad would never forgive her for stirring up trouble. And he certainly wouldn't be happy about her getting into debt.

Yvonne hadn't finished. 'The IMLT has specialist investigators who collect evidence in order to bring about a prosecution. What strengthens a case and the chances of a successful outcome is having people come forward with examples of illegal moneylending. As you can see from my business card, I'm a Victim Support Officer. My job is to ensure that anyone giving evidence is safe, protected, and supported throughout the process.'

The room began to spin, the brown carpet rising up to meet the distorted colours in the sofa. Lauren needed a drink.

She got up and poured herself a glass of water, taking a moment to collect her thoughts. It was true that Glenda's behaviour had switched from pleasant and understanding to hostile and demanding, but that was only because she needed the money back so she could help other people in a similar situation. Glenda was filling a gap in the market, providing a community service... at least, that's how she'd always described it. Now Lauren was having serious doubts. God, her head hurt.

Yvonne waited until she'd returned to the lounge before continuing. 'Would you be willing to provide us with evidence against Glenda Graham?'

Lauren shook her head. 'There's nothing to investigate. Everything's under control.' Except it wasn't, was it? Her hands were trembling like Freddie's favourite strawberry jelly. But the thought of her kids only strengthened her resolve. No way was she about to humiliate them. If word got out that she was in debt and had reported Glenda to the authorities... Well, there was no coming back from that. She'd be ostracised in the community. A social outcast.

Yvonne watched her closely. 'Are you sure about that?'

'Positive.' Lauren handed back the business card and identity badge. 'I'd like you to leave now.'

Yvonne took the badge. 'You keep hold of the card, just in case you change your mind.'

'I won't.' Lauren kept her hand outstretched, but the woman didn't take the card.

'Call me anytime,' Yvonne continued, as though Lauren hadn't spoken. 'My mobile is always switched on, day and night.' She paused, as if hoping Lauren might reconsider. When she didn't, Yvonne picked up her bag. 'I'll see myself out.'

Lauren followed her over to the doorway, realising that someone else must know she owed Glenda money. 'Can I ask who gave you my details?'

Yvonne hooked her bag over her shoulder. 'That's confidential information, I'm afraid.' But then she hesitated. 'I can't give you his name, but we received an anonymous tip from a concerned friend. He sounded very worried about you.'

He…?

'Take care, Lauren. You have my number. I hope to hear from you.'

Lauren waited until the door had closed before sinking to the floor, her legs no longer able to hold her weight. She was sure her howl could be heard in the next town. A mixture of emotions raged within her: guilt, disgrace, embarrassment, anger. Who had done this? Shamed her in such a way?

She pummelled the floor, but there was no energy behind her anger, she was too spent. Tears filled her eyes as she lay on the floor contemplating who had given her name to the authorities.

All she knew was that the person was male. It wasn't her dad; he would have confronted her himself. And besides, he would never have suspected his friend Glenda of being a loan shark. So, if it wasn't her dad, who could it be…? Like a hammer blow, she realised it could only be one person.

Without pausing to check her appearance or curb her anger, she shoved her feet into a pair of flip-flops, snatched up her keys and left the flat.

She ignored the blare of a car horn as she ran across the road, narrowly avoiding a collision with a Fiesta. Pain nearly derailed her when she grazed her toes tripping up on the pavement in her flimsy footwear, but she didn't care. She kept moving, pushing open the door to the post-office collection depot and heading for the counter.

A fellow postman nudged Nate, his face registering that a scene was about to unfold.

Too bloody right!

Nate turned, his face instantly full of concern. 'Lauren? What's wrong?'

She wouldn't allow his kindness to derail her anger. 'It was you, wasn't it?'

Thankfully, the other postman disappeared into the back office.

Good. She didn't need an audience.

Nate took a moment to answer, his deliberation confirming her suspicions. 'Yes, it was me.'

His honesty momentarily threw her. 'How could you?'

He reached for her hand. 'Because I'm worried about you. We all are.'

She batted his hand away. 'We…? Who is *we*?' Oh, God, who else knew about this?

'No one.' He shook his head, as if realising his mistake. 'Just me. It was only me.'

'Liar!' She shoved him hard in the chest. He barely moved. She really had no strength left. 'Let me guess, Paul and Barney? I can just imagine the three of you sitting around laughing at stupid... gullible... pathetic Lauren.'

'It wasn't like that, I promise. And there was no one else, it was me who reported Glenda.'

His admission only fuelled her fury. 'Why...? Why would you do that? Do you have any idea how humiliated I feel?'

He closed his eyes. 'That wasn't my intention. I was trying to help.'

'How was it helping?' She shook him by the shoulders, forcing him to open his eyes. 'Look at me!' She dropped her hands, suddenly not wanting to touch him. 'Do you realise you've put my kids at risk? Social Services will probably have a field day. The dumb single mother who can't provide for her kids.'

'Stop it, Lauren. That's not going to happen.' He stepped towards her.

'How do you know?' She stood her ground. 'Suddenly you're an expert, are you? You know what I need?'

'Yes... I mean, no.' He looked confused, his dark eyes radiating panic. 'What I mean is, you're too nice. You only see the good in people. You'd never have reported Glenda. I did it for your own good.'

'My own good?' The fury in her voice caused him to step backwards. 'You sanctimonious prick. I don't need you or anyone else telling me what to do. My life is none of your concern. Do you hear me?'

He flinched. 'Please listen to me, Lauren. The debt is unenforceable.'

'What debt? I don't know what you're talking about...'

'Stop pretending!' His raised voice stunned her. It was the most animated she'd ever seen him...

Well, apart from when he'd rescued her daughter, but she wasn't going to think about that, not when she needed to stay mad at him.

'You're angry with me, I get that. But please don't punish yourself for something I've done.' His voice softened. 'I see how stressed and unhappy you are. Glenda's making your life a misery. I'm not blind, Lauren. I've seen her bullying you, hounding you for money. It's got to stop. *She's* got to be stopped.'

The truth of his words only flamed her humiliation. 'No one's being bullied! And you know what, so what if I owe her money? It's my life, my business, no one else's. And I pay my debts. I have every intention of repaying every penny I owe.'

'Lauren, please...'

'Butt out of my life, Nate. This has nothing to do with you. You're nobody to me.' With one last weak shove in his direction, she sprinted back across the road, adrenaline the only thing fuelling her legs.

It was only once she was inside the sanctuary of her flat that she allowed the tears to flow. Hot, angry tears that stung her eyes and made her chest heave as she tried to suck in enough air to breathe, cry, and yell simultaneously. Falling onto the couch, she buried her head in the cushions, sobbing until every muscle in her body ached. It was only later, much later, when she was done crying and replaying the argument in her head, that she bitterly regretted her choice of words. He meant *everything* to her.

Chapter 21

Saturday, 13 August – 10 days till curtain-up

Charlotte stirred slowly, her eyelids heavy with sleep, her right arm tingling with pins and needles. It was an effort to roll over, the cushions seemed softer, bigger and less lumpy. Her toes usually collided with the wall when she stretched out on the daybed; they didn't this morning. The duvet smelt different too, less spilt Ribena and more... what was the word she was looking for? Manly? A warm, musky scent. Her eyes pinged open. She wasn't on the put-you-up in Lauren's flat. She was lying naked in Barney Hubble's bed. *Holy crap.*

She tried sitting up, hindered by the rumpled duvet and dead right arm. She blinked furiously, trying to encourage her eyes to focus so she could assess how bad the situation was. Bright, morning sunlight sneaked through the small crack in the blue curtains, highlighting the white walls, pine furniture and single armchair in the corner of the room.

What time was it? She looked around for a clock. Discarded clothes lay strewn around the room: a man's shirt lying on the floor, her top from last night bunched into a ball... her bra dangling from the arm of the chair. *Oh, shite!*

Mortification proved to be a good antidote to sleep. Shaking her arm, trying to restore blood flow, she forced her brain into gear. How had she ended up here? Her memory was sketchy. She remembered not wanting to stay home last night; her sister was in another bad mood and she didn't want Lauren discovering she'd paid her catalogue bill. Lauren had complained of a headache – the same headache that had kept her away from rehearsal the previous night – and had retired to bed early. Declining her dad's invitation to join him and the kids for a weekend away on his boat, Charlotte had headed out to Smugglers Inn to watch Barney's gig.

She remembered enjoying his Beatles set, knocking back a couple of glasses of Prosecco, and dancing with Dusty. Dancing? Crikey, she never normally danced. Maybe she'd had more than two glasses? Suddenly the rest of the night's events tumbled into her psyche: kissing Barney outside the pub, going back to his place, lying on the kitchen table minus her underwear, barely making it up the stairs before... *Oh, God!* Where were her knickers?

She scrabbled to an upright position, needing to get dressed and out of there as soon as possible, but the sound of the bedroom door opening scuppered her plans.

'Morning, sleepy.' Barney backed into the room carrying a tea tray. He was wearing snug-fitting boxer shorts, nothing else. 'Hope you like crumpets.' The sight of his tanned body, messy black hair and open smile was enough to still her efforts to flee.

Plus, she was naked.

She pulled the duvet closer. 'What time is it?' Her voice sounded croaky.

'Just gone nine.' He came around to her side of the bed and placed the tray down on the lamp table. 'Did you sleep okay?'

She remembered now that she hadn't meant to stay the night. Her attempts to leave had been overridden by Barney's desire to 'cuddle' after they'd... Well, she didn't want to think about exactly what they'd got up to. Suffice to say, it wasn't her normal behaviour. What was wrong with her? She usually showed a lot more decorum. 'I need to go.'

'No, you don't.' He sat down on the bed, his weight pinning the duvet to the mattress.

'Yes, I do.' She tugged at the bedclothes. 'I have somewhere to be.'

'You told me last night you had nothing planned for the weekend. You were going to spend the day learning lines.'

Her irritation kicked up a notch. 'Exactly. So, I'd better get on with it.'

'Eat something first.'

'I'm not hungry.'

He responded by kissing her. It was so unexpected that it took her a good few seconds to object. His lips were warm and soft, the gesture so tender and very unlike the frantic exertions of the previous night. It was quite alarming. He pulled back. 'Are you cold?'

'No.' Her shivers had nothing to do with the temperature. She tried to move, but was trapped by the entangled duvet and solid headboard. 'Could you move, please?'

'Not until you've eaten.' He tore off a small piece of crumpet.

'I told you, I'm not—'

He popped it into her mouth, the sensation almost as seductive as his kiss: hot, buttery and utterly delicious.

He watched her chew, a hint of smugness creeping into his smile. 'Good?'

She nodded, albeit reluctantly.

He broke off another piece of crumpet.

She tried to take it from him. 'I can feed myself.'

'I know, but this way we both get to enjoy it. Open up.' His gaze remained fixated on her mouth.

One more bite, she decided, and then she'd regain control.

'How are you getting on with your lines?' He licked his lips, mirroring her when she did the same. 'You have a great mouth.'

'Stop staring, you're making me self-conscious.' She swallowed another piece of crumpet. 'It's hard work and time-consuming.'

'You did really well at rehearsal on Thursday.'

'Liar.'

'I'm not lying.' He laughed, no doubt at her peeved expression. 'The part is perfect for you.'

'Excuse me?' Had he lost his mind? 'A mischievous green goblin who lives in a wood with a bunch of imps, has a highly suspicious relationship with the King of the Fairies, and flies around the forest planting spells on people whilst turning into various apparitions – including a horse?'

His laughter increased. 'See? You've got it nailed.'

She poked her tongue out. 'I'm still not happy about being coerced into taking the part.'

'I know, but you're very cute when you're disgruntled.' He fed her more crumpet, preventing her from speaking. 'And I for one am very grateful.'

She accepted the mug of tea and took a sip. It was delicious. She certainly couldn't fault his tea-making skills. She watched him take a bite out of his own crumpet, thinking about his other talents – and not just in the bedroom. The role of director suited him. He'd shown real maturity and sensitivity over the last two weeks, dealing with everything from upset actors, tearful children, and demanding backstage crew, to assuring Lauren he wouldn't make her wear the awful dress Glenda had made for her. However much he protested, picking up responsibility and taking leadership suited him. He might not like it, but he was very good at it.

He seemed to sense her watching him and wiped his fingers on a paper towel. 'So, you think Puck has a highly suspicious relationship with Oberon, huh?'

She sipped her tea. 'Oh, please. All that master and servant stuff? Very dubious.'

'I'm not sure Shakespeare intended it that way, but there's no reason why we can't develop our own interpretation' – his lips brushed against her shoulder – 'and explore their relationship in more depth.'

'Stop it, you'll spill my tea.' He took the mug from her and placed it on the tray. 'Hey, I was enjoying that...'

He kissed her.

However much her mind tried to fight it, her body betrayed her. He tasted of tea and hot buttered crumpet. Her senses flooded with pleasure as his weight settled on top of her. The kiss deepened... and then someone tapped on the bedroom door.

At the sound of Paul's voice, Barney sat up, dislodging the duvet.

Frantically grabbing the cover, she only just managed to dive beneath it before the door opened. She lay perfectly still, hoping Paul hadn't spotted her, or at least wouldn't know it was her.

'I'm off to work.' Paul's voice was muffled through the duvet. 'I'm meeting Will for a drink tonight. Chances are I won't be home till late.'

'You're not coming back to change into Dusty first?' Barney's movement made the mattress bounce, threatening to blow her concealment.

Sit still, damn you.

'Will says he can't have a serious conversation with me when I'm *dressed up*, as he puts it. He says Dusty's too sarcastic.'

Barney laughed. 'He has a point.'

Paul's sigh conveyed his sadness. 'That's family for you.'

Charlotte had another flashback from the previous night. She remembered consoling Dusty for not being allowed to attend her brother's wedding. She still found it hard to reconcile the mild owner of the boutique with his outrageous alter ego. They were very different beings.

'See you later.' Paul was leaving. Good. He hadn't spotted her. She'd been saved from the indignity of being caught in a compromising position. 'Bye, Charlotte.'

Damn it!

'Nice bra, by the way.' Paul's laughter reverberated into the hallway.

She groaned. Would the humiliation ever end?

Barney peeled away the duvet. 'You can come out now.'

She peeked over the top. 'How did he know it was me?'

Barney smiled. 'Who else was it likely to be?'

She gave him a knowing look. 'Oh, I don't know. Kayleigh, perhaps?'

His smile switched to a frown. 'How many times...?'

'Ah, so it's okay for you to tease me, but not the other way around?' She shuffled onto her elbows.

It took him a moment to realise she was joking. 'That's your idea of humour, is it?' His hand slid under the duvet.

'Stop it!'

'No.' His fingers found her midriff. 'I deserve revenge. I'm still having nightmares about that woman.'

'And so am I.' She tried to wriggle away. 'She's the reason I got roped into playing Puck. Stop tickling me or I'll go home!'

His hand stilled. 'That's blackmail.'

'So is pinning me to the bed and force-feeding me crumpet.'

'Yeah, but you secretly enjoy it.' He delivered it almost as a question.

There was no way she was about to admit anything of the sort – even if her sister had been right when she'd said letting go would prove to be a great antidote for stress. Barney Hubble didn't need any further encouragement in that department. He was a charming sweet-talker who'd coerced her into jousting, having intimate relations in public places, and had hoodwinked her into taking the role of Puck. Christ only knew what else he'd 'persuade' her to do if she let her guard slip any further. She needed to stick to her plan and ensure she was focused and ready for her employment tribunal in three weeks' time. She couldn't allow anything to derail her return to London, not even the enticement of a fit guy with an annoyingly engaging personality.

She shuffled back against the headboard, tucking the duvet under her arms so her breasts were covered. 'Could you pass me my tea, please.'

'Nice change of topic.' He obliged, and then climbed into bed next to her. She tried to ignore the sensation of his arm brushing against hers.

'Is that yours?' She nodded to a framed picture of a George Eliot quote which hung on the wall. *It's never too late to be what you might've been*.

He nodded. 'It was my gran's. It used to hang on the wall in her house. I always liked it.'

She sipped her tea. 'Was she a doctor too?'

'God, no. Gran ran her own catering company. She worked right up until she died aged seventy-four.'

'Were you close?'

'Extremely.' His arms rested on his bent knees. 'My parents worked long, unsociable hours, so I spent most of my youth at her house. She's the one who encouraged my love of music. She'd put on Elvis films and we'd play along, her on the piano, me on guitar.'

He painted a nice picture. 'Did you want to be a musician then, rather than a doctor?'

He rolled his head to look at her. 'I don't think I knew what I wanted. I still don't.' He sighed, his frustration evident. 'My parents have decided they've been patient enough and have enrolled me on a specialist medical programme starting next month.'

'And you don't want to do it?'

'Honestly? I don't know.' His head flopped back against the headboard. 'My heart's not really in it.'

'Because you don't think you'd be any good? Or because you genuinely don't want to be a consultant?'

'A bit of both.'

She handed him the empty mug. 'Lovely cup of tea. Thank you.'

'You're welcome.' He stretched across to put the mug down.

She had to resist the temptation to trail her fingers down his back.

'I don't hate medicine, and I love helping people, it's just the constant pressure and long hours I can't stand. It's relentless.

Depressing.' He settled next to her, closer than before. 'I know you think I'm irresponsible and a waste of space.'

'No, I don't.'

He raised an eyebrow.

'Okay, I did.' Her remark evoked another smile. 'But that was before I got to know you. You're not a bad doctor, whatever you might think. I've seen you in action. Look how you saved Jonathan.'

'Not a good example.'

'Why, because it left you traumatised?'

He flinched.

'It was a life-or-death situation and you didn't have any professional back-up. I'm not surprised you found it upsetting. Anyone would've done, medically trained or not. Under the circumstances, you did amazingly well.' She patted the back of his hand, feeling the need to offer some form of comfort, but not wanting to do anything too intimate. 'But think of the other stuff, like how great you were with the kids on Wednesday. Freddie and Florence haven't stopped practising their first-aid skills. I had to sit with my arm in a sling for an hour yesterday afternoon, and when Dad arrived to pick them up, they insisted on putting him and Sylvia into the recovery position. You made a real impact on them.'

He looked dejected. 'So, you're saying I should suck it up and return to medicine?'

'No, I'm saying you should find a way of using your talents in such a way that it makes you happy. You're fixated on what your parents want and how they see your career panning out. Surely all that medical training must be useful for something other than being a consultant?'

He raised both eyebrows. 'You mean like working on a cruise ship, or something?'

She shrugged her shoulders, which was a bad move, as it dislodged the duvet, revealing a little too much flesh. 'Possibly, but there must be other roles, like working abroad helping with emergency relief, or running clinics. Maybe even getting into education. You're a natural teacher. I bet there are all manner of opportunities once you start looking into it.'

It was a mistake to get onto such a personal topic, especially as she'd just flashed her breasts at him. They weren't in a relationship, they were 'friends with benefits', two people needing the distraction of physical pleasures to occupy their bodies and minds whilst they both sorted out their lives. Nothing more.

It was time to switch focus, particularly as his pupils had dilated and he was staring at her neck. 'So, are you going to help me with my lines, or not?'

He moved her hair away from her shoulder. 'Of course. Do you need me to get my script?'

'Let me try without first, see how I get on.' She refused to acknowledge the flutter of butterflies in her tummy when he kissed her shoulder. 'I've learnt the bit with Oberon in the forest.'

'Okay.' His fingers slid up her arm. 'Let's hear it.'

Her brain told her to move away from his touch, staying put was only encouraging him, but her body screamed, *don't even think about it!*

'"Believe me, King of Shadows, I mistook. Did not you tell me I should know the man by the Athenian garments he had on?"' She paused, trying not to be distracted by his hand, which had started massaging her shoulder. Christ, the man had nimble fingers. '"And so far blameless proves my enterprise, that I have anointed an Athenian's eyes. And I am glad it so did sort, as this their jangling I esteem a sport."'

'Perfect.' His palm circled her shoulder, his fingers gently working the muscles leading up to her neck. '"Thou seest these lovers seek a place to fight."' His words were even more seductive than normal, his breath tickling her skin as he spoke. His touch was warm and enticing, his body both soft and hard against hers. '"Like to Lysander sometime frame thy tongue."' On the word 'tongue' he licked her neck, then gently blew on her damp skin.

A bolt of something liquid shot from her toes right up her spine, rendering her unable to resist when he pulled her down the bed. He slid on top of her, his face hovering above hers, kissing her shoulder, her neck, her collarbone.

How the hell was she supposed to remember her words under such an onslaught? His fingers laced with hers and he tightened his grip, sliding her hands up and over her head, pinning them to the headboard. The duvet no longer covered her dignity. 'My God.'

'I think you'll find the line is, '"My fairy lord."'

Smart-arse. He was clearly enjoying toying with her. She closed her eyes, hoping to shut out the distraction of his closeness, his kisses, his mouth as it moved south. Concentrate, she told her brain. '"My fairy lord, this must be done with haste, for night's swift dragons cut the clouds full fast."' She said it on a rush, knowing her ability to recall words was rapidly slipping away.

His kisses moved lower. He was getting perilously close to her...

Everything within her tightened. A mixture of pleasure and fear, like she was about to shatter. She tried to free her hands so she could move away from his mouth, but he held firm. '"Up... and... down."' The words would barely come. '"I... will... lead them..."'

'Stop talking.'

'But I—'

The intensity of his kiss ratcheted up a notch.

She tried again when he pulled away, albeit with a little less protest. 'But...'

'Shush.' He smiled, a curiously wicked glint in his eye. 'Don't make a sound.'

She realised he was getting his own back for the other night at Smugglers Inn when she'd accosted him in his dressing room. He was turning the tables, the one giving instructions, calling the shots. The one... *Oh, Christ*. What was he doing now...?

Yes, indeed. However you looked at it, Puck was engaging in a highly inappropriate relationship with the King of the Fairies.

Chapter 22

Sunday, 21 August – 2 days till curtain-up

Barney flinched when the stage manager's voice crackled over the headset. No one had responded to her requests to cue the fog machine and she was getting increasingly irate. Technical rehearsals were never easy. The cast got bored from hanging around waiting for the backstage crew to set the cues, the kids became fractious and distracted the more the day progressed, and the SM spent the entire time shouting at everyone for not listening to instructions. As director, Barney was expected to manage the whole debacle, remaining calm and positive as he was pulled in all directions, trying to sort out a multitude of queries, from issues with the props, to wardrobe malfunctions. Not exactly a restful way to spend a sunny afternoon in August. He'd been at the theatre since nine a.m. trying to coordinate the merging of the backstage team with the onstage team and it was proving testing.

'Is anyone going to answer me?' The SM's yell almost deafened him.

He looked around, trying to work out why Sylvia wasn't responding. She was in the makeshift wings frowning at the fog machine. He went over. 'Everything okay?'

'I've followed the instructions, but the start button won't work.' She pressed the big red switch to emphasise her point.

Barney picked up the cable and followed the trail to the extension socket tucked against the flats. 'It's not switched on at the wall, Sylvia.'

She came over to check, as if not believing him. 'I was sure I'd switched it on.' She smacked her forehead with her hand. 'I'm so stupid.'

'It's an easy mistake.' He flicked the wall switch on. 'Try it now.'

She went back to the machine and pressed the red switch. A burst of fog exploded from the vent. 'It works!'

Yeah, funny that. Leaving Sylvia to deal with the fog machine, he returned to the stage, only to be accosted by an irate Glenda. 'Lauren tells me she's not wearing the dress I made for her.' She stood in front of him, hands on hips, making it clear she wasn't budging. 'I put her straight. I said, "You're wearing it, my girl," but she's refusing.'

Barney knew tact was required. 'Unfortunately, the dress you'd made didn't quite work, Glenda. Sorry about that. I know you've put a lot of effort into the costumes.'

Everybody else's costumes, anyway. Lauren's dress looked like a drab rag compared to the rich fabrics used to dress the other characters. He was starting to wonder if Nate's 'bullying' theory was right.

'No one else has complained. I don't see why she should get special treatment just because she doesn't like her costume.' Glenda pointed to where Lauren was sitting with Tony, her voice deliberately loud.

At that moment, Sylvia appeared from the wings and went over to squeeze Lauren's hand, a show of support against the might of Glenda's verbal attack. Tony remained oblivious. It was hard to tell whether he genuinely didn't notice, or just didn't want to get involved.

Barney kept his voice low, indicating this wasn't a discussion that needed to include anyone else, especially not Lauren. 'It isn't that she doesn't like it.'

'Then what is it? She's too vain, that girl. She needs to stop fussing over her appearance and wear what she's given.' Glenda's voice rose another notch.

Lauren stumbled to her feet and ran towards the loos.

Sylvia gave Glenda a pointed look and followed Lauren into the loos, not before scolding Tony with, 'You shouldn't let her speak to Lauren like that.' But the remark was lost on Tony, who looked around with a puzzled expression, as if confused by what had just happened.

Barney reverted his attention to Glenda, wondering if he should point out that Lauren was the least vain person he knew. But he suspected this had more to do with issues outside the drama group than a spat over costumes. 'You've done an amazing job with the costumes, Glenda. We just need to put Hermia in something more fitted and less likely to trip her up.'

'If that's the only issue, then I'll take up the hem.'

'It's also too baggy. Hermia's supposed to be petite. We need the visual contrast between her small stature and Helena's tall stature, otherwise the fight scene in the forest isn't funny.'

'I'll take the dress in.'

'No need, Glenda.'

'Jonathan liked my designs.' Glenda was used to getting her own way. No wonder she made such a formidable money-lender.

'I'm sure he did, but this particular dress isn't working.' He hoped his tone indicated it was discussion over. 'The show starts on Tuesday, it's easier if we use the hire dress I picked up yesterday.' He made a point of moving past her. 'Now, if you'll excuse me, we need to get on with the tech.'

He ignored her grunt.

Directing a play was similar to working on the wards, he'd decided. Endless pacifying, juggling a multitude of tasks, and bouncing from one issue to another. The only differences were that no one was likely to die on his shift, and he got to go home at a reasonable hour... at least, he hoped so.

He took a moment to look around the stage, wondering what else needed resolving.

Nate was looking after the kids, handing out packets of crisps in a bid to keep them quiet. Good. That was one less thing to worry about.

Paul was up a ladder moving spotlights. It was all hands on deck in amateur dramatics. Thankfully, the theatre supplied a backstage crew for the run, so he didn't have the hassle of trying to find volunteers to work lighting and sound.

Daniel was sitting alone, his head buried in his script. It would be nice if he made himself useful, but he wasn't causing any grief, so Barney left him to his own devices.

That just left Charlotte.

He found her standing next to the tree house. She was wearing her snug-fitting jeans with a red top and what looked like white school plimsolls. Having admitted she didn't own any trainers, he'd suggested she buy a pair to rehearse in. High heels weren't exactly suitable for playing the part of a woodland nymph.

As he neared, he could see a frown creasing her forehead.

She was clinging hold of the scaffolding, shaking her head. 'I'm sorry, but I can't do it.' There was a genuine sense of panic in her voice as she looked up at Quentin and Vincent Graham.

'I see you've met Glenda's sons.' Barney realised that the Neanderthal pair were trying to get Charlotte to test out the fly rig. Both brothers were built like Thor, only with substantial beer bellies and significantly less hammer skills.

Charlotte turned at the sound of Barney's voice. 'They want me to climb up there and jump off!'

'She's gotta wear the harness.' Quentin held out the leather belt. 'Mum said so.'

Despite being well into their thirties, both brothers still obeyed their mother. Sad, really. Or maybe it was just him that disobeyed parental orders? 'Give me five minutes, will you?'

With some reluctance, they repositioned themselves a few feet away. They weren't very good at switching focus, he'd discovered. Still, as muscle was needed backstage, he had to keep them sweet.

'There's nothing to sort out.' Charlotte's whole body was physically shaking. 'I'm not jumping off six feet of scaffolding.'

Barney tried to take her hand, but she wouldn't let go of the support pole. 'No one's asking you to.'

Her expression turned hopeful. 'I don't have to jump off?'

'It's more of a gentle swing down.'

Her eyes grew wide. 'From up there?' More head shaking. 'No way, I… I can't.'

He'd forgotten about her fear of heights. How to tackle this? he wondered. Coercion? Bribery? Or just plain diversion tactics? He prised one hand away from the scaffolding. 'If you can't do it, then I won't make you.'

She looked wary. 'You won't?'

'Of course not. But I think it's a shame. Puck flying across the stage would look fantastic, quite a spectacle for the audience.'

'Not if I throw up halfway across!'

'Oh, I don't know. I quite like the idea of you splattering Daniel's head with last night's dinner.'

She didn't laugh.

Okay, time to switch tactics. 'Forget the show for a moment. Think about what this could do for you personally.'

'Flying through the air on a harness is not on my bucket list.' Her disgruntled expression made him smile.

'Maybe not, but you have to admit that you've tried all sorts of new things over the summer, and for the most part, you've enjoyed them.'

She faltered, almost as if she wanted to contradict him, but couldn't.

'You don't like heights, I get that. But think what an achievement it would be if you overcame that? Imagine how empowering it would be to conquer your fears and feel the elation of flying.'

'I... I don't know.'

'You'd be perfectly safe, I promise you. The harness is very secure, and look at the size of the men controlling the rig?' He pointed to where Quentin and Vincent were standing, waiting for their next instruction. Dumb fucks, the pair of them. 'No way are they going to drop you.' At least, he bloody well hoped not.

She chewed on her lower lip, her eyes assessing the gap between the stage and the tree house. 'How... how far would I be off the ground?'

'Just a few feet. You swing down from the tree house, across to the fairy grove, and then back again. Simple.'

'Oh, God. I can't believe I'm actually contemplating doing this.'

He took her by the shoulders. 'You're a remarkable woman. Brave and resilient. Under that buttoned-up exterior is an adventurous spirit waiting to be unleashed.'

She raised an eyebrow. 'You do talk bollocks sometimes.'

He laughed. 'Is it working?'

She hesitated. 'You promise to stop if I don't like it?'

He leant closer. 'I promise. But maybe once you give it a go, you'll love it.' She smelt amazing: fruity and summery. 'I can think of a few other instances where that's happened.' He gave her a teasing smile.

'Yes, well, you have a very persuasive nature.' She shrugged free from his grasp. 'I haven't quite worked out whether that's a good thing or not.'

'Have you had fun this summer?'

'Much as I hate to admit it, yes.'

'Any regrets?'

With some reluctance, she shook her head. There was a time when she'd be fiddling with her hair or searching out a button when faced with adversity, but no more. She was definitely less wired.

'Do you trust me?'

She raised an eyebrow.

'Well, do you?'

She sighed. 'Yes, I trust you.'

'Good. Because I honestly believe you'll love it.' He moved closer, intending to kiss her, but she pulled away like he was about to strangle her. 'Stop it!' she said, glancing around. 'People will assume something's going on.'

He smiled. 'Well, it is... isn't it?'

She gave him a look. 'There's no need to advertise. And it's not like it's going anywhere. It's a short-term arrangement. The fewer people that know, the better.' Her cheeks coloured.

He laughed, mostly to cover his disappointment. Foolishly, he'd thought their 'relationship' was shifting. It wasn't. 'Discretion it is.' He beckoned over the Graham brothers and held open the harness for Charlotte to step into. 'One leg either side of the strap.'

After a moment's hesitation, she obeyed and let him fasten the clips.

'Do you need a hand getting into the tree house?'

She straightened her shoulders. 'No, thanks. I can do it on my own.'

'See? Remarkable and brave.'

She shot him a look. 'Quit with the sales pitch. I've succumbed.'

He watched her climb up the ladder, resisting the urge to touch her.

When she reached the top, she hesitated. 'What do I do now?'

'Ease yourself onto the ledge. Quentin and Vincent will control the fly rig from the wings.' When they didn't move, he pointed to the wings. 'Over there, guys.'

Vincent shifted his bulk, followed by Quentin. Brainless pair.

Barney looked up at Charlotte, who'd edged her way onto the ledge, clutching hold of the camouflage netting. 'When the rope goes taut, push yourself away from the ledge.' He waited for everyone to clear the stage. 'Quentin? You ready?' Satisfied they were set, Barney gave Charlotte a thumbs up. 'Whenever you're ready.'

It took a few aborted attempts before she finally let go, the fear in her body rendering her as stiff as a mannequin. Part of him felt bad for making her do it. Was it really a good idea to force someone into facing a phobia? Especially when that person was someone you cared about. Because, despite his best efforts to keep their relationship purely physical, he'd failed. Over the last week, when they'd practised their lines together, gone for long walks along the beach, and ended up in bed each time, exhausted and laughing, a connection had been formed… on his part, at least. But Charlotte had made it clear she only wanted a fling. And he wasn't quite sure how he felt about that.

As he watched her now, battling her instincts to cling hold of the scaffolding, he was overcome with something powerful. Pride? Admiration? Or just lust? He didn't know, but seeing her flying across the stage, screaming with a mixture of exhilaration and fear, gave him a sense of satisfaction like no other.

It wasn't the most elegant of flights, but when she swung back across the stage, her scream was a little less 'I'm being murdered' and more 'this might be fun'.

'How was it?' he shouted.

She grabbed hold of the scaffolding, taking a moment to ensure she wasn't about to fall off. 'Okay… I think. As long as I don't look down.'

He smiled. 'You did it!'

She nodded, slightly manically. 'I did, didn't I?' Her hair moved softly in the breeze, and for a moment he was stunned by how beautiful she was.

He tried to clear his mind. 'Can we try it again with the lines this time?' He waited for her to nod, before checking that the Graham brothers were paying attention and weren't about to drop her.

She only faltered for a moment before pushing herself away from the ledge. '"I go – I go – look how I *gooooooo*!"' She flew across the stage, her hands outstretched, landing on the raised fairy grove with all the grace of a prop forward entering a rugby scrum. It didn't matter. She'd done it. Her return flight was a little more fairy-like, and she nailed the landing perfectly. '"Swifter than arrow from the Tartar's bow."'

The rest of the cast, who'd gathered below to watch, clapped enthusiastically and cheered. Tony shouted, 'Well done, love,' evoking a smile from his daughter.

Barney stood at the bottom of the ladder. 'Need a hand down?'

She shuffled around to the top. 'Nope, I got this.'

When she reached the last rung, he placed his hands on her waist. 'Like I said, remarkable woman.'

She turned in his arms. 'Thank you for pushing me out of my comfort zone.'

'My pleasure.' Her cheeks were flushed, her hair was wild, and he'd never wanted a woman more in his life. But she broke free from the embrace, taking all warmth with her.

Right, yes. He needed to direct a show. The sound of the SM's voice telling him they were ready to set the cues for the fog machine brought him to his senses.

He returned to the stage and called the cast to join him. When they'd run the fight scene on Thursday, it had been a mess. Partly because Daniel still wasn't comfortable touching Paul, but mostly because the tension between Lauren and Nate was at breaking point. All he knew was that an argument had taken place following a visit from the authorities regarding Glenda, and Lauren hadn't taken the interference well.

Barney looked at the four unhappy faces in front of him. It was going to be a long afternoon. 'We'll start from when Hermia runs on stage. Nate, can you give Lauren her cue?'

Nate glanced at Lauren, who wouldn't look at him and disappeared into the wings. A despondent Nate took up his position at Paul's feet.

Barney moved in front of the stage. 'Ready when you are.'

As directed, Nate tried to divert Daniel's attention away from Paul. '"Look where thy love comes, yonder is thy dear."'

Lauren ran onto the stage and flung herself at Daniel, who, being a bit of a weakling, staggered backwards and nearly fell off the side of the stage. Regaining his footing, he shoved her to the ground, a little too forcefully, making her yelp when she hit the stone floor.

Nate jumped up. 'Mind what you're doing. You don't need to push her that hard.'

Lauren ignored Nate's offer to help her up. 'I can fight my own battles, thank you.' She brushed dust away from her shorts, refusing to look at him.

'I know you can.' Nate looked stung. 'I thought you might be hurt.'

'Well, I'm not.' She resumed her position by Daniel. 'Can we get on with this, please? I don't want to be here all day.'

Barney forced a smile. 'Pick it up, guys.'

Paul marched over to Lauren. '"Will you join with these men in scorning your poor friend?"'

Lauren looked genuinely confused. '"I understand not what you mean by this."'

Paul towered over her. '"Tis partly my own fault, which death or absence soon shall remedy."'

Daniel scurried over and blocked his exit, one eye warily on Nate, as his nemesis grabbed Paul around the waist. Paul's next move should have been to push Daniel into Lauren's arms. Unfortunately, Lauren ducked at the wrong moment and Paul fell over her, landing on Daniel, taking Nate down with him. All four lay in a crumpled heap on the floor.

'Ow! Get off my hand,' cried Daniel.

'Then let go of my arm, you idiot.' Paul tried to roll off Daniel, but his foot connected with Nate's head. 'Sorry, mate.'

Nate was too busy trying not to squash Lauren, who'd landed under him.

A sudden burst of fog shot from the wings, covering all four of them.

'Not yet, Sylvia!' Barney pressed the button on his headset. 'Sylvia, cut the fog. You're too early.'

Another burst of fog engulfed the stage.

Daniel crawled out from the fog, coughing. '"Helena, I love thee. By my life, I do."'

Sylvia's voice came over the headset. 'Sorry!'

'It's okay, Sylvia. That's what technicals are for, so we can iron out any wrinkles.' Barney rubbed his temples. Keeping up such positivity was draining. 'We'll come back to this scene once the fog has cleared. Can I have the principals down the front so we can block the finale.'

When everyone had gathered, he outlined his ideas for the end of the show. 'Instead of a traditional curtain call, I'd like to set a tableau depicting the various relationships throughout the play. I thought we could call it, Unrequited Love.'

A series of blank expressions stared back at him.

'It'll make more sense when you're in position. Nate, if you could come to the front and lie down.' Nate did as he was asked. 'Lauren, if you could kneel in front of him, but with your back to him. The idea is that Demetrius is pining after Hermia.'

He only realised the significance of this scenario when several people raised their eyebrows.

He quickly moved on. 'In front, we'll have Glenda. If you could adopt a seated position here.' Again, he hadn't though this through. Lauren refused to look at Glenda. 'Next, we have Sylvia and then Tony.' He guided them into position. 'Paul and Daniel, if you could come to the other side and form a circle. Finally, myself and Charlotte will finish the loop.'

He stood back to assess the impact.

Talk about awkward. You could cut the tension with a knife. It wasn't quite what he'd envisaged. 'At the moment, you all look a little detached. The idea is that each of you is in love with the person in front of you, but they're in love with the person in front of them. Does that make sense?'

A few murmured responses.

'So, if everyone could get into character and, on the count of three, adopt a pose that depicts "unrequited love". After three. One... two...'

Glenda scowled. Lauren looked close to tears. Daniel overplayed it, and Paul's expression conveyed sarcasm. Only Nate and Sylvia pitched it right, their faces showing the pain of a hopeless cause – but then Barney guessed that they didn't have to act much.

He moved into position next to Charlotte, wondering how to depict Oberon's emotions. He didn't have to try very hard. One look at Charlotte in her white plimsolls, looking relaxed, happy, and a total contrast to the woman who'd bitten his head off the first day she'd arrived in Cornwall and the bottom dropped out of his stomach.

She was frozen in her pose, reaching for him, suspended in animated desire for her master. It was oddly arousing. Not helped when she mouthed, 'Highly suspicious relationship,' making him laugh.

He liked her, didn't he? As in, *really* liked her.

He was in big trouble... and not just with the play.

Chapter 23

The Isolde Players present *A Midsummer Night's Dream*

Lauren usually loved the opening night of a show. The mixture of excitement and nervous energy bubbling through the cast created a buzz of anticipation. The communal dressing area was a bustle of noise, with people warming up their voices or going over their lines, convinced they'd forget them the moment they stepped on stage. Hanging rails were crammed full of costumes, with people's discarded personal belongings creating trip hazards on the floor. Cast members walked about in various stages of undress, some made-up, some waiting to have their wigs fitted. Bright spotlights surrounded the large dressing mirrors, even though dusk had yet to descend on the amphitheatre and the stage glowed in the early-evening sunlight.

But, despite the smell of greasepaint and the sight of her children dressed in their respective costumes, looking both mischievous and angelic, she didn't want to be there. A pastime that was normally so joyous had become torturous.

Slipping her dress off its hanger, she took it into one of the loos to change. She didn't want to undress in front of people and invite stares or questions as to why she'd lost more weight.

It had been nearly two weeks since the woman from the IMLT had called at her house. Lauren wasn't sure she'd slept a wink since. She kept expecting Glenda to burst into her flat and accuse her of contacting the authorities, using her sons to inflict some sort of physical punishment. Living under the constant threat of being 'outed' was shredding her nerves to pieces. She'd become forgetful at work, snappy with the children, isolated from her friends. Not to mention she'd been crying all the time. It was exhausting.

She zipped up the hire dress. It fitted better than the dress Glenda had made, but it was still loose around the middle. She sat down on the closed loo seat, dropping her head in her hands, tired beyond belief. Every night, she lay in bed staring at the cracked ceiling, praying for a way out of her predicament. Numerous times she'd been tempted to tell Charlotte what was happening, especially as she suspected that her sister had guessed something was up. Why else would she have paid her catalogue bill? But something always stopped her. Shame? Humiliation? Guilt?

And she had a lot to feel guilty about.

She tugged on the loo roll and blew her nose, wiping away tears from under her sore eyes. She'd been so quick to criticise her sister's failings when she'd arrived in Penmullion, untactfully pointing out her compulsive tendencies, lecturing her on how she needed to 'live a little'. As a consequence, her sister had made a real effort to change. Her set designs for the show were magnificent, and she was ingraining herself into community life. Seeing her smiling and joining in with the production was a true delight. There was no way she could ruin that for Charlotte, not when her sister was finally learning how to be happy.

She got up and flushed the crumpled loo paper away. Her make-up would need touching up, she probably had mascara smudges running down her cheeks. Exiting the loo, she headed back to the dressing area, spotting Barney giving last-minute instructions to the front-of-house team. He was already in costume, his dark-red and gold velour slashed top and trousers making him look like a Shakespearean Ziggy Stardust.

Avoiding eye contact with him, she hurried through the wings, wishing she could find a quiet place to hide until she was needed. The audience had started to arrive. She could hear murmurs of appreciation filtering through the flats as those new to Penmullion took in the stunning location of the theatre. Tickets for every night had sold out, which only added to the pressure.

No sooner had she entered the dressing area than Glenda appeared like an unwelcome apparition. 'Sit down, love. I'll do your hair.'

Panic raced through her. 'That's kind of you, Glenda. But I can do it myself.'

'No need. Always happy to help.' Lauren wasn't quick enough to avoid being manhandled into the chair. 'Plaiting is tricky, it's easier if someone else does it. Isn't that right, Tony?'

Her dad, who was standing by the hanging rail buttoning up a gold-brocade waistcoat, laughed. 'It's not something I've ever tried, Glenda.' He smoothed back his short reddish-blond hair.

Glenda winked at him. 'You'd look rather fetching with a few plaits.'

Sylvia glanced up from applying her make-up and glared at Glenda. 'What nonsense.'

Glenda pulled a face. 'All right, keep your hair on. It's just me and Tony having a bit of a laugh.' Her expression switched to flirtatious. 'Isn't that right, Tony?'

Her dad's eyes darted from Glenda to Sylvia and then back again. He didn't look like he wanted to get involved.

Nope, telling her dad wasn't an option either. He was integral to the community, friends with Glenda, part of a tight-knit group. She couldn't take that away from him. Besides, would he even believe her? Looking at Glenda now, no one would suspect she was anything other than a jolly, kind-hearted woman who 'wanted to help'. But the woman had threatened to report her to Social Services for being an unfit parent. Maybe not in so many words, but the warning hung in the air. Who knew what else she was capable of? For the sake of her family, Lauren needed to keep quiet and deal with it herself.

Glenda tugged at the knots in Lauren's hair, showing little consideration for her scalp. After a moment, she turned to Sylvia. 'Can I help you?' That was the problem with so many mirrors, nothing went unnoticed.

Flustered at being caught watching, Sylvia resumed applying her lipstick. 'I don't want anything from you, thank you very much, Glenda.'

'Hark at her, all snooty. What's her problem?' Glenda angled her body away from Sylvia, before reverting her attention to Lauren. 'Don't forget to remove your jewellery before curtain-up, love.'

Lauren noticed Glenda eying up her charm bracelet in the mirror. 'Thank you for the reminder.'

'Looks expensive.' To anyone watching, it was an innocent enough remark, but Lauren sensed a hidden meaning.

Her hand went instinctively to the bracelet. 'It was my mother's.'

'I hope it's insured. It would be a shame to lose something so valuable.' Glenda smiled into the mirror.

Lauren felt her insides tighten. Next to her, she could sense Sylvia itching to say something. Whether she would have done, Lauren would never know. The SM's head appeared around the door, asking Sylvia to come backstage so they could fit her mic.

With a show of reluctance, Sylvia got up and squeezed Lauren's shoulder as she passed by. 'Break a leg, sweetheart,' she said, giving Glenda a look that said she'd like to break *her* leg, but was far too much of a lady to do so.

Lauren lowered her eyes, hoping Glenda wouldn't engage in further conversation. Remaining civil was becoming increasingly challenging.

'I've been thinking.' Glenda checked the top of the plait was straight. 'I think we need to increase your weekly repayments to seventy-five quid.'

Lauren's head jerked up.

'Keep still, love. I'm trying to do your hair.'

Air seemed to get stuck in her lungs, like when she'd been winded falling down the stairs as a kid. She tried to breathe, but her throat wouldn't work. All she could do was shake her head.

Glenda continued plaiting. 'It makes sense. You don't like owing me money.' Her eyes checked the mirror to ensure no one was listening. 'I can see it's stressing you out.'

Lauren tried to breathe.

'And that upsets me, because you mean a lot to me. I figure, the quicker we get this debt settled, the better for everyone.'

She smiled, as though she was offering Lauren an all-expenses paid holiday to the Seychelles.

'I… I can't.' Finally, she could speak, albeit in a whisper. 'I can't afford to increase the repayments, Glenda. I'm struggling to find fifty pounds as it is.'

Glenda nodded, as if in understanding. 'You say that, but then I see you wearing flash jewellery, and I think, well, she's clearly got more money than she's letting on.'

'I told you, the bracelet was my mother's. It was left to me in her will. I didn't buy it.'

'No, but you could sell it.'

'Wh-what?' A few heads turned at the sound of Lauren's panicked voice.

'Keep your voice down, love. No need to involve anyone else. This is a private arrangement.' Her grip tightened, pulling Lauren's head back slightly. 'That's right, isn't it?'

Did Glenda know? Had she found out about the IMLT investigation? A throb thumped in Lauren's temples. Guilt gave her away, her eyes searching the room until they locked on Nate's. He was looking over, his expression intense as if he knew what they were discussing.

Sweet, kind, wonderful Nate. Who'd done nothing but be a friend and look out for her and her kids since they'd moved to Cornwall. He was dressed in his Athenian costume, his hair tamed into a neat style, his beard trimmed. She missed him. The kids missed him. But she couldn't rely on him to rescue her. And besides, she was still mad at him.

She dropped her gaze. Shame burned deep within her as she recalled their argument. But why hadn't he come to her first with his concerns before reporting Glenda? She could have assured him she was dealing with it. Except she wasn't, was she? Her life was unravelling, and she had no idea how to stop it.

Glenda's face lowered next to hers, close enough that Lauren could smell stale coffee. 'Maybe you didn't hear me. I said, this is a private arrangement... right?'

Lauren nodded, which was hard when Glenda had hold of her hair.

'Good girl. Pass me that band.' Glenda fastened the plait. 'Perfect.'

'Please don't ask me to sell my mother's bracelet. It has sentimental value.' She could feel the tears running down her face.

Glenda rested her hands on Lauren's shoulders, her grip a little too firm. 'You don't need to tell me about family, love. I have boys of my own.' On cue, the Graham brothers came into the dressing room, blocking out most of the natural light. 'And they'd do anything for their old mum. Protect me, they do. A little too much, at times, if you know what I mean. You wouldn't know it to look at them, but they've got quite a temper.' Glenda reached out and chucked Vincent under the chin. 'But they mean well, and I'd do anything to provide for them. Which is why, sometimes, I have to make tough decisions.'

Lauren heard Nate's voice before she saw him approach. 'Cast only in the dressing room, boys. You know that.'

Glenda's hand left Lauren's shoulder as she turned to Nate. 'Since when have you been a stickler for the rules?'

'There's not enough room and people are getting changed.' Nate's tone remained polite, but firm. He pointed to the door. 'Leave, please.'

Barney appeared in the doorway. 'Everything okay in here?'

Everyone looked at Lauren, except for Glenda, who stared at Nate. 'Someone's getting a bit full of himself.'

Lauren's humiliation grew, but Nate wasn't backing down. 'You'd know all about that, wouldn't you, Glenda?'

Glenda turned to him. 'What's that supposed to mean? You got something to say?'

Lauren jumped to her feet. 'Stop it, please.' Her hands covered her ears like a child trying to block out noise. 'I can't take this. Can we just focus on the play?' She ran from the room, trying to hide the sobs forcing their way past the lump in her throat.

Behind her, she heard Barney say, 'It's just first-night nerves.'

If only.

Chapter 24

Act One

Charlotte's ten-minute cue jolted her from her thoughts. She'd been hiding behind one of the large stone pillars, going over her lines, listening to the others on stage, and trying to quash the overwhelming desire to jump in her car and head back to London. But it was too late. People were relying on her. She needed to dig deep, focus, and adopt the role of 'woodland nymph'.

Grabbing her green-velvet tunic and shorts, she dived for the loos, cursing herself for leaving it so late to finish dressing. As reluctant as she was to appear in public wearing what could only be described as 'hot pants', she now wore the once dreaded items with much more enthusiasm than she could ever have imagined. Along with the green face paint, and orange feathers threaded into her backcombed hair, they acted as a shield, a mask to hide behind so no one would recognise her. Not that she was likely to know anyone in the audience, but remaining anonymous certainly helped to calm the trembles. A bit, anyway.

With shaking hands, she fastened her shorts over her

bottle-green tights, and slid her feet into her plimsolls, which were still damp from being spray-painted green.

Throwing open the loo door, she almost ran smack into Barney.

'There you are.' He reached out to steady her. 'You had me worried, I thought you'd done a runner.'

'Tempting, but no. I was getting changed. How's it going out there?'

'Good. Only a couple of minor mishaps. Nothing the audience would've noticed.' And then he spotted her shorts. 'Whoa, nice fit.'

Her hand tugged self-consciously on the hem. 'I feel like a mouldy Kylie Minogue.'

'Well, you've got *me* spinning around.' He grimaced at his own joke. 'You look hot.'

So did he. His midriff was on show beneath his red-velour tunic, a flash of gold paint highlighting his stomach muscles. She refrained from telling him as much. He didn't need any encouragement.

He was still checking her out. 'Turn around.'

'Stop perving.'

'I'm not perving, I'm appreciating.' His smile was disarming.

She shook her head. He had an answer for everything. 'No time. We're on stage soon.'

The SM appeared from the wings. 'Puck, we need you in your starting position.'

'See? We need to go.' She made to leave.

He caught her arm. 'Ready to do this?'

She shrugged. 'Whether I am or not, there's no turning back.'

He kissed the back of her green hand. 'Break a leg.'

'You theatre types are a strange bunch. Break a leg, indeed.' She moved away from him. 'See you on stage... And stop staring at my backside.'

'I can't help it,' he called after her. 'It's hypnotic.'

She made her way through the props area, which currently housed various items, including the makeshift wall she'd made for the play-within-a-play. The wings were equally precarious – dimly lit, a minefield of ropes and scenery.

Standing at the side, ready to go on stage, were her niece and nephew. Flo was playing the part of Cobweb, one of the fairies. She looked so cute in her floaty white dress, which was covered in large pastel-coloured petals, and net wings. Her hair was adorned with flowers sprayed with glitter. She was holding an ornate wand. Freddie was dressed as a mini Oberon, having jumped at the chance to upgrade his part and wear the same outfit as Barney.

Charlotte made her way over to them. 'You okay?' she whispered.

Flo nodded. 'Excited.'

'I need a pee.' Freddie's voice was a little too loud, causing the SM to shush him.

Charlotte patted his shoulder. 'Me too. I think it's nerves. How's your mum doing?'

Flo pointed to the stage. 'She's amazing. Uncle Paul forgot a line, but she whispered it to him, so it was okay.'

Charlotte looked through the gap in the wings. Lauren did indeed look amazing. She was animated, beautiful and confident, which just proved what a good actress she was. Off stage, she was anything but. Whatever was going on, it had reached crisis point. Charlotte couldn't stand back any longer and watch Lauren deteriorate. Whether her sister liked it or not, she was going to confront her and insist Lauren confess all.

The SM appeared next to Charlotte. 'Time to climb into the tree house, Puck.'

This was the bit she dreaded. Well, that and jumping off it, but that was the next act, so she had a while to steel herself.

Giving Freddie and Flo a quick thumbs up, she followed the SM through the obstacle course of props, and accepted the offer of a leg-up onto the scaffolding. It was easier to deal with her aversion to heights if she closed her eyes, so she shut them tightly as she climbed up. With a firm shove from behind, she landed in the cramped wooden tree house, her home for the next few minutes. The matting beneath her was scratchy, making it hard to lie still. She tried to settle, allowing her eyes time to adjust to the darkness.

Against a backdrop of crashing waves, and the actors projecting their lines on stage, she could hear murmured voices emanating from the audience.

Lauren and Paul finished their scene. It was now the turn of the Mechanicals, meeting to rehearse their play for the Duke of Athens. Her dad appeared, dressed in workmen's attire, complete with leather apron, in his role of Bottom, the weaver. His first line was a little shaky, but he soon warmed up as the audience began laughing at the players' shenanigans.

As Charlotte watched him, it struck her just how far her dad had come. When he'd sunk into a depression after their mum had died, no way would he have been able to act in a play. But look at him now, speaking to the audience, making them laugh with his comic timing. He was a different man. It brought a lump to her throat.

Great as it was to see her dad's recovery, it wasn't enough to eradicate the nerves itching beneath her skin, making her feel like her bladder was full and her mouth was dry. No amount of rehearsal had improved the trepidation of launching herself off six feet of scaffolding. Whether it was jumping off the ledge while attached to the harness, or merely climbing down the ladder onto the stage for her other entrances, her fear of heights still hampered her. She'd tried to 'speed up' as Barney had requested, but with shaking hands, wobbly legs, and a feeling of encroaching nausea, it was hard to do anything other than descend at a snail's pace. Hardly 'sprite-like'.

The scene below drew to a close. No going back now.

God, she needed a pee.

As the Mechanicals exited the stage, and the fairy music started, all she could envisage was the horror of her shorts catching on the ladder rungs and being catapulted into the audience. Oh, well, it would be one way of making a dramatic entrance.

She edged closer to the opening, trying not to make too much noise, and watched as Flo sprang onto the set to begin her ballet sequence.

This really was it. Why had she agreed to do this? Was she out of her mind?

Flo leaped across the stage and twirled, giving Charlotte her cue to appear.

She was in such a state of anxiety about descending the ladder too slowly that she simply closed her eyes and hurled herself from the planking. It was therefore something of a relief that she landed, with the precision of a highly trained parachutist, on the target marked X. The shock of successfully arriving on stage at the right time, and in the right place, momentarily threw her. She nearly forgot what to do next.

Thank God that Flo was concentrating. Her niece sprang into action, dancing up to her and giving her a gentle prod with her wand.

Right, her opening line. What was it again...?

Flo mouthed, *how now spirit*.

Oh, yes. '"How now, spirit. Whither wander you?"'

Flo waved her wand in the air. '"Over hill, over dale, I do wander everywhere."' She hopped, she sang, and she charmed the audience, inviting collective oohs and ahhhs with her precocious cuteness. '"I must go seek some dewdrops here, and hang a pearl in every cowslip's ear."' She twirled back to Charlotte. '"Farewell, thou lob of spirits. I'll be gone. Our Queen and all her elves come here anon."'

It was Charlotte's turn.

With dangerously high levels of adrenaline, she raced through Puck's opening lines, exhausting herself, and – she was sure – everyone watching. '"The King doth keep his revels here tonight. Take heed the Queen come not within his sight."'

She whizzed around the stage like a hyperactive child on speed, trying to emulate a mythical being. By the end of the first paragraph, she was perspiring, knackered, and running out of air. Breathe, she told herself.

Flo looked slightly dazed by her auntie's antics, but kept smiling, like the little pro she was.

Charlotte skipped across the stage as instructed. '"I am that merry wanderer of the night."' She made the mistake of looking at the audience. There were so many of them, filling the rows of seating, all looking at her expectantly. She forced her head up, aiming her words at the darkening sky. It was an impressive sight: dark blue, streaked with smudges of red and pink. *No time for sightseeing. Concentrate.*

'"Neighing in likeness of a filly foal."' She trotted on the spot, her playful neigh sounding more like an injured sheep. Belatedly, she remembered she was supposed to be entertaining the fairy and darted over. '"The wisest aunt telling the saddest tale."'

Flo giggled, no doubt as a result of her aunt's poor acting skills, rather than because she was genuinely funny, but either way Charlotte was glad to be nearing the end.

'"... Then slip I from her bum. Down topples she ..."' As had been carefully choreographed, she toppled down and rolled over on the floor, with the aim of springing back up on, '"And then the whole choir hold their hips and laugh."' But as her knee gave way at the crucial moment, she stayed where she was.

Unperturbed by her auntie's continued kneeling position, Flo tapped her with her wand before elegantly pirouetting off stage. '"Good friends. Would that he were gone!"'

Charlotte remained firmly rooted to the spot, a fear of falling flat on her face preventing her from moving.

Thankfully, Barney came to her rescue, striding across the stage and hauling her up off the floor. '"Ill met by moonlight, proud Titania!"'

She'd thank him later.

He turned to address Sylvia, who'd made a nervous entrance, her long gown catching under her feet, making a few people in the audience snigger.

Freddie copied Barney's regal stance, thrusting his little chest out. Barney placed a hand on his sidekick's shoulder, guiding him to face the audience.

It was nice how he looked out for the kids. Protected them. He was a good man, trustworthy... and not what she'd first thought when she'd arrived in Penmullion.

She felt a twinge in her chest.

Deciding that she must have pulled a muscle launching herself from the scaffolding, she slunk behind the fairy throne and remained there for the rest of the scene.

It was safer that way.

Chapter 25

Act Two

Barney stood in the wings, waiting to go on stage. The first act had gone almost without a hitch. The actors had upped their performances, gaining in confidence and perfecting their comic timing, and the audience were laughing and clapping loudly. They were reaching the midway point, and Lauren and Paul were throwing themselves into the fight sequence.

'"You thief of love!"' Lauren ran full speed towards Paul. '"Have you come by night and stolen my love's heart from him?"' Nate blocked her path, picking her up and swinging her around as she flailed and kicked about.

Paul backed away. '"Have you no modesty, you puppet!"'

'"Puppet?"' Lauren dug her elbow into Nate's ribs, causing him to drop her. He rolled around the floor groaning, leaving Lauren free to advance on Paul.

Yep, it was all very frenetic, very convincing, and nearly all of it was acting.

Barney glanced across to where Charlotte was standing on the other side of the stage, hooked up to the fly rig. She still didn't look completely happy about flying, he guessed she never would, but no one watching her would suspect a fear of heights.

It was quite something to defy the clutches of a phobia. But then, she was quite a woman... as he was discovering.

Behind him, the Graham brothers stood silently, flanked by their mother, watching the fight scene. Glenda had no valid reason for being in the wings, she wasn't due on stage anytime soon, but theatre etiquette stated that, once a show began its run, the director was no longer top dog, the SM was in charge – something Glenda had been quick to point out when he'd suggested she return to the dressing area and await her cue. And he'd thought working in medicine had been tricky. It was a piece of piss compared to this.

On stage, Lauren kicked Paul in the shins. Daniel grabbed her by her hair and pulled her away. '"Get you gone, you dwarf."'

Nate knocked Daniel away, his frustration at Daniel's exuberance all too evident. '"You are too officious!"'

The chase scene followed, with Paul trying to hide behind Nate and Daniel. The audience were rocking with laughter, unaware that Nate tripping up Daniel wasn't part of the rehearsed choreography.

Paul ran into the wings, annoyed to find bodies blocking his path. Nate and Lauren appeared a moment later, and discovered the same issue.

Amongst Paul's whispered requests for people to 'budge out the way', Barney prepared for his entrance. He was just about to step on stage when Paul fell against him – his cry of, 'Mind who you're pushing,' followed by the sight of Nate pointing a finger at Vincent. Glenda and Lauren were tugging on his arm, trying to drag him away. Barney had no idea what had happened, but clearly something had gone down. He'd never seen Nate look so angry.

Paul looked equally perplexed. 'What the hell's going on?'

The SM appeared. 'Barney! Get on stage!'

Shit! He'd missed his cue.

Leaving the SM to deal with the fracas in the wings, he stepped on stage. '"What fools these mortals be! Come, hobgoblin Puck!"'

With perfect timing, Charlotte appeared on the tree house ledge, one hand gripping the camouflaged scaffolding. She looked suitably impish in her cute shorts and matching waistcoat.

He strode towards her. '"This is thy negligence."'

She did an adorable shrug, conveying both mischief and defiance. '"Believe me, King of Shadows, I mistook. Did not you tell me I should know the man by the Athenian garments he had on?"'

Her confidence had been growing all night, which was great to see. She'd transformed from an uptight woman into a playful nymph. Her reactions were natural and her comic timing was spot on. But the flow of the current scene was marred by raised voices filtering through from the wings. Instinct made him glance over. Quentin was having a go at Nate.

'You... you did.' Charlotte had deviated from the script. 'You said he'd have Athenian garments on, and I went into the woods and I squirted love potion in his eye. I didn't know it was the wrong one...' She tried desperately to regain his attention. '*Oberon!*'

Barney realised he'd missed his cue... again. '"Hi Puck."'

'Hi.' Looking relieved, she launched herself from the ledge and flew across the stage, arms outstretched, her toes pointed downwards.

The scuffle in the wings increased with a muffled thud, followed by a wooden toadstool rolling onto the stage.

Realising her master was somewhat distracted, Charlotte continued to ad-lib. 'Well, I didn't know there were two Athenian men, did I? You should have been more specific.'

Barney could see pushing and shoving in the wings, although who was shoving who, he wasn't sure. One of the flats tilted precariously. He moved just in time before it crashed onto the stage.

The audience gasped.

He was a little shocked himself.

He tried to look nonchalant, as though it was supposed to happen and continued with his speech, '"Crush this herb into Lysander's eye, and when they wake, all this derision shall seem like a dream, a fruitless vision."'

A yelp from the wings preceded the sight of Tony trying to break up what looked like Nate and Paul wrestling with Quentin and Vincent.

Barney stepped around the fallen flat. '"Whiles I in this affair do thee employ, I'll to my queen and beg her Indian boy."' He dived into the wings and thumped someone on the back – he didn't know who. 'For fuck's sake! Pack it in, will you?'

Nate and Quentin were locked in battle.

Tony and Paul were holding on to Vincent.

Glenda was tugging on Nate's sleeve, hissing at him to 'let go of her boy!'

Lauren was crying, pleading with everyone to 'stop fighting!'

The SM was on her headset calling for back-up.

It was then that Barney heard Charlotte's scream. He spun around in time to see her swinging wildly across the stage. *Shit!* No one was controlling the fly rig.

'"My... my fairy lord, this must be done with haste!"' Her voice sounded panicked as she wobbled on the end of the rope.

He ran onto the stage and tried to grab her, but she sailed straight past.

The audience laughed.

He ran across to the assistant stage manager's side and into the wings. 'Get someone on the fly rig.'

The ASM looked at him blankly. 'But I have to cue the fairies.' She pointed at her script.

'Fuck the fairies,' he said, realising a beat too late how inappropriate that sounded. 'This is more important.' When she remained frozen, he bellowed, 'Do it now!'

On stage, Charlotte was desperately trying to hold it together as she swung from one side to the other, like a wayward pendulum. 'And, basically, there's a very long speech here, ladies and gentlemen, and all the spirits have gone to bed... er... isn't that right, *Oberon*!'

The audience's laughter increased.

Barney ran onto the stage. '"I with morning's love have oft made sport..."' He tried to grab her. '"Even till the eastern gate all fiery red..."' He jumped again, only managing to dislodge one of her plimsolls. '"Opening on Neptune with fair blessed beams, turns yellow gold, his salt green streams."' He almost caught her, but lost his grip.

She was now 'spinning around', as well as swinging from side to side, and minus one shoe. 'I feel sick.' Not exactly Kylie.

He rattled through his speech. '"Make no delay, we may effect this business yet 'ere day."' He ran off stage, pushing his way into the scuffle. 'Stop fucking about, you selfish arses!'

On stage, Charlotte had managed to grab one of the stone pillars and was now clinging hold, her legs wrapped around it. '"Fairies! Flowers, please!"'

Freddie and Florence stumbled onto the stage, confused at finding Puck clinging hold of a pillar. They stopped in their tracks, looking around for adult guidance. No chance. The adults were behaving like five-year-olds. Florence recovered first, waving her wand about, nudging her brother, gesturing for him to start scattering petals.

In the wings, Barney pleaded with Paul and Tony. 'Get him out of here,' he said, pointing at Nate, before turning to Glenda. 'Tell your sons to pack it in and take control of the fly rig.'

'Don't you blame this on them. This was all *her*.' Glenda jabbed a finger at Lauren, who was still crying.

'I don't give a flying fuck whose fault it is. We're in the middle of a show, in front of a paying audience. They deserve better.' He overrode any attempts to interrupt. 'Charlotte has a fear of heights, so to leave her hanging out there is a fucking disgrace. Stop acting like kids and get a grip.'

The SM bustled her way into the group. 'You heard the man. *Move!*'

On stage, Charlotte was still clinging hold of the pillar, her eyes wide, her toes no longer pointed. '"Up and down, up and down, I will lead them up and down."' Bless her, she was trying her best to stay in character, showing more professionalism than the rest of the cast put together.

Trying to refocus, Barney headed onto the stage and went over to her. As he looked up, noticing her locked knees and her hands gripping the pillar so hard they shook, something inside him shifted. 'I love you,' he whispered, prising one leg away from the pillar.

He was left in no doubt that she'd heard him. Her shock was understandable, but it was the look of horror on her face that stung the most. What had he been thinking? Well, he hadn't. Good one, Barney. Avoiding eye contact, he eased her away from the pillar and gently swung her towards the wings.

Thankfully, Daniel made his entrance, diverting attention elsewhere. '"He goes before me, and still dares me on. I followed fast, but faster did he fly."'

As Barney swung Charlotte across the stage, she clipped Daniel's head with her foot, causing him to stumble forwards with all the theatrics of a footballer appealing to the referee for a penalty. Rubbing his head, Daniel stared daggers at a retreating Puck. '"That fallen am I in dark uneven way."'

The audience were in hysterics. They clearly found the whole mess extremely funny.

Would anyone be laughing later? Barney wondered.

Chapter 26

The Interval

Lauren wanted to hide, curl up in a ball, and never face anyone ever again. Knowing she'd been the cause of such a monumental meltdown had shamed her beyond belief. The urge to grab her kids and run from the theatre was overwhelming, but she had to dig deep and finish the show. She'd caused enough trouble as it was.

Unsurprisingly, when she entered the dressing area, a hush descended. Nate looked up from tying his bootlaces, but refrained from comment. His face didn't light up like it normally did when he saw her. Part of her wondered if he'd told people what he'd overheard – how Glenda had suggested Vincent call around to her flat after the show to collect the money she owed. But he couldn't have, otherwise all hell would have broken loose.

Glenda appeared, blocking her path. 'Sit down so I can tidy your hair.' It wasn't a friendly request. She was wearing her Hippolyta headdress, looking even more intimidating than normal.

Lauren's gut twisted into a tight knot.

Before she could respond, Charlotte stepped in front of

Glenda. 'I'll see to Lauren's hair.' Her tone didn't invite debate, despite the joviality of her green make-up and playful shorts. 'Move please, Glenda.' She held a chair out for Lauren to sit on.

Glenda harrumphed and moved away. 'Talk about ungrateful.'

Lauren almost collapsed onto the chair, a mixture of relief and tiredness draining the strength from her legs. 'Thank you.'

Charlotte gave her a sympathetic smile. 'No problem.' And then she bent down so her mouth was next to Lauren's ear. 'Get through tonight as best you can. Later, you're going to tell me what's going on. Whatever it is, we'll deal with it together. Okay?'

Tears pooled in Lauren's eyes. 'You'll be so disappointed in me.'

Charlotte shook her head. 'Not possible. You're my sister. I love you.' She rested her hand on Lauren's shoulder. 'I have your back.'

Lauren reached up and placed her hand over Charlotte's. 'Thank you.'

They were interrupted by Barney climbing onto a chair, asking for quiet. He waited until the room had descended into a hush. 'I know the director isn't normally supposed to get involved once the show has started its run, but the SM agreed with me that tonight was an exception.' He looked around the room, daring anyone to challenge him. 'You've all worked incredibly hard to make this show a success. As a group, we've had to overcome adversity, and numerous challenges, along the way. It's only come together through teamwork and sacrifice. So, I'm asking you to put aside any personal grievances and show each other some respect. Let's make this production one to remember, and for the right reasons.' He looked around the room. When no one spoke, he added, 'Okay?' He waited until everyone, including Nate and Glenda, had nodded in agreement, before stepping down from the chair. 'Thank you.'

Lauren couldn't help noticing the way her sister watched Barney deliver his pep talk. She looked conflicted, her expression part bewilderment, part wistful. Charlotte was definitely developing feelings, although whether she would acknowledge as much remained to be seen.

The fifteen-minute bell rang.

Her dad's face appeared in the mirror. 'Where have you been, love? I've been looking everywhere for you.'

Charlotte came to her sister's rescue once again. 'It's fifteen minutes till curtain-up, Dad. I need to get Lauren's hair done. You can talk to her later, okay?' She picked up a brush and busied herself replaiting Lauren's hair.

Her dad looked a little perplexed, but didn't push the matter, something Lauren was incredibly grateful for. There was no doubt about it, she was going to miss Charlotte when she returned to London next week.

Thankfully, everyone seemed to take on board Barney's words, and the tension eased slightly. Craving some air, Lauren ducked out of the dressing room and found a place to hide in the wings. Trying to clear her mind, she focused on how much Freddie and Florence were loving acting in their first proper grown-up show. She couldn't be prouder of them. They weren't afraid to shine, relishing the buzz of the audience rather than shrinking away from the attention, as some children did.

She was so engrossed in her thoughts that she didn't see Nate approach, until he said, 'I'm sorry about the disruption earlier.' He didn't sound remorseful. If anything, his manner was a little cool. 'But I'm not sorry for making a stand. I won't apologise for that.'

Agitation made her look at him. 'It's not up to you to make a stand, Nate.'

He nodded. 'You're right.'

'I'm glad we agree.'

'It's up to you.' The tone of his response made her baulk.

She folded her arms across her chest, needing a barrier. 'There are reasons why I can't say anything. You have no idea what Glenda is capable of. What she's threatening to do if I don't toe the line. I need to protect my kids.'

'But this isn't the way to go about it.'

'Oh, so you're an expert at parenting now, are you?' She glanced around, checking that they were out of earshot from the backstage crew. 'Well, it's not your concern...'

She couldn't have been more surprised when he pulled her behind a lowered backdrop, away from prying eyes. Her back was pressed against one of the flats, preventing her from escaping.

He stood in front of her, close enough that she could feel his beard brushing against her cheek. 'And what kind of example are you setting those kids by keeping quiet, eh?' His hands were either side of her head, his body hovering close to hers. 'That it's okay to be scared and miserable? That giving into a bully and not standing up to them is the right thing to do? How is that protecting them?' The intensity of his gaze rendered her speechless. 'I'm so disappointed in you, Lauren. I thought you were better than that.'

His words were like nails puncturing her heart. She'd disappointed him? 'I don't know what to do.' Her voice was barely a whisper; she was surprised he even heard her.

'One phone call, Lauren. That's all you have to do, and this whole mess will disappear. But instead, you live in fear, punishing your family and your friends for having the audacity to care about you. And why? For the sake of your pride.' His palm smacked against the flat, making it wobble. 'So, you needed a loan? Big deal. Money's a bit tight? So what? You need to take responsibility for the situation you've found yourself in and be the capable, strong, fantastic mother I know you are, before someone gets really hurt.' His glare rooted her to the spot. 'And that someone is likely to be you.'

'I... I can handle that.'

'Can you? And what happens to Freddie and Florence if you're not around to look after them?'

Her chest contracted. It wouldn't come to that, would it? But the truth was, she was scared of Glenda. The woman was intimidating and relentless. Making a stand wasn't easy.

'The only person you're protecting by keeping quiet is Glenda.'

'Not now, Nate.' Lauren had begun to shake. 'I'll deal with it, I promise. Just not now.'

'You're not the only one affected by this, Lauren. Remember that.' He pushed away from the flat and disappeared, leaving her shaking and bereft. She sank down onto the floor, resting her head on her knees. Nate was right. Beautiful, sweet, kind, Nate. Who hated her.

Wiping her eyes, she stood up and headed back to the dressing area. If she could just get through the rest of tonight, she'd think about how to tackle the mess that was her life tomorrow. She'd confide in Charlotte, and together they'd work out how to deal with Glenda.

She'd just sat down and begun touching up her make-up, when Freddie appeared, eating a small tub of ice cream.

'Where did you get that?' She frowned at her son in the mirror. 'Did Auntie Charlie get it for you?' Her sister knew Lauren didn't like them eating during a show, in case they spoiled their costumes.

'Glenda bought it for me.' He scooped up a mouthful.

'Glenda?'

He licked the plastic spoon. 'She said it was a thank you for running an errand.'

Lauren's heart rate started to speed up. 'What errand?'

'A message.' He slumped against the back of her chair, as if trying to remember what he was supposed to do. 'Glenda said, if we're good children, she'd take me and Flo to the funfair tomorrow so you could have a day off.' He ate another mouthful of ice cream. 'And she'd bring us home when you settled up.' He frowned. 'I think that was it.'

Something cold and liquid caused Lauren's heartbeat to falter. It was like she was having an out-of-body experience. No way was she letting Glenda take her kids anywhere. Without conscious decision, she found herself standing up and moving towards Barney, almost as if in a trance.

He immediately sensed that something was wrong, reaching out to catch her before she fell. 'Lauren, are you okay? What's wrong?'

'Can... can you take Freddie and Florence outside for me.'

'Well, sure, but...'

'Don't let them out of your sight.' She gripped his hand. 'Not even for a second. Okay?'

A confused-looking Barney ushered her kids from the room.

Once she was sure that her kids were out of earshot, Lauren

climbed onto the same chair that Barney had used earlier to deliver his pep talk. But what she had to say wouldn't be uplifting, of that she was certain. She didn't care. It was one thing to threaten her, to bully and hound her until she paid up, but to involve her kids? No way was she putting up with that. Glenda had gone too far. She'd crossed a line. Nate was right. It was time to make a stand.

The noise around her faded into a pounding rhythm in her head.

A couple of people questioned why she was standing on a chair. Most people hadn't noticed, until she said, 'Can I have everyone's attention, please.'

Her dad and Sylvia were sitting close by drinking a cup of tea.

Paul was chatting with Charlotte.

Glenda was sewing a button back on to Daniel's jacket.

'I have something to say.' She looked at everyone's puzzled expressions. All except Nate, who'd lowered his gaze as if not wanting to put her off.

Glenda made a point of not looking at her. 'People have got better things to do than listen to you.' She dug the needle sharply into the fabric, causing Daniel to suck in his stomach.

Lauren steeled herself. 'Maybe, but I have to do this now.'

Her dad stood up. 'What's wrong, love?'

'I'm in debt,' she said on a rush. 'I borrowed money from Glenda, and I'm struggling to pay it back.' If she thought that unloading might ease the tightness in her chest, she was mistaken. The grip squeezed harder, reducing the airflow to her lungs.

The look on her dad's face radiated disapproval. 'Which is

very disappointing to hear, but not really appropriate for discussion here and now.'

Sylvia placed a hand on her dad's arm. 'Let her finish, Tony.'

He frowned at Sylvia. 'She knows how I feel about borrowing money, not to mention airing dirty linen in public.'

Lauren's shame was acutely overwhelming, but she had to continue, or she never would. 'Glenda is a loan shark.' There, she'd said it.

This announcement was met with a series of varying responses.

Daniel snorted in disbelief.

Her dad looked puzzled, and said, 'She's a what?'

Sylvia covered her mouth.

Glenda said, 'Don't be ridiculous.'

And Charlotte gasped.

Her dad nudged Sylvia, urging her to take his mug so he could move towards his daughter. 'Stop this, Lauren. You're being very disrespectful to Glenda. Now come down from there...'

Lauren didn't budge. 'Glenda is charging me an extortionate interest rate. The amount I owe keeps increasing. The repayments started off at twenty-five pounds per week, then fifty, and now seventy-five. I can't afford the increases, but Glenda keeps pestering me for more money, which I don't have. She says we have a legally binding contract which allows her to vary the repayments.'

This stopped Tony in his tracks. He looked at Glenda. 'Is that true?'

Glenda waved the question away as if Lauren was being unreasonable, although her face had coloured a little. 'Your daughter was in a tight spot, so I loaned her a few hundred quid. What's the big deal? That's what mates do. They help each other out.'

Lauren steeled herself. 'But with two hundred and fifty per cent interest being added, I still owe eight hundred and forty pounds, despite having paid back a thousand pounds already.'

A collective gasp filled the room.

Charlotte appeared next to her. 'That's your idea of helping, is it, Glenda?'

Glenda was beginning to look flustered. 'How else am I supposed to make ends meet? You've seen where I live, in a bleedin' caravan park. I don't have money to throw round. I'm not running a charity.'

Tony was shaking his head, but his annoyance was directed at Lauren. 'Nonetheless, you shouldn't have asked Glenda for money.'

Lauren's arms felt heavy, weighted down with remorse. Despite everything, this was still her fault.

Sylvia smacked Tony's arm. 'If you didn't want her borrowing money from Glenda, then you should've given it to her yourself when she asked for help.'

Tony didn't look happy about being reprimanded. 'Never a borrower nor—'

'—a lender be. Yes, Tony, we know the saying. But being a single parent is hard work, and running a home isn't cheap, so a little compassion wouldn't go amiss.'

Lauren had never heard Sylvia rebuke her dad before.

Charlotte took Lauren's hand. 'Is there anything else you want to say?'

Lauren took in a shallow breath. 'No, that's it. I just wanted everyone to know that I have a debt.' She tried to look defiantly at Glenda, but the woman wasn't about to be intimidated. 'It's out in the open now.'

'You try and help someone out, and that's the thanks you get.' Glenda cut the cotton with her teeth.

Charlotte squeezed Lauren's hand tighter. 'Just so we're clear, Glenda. Lauren won't be giving you another penny.' She glared at Glenda. 'Do you understand? Not another penny. Unless, of course, you'd like me to check the validity of this so-called contract with the Financial Conduct Authority?'

Glenda didn't say a word.

Charlotte helped Lauren down off the chair. 'Just as I thought.'

Lauren had never been so glad to hear the three-minute bell.

The SM's head appeared around the door. 'Beginners to the stage please.'

Chapter 27

Act Three

All the cast, except for Charlotte, were either on stage or about to make their entrance for the Mechanicals' play. Standing quietly in the darkened wings allowed her breathing space to gather her thoughts. Not that there was much chance of reaching any satisfactory conclusions tonight, her head was fit to burst. Questions whizzed around her brain that were both confusing and unbelievable. Glenda was a loan shark? Barney loved her? Seriously? How the hell was she supposed to deal with all that?

Laughter erupted from the audience as Paul appeared on stage wearing the makeshift wall costume she'd made for him. He shuffled sideways across the stage, his head poking out from the top.

Her dad made his entrance as Pyramus, the love-struck hero of the play-within-a-play, and pretended to look through the hole in the wall. '"But what see I? No Thisbe do I see."' His hand went to his forehead, hamming up the melodrama of the piece.

Although it was great to see her dad enjoying himself – a far cry from the miserable wreck he'd been in the early months following their mother's death – she couldn't help feeling a bit disappointed in him. She hadn't known that Lauren had asked him for money. And whereas she appreciated he wasn't rolling in cash, surely he could have helped her out. That's what families did, didn't they? Made sacrifices, even if it caused hardship. And knowing how proud Lauren was, she couldn't imagine that it had been easy for her sister to ask for help. Even more reason as to why her dad shouldn't have refused.

Further hysterical laughter followed when Nate appeared as Thisbe, wearing a Roman toga dress, his expression forlorn as he acted the reluctant heroine. As he turned around and the audience spotted that the back of his dress was hitched up, revealing his bare backside, they roared with laughter. Nate bent down and pressed his lips against the hole. '"My love! Thou art my love, I think?"'

Glenda ran forwards and unhooked his dress, pretending that 'mooning' the audience hadn't been intentional. The audience rocked with laughter.

As Charlotte watched Glenda fuss over Nate's costume, she felt a surge of anger towards the woman who'd extorted money from her sister. A woman who'd threatened, coerced and abused their supposed friendship. A woman who'd appeared sweet, funny and helpful, but was anything but. No wonder Lauren had been so utterly miserable.

Sylvia appeared high on the raised fairy-grove platform, carrying a lantern. The lights on stage faded, leaving only the lantern aglow. Unlike Glenda, Sylvia was a decent woman, who obviously cared deeply about Lauren as well as her dad. And that meant a lot. So what if she was a bit clumsy? It was nothing compared to Glenda's crimes. '"This lantern doth the moon present!"'

Freddie roared loudly in his role as Lion. Florence carried on the sword for Pyramus, which was dripping with tomato ketchup.

Her dad took the sword and stabbed himself, ensuring the tip of the blade poked out from underneath his arm comically. '"Now I am dead."'

Nate gasped and ran over, tripping on his dress and stumbling to his knees. '"Asleep, my love? What, dead, my dove?"' He picked up the sword, struggling to yank it free from under Tony's weight and stabbed himself. '"Thus Thisbe ends."' It took a while for Thisbe to die, mostly because the audience were laughing so much, but eventually the stage faded to black.

Charlotte prepared for her entrance. She picked up the large donkey head and placed it over her own. During the dress rehearsal, Barney had decided to move the scene where Bottom awakes from his dream to the end of the show. The first thing Bottom would see when he awoke would be Puck wearing the ass's head, moving spookily about the stage. It was a great idea... in theory.

In reality, because she'd only had one opportunity to practise wearing the head, which was covered in horsehair and weighed a ton, she hadn't appreciated how unstable the ruddy thing was. During the dress rehearsal, she'd almost toppled over, only remaining upright through sheer determination and improved core stability thanks to spending the summer negotiating the steep inclines of Penmullion.

Holding the thirty-inch head steady by its protruding ears, she quietly took up her position behind the backdrop of camouflage army netting. Through the narrow eye-slits, she could just make out her dad yawning and stretching as he awoke from Bottom's dream. '"I have had a most rare vision,"' he said, sitting up. '"I have had a dream past the wit of man to say what dream it was."'

At this point, Charlotte was supposed to dart forwards and reveal herself to Bottom. Unfortunately, she didn't realise the ears of the donkey head were caught in the army netting. Her entrapment only came to light when she made a move forwards and the netting locked tight like a well-designed seat belt. The ass's head swivelled ninety degrees, blinding her view and masking her mouth. Unable to see, and with her arms and legs entangled in army netting, she realised there was no immediate escape. She yelled her muffled line from the back of the stage, hoping no one would notice.

Her dad faltered slightly over his speech, no doubt wondering why Puck's head and body were facing in opposite directions.

She persevered as best she could, exhausted from having to shout her lines through two inches of wicker, her movements restricted to two steps either side of where she was entangled. She'd never been so relieved to reach the end of a scene. Well, except for the fly-rig scene, which she was still having nightmares about... and not just because she'd been forced to mount a concrete pillar. Barney's declaration of love had been both startling and unexpected. She'd had no idea he felt that way. And why would she? He was attentive, yes. Affectionate, definitely. No man had ever paid her so much attention. Whether it was feeding her, massaging her, or showing her the delights of physical intimacy. But love? It didn't make sense. People didn't fall in love after a few weeks messing around... did they? It wasn't logical.

The lights cut to black. Several pairs of hands sprung from

nowhere and began groping her in the dark. Despite encouraging whispers that '*no one will have noticed*', she remained sceptical. A green goblin wearing a back-to-front ass's head, and stuck in army camouflage netting, was something most people would notice.

Eventually, she was freed from the netting, and able to deliver the show's closing speech. As she moved forwards, carrying the donkey head under one arm, she was lit only by a follow spot. There was no one else on stage, it was just her and the audience.

She placed the donkey head on the ground. '"If we shadows have offended, think but this, and all is mended. That you have but slumbered here, while these visions did appear. So, give me your hands if we be friends, and Puck shall restore amends."'

As she took her bow, she had to admit that receiving a rapturous round of applause was a nice experience. She could see the appeal.

The rest of the cast moved onto the stage and took up their positions for the end tableau.

As she turned and reached out to Oberon, he smiled and winked at her. Something gave way inside her, as if the last remnants of stress had finally melted away. She'd loved her time in Penmullion. She'd participated in amateur dramatics, made new friends, and enjoyed reuniting with her family, not to mention spending time with Barney, but she was returning to London next week and her Cornish adventure would be over.

As the clapping continued, Barney stood up and led the bows, which was an awkward affair as Lauren, Glenda, Sylvia and Nate all refused to hold hands. Never one to panic, Barney stepped forward and addressed the audience.

'Thank you, ladies and gentlemen. We hope you enjoyed tonight's show and we appreciate you coming along to support the Isolde Players' production of *A Midsummer Night's Dream*. As you leave the auditorium tonight, you will see front of house personnel carrying buckets and collecting money for Hearty Lives Cornwall. This is a local project run throughout the county, encouraging children and families to adopt healthier lifestyles and, as such, lower the risk of heart disease. It's something that has affected all of us only recently.' He nodded at Sylvia, who disappeared off stage and returned with a huge bouquet of flowers. 'Tonight's performance is dedicated to our director and special guest this evening, Jonathan Myers.'

Sylvia carried the flowers over to Jonathan, who stood up and took a bow as the audience, cast and crew clapped loudly.

Charlotte hadn't realised that Jonathan was in the audience. Amongst the clapping and whistling, she watched Barney step away from centre stage, allowing Jonathan to take the limelight. Jonathan's cheeks reddened as he soaked up the applause. Considering how close the man had come to expiring, it was a miracle to see his recovery. A recovery that was only possible thanks to Barney.

There was no getting away from it, Glenda wasn't the only person who she'd misjudged this summer. Barney Hubble wasn't a lazy layabout, with no focus or prospects, but a born leader who worked extremely hard and had a lot to offer the world. It was just a shame he didn't have a life plan, or a stable career like her – or at least she would have one, once she returned to London. Otherwise they might... What? Have continued their acquaintance?

Whatever. No point dwelling. It wasn't like she'd developed

feelings for him, was it? It was a summer fling. A dalliance. A temporary distraction. The ache in her chest was nothing more than the sadness everyone felt when a particularly good holiday was drawing to an end. It would fade soon enough... wouldn't it?

Chapter 28

Sunday, 28 August

Barney unbolted the fairy-grove construction, mulling over what a massive comedown the clear-up session was – like suffering a particularly bad hangover after a wild night partying. Without the softening of moonlight and mesh filters, the set looked battered and tired; no longer a magical space, but an empty cauldron of scattered rubbish and discarded programmes. The cast looked equally weary, their once energised movements now lethargic as they cleared the theatre ready for the next group of players to take over.

The hairs on his arms lifted as the wind picked up, flapping the cloth against the scaffolding. The weather had cooled overnight. It was taking longer for the sun to emerge from behind the clouds this morning. Technically it was still summer, for a few more days at least. Tomorrow's bank holiday would see the last of the holidaymakers soaking up Cornish life before the kids returned to school and a new term began. For him, too. Student life beckoned.

He searched for a screwdriver, needing an implement to lever out the staples holding the cloth in place. Returning to his medical studies didn't fill him with unadulterated joy, but he wasn't quite as averse to it as he'd once been. Directing the show had unearthed a set of skills he'd never known he had. The most significant being his ability to overcome adversity. If directing had been a breeze, then it might not have felt quite so rewarding when everything came together. Last night's performance had culminated in a standing ovation and the promise from the *Cornish Times* reporter of a glowing review in next week's edition. It was heady stuff. Addictive.

He found a screwdriver and returned to the task of dismantling the fairy grove.

He'd always thought he lacked the necessary mettle to cope with adversity, so it had been something of a shock to discover that wasn't the case. Maybe he could use these new-found skills to improve his attitude towards medicine? It was worth a try. The words 'clutching' and 'straws' sprang to mind.

Sylvia appeared wearing illuminous-yellow rubber gloves, complete with floral cuff and matching apron. 'The loos are cleaned. What would you like me to do next?'

He looked around the theatre. Nate was helping Tony dismantle the tree house. He couldn't imagine Sylvia wanting to join them – manual labour wasn't her strongest suit – but also because things were a little cool between her and Tony.

Barney was just glad that Glenda wasn't around to add to the tension. Despite quitting the show after the opening night, she'd contacted him yesterday to say she'd be collecting the costumes this morning. Being outed as a loan shark can't have been fun, so he understood why she couldn't face everyone, but it was selfish nonetheless, and had nearly ruined the show. Lauren had taken on the role of Hippolyta, and Sylvia had covered the smaller parts, but it hadn't been without its headaches, namely a day spent at the theatre re-blocking and training a new team to control the fly rig. But it had come together in the end, thanks to the commitment of the cast and backstage crew. The atmosphere had dramatically improved without the Graham family's involvement, so, as annoyed as he'd been when all three had stormed off, he'd ended up being grateful that his new-found leadership skills could take the rest of the week off.

'You could help Lauren sort out the costumes when she returns from taking the props to the hall with Charlotte. They should be back soon.'

'Righty-ho.' Sylvia peeled off her gloves. 'Shall I make tea in the meantime? Looks like everyone could do with a brew.'

'Sounds great. Thanks, Sylvia.'

He watched her take everyone's drinks orders. Tony replied with a one-word answer, Daniel ignored her, and the SM seemed flustered at being interrupted whilst trying to tally the bar takings. Only Nate responded with a smile, his gaze drifting to the steps leading up to the car park in the hope that Lauren would appear soon.

Barney might deem this love-struck behaviour slightly pathetic, if he wasn't afflicted by the same condition.

Laughter drifted down from the auditorium. Paul was helping Freddie and Florence pick up rubbish, but was currently chasing them around the seating wearing the ass's head from the show. Their smiling faces and infectious laughter brought on another bout of longing for kids of his own. It also served to cement the decision he'd made to return to medicine. Aside from accepting the fact that he needed a challenge, he'd also realised that floating along, living a care-free, hand-to-mouth existence, would not be conducive to achieving his long-term goal of a family. For that to happen, he needed to be in a relationship. More specifically, he wanted to be in a relationship with Charlotte. And Charlotte had made it clear she wasn't interested in being with a man who didn't have a stable job.

Having removed the staples from the cloth, he rolled the now faded and torn midnight-blue fabric into a tight ball.

Knowing that Charlotte would be returning to London herself soon had helped soften the blow of succumbing to his parents' coercions. Having realised that he'd fallen in love with her, he needed to take drastic action to convince her that moving from a casual fling into a serious relationship was a good thing. And for her to view him as a serious prospect, he needed a more focused career plan. Being a specialist might not hugely appeal, but, with any luck, his lengthy sabbatical might have strengthened his resolve. His parents had assured him that things got easier once you'd specialised, so maybe this time he'd rise to the challenge and not falter at every hurdle. He could only hope.

As he unbolted the legs of the scaffolding, he spotted Charlotte descending the theatre steps. He was struck by how stunning she was. Dressed in jeans and a cream top, she was scrubbed clean of all traces of green. Her hair was wavy and free, dancing about in the breeze as she skipped down the steps. His heart missed a beat, something his medical brain told him wasn't possible unless he suffered from premature ventricular contractions, which he didn't. He didn't care. He was in love. He'd never been in love before. It was strangely liberating.

When it became apparent that she hadn't welcomed his declaration of love at a very inopportune moment during the opening night, his initial disappointment had given way to a determination to win her over. Of course she'd panicked. Charlotte was a cautious, conservative and slightly obsessive woman. She needed careful handling. If he came on too strong, she'd bolt. He needed to gently persuade her that letting him in to her life was a positive thing, and not scare her off.

Her coolness towards him during the rest of the run had thawed after last night's performance when, riding on the coattails of adrenaline, she'd accepted his offer to continue partying back at his place, and they'd spent the night drinking champagne and rolling about his bed entangled in the sheets. It had been playful, intimate and hugely enjoyable. He'd also been careful to steer well clear of anything resembling 'feelings'. He wasn't that stupid. He'd made her breakfast in bed this morning, joined her in the shower – under the pretence of needing to help remove all traces of greasepaint – and teased her over the various mishaps she'd encountered during the show. All of which she'd accepted with good humour, proving she was no longer mortified at being emotionally exposed, but rather empowered by it.

He might have seen this as a breakthrough, if it hadn't felt quite so much like a goodbye. One final fling before reality kicked back in. A feeling he was desperately trying to ignore, hoping he was wrong.

But, as she neared the stage, he realised her animation wasn't as a result of happiness following their playful night together, but anger. It radiated off her in waves, like an electrical current. Why was she so cross? More worryingly, why did her anger appear to be directed at him?

'I want a word with you.' Without waiting for a reply, she grabbed a fistful of his T-shirt and dragged him away from prying eyes.

He let her, mostly because she'd rip his T-shirt if he resisted. *Hawaiian Elvis* was his favourite. 'What have I done?'

He might not have experienced love before, but he knew enough about women to know when he'd fucked up. Although quite what he'd done to piss her off in the hour or so she'd been gone, he didn't know.

She let go of his T-shirt and folded her arms. 'Lauren received a call from the police this morning.'

'Okay.' He had a feeling more was coming.

'Glenda Graham and her two sons have been arrested.'

He was right.

'The police raided Glenda's caravan late last night and removed evidence.'

So that's why she hadn't shown up this morning. 'What kind of evidence?'

Her gaze narrowed. 'Take a wild guess.' There was no volume in her words, her anger was being contained – barely – almost as if she was waiting for the opportune moment to unleash it. 'You're a smart man. What do you think the police might find in Glenda's home?'

He was being tested. There were two possible answers. The truth, or a lie. Both would result in his demise. 'Evidence of illegal moneylending?'

'Bingo.' Her cheeks were no longer nymph-green, but warning-red. 'A notebook listing all Glenda's customers, and several handwritten contracts. Not to mention a stack of cash.'

He still wasn't sure what he'd done wrong. He'd missed Lauren's big declaration on the opening night, about owing Glenda money. Nate had filled him in afterwards. As far as he knew, his name hadn't been mentioned. Why would it? 'That's good, isn't it?'

'For Lauren, yes. Anyone doubting my sister's honesty will now see Glenda for what she really is, a manipulative, mean-spirited woman who preys on the financially vulnerable.'

He nodded his agreement, feeling it unwise to offer anything else.

'As you can imagine, I was completely stunned when the police contacted Lauren this morning.' Her tone had switched to sarcastic. 'I mean, who knew they'd been tipped off and had been carrying out surveillance on Glenda for almost three weeks.' Her gaze was locked on his, daring him to concede, as if playing some kind of Russian roulette.

Being a sensible man, he kept quiet.

'But Lauren wasn't surprised. Oh, no. Turns out a rep from the Illegal Money Lending Team had called round to Lauren's flat. Ever heard of them, Barney?'

Again, he said nothing.

'But even after Lauren was told that Glenda's behaviour was illegal, my sister was too frightened to make an official complaint.' Her fists were bunched so tightly that the skin around her knuckles had turned white. 'She was so scared of the repercussions, of the shame of anyone knowing about her situation, that she refused to give evidence. Can you imagine that?' She advanced on him. 'How it feels to be that scared?'

Right at that moment? Yes, he could. He figured that was the point.

She lifted a finger. 'I can think of only one thing worse.'

Here it came.

'People knowing who Glenda really was and not saying anything.'

And the guillotine dropped. One swift slice and his balls

lay in a basket by his feet. So that was his crime. She'd found out that he had known.

'Not even just people... *friends*.'

Guilt flooded him. 'I only suspected.'

'Oh, you only suspected?' Her voice rose another notch. 'So you didn't exchange playful banter with your mates, referring to the woman as Glenda-the-Lender?'

Shit. His eyes closed involuntarily.

She shoved him in the chest. There was no strength behind it, despite her fist being clenched. 'How long have you known?'

The time for denial was gone. What was the point; she knew anyway. 'A while.'

'How long is a while? A month? A year?' When he didn't reply, she became incredulous. 'You've always known, haven't you? Ever since you came to Penmullion?'

The flicker of his eye movement must have given him away.

'And you never said anything?' She was yelling now.

'It wasn't my place.'

'Not your place?' She raked her hands through her hair, a gesture so out of character and so unlike Charlotte that he didn't know whether to be pleased or afraid. She was finally unravelling. Unfortunately, he was the cause. 'Whose place was it, then? You're her *friend*. You socialise with her, babysit her kids, constantly tell me how special she is...'

'She is—'

'Then why the hell didn't you help her?' Angry tears fought their way down her cheeks. 'Why did you stand back and let Glenda bully my sister? Tell me?'

'Because...' but nothing would come. He wanted to find the right words, something that would defend his actions, justify keeping quiet, but the enormity of his fuck-up meant that excuses were pointless. 'I wasn't certain. None of us were. We suspected that Glenda loaned people money, but we had no idea she was a loan shark. Not really. We just thought it was something she did on the side, you know, a part-time business.'

'Just a harmless bit of illegal moneylending, eh? You saw how miserable Lauren was, how much weight she'd lost, and yet you did nothing.'

'That's not true... Well, not entirely.' He jumped in before she could interrupt. 'Lauren's a private person, proud too. She wouldn't have wanted everyone knowing her business. So we kept quiet, hoping she could sort it out herself.'

'Oh, great plan.' Charlotte's sarcastic nod was accompanied by a slow hand clap. 'What a bunch of cowards.'

'You're right.' And then he felt the need to clarify. 'I am, at any rate, but not Nate. He wanted to intervene.'

She didn't look like she believed him. 'Then, why didn't he?'

Oh, hell. 'Because we persuaded him not to.'

She stilled, which was worse than when she was raging. 'You did what?'

'We...' And then he realised there was no point shafting Paul as well. '*I* thought he was overreacting, that he'd got it wrong. In the end, he decided to report Glenda anyway, even though he risked Lauren hating him.'

She shook her head. 'The only one with any balls.'

He looked down at the floor. This was true.

After a moment's silence, she said, 'It doesn't explain why you didn't mention it to me, though, does it? All this time we've spent together, and not once did you think to alert me to what was happening.'

He shrugged. 'I didn't want to complicate what we had.'

'Complicate it?' She seemed genuinely confused.

'You know, by making it too… personal. You wanted to keep things purely physical.'

Her confusion turned incredulous. 'So, this is my fault?'

'Of course not.' He reached out, but she batted him away. 'I'm just trying to explain why I didn't tell you. I made a mistake.'

'You certainly did.' Her fingers searched for a non-existent button on her top. 'Well, thank God I found out now. Thanks for making leaving Penmullion so much easier for me, Barney.' She backed away.

'You're not going?' He needed more time. He had to tell her about his move to London. Try to persuade her that they could make a go of things.

'I have no reason to stay.'

'Yes, you do.' He moved quickly, catching her arm before she could escape. 'For a few more days, at least.'

But she yanked free from his grip. 'Like I said, this was only ever a short-term arrangement. It was never going to last.'

He couldn't believe how quickly everything was slipping away. How had things gone from laughter to loathing in the space of a few hours?

'Goodbye, Barney.' She turned and made her escape.

He watched her walk off, knowing it was pointless to try and stop her. He'd apologised, admitted that he'd made a mistake, even told her he loved her. None of it had mattered. He'd laid himself bare, and still she'd rejected him.

So much for her not bolting.

Chapter 29

Monday, 29 August

Charlotte was glad she'd listened to Lauren, and not rushed back to London the previous evening. Her sister was right: the bank-holiday traffic would be a nightmare. She was better off staying one more day and heading off early Tuesday morning. It also meant she could say a proper goodbye; something she would've regretted not doing if she'd left in a haze of anger. So, she'd spent her last day with Lauren and the kids, enjoying a picnic on the beach, followed by a game of Scrabble back at the flat. The kids were now tucked up in bed, and she was recovering from the trauma of saying goodbye to them.

'You okay?' Her sister was standing in the bathroom doorway, leaning against the door frame.

She stopped packing her toiletries. 'Not really. I'm going to miss them.'

'They're going to miss you too. Flo's still crying.'

The recollection of both kids hugging her and begging her not to leave would probably haunt Charlotte for the rest of her days. 'I didn't realise leaving would be so hard.'

'I'll take that as a compliment.' Lauren moved away from

the doorway and sat down on the closed loo seat. 'When you first arrived, you hated the place.'

'Not hated, just... I don't know, it wasn't where I wanted to be. I was a mess.' Charlotte dropped her hand sanitiser into her washbag. 'Thanks for putting up with me. I needed sorting out.'

Lauren smiled. 'Likewise. I couldn't have got through the summer without you. You've no idea how much I appreciate your support.'

Charlotte perched on the rim of the bathtub. 'Was that the police on the phone?'

'No, it was Yvonne from the Illegal Money Lending Team. She wanted me to know that Glenda and her sons have been bailed pending a trial. They're not allowed to contact me. I can apply for a formal restraining order if they don't adhere to the conditions of their bail.'

'That's good.' Knowing that Lauren had someone in her corner eased Charlotte's guilt at leaving earlier than intended.

'She asked me if I'd reconsider being a witness.'

Charlotte looked at her sister. Lauren was painfully thin and drawn, but there were also signs of recovery. She certainly seemed less tortured than before. 'What did you say?'

'I agreed to do it.' Lauren shrugged. 'Seems stupid not to, now everyone knows.'

Charlotte took Lauren's hand. 'You made the right decision.'

'Not sure Dad will agree with you.'

'He'll come around.' At least, she hoped so. Surely, he'd realise that Lauren was the victim now that Glenda had been formally charged.

'Yvonne will be my support officer throughout the trial, so that's a comfort.'

'For me too. I'm only a phone call away, but I'll sleep better knowing someone's looking out for you.' Charlotte patted the back of her sister's hand. 'By the way, I've left some money for you in the bill jar in the kitchen. And before you jump down my throat, I won't take no for an answer.'

'But—'

'No buts.' She held up a hand. 'You wouldn't accept any rent money, so let me contribute something to tide you over. I'll be seriously offended if you refuse.' She resumed packing her toiletries. 'Plus, it helps to ease the guilt of leaving you.'

'You've got nothing to feel guilty about. This is my mess. Your life is back in London. Mine is here. I have plenty of people to help me.' Lauren handed Charlotte her flannel. 'Like Sylvia, for instance. Did you know she left me a voicemail apologising for not realising what was happening, and vowing to support me going forwards?'

Charlotte rung out the flannel. 'That was nice of her.' But then, Sylvia was a nice woman – something she'd been slow to pick up on. Or maybe it was just a reluctance to accept another 'mother figure' into her life. Like she was somehow betraying her real mother, which was nonsense. Whatever the reason, she was glad Sylvia was in her sister's corner.

Realising she didn't have a plastic bag to hand, she shoved the damp flannel in her washbag. Goodness, she was living dangerously. 'You also have Nate.'

Lauren looked down at her feet, her worn slippers suddenly capturing her attention.

'Look, the last thing I want to do is fall out with you before I go. I know the whole Nate thing is a sensitive subject, but can I just say one thing?' Without waiting for an answer, she lifted her sister's chin. 'Nate's a great bloke. He's funny, kind, and he adores you. He'd do anything for you or your kids. So much so, he reported Glenda even when he knew it risked losing your friendship.'

Lauren folded her arms across her chest. 'And your point is?'

'Do you think that maybe you're using your anger towards him as an excuse for keeping him at arm's length? Because if you stop being angry and forgive him, then it lets him back into your life, and that scares you?'

Tears pooled in her sister's eyes. 'I can't rely on anyone else. I have to be the one who supports my family.'

'And you do, Lauren. You've proved that you're strong and capable. Letting Nate in won't undermine that, but it might make your life easier and happier. Don't you want that?'

'Suppose he leaves, like Joe did? What would that do to Freddie and Florence?'

'Lauren, I hate to break it to you, but they're already hurting. They miss Nate, they told me tonight when I was putting them to bed.'

Her eyes grew wide. 'They did?'

'They don't understand why Mummy is so angry. They think they've done something wrong and that's why they're not allowed to see Nate.'

'Oh, God.' Lauren's head dropped into her hands.

Charlotte squatted down next to her. 'You gave me some very valuable advice a while back, and I'm glad I listened to you, because you were right. So, I'm going to do the same for you now.' She rubbed Lauren's arm. 'Nate is a good guy. The kids adore him. And if you're honest, so do you. Give him a chance to make your life even happier than it already is – or was, before Glenda made things miserable. Take a risk. Live a little.'

Lauren's head was shaking in disagreement. 'It's too late, I've pushed him away. He might not want me anymore.'

'Only one way to find out.'

They were interrupted by a knock on the front door.

Lauren wiped her eyes. 'God, who's that at this time of night?' She checked her watch. 'It's gone nine.' She went to answer the door.

Charlotte checked her reflection in the cracked bathroom mirror. Her hair was wavy and relaxed, a far cry from the straightened style she used to wear. Strangely, she didn't mind so much. She'd grown to like it.

Voices in the lounge preceded the sight of Dusty appearing in the cramped bathroom, wearing a black and white dog-tooth-check dress and white beehive wig. 'What are you doing hiding away in here?'

Charlotte picked up her washbag. 'I'm not hiding, I'm packing. I leave tomorrow.'

'A fact I'm well aware of.' Dusty looked disgruntled. 'If you think I'm going to let you disappear without a proper goodbye, then you're mistaken. Come on, we're going to the pub.' Charlotte's washbag was removed from her grasp and slung into the bath.

'But I haven't finished packing.'

'You can do it later. I won't take no for an answer.' Dusty stopped by the doorway. 'You don't mind if I steal your sister away, do you? I'm guessing you can't join us?'

'Afraid not, the kids are in bed. But you go. We've had Charlotte to ourselves all day, it'll be good for her to say goodbye to everyone else.'

'Exactly.' Dusty dragged Charlotte into the lounge. 'Where are your shoes?'

'Do I get a say in the matter?'

'No.' Dusty thrust Charlotte's jewelled sandals at her. 'Put these on.'

With no opportunity to touch up her make-up or change out of her jeans, she was bundled out of the door and down the metal staircase towards a waiting taxi. 'Why do we need a taxi? Where are we going?'

Dusty opened the car door, waiting until Charlotte had climbed inside before replying. 'The taxi is for my benefit. These shoes are not designed for walking.' She climbed in next to her. 'It also has the added bonus of ensuring you don't escape.'

Charlotte looked at her. 'Why would I want to escape?'

'Because we're going to Smugglers Inn.' Dusty's beehive was so high it touched the roof of the taxi. 'Barney's performing there tonight.'

'Let me out.' Charlotte went for the door handle.

'Drive,' Dusty instructed the driver, ignoring her companion's protests. When they'd pulled away, she patted her friend's knee. 'You can thank me later.'

'Thank you? I want to throttle you.' No way did she want to see Barney again. And definitely not singing. Her fragile resistance couldn't withstand that.

Dusty's phone rang. 'Later, babes. I need to take this – it's my brother.' She turned away and answered her phone. 'Will, honey? What's the verdict?'

Charlotte folded her arms. She wasn't sure what she was angrier about: being kidnapped, or being forced to see Barney again. She didn't want to see him. It was easier to stay mad at him if she didn't have to look at his handsome face, or succumb to his attempts to make her laugh. Distance was her only barrier. She needed to stay strong, focus on her life plan, and avoid thinking about what might have been.

Her stomach lurched as the taxi descended the hill. As they drew closer to Smugglers Inn, her reluctance to re-engage with the man who'd declared undying love for her grew. Well, perhaps not undying, but it had shocked her just the same. She certainly hadn't seen it coming. But the exchange had forced her to reassess her feelings. And there was no denying that Barney Hubble had got under her skin. He'd shown her what was possible, in terms of physical satisfaction, but also what it was like to be... what was the word she was looking for? Adored? It was probably too strong a description, but that's what it had felt like. He'd challenged her boundaries, stripped away her defences, and bulldozed right through her protective barrier. She wasn't sure whether she should be mad or grateful.

She focused on her surroundings, trying to divert her mind elsewhere. The quayside was lit up, bright lights reflecting off the water as the tide washed over the bay. The sea looked almost black, infinite and foreboding. She opened the window a crack so she could hear the sounds of the waves and smell the salty air. She'd certainly miss living by the sea. There was something so life-affirming about fresh air filling your lungs.

The taxi pulled up next to the footbridge by the moored boats. Dusty paid the driver, batting away Charlotte's attempts to pay.

Letting Dusty finish her conversation with Will about his upcoming wedding, Charlotte crossed the footbridge, pleased to note that her fear of heights was less disabling than it had been before arriving in Cornwall. Maybe dangling from a fly rig had been a blessing after all. Not that she'd felt that way at the time. It had been truly horrifying.

She glanced over the rope-lined edge. The water rushed below, hypnotic as it sped past, bleeding into the sea. High up on the clifftops, she could make out the silhouette of Morholt Castle standing proud against the skyline. Yep, she was going to miss Penmullion.

Dusty finished her call, and teetered over, dropping her phone inside her Marc Jacobs handbag. 'Sorry about that.'

'What's the verdict?'

'We're both going to the wedding.' Her smile was infectious. 'Paul will attend the day, and Dusty will attend the evening reception.'

'Nice compromise.'

'I thought so. The bride isn't happy, but my brother has agreed to the releasing of doves at the church ceremony, so she's relented.' Dusty slipped her arm through Charlotte's. 'The moral of this story is that some things are worth fighting for. Even if fighting causes conflict and drama along the way.' They crossed the footbridge, walking past the lit-up restaurants, still bustling with holidaymakers. 'Paul wasn't satisfied with the life he was living, so he made the decision to change. Hence the creation of Dusty.' She gave a little curtsy. 'As a consequence, Paul is a much happier man.'

Charlotte stopped walking. 'I know what you're doing. You don't fool me for a second.'

'I wasn't trying to.' Dusty manoeuvred her towards Smugglers Inn. 'I'm simply saying, there's no shame in admitting you want something different out of life.'

'I don't want a different life. I'm perfectly happy with the one I have.' Charlotte entered the pub, immediately hit by a wave of music and chatter. 'Or the life I *had*, at any rate.'

Dusty raised a perfectly shaped eyebrow. 'Sure about that?'

'Absolutely.' It was only after she'd said it that doubt crept in.

'I've seen politicians look more convincing. What are you drinking?'

'Prosecco. A small one. I'll get these.'

Dusty prevented her from opening her purse. 'I'll get the drinks. Go and say hi to Tony.' She was shoved in the direction of her dad, who was sitting alone watching Barney's gig.

Despite avoiding looking at the stage, the sound of Barney's voice still had the ability to derail her. She recognised the song; Lauren had played it in the flat on numerous occasions. Biffy Clyro's 'Many of Horror'. He captured the torment of the song, but then, he was a good actor. It didn't mean he meant what he was singing.

Keeping her eyes fixed on her dad, she went over and sat with her back to the stage. 'Hi, Dad. No Sylvia tonight?'

He glanced up, looking forlorn. 'Oh, hi, love. No Sylvia tonight. She's busy.'

'Is she still annoyed with you?'

He shrugged, looking worryingly down in the dumps. God, she hoped his depression wouldn't rear its ugly head again. That wouldn't be a good development.

'She has good reason, Dad.' She waited for him to look at her. 'It was hard for Lauren to ask you for help. I know you don't agree with borrowing money, but that principle only works in an ideal world, and we don't live in an ideal world. Life is messy and complicated.'

'That's no excuse for not budgeting. You girls were brought up to be responsible.'

Irritation rose within her. 'Has Lauren ever asked you for money before?'

He frowned. 'No.'

'Has she ever shown herself to be irresponsible or reckless?'

He raised an eyebrow.

'Well, okay, apart from falling pregnant in her teens. But that was only partly her fault. It takes two people to make a baby. She didn't know Joe would turn out to be a complete waste of space. He never supported Lauren or his kids and left her to raise them single-handedly. She was dealt a bum deal, Dad.'

'I agree.'

'My point is that, against all the odds, Lauren's done an amazing job of raising two beautiful, smart, well-adjusted kids. Freddie and Flo are happy and healthy. You should be really proud of her.'

He looked put out. 'I am.'

'Then stop acting like she's an embarrassment. It's unfair, and she doesn't deserve it. She's wounded and upset. Glenda's the bad guy here, not Lauren. So, will you please show what a good dad you are and support her through this, because things are likely to remain crappy for a while before they get better. She needs you. Okay?'

He let out a long sigh. 'Sylvia said pretty much the same thing.'

'Then listen to her. She's a smart woman.'

He looked morose. 'When are you leaving?'

'First thing tomorrow.'

He took a long swig of his beer. 'I'm going to miss you.'

'I'll miss you too.' She gave him an awkward hug. 'Say

goodbye to Sylvia for me.' She got up and made her way to the bar, before she started blubbing.

Despite making good progress with her dad over the summer, it still felt like they were being too cautious, each one fearing that the other might shatter if pushed too far into anything resembling real emotion. It saddened her.

On stage, Barney had finished his song. Without any preamble, he went straight into Charlie Simpson's 'Parachutes'. Somehow, she still managed not to look at him.

She reached the bar, and climbed onto the bar stool. The quicker she left Penmullion, the quicker she could resume her old life and forget all about Barney Hubble.

Nate was serving behind the bar. 'I didn't realise you were still here.'

She angled herself away from the stage. 'I leave tomorrow.'

His gaze flickered towards Barney before coming back to settle on her. 'You'll be missed.' He stretched across the bar and kissed her cheek. 'Take care. Visit again soon.'

'I will… And Nate?' She caught his hand before he could disappear. 'Please don't give up on my sister. She's scared, but it doesn't mean she's disinterested. Hang in there, okay?'

He gave a non-committal shrug, and wandered off down the other end of the bar.

Dusty got up and moved stools. 'Talking of relationships.'

'Which we weren't.' Charlotte was forced to look in the direction of the stage, which she guessed had been Dusty's motivation for moving.

'We need to talk about you and Barney.' Dusty crossed her legs.

'We really don't.'

'I want to know why you're so angry with him?'

'Are you serious?' She stared at Dusty, more as a means of avoiding looking at Barney than anything else. 'He watched my sister being bullied by that witch Glenda Graham and did nothing about it.'

'So did I, but you're not angry with me.'

A pause followed. Charlotte tried to reason this piece of logic. 'It's not the same thing.'

'How is it different?'

'Because I'm not in—'

'—love with me?'

It was hard to look stern when faced with fluttering false eyelashes. 'I was going to say, I'm not *involved* with you.'

'Maybe not, but we're friends. So why was it okay for me to keep quiet, but not Barney?' Her smile was mischievous.

'When you put it like that, you're right. You were totally out of order, and I'm mad at you too.' She play-slapped Dusty's knee.

'Except I don't believe you.'

'Want me to pull your hair to prove it?'

'It's a wig, you daft woman. It'll come off.' Dusty scowled at a chip in her French-polished nails. 'Now listen, I have a question for you.'

'Here it comes.' Charlotte took a slug of wine, preparing herself.

'Do you think that maybe you're using your anger as an excuse to leave?'

A sense of déjà vu settled over her. Hadn't she just had a conversation with her sister about holding on to anger as an excuse not to do something? 'Of course not. My life is back in London. My ET hearing starts on Monday. I have to go back.' Her denial was scarily similar to her sister's.

'Actually, you don't.'

Charlotte placed her glass down on the bar. 'Excuse me?'

'At this precise moment in time, you have no job and no home. Technically, there's no reason for you to return to London.'

'Maybe not, but I want to go back. It's where I belong.'

Dusty took her hand. 'Are you sure you're not running away because you're scared?'

She withdrew her hand. 'What on earth have I got to be scared about?'

Dusty shrugged. 'Admitting you want a different life? Risking a change of direction?'

'I love being an interior designer,' Charlotte said, which was true. 'I don't want to change.' This was entirely untrue.

'I don't mean your career.'

'What, then?'

Dusty leant forwards. The stage was now in full view. 'Do you remember that first day in Penmullion, when you found me handcuffed to a tree?'

Charlotte could see Barney strumming his guitar in her peripheral vision. 'How could I forget?'

'You were wound tighter than an old lady's perm. You turned your nose up at everything and found fault in everyone.'

'I know who to come to for a character reference.' She ignored Dusty's laughter. 'May I remind you, I was in a bad place? I'd just lost my job, my home and my boyfriend. I was allowed to be stressed.'

Dusty looked reproachful. 'Honey, it takes a lifetime to get that wound up. You can't tell me that hadn't been building for years?'

True, but she refused to admit as much.

'Over these last few months, I've seen a complete transformation. You've learnt how to laugh, love and be happy. I just figured staying here and continuing to grow might appeal, that's all.'

Charlotte would be lying if she didn't admit similar thoughts had crossed her mind, but she figured this wasn't just about Penmullion, it was about a change in mindset. 'I'll admit that what you're saying isn't complete rubbish – but it's only because I haven't had the stress of work to contend with. I've been on holiday. I've been playing at life, indulging in creative activities and letting my hair down, but that can't continue.'

'Why not?'

'Because it's not based on reality. It's wishful thinking, it's a... a midsummer night's dream. It's based on fantasy, not real life.' She climbed off the bar stool. 'I know you mean well, and thank you for being a wonderfully good and eccentric friend, but the sooner I resume my old life, the better it'll be for everyone.'

'You sure about that?' Dusty gestured to the stage. 'Did you know he's decided to return to medicine? He's accepted a place at Hammersmith, starting in September. Now, I wonder why he did that?'

Charlotte glanced at the stage, wondering the same thing. Why hadn't he told her? But then, she supposed she hadn't given him the opportunity. 'It doesn't change anything. I still don't want to be with a man who stood by and let my sister be bullied by a loan shark. How could I trust someone who didn't have the decency to protect her, or support his friend when he decided action was needed?'

Dusty sighed. 'Because, despite messing up, he loves you. I

don't think he meant for it to happen, but it did. He fell in love with you. And I rather suspect you feel the same way.'

What nonsense. Charlotte shook her head, refusing to hear what Dusty was saying. It was ludicrous to think she'd fallen in love. She just needed some distance. A return to being in control... just without the headaches and obsessive behaviour. 'Whatever we had is over. We're not compatible.'

Dusty raised an eyebrow. 'You sure about that?'

Refusing to look at Barney, Charlotte kissed Dusty's cheek. 'Positive. Take care of Lauren for me. I'll send you my new address when I've found somewhere to live.'

Dusty kissed her back. 'Think about what I said, okay? Stop being stubborn. And when he's back in London and calls you, forgive him.' She nodded to the stage, where Barney had just started singing, Gotye's 'Somebody That I Used to Know'.

The irony wasn't lost on Charlotte.

She shook her head. 'He won't call.'

'I guess only time will tell. Bye-bye, sweetie.'

Charlotte headed for the door, unable to resist one quick glance at the stage. The impact was hard and fast. Barney was looking right at her. The intensity in his eyes made her gasp.

Fumbling for the door, she almost fell out of the pub, eager to distance herself from the what-ifs filling her brain. What was the point? It wasn't like she was ever going to see him again. She was better off keeping her distance. There was nothing to be gained from prolonging the agony.

Her life was back in London, and it didn't include Barney Hubble.

Chapter 30

Wednesday, 21 September

Flicking off the lights, Lauren locked the café door. A gust of wind blew a shower of sand against her legs. The wind was picking up now the nights were drawing in. It was mid-September, so even at six-thirty the sun was beginning to set, the sky dulling into a mottled grey. As the sun faded, the silvery light reflected off the sea, the dusk bringing with it a chill. It wasn't coat-weather yet, but she wrapped her waterfall cardigan around her as she walked across the bay, making her way home. She'd received a text from her dad saying he had the kids. Sylvia had cooked egg and chips for tea, and they were planning to watch a Harry Potter film. Was it okay if they stayed the night?

How could she refuse? No matter how lonely she felt, there was no way she was going to deny her kids a fun night with their granddad. She was just glad her dad and Sylvia had made up. It would be a shame for them all to be miserable.

She ambled slowly up the hill, in no rush to reach her empty flat. She wasn't sure why she felt so morose. All things considered, she should be feeling elated. Her life had reverted to where it had been six months ago. She was a single mother with a part-time job, she had good friends, and lived a happy, simple life with two adorable children. She didn't need or want for anything more. So why did she feel as though something was missing? Yes, living with Charlotte had proved challenging. Add to it the trauma of owing Glenda money, and she should be glad things were back to normal, but she wasn't. She was lonely and bored. She missed Charlotte. Not to mention Nate.

Every time her phone beeped, a customer entered the café, or the doorbell rang, she hoped it might be him. But it never was. And it was her own stupid fault. She'd done nothing but push him away. She'd taken his friendship for granted, rejected his kindness, and had never once offered him anything in return. No wonder he'd got fed up. She couldn't blame him. He'd only been trying to protect her. She should have thanked him, not yelled at him. And now it was too late. If only she'd realised her mistake at the time, she could have saved herself a lot of heartache.

Her legs felt heavy as she climbed the metal steps leading to her flat. The potted plants and hanging baskets filling the rooftop space had been neglected, their once vibrant foliage was now brown and brittle, snapping when her fingers brushed against them.

It was only as she neared her front door that she realised Dusty was sitting on the bench seat holding a large vanity case. 'You took your time.'

Lauren tried to recall what she was supposed to be doing tonight, but nothing sprang to mind. Her diary was depressingly empty now the show had finished, and Charlotte had returned to London. 'I wasn't expecting you... was I?'

'No, sweetie. I'm just being impatient. Ignore me. It's the excitement.'

'Excitement?' She headed for her front door, Dusty hot on her heels. 'Does this have something to do with a man?'

Dusty smiled. 'It does.'

No surprise there. Lauren stepped inside her flat and kicked off her shoes. 'Big date, huh?'

'The biggest.' Taking her hand, Dusty almost dragged her towards the bedroom. 'We need to get a move on, we don't have much time.'

Lauren's puzzlement increased. 'Time for what?'

The vanity case caught on the bedroom door as Dusty burst through it. Not that it mattered, the door had seen better days. 'To get ready.'

'But you are ready, aren't you? You look great.' And Dusty did. The navy shift dress and dog-tooth kitten heels looked surprisingly elegant.

'Ah, thanks, sweetie. But it's not me who needs to get ready.' Dusty unzipped the vanity case and removed a long floaty dress with layers of sheer grey and white fabric. 'Your taste differs from mine, so I tried to choose something more bohemian and less showgirl-slapper. What do you think?'

'It's beautiful, but—'

'Excellent. Quick shower, and then we need to get your make-up done.' Dusty laid the dress on the bed.

Confusion still clouded her brain. 'I don't understand. Is the dress for me?'

'Well, of course it's for you.' Dusty steered her towards the bathroom. 'Who else would it be for?'

'What do I need a new dress for?'

'Your big date.'

'*My* big date?' Stopping dead, she turned to face Dusty, although she barely reached her chest.

'No time for talking, get showering. All will become clear.'

Realising that arguing was pointless, and lacking any real energy to resist, Lauren undressed as instructed. She was going on a date?

In truth, there was only one person she wanted to date, but that person was currently avoiding her. There'd been no chance meetings at the post office over the last three weeks. No casual 'bumping into one another' when out shopping, like there used to be. He'd made it clear he didn't want to see her, let alone date her. So, what did that mean? Was he being coerced as well? Was he at this very moment being shoved into a shower? And by whom? Barney was back in London, starting a new life as a doctor, so there was no one on hand to assist Dusty's scheming.

As she climbed out of the shower and dried herself, a horrible thought occurred. She slipped on her dressing gown and went into the bedroom. 'Please tell me this isn't a blind date?'

Dusty had unpacked the contents of the vanity case, and had lined up an array of beauty products on the dressing table. 'Come and sit down.'

Lauren sat down in front of the mirror, trying not to look at the dark circles shadowing her eyes. 'Seriously, Dusty. I'm not up for being paired off with some random bloke.'

Dusty twisted the lid off a bottle of foundation. 'Relax, will you? Credit me with some sense.'

'Who is it, then?'

Dusty began lightly brushing her face with the liquid. 'Take a wild guess?'

Dare she even think it? A heavy thud pounded in her chest. What was she feeling? Dread? Hope? Panic?

Dusty lifted her chin. 'Now, we could waste time discussing this, or you could stop overthinking and let me work my magic. And stop frowning, it wrinkles your skin.'

It was easier to obey, so she stopped resisting.

For the next twenty minutes whilst Dusty worked on her, she tried to unscramble the multitude of thoughts crowding her brain. None of them made sense. All she knew was that continuing to deny her feelings for Nate was stupid and self-destructive. Charlotte was right, she needed to take her own advice and let go a little. Take a risk. She was strong enough to deal with whatever happened... wasn't she? God, she hoped so.

'There you go. What do you think?'

She glanced up at her reflection in the mirror. Her eyes no longer looked sunken, but benefited from Dusty's clever smoky-effect shading. Her lips were dark red and her hair was loose and curled into waves. 'You're a miracle worker.'

'I know.' Dusty beamed, revealing recently whitened teeth. 'Although to be fair, nature did most of the work for me.'

Lauren was handed an ivory-coloured bra and knicker set. 'Put these on. The taxi will be here in five minutes.'

'New underwear?' The items were exquisite, delicate and feminine.

'And shoes.' Dusty picked up a pair of jewelled sandals, similar to the ones Charlotte owned and Lauren had often admired. 'No point being half-hearted.'

'All this must've cost a fortune. I have to give you some money.'

Dusty's hands went to her hips, the red of her nails contrasting against the blue of her dress. 'Don't even think about it. What's the point of owning a boutique if you can't use it to spoil your friends? Now, I want no further mention of money. It's my treat. You deserve it.' Her stance softened into one of awkwardness. 'It's also my feeble attempt at an apology. I'm sorry for the whole Glenda thing.'

Lauren broke eye contact. 'No apology necessary. It was my mess and my responsibility to sort it out.' She still felt uncomfortable talking about Glenda.

'I disagree. I think it was all our responsibility. The whole community. This was happening on our doorstep and we did nothing to stop it. Everyone suspected Glenda of shady dealings, but no one had the balls to confront her. We were all guilty of turning a blind eye.' Dusty kissed her cheek. 'All except Nate, of course.' She wiped away a smudge of lipstick left on Lauren's cheek. 'Anyway, enough with the sentiment. The clock's ticking. Underwear on, please.'

Five minutes later, wearing her gorgeous new outfit, Lauren was escorted to the waiting taxi, where Dusty instructed the driver to take them to Piskies café.

Lauren's confusion increased when they pulled into the car park by the bay, and she could see a light flickering inside the wooden shack. She'd definitely turned off all the lights before she'd left. What was going on?

When they reached the door, Dusty tucked the label inside Lauren's dress. 'I'm off to take over childminding duties. Your dad and Sylvia will be here shortly to serve dinner. Enjoy.' Blowing an air kiss, Dusty darted back to the waiting taxi before Lauren could assemble her thoughts and quiz her further. Her dad and Sylvia were cooking dinner? The evening was getting more surreal by the minute.

As she pushed open the door, she was greeted by music, candlelight and the scent of flowers. Each table was decorated with tea lights and scattered rose petals. Fairy lights hung from the ceiling. Lengths of white voile were draped across the room creating a soft canopy, drawing her eye to the centre table, which was covered in a white tablecloth. A display of red roses sat in the middle, surrounded by more tea lights. Next to the table stood Nate.

Her heart gave a little kick.

He smiled when she appeared in the doorway. It was tentative at first, as if unsure of her reaction to the overtly romantic staging. 'You look beautiful.' His voice cracked as he delivered his line. 'I was worried you might not come.'

He was wearing a suit. Not a business suit, but a casual linen affair, teamed with a soft white shirt. It was unbuttoned at the neck, revealing a little chest hair. She'd never seen him in a suit before. He looked different. Not unattractive, just very un-Nate-like.

'Would you like a drink?' He lifted a bottle of champagne from an ice bucket, his hands shaking as he fumbled over the cork. He was nervous.

Somehow this relaxed her a little. 'That would be lovely.' The table was laid out with cutlery for two. 'Did you do all this?'

The cork shot from the bottle with a loud pop. 'With a little help from Freddie and Florence.'

Freddie and...? She moved to the table. 'But... how? I mean, they're with their granddad... aren't they?'

'Cover story.' He looked sheepish. 'We were hiding in the car park waiting for you to leave. They wanted to make it special for you.' Bubbles of fizz ran down the neck of the bottle and over his fingers.

She noticed cut-out hearts and stars attached to the fairy

lights, recognising the handiwork of her daughter. A home-made menu lay on the table covered in glitter and her son's wonky handwriting. Tears pooled in her eyes.

'You're not angry, are you?' He handed her a glass of champagne.

She shook her head. 'A little confused, but not angry.'

He looked relieved. 'Here's to… new beginnings?' He raised his glass.

She clinked glasses with him. 'New beginnings.'

An awkward silence followed, during which they both sipped champagne, looked anywhere but at each other, and fiddled with their glasses.

Eventually, Nate said, 'How's Charlotte getting on in London?'

'Okay, of sorts. She won her tribunal case for unfair dismissal. She returned to her old job last week.'

'That's good.'

She offered him a napkin, his fingers were still dripping with champagne. 'It should be, but it's not without its problems.'

'How come? Oh, thanks.' He took the napkin, his eyes flickering with something unreadable when their hands touched.

'I don't think she realised quite how uncomfortable it would be returning to work for someone you've sued.'

'Yeah, I guess that would be tricky.' He looked around for somewhere to dispose of the soiled napkin.

'Still, it's only been a couple of weeks. Maybe things will improve.'

'Let's hope.' He scrunched up the napkin and threw it, basketball-style, into the bin by the door.

More awkward silence, followed by more sipping of champagne and admiring the surroundings.

It was Lauren's turn to make small talk. 'How's Barney getting on with his training?'

'Miserable. He hates it.'

'Oh, dear. That bad?'

'He says it's the long hours and depression of being stuck inside all day, and not being able to surf, but I think there's more to it than that.' He looked like he was debating whether to elaborate.

'Do you think it has something to do with my sister?'

He seemed relieved that Lauren had been the one to mention Charlotte. 'I think the only reason he agreed to return to London was so he could be with her.'

'The things people do for love, eh?' Lauren had meant it as a joke, but regretted her words the second they left her lips.

Nate raised an eyebrow. 'Crazy, huh?'

A soft knock at the door came as a welcome interruption.

'Okay to come in?' Sylvia's head appeared around the door. 'Not disturbing anything, are we?'

Lauren felt her cheeks burn. Why, she wasn't sure. It wasn't like they'd been doing anything.

Nate's face had coloured too, obviously sharing her discomfort. 'Come in, Sylvia. Would you like some champagne?'

'No, dear. We don't want to intrude. Ignore us, we'll be in the kitchen. Carry on as you were.' Head down, she marched into the kitchen, a woman on a mission.

Lauren's dad followed, carrying a cool box. He nodded at Nate. For a moment, she wondered if he was going to ignore her, but thankfully he looked over and smiled. 'Having a nice time, love?'

They'd barely spoken in the last three weeks, so this was something of a white flag. The uncomfortable stand-off had been broken. It hadn't been a good feeling knowing she'd disappointed her father in such spectacular fashion.

Swallowing back the lump in her throat, she nodded. 'Lovely, thank you. Where are the kids?'

'Watching Harry Potter with Dusty. We'll head back when we're done here.' He moved towards the kitchen, but not before turning back. 'Can I have a quick word, love?'

Lauren glanced at Nate. It wasn't the best timing for a heart-to-heart.

'You go. I'm fine here,' Nate said. He lifted his glass and gulped down a mouthful of champagne.

She followed her dad into the kitchen, her heels clicking on the wooden flooring.

Sylvia was busy lighting the oven and unpacking the cool box. 'Leave this to me. Talk to your daughter,' she said, pushing him in Lauren's direction.

Her dad coughed, as if trying to clear his throat. 'Nice dress.'

Sylvia tied a floral apron around her middle. 'Stop procrastinating. Lauren has a date to get back to.'

'I'm not procrastinating,' he said, looking flustered. 'But this is hard.' He turned to his youngest daughter. 'I've never offered you advice before, not about matters of the heart.'

'It's a little late for the "birds and bees", Dad. That horse bolted nine years ago.' Her attempt to lighten the mood fell flat.

He looked serious as he took her hand. 'When Iris – your mum – died, I vowed never to love again. It devastated me. I was afraid of getting hurt. I didn't think I could cope with the pain of losing anyone else.'

A quiet sound escaped Sylvia, but she hid it by rattling a saucepan.

'I now realise that life hurts either way, whether you love someone or not. You can't protect yourself from getting hurt. You're better off loving someone and losing them than never loving them in the first place. Does that make sense?'

This was quite a turnaround. Her dad had always maintained that being alone suited him, it was his choice. Who knew he was as insecure as both his daughters? She glanced at Sylvia, who was doing a terrible impersonation of someone pretending not to listen. 'Does this mean you and Sylvia are, you know, together...?'

A beat passed before he nodded.

'Took his bleeding time,' Sylvia said, looking miffed, as she grated a lemon.

Her dad smiled. 'Sometimes the person we want is right in front of us, and we don't see it. Or maybe we do, but we mistakenly believe that having them as a friend is safer than loving them and risking losing them.'

Sylvia gave him a reproachful look. 'How dumb is that? No logic, some people.'

Lauren sensed Sylvia's words were directed at the both of them, not just her dad. She braced herself for a lecture about love, but her dad surprised her by switching topics. 'I'm sorry I didn't give you money when you asked for it. I should've done more to help you. I feel terrible you had to carry that burden for so long.' He took her hand. 'And I'm sorry I didn't believe you when you told me about Glenda. I was wrong. I've not been a good father.'

A tightness contracted in her chest. 'Oh, Dad, don't say that.

Glenda fooled us all. Of course you're a good father. You help me out with the kids all the time.'

He shook his head. 'Only when it suits. I don't exactly put myself out to make myself available. It's always been on my terms. I've been so preoccupied with trying to recover from my grief that I've become insular and selfish.'

This was shocking to hear. And untrue – for the most part, at least. 'Nonsense. You volunteer for the RNLI. You risk your life every time you get a shout, to save others. That's not selfish. That's incredibly brave.'

'But I do more to help strangers than I do my own flesh and blood.' There was a smidgeon of truth to this statement. 'And I'm sorry for that. I thought encouraging you to become independent, and stand on your own two feet, was helping. I now realise it's made you afraid of sharing your life with someone. If it didn't work out, and the fella left, you were scared I'd judge you and blame you for making a mistake.'

Her sharp intake of breath made her dizzy. It was the sudden realisation. It hadn't occurred to her until that moment, but that was exactly how she felt. When Joe had left, she'd felt like a failure. She'd believed her dad felt that way too, that he thought her irresponsible and stupid. That's why she'd been so afraid of letting someone else get close.

Her dad looked tortured. 'But that wasn't my intention. I'm so sorry, sweetheart. You're a fantastic mother, and I'm very proud of you.' He kissed her forehead.

'Stop it, Dad, you'll ruin my make-up.' She wiped away the tears threatening to smudge her mascara.

'From now on, I'm going to help out more with the kids, so you have the opportunity to have a life of your own. You deserve to be happy. And you deserve to be loved.' He glanced at the door, where, on the other side, Nate was waiting. 'Can you forgive me?'

'There's nothing to forgive. But thank you for opening up like this, I know it can't have been easy.'

He glanced at Sylvia. 'I had a little help.'

Sylvia feigned innocence. 'Who, me? Interfere? Never.'

Lauren's dad laughed. 'Sylvia told me a few home truths. Thanks for listening, love. I wouldn't normally interrupt an evening like this, but I – or rather, we – felt that it needed to be said, so you didn't react negatively to—'

'Shut up, Tony.' Sylvia waved a spoon at him. 'Let them sort it out themselves.'

The last thing that Lauren saw as she exited the kitchen was the sight of her dad kissing Sylvia. Awkward as it was to see your parent smooching, it also showed that it was never too late to make a leap of faith.

Inspired by such a public display of affection, she returned to where Nate was waiting, and when he greeted her with, 'Everything okay?' she kissed him. It was a clumsy attempt, involving a clash of noses, treading on his foot, and knocking into the table as she tried to make an impression – something she was pretty sure she hadn't done. Not in a good way, at least. Mortified, she pulled away, scolding herself for believing it was as easy as they made it look in the movies.

Nate caught her as she stumbled backwards. 'Hey, where are you going?'

'I'm sorry, I don't know what I was thinking.'

'I don't care. Come here and do it again. You caught me by surprise, that's all. I wasn't ready.' Typical Nate: caring, sweet, trying to spare her feelings.

'You're just saying that. You don't really want me to—'

Her objections were cut short. Unlike her pathetic attempt, he didn't make a hash of it at all. Far from it. Quiet, shy, and sometimes insecure, Nate Jones, proved he was anything but, when it came to kissing. His arms held her close, his beard was both rough and smooth against her skin, making her dormant senses jump to life, and her heart fizz like a wayward sparkler, leaving her breathless and struggling to keep pace.

And then he let go, and dropped to one knee. 'Lauren Saunders, will you marry me?'

Music and lust still filled her head, creating a buzzing in her ears, her body reluctant to let go. But as the sensations lulled, and the realisation of what he'd said dawned, she backed away. 'What...? No. Of course not. Are you crazy?'

He held her hand, preventing her escaping. 'Not quite the answer I was hoping for.' He stood up, his smile rueful. 'Hear me out, okay?'

'There's nothing you can say...'

'I love you.'

That shut her up.

'I've loved you ever since you came to Penmullion. There's never been anyone else. I've only ever wanted you.'

The buzzing in her ears returned.

The intensity in his gaze was alarming, like the night at the play when he'd scolded her for not standing up to Glenda. It made her skin tingle. 'No other girlfriends. Only you. I've been waiting all this time. Hoping if I was patient, you'd see I was serious and trustworthy, and you'd give me a chance.' His hand gripped hers, as though he was afraid that if he let go, she'd run. 'You don't need to tell me proposing is crazy. It's rash and naive, but I needed a big gesture. Something to show you this is the real deal. That I'm in it for the long haul. That I won't ever leave you, or let you down, and that your heart is safe with me.' His free hand settled on her chest, covering her heart.

'But we haven't even been on a date. Let alone... you know?' She felt it was necessary to point this out, however obvious.

He nodded. 'I know, but that's the easy stuff.'

You could've fooled her. Sex had always been a bit of a clumsy affair.

'What I mean is, we already know we like each other. We're attracted to each other, and we have common interests. We make each other laugh, we've even argued and pissed each other off. And yet we're still here, drawn to each other.' The warmth of his hand penetrated the thin fabric of her dress. 'I love your kids as if they were my own, and I'm crazy about you. So, from my perspective, the other stuff isn't what's important, not in isolation, anyway. I'd be lying if I said I didn't want to... you know?' He blushed, looking much more like the Nate she knew. 'So, the only real question is, whether you want me? Whether I'm who you want to have a relationship with? And I think I can answer that for you.'

'You can?'

He sucked in a long breath, the same movement he did when he was preparing to walk out on stage. She sensed a speech was coming. She was right.

'I think you want someone who isn't afraid to admit they miss you. Someone who knows you're not perfect, but treats you as if you are. Someone whose biggest fear is losing you. Someone who'll give you their heart completely. Someone who'll say I love you, and mean it. And someone who'll wake up with you every morning, and fall in love with you all over again.' He waited a beat, pausing for effect. 'And in case I haven't made it clear, that someone is me.'

Something within her calmed, like the sea after a raging storm. Her grip on his hand relaxed, allowing him to pull her close and kiss her again. She succumbed, allowing her mind and body freedom to enjoy, to feel and to let go. All without fear, constraint, or doubt.

When the kiss broke, he looked at her tentatively. 'Is that a yes?'

She smiled. 'It's not a no.'

He frowned. 'Anything I can do to turn it into a yes?'

She nodded. 'Ask me again, a year from now. Let's see if this thing between us is as amazing as we both hope and want it to be. If it is, one year from today, I'll say yes.'

He smiled. 'Deal.'

'One last request.'

'Anything.'

She glanced at the kitchen door. 'Next time you propose, can you make sure my dad and Sylvia aren't listening in?'

There was a soft thud from the kitchen, followed by muffled voices.

Nate laughed. 'I didn't think that one through, did I?'

'Not really.' She kissed his cheek. 'Thank you, Nate.'

'What for?'

'For everything. For waiting for me, for rescuing my daughter, for reporting Glenda, and for making me believe in love again. I'm a very lucky woman.'

And wasn't that the truth.

Chapter 31

Friday, 30 September

Barney had encountered many depressing scenarios during his medical training, from the results of knife crime, to the utter hopelessness of drug use, but this had to be the ultimate low point. It wasn't that his patient was a prostitute, or that she had the distinctive pallor and track marks of a regular heroin user. His instinct to heal had kicked in the moment he'd seen the cuts and bruising on her face and body, the result of a vicious assault. He wasn't there to judge, only to treat, and returning to medicine had reinforced that. Discovering that beneath his uncertainty was an intrinsic desire to cure made up for the monotony of long shifts and a lack of free time. But the discovery that the woman's request for an HIV test wasn't about a fear of illness, or a step towards improving her health and lifestyle, but a way of charging her clients more for her services by proving she was 'clean', depressed the hell out of him. She couldn't care less about her cuts and bruises, she just wanted to be back on the streets earning money. And he thought the life of a doctor was hard?

Signing off the woman's paperwork, he left the cubicle and headed for the canteen, needing a strong coffee before finishing up his shift. He'd been back in London for a month, but it had only taken two weeks before he'd experienced an epiphany. It wasn't medicine he had a problem with, it was hospitals. The cloying smell of disinfectant, the constant threat of death looming around every corner, the stark white walls, and clinical uniforms. Even the artwork decorating the corridors, designed to soften the view, didn't wipe out the grating of trolley wheels on lino, or the painful sounds of crying, wailing, and drunken ramblings that accompanied each shift. It was miserable and claustrophobic. No wonder patients complained. He didn't like it either, and he wasn't ill. But resuming his training, and being assigned to A&E to refresh his skills, hadn't been a complete waste of effort. In fact, more than anything, it had clarified things for him. He knew what he had to do next.

A vibrating in his pocket alerted him to his phone ringing. Balancing the device between his ear and shoulder, he dug out enough change to pay for his coffee, and headed for the back of the canteen. 'Hi, Paul. How's the wedding going?'

Two women were seated at a nearby table. They were crying, the younger one consoling the older one. A familiar sight that never got any easier to witness. Next to them, a man balanced his plastered leg on a chair. One of his crutches slid to the floor when he tried to shuffle closer to the table. Barney picked it up and handed it back to the man, who thanked him, wincing as he tried to get comfortable.

The noise crackling down the phone indicated that the evening reception had started. Paul's voice slurred as he spoke. 'The bride looked beautiful. The groom cried. My gran is tipsy, and Uncle Bob nearly got removed by security for pinching a waitress's bottom.'

Barney smiled. 'And how about you?'

'Pissed as a fart, and counting down the minutes until I can unleash Dusty and end the torture of tiresome small talk with distant relatives who begin every conversation with "goodness me, you've grown". Considering I haven't seen most of them for twenty years, it would be rather alarming if I hadn't.'

Barney settled into one of the battered sofas. It had been a long shift, and his body was complaining about a lack of exercise. What he wouldn't give to be back in Cornwall surfing. 'How will they cope with Dusty?'

'With shock, I'm guessing. But at least it'll liven things up. And it might stop my gran trying to pair me off with one of the bridesmaids.'

'Your nan doesn't know you bat for the other team?'

'I rather think she views it like having a bad cold. At some point I'll get over it.'

Barney laughed. 'Has she met Dusty before?'

'Lord, no.'

Barney sipped his coffee. 'You might want to check your gran's blood pressure before unveiling her.'

'She'll be fine. She's part of the stoic generation. What's a little cross-dressing when you've survived a war, and all that? And besides, Dusty is so much better at coping with social engagements. I've every confidence she'll win Gran over. It's the bride I'm not sure about.'

Barney could hear 'Dancing Queen' blaring in the background. Talk about irony.

'Enough about me. Have you told your parents the news yet?'

'Not yet. My shift's just ended. I'm summoning up the

courage to head home and break it to them. Telling them I cross-dress would be a breeze by comparison.'

'True, but you'd make a terrible woman. And remember, you're doing the right thing.'

'I know. I just need to convince them.' Barney undid a button on his shirt, an action that reminded him of Charlotte. He took another swig of coffee, trying to eradicate the memory. He'd hoped that moving away might dull the ache – it hadn't. If anything, he missed her more.

The background music switched from recorded to live, feedback from the speakers forced Barney to hold the phone away from his ear.

'The band are up,' Paul yelled. 'My cue to switch personas. Talk soon. Good luck!'

'You too…' But the line had already gone dead.

Smiling, Barney relaxed against the sofa, and finished his coffee. He wasn't relishing talking to his parents, but it had to be done. Delaying the inevitable wouldn't make it any easier; the sooner he ripped off the plaster, the better.

Steeling himself for a battle, he downed the remnants of his coffee, and headed for the train station.

The journey from East Acton to East Dulwich took nearly an hour, and he had to change at London Bridge, all of which gave him plenty of time to dwell on what he was about to do.

As nervous as he was about disappointing his parents, it was different this time. Mainly because last time he'd told them he was dropping out of his studies, he'd had no idea what he wanted to do instead. They'd accused him of running away, and they'd been right. He'd had no 'life plan' – as Charlotte had referred to it. The reminder caused another momentary flicker of pain to surface. He'd hoped that time and space apart would have healed the rift and she'd get in touch once they were back in London. But despite Dusty's assurances that Charlotte would call, she never had. Gutted didn't come close to describing how he felt about losing her. But then he'd never really had her in the first place, had he? It had been a summer romance, a brief liaison with a pre-determined expiry date. It was only him who'd been stupid enough to fall in love.

By the time he reached his parents' house, it was dark. Both cars were in the driveway. Shifts rarely finished on time, so it was impossible to rely on their schedules, but on this occasion, fate was on his side... or not, depending on how things went.

As he opened the front door, he was greeted by music. Nothing like the raucous blare of Abba at Will's wedding, but Chopin, the melodic piano recital accompanying his mother as she cooked dinner.

'Good timing,' she said, carrying a bowl of green beans through to the dining room. 'Fetch a bottle of white, will you? We're having fish. Henry, dinner's ready!'

His dad appeared from the lounge, still wearing his suit trousers, shirt and tie. It looked strangely at odds with his tweed slippers. 'Good day at the office, son?'

Barney was treated to a manly slap on the back, a father displaying approval towards his son. Whether Henry Hubble would still be proud after hearing his son's latest plans for a career change remained to be seen. Somehow, Barney doubted it. 'Not bad. Any reason why we're eating in the dining room?' He had a sudden concern they'd invited guests over. An audience would not be welcome, not when he was about to drop a bombshell.

His mum danced past with a huge plate of roast potatoes. 'We just thought it would be nice to enjoy a family dinner with our lovely son. Isn't that right, Henry?'

Shit.

His dad smiled. 'We want you to know how proud we are of you.'

Double shit.

'Come on, sit down. Dinner will get cold.' His mum ushered his dad into the dining room, leaving Barney to fetch the wine.

This was going to be tougher than he'd imagined, and that was saying something.

Uncorking the wine, he carried it through to the dining room. How should he play this? Quick and painful, or soft and gentle? Preamble, or cut to the chase?

'Giles tells me you're doing well, considering the break you've had from your studies.' His mother seated herself at the end of the table, and shook out a folded napkin.

Barney poured her a generous helping of wine. Not that he was trying to get her drunk or anything.

'He was surprised at how quickly you've got back into the swing of things.' Her hand reached out to stop him. 'Not too much wine, dear. I'm working tomorrow.'

'He's a good consultant.' Barney headed to the other end of the table.

'You'll learn a lot from him,' his dad said, not objecting when his son filled his glass to the brim.

Barney took his place in the middle of the table. The table, like the house, was far too big for three people, but it seemed that buying bigger, whether it was a house or a car, was an advert for how well your career was developing. The more successful a person became, the more trappings they were expected to accumulate. It seemed wasteful and pointless to him. Surely there was more to life than just working towards retirement? He wanted more.

'I have something to tell you,' he said, pouring his own large glass of wine.

'I can't tell you how nice it is working together in the same hospital,' his mother said, overriding his attempts to confess his crime. '*That's my son*, I say whenever your name comes up in conversation, which it does frequently,' she added, tucking into her salmon. 'You're making quite an impression.'

'Which is great, but—'

'And don't get me started on the nurses. I've lost count of how many times I've been asked for your phone number.'

'Takes after his father.' Henry raised his glass.

Alexa lifted her own glass. 'Indeed.'

Tempting as it was to keep quiet and enjoy his parents' praise, Barney knew that telling them was only going to get more difficult the longer he left it. He lowered his knife and fork. 'I'm sorry to tell you, but I'm leaving.'

There was a brief pause before his mother said, 'Leaving? Leaving where?'

'The hospital. The programme. I advised HR today.'

An almighty clatter filled the room when his mother's knife fell from her hand, hitting the ceramic dinner plate. 'No, no, you're not—'

'Please, Mum, hear me out.'

'Don't you dare, *please Mum*, me!' She threw her napkin at him. 'We are not going through this again!'

He recoiled at her ferocity. Thank God she'd only thrown a napkin and nothing more lethal. 'Will you let me explain?'

His dad signalled for his wife to quieten. 'Let him speak,

Alexa.' His father didn't look happy, but at least he was prepared to listen before commencing with a bollocking.

Supressing the urge to run off to the pub and get blindingly drunk, Barney knew he had to face the backlash. It was the mature thing to do. 'Firstly, you were both right when you encouraged me to give medicine another go, so thank you for that.'

'Well, of course we were right!' His mother's hand banged on the table.

Henry glared at her. 'Alexa? Let him finish.'

Ignoring the sight of his mother physically vibrating in his peripheral vision, Barney focused on the candelabra sitting in the middle of the table. 'I know I've frustrated you. Believe me, I've frustrated myself. It's taken me ages to work out what I wanted and, more importantly, what the problem was. And it's not medicine. It's working in a hospital.'

'So finish your training and become a GP, then you don't have to work in a hospital,' his dad offered by way of reason, even though Barney could see it pained him to do so.

'That wouldn't work for me either. I've realised that I need to be outdoors. I can't stand being cooped up inside all the time. That's why I've decided to return to Penmullion.'

His mother almost screamed. 'What? No!'

'I miss the beach, my friends, singing and acting. I want it all.'

Once again, his dad tried to shush his wife. 'Wait a sec, Alexa.' He turned to his son. 'I don't understand what you're saying. Are you giving up medicine?'

Barney shook his head. 'No, but I am changing direction. I've applied for a job as a medic with Cornwall Air Ambulance. They're a charity, funded by the people of Cornwall. The scattered population and rugged landscape means that having a prompt response team is essential. I have an interview scheduled for Monday, so nothing's certain, but they seem pretty keen to have me. I'm also planning to volunteer for the RNLI. It's about time I gave something back to the community that took me in and welcomed me into their lives.'

His mother wasn't impressed. She dismissed his words with a shake of the head. 'Idealistic nonsense.'

Barney took a large slug of wine. 'I know it's not what you wanted, but I thought you'd be pleased my training isn't going to complete waste.'

Pleased wasn't an adjective that accurately described the look on his mother's face. Incredulous would better describe it. 'It's hardly the cutting edge of medicine, is it?'

His dad sat back in his chair. 'I think what your mother means is, it feels like a backwards step, son. It's a far cry from being a consultant.'

'But I don't want to be a consultant.'

'How much does this charity job pay?' His mother's emphasis on the word 'charity' revealed her inner snob. It certainly wasn't one of her better qualities. 'I can't imagine the salary is competitive, certainly not with London rates?'

'The salary isn't great, but it's enough for me.'

His dad joined in. 'What about prospects? Your career development? How do you envisage that progressing?'

'Honestly?' Barney looked between his parents, both equally disappointed, one slightly less scathing than the other. 'I don't know. All I can tell you is that this opportunity excites me. I feel more motivated than I've ever felt in my life. It's the job of my dreams. I don't know why I didn't think of it before.' He had Charlotte to thank for his new career path: she'd been the one who'd suggested thinking outside the box. Shame she'd never know he'd taken her advice. 'Not just that, I get to combine all the things I love. Theatre, music, surfing, adventure, the outdoors, and medicine. It's the perfect life...'

Well, almost. Charlotte wouldn't be a part of it, but sometimes you couldn't have it all. No matter how much you wanted it.

His dad sighed. 'Sounds like you've made your mind up.'

Barney smiled at him. 'I have, Dad. This is what I want.'

He was going home. Back to where he belonged. Back to where he was happy, and could make a life for himself... he just wished that life included Charlotte.

Chapter 32

Monday, 3 October

Charlotte was struggling to keep her frustrations hidden from her client. The woman was only in her twenties, but she was one fifth of the latest girl-band phenomenon to sweep the music charts, and she'd used her new-found wealth to purchase a plush town house in Notting Hill. Despite it being mid-afternoon on a particularly dreary day in early October, Freya was dressed as if she was about to shoot an erotic video. Ripped fishnets adorned her legs, teamed with patent lace-up boots and a leather miniskirt that looked more like a large belt. Her make-up was thick, her eyelashes false, and she was chewing gum as she flicked through numerous interior design magazines, dismissing each image with a sneer.

Charlotte tried once again to focus her client's attention. 'Can I suggest we look through the mood boards I've prepared, and see if they meet your brief?'

Freya chucked the latest magazine onto the floor. 'I know what I want, but it's, like, hard to describe.'

Tell me about it, Charlotte thought, laying out her mood boards on the enormous stone coffee table. Freya 'didn't do chairs' apparently, so they were sitting on beanbags, an uncomfortable experience that Charlotte wasn't keen to repeat anytime soon. Lounging around on the floor, in an inelegant fashion, hardly helped to maintain a professional demeanour. The client's brief had been a confusing mix of styles that would challenge the most experienced designer. It was probably why Lawrence had given her the job. He was testing her. Punishment for forcing him to rehire her.

Winning her tribunal case hadn't been as rewarding as she'd imagined. The judge had given her two options: monetary compensation or overturning the dismissal. It was widely acknowledged that looking for another job was much easier if you were already employed, so she'd opted for returning to Quality Interiors, figuring this would tide her over until she found a new position. Big mistake. Aside from having to deal with the strain of damaged professional relationships, she'd discovered that she had no appetite for job hunting, and she wasn't quite sure why.

She moved from a seated position to kneeling – which proved tricky when wearing her snug Karen Millen suit. She had to roll off the beanbag and shuffle across the rug to start her presentation. 'The good news is that we have plenty of space to work in. The master bedroom is beautiful.'

Freya's iPhone pinged with another message. The draw of social media was too enticing. The girl was popular, if nothing else.

Irritation itched beneath Charlotte's skin. Her client had the attention span of a goldfish. Once around the bowl and she was onto something else... which made trying to present a sales pitch extremely difficult. All she could do was wait... and wait.

God, she was bored. Plus, her suit felt too tight. Had she

put on weight over the summer? Or had she just got used to wearing more relaxed attire? Either way, she felt constricted and uncomfortable.

When Freya's attention finally reverted to the task in hand, Charlotte angled the three mood boards for her client to peruse. 'You mentioned Scandinavian, Romantic, and Moroccan styles in your brief.' This confusing mixture was probably another factor in Lawrence lumbering her with the pitch. Anyone who could make three contrasting themes work together would certainly earn their commission. 'I have three designs for you to look at. I've tried to keep a neutral colour palette, so we get that bright, clean Scandinavian look you're after. I've done this by using a mixture of whites and soft greys for the walls and ceiling.'

Freya screwed up her nose. 'I like colour.'

'Which is why I've introduced splashes of mink, mushroom, and a hint of lime green to accent the room, with a collection of sheer fabrics for the soft furnishings. If we use silk and satin, it will give the room that romantic feel you're looking for.'

Freya didn't look impressed. 'I dunno. It doesn't look very Eastern.'

The client is always right, Charlotte told herself, and moved on to the last mood board. 'I was thinking that we could use the alcoves in the room, building the arches into the design, and backlighting them to create warmth and give it a hint of Morocco.' Plus, it would enable her to hide the client's sixty-inch plasma TV, the curse of many a designer.

Freya's phone rang. She answered it with lightning speed, like a modern-day gunslinger. 'Babe!' She was up and out the room without so much as an 'excuse me'.

Don't mind me, Charlotte thought, trying to stand up so she could stretch her legs.

She hobbled over to the large glass doors which led out to the garden. The house was currently of modern design, which suited the layout much better than the latest occupant's suggestions. But who was she to question her client's brief? As the professional, it was up to her to make the scheme work, no matter how conflicting it might be. After all, she'd always enjoyed a challenge. Trying to satisfy a client's wishes whilst pushing the concept to incorporate her own sense of style had always been what had inspired her, what drove her on. So why was it no longer enough?

The view from the window was stunning. The grounds were landscaped and vast. Despite the miserable weather, the garden looked lush and green, a brief reminder of what she'd left behind in Cornwall. She felt another pang of longing.

Resting her hand on the window frame, she reasoned this was only to be expected. It was bound to take a while to readjust to city life. Five weeks really wasn't that long. Her enthusiasm would return soon enough... wouldn't it?

Her GP seemed to think so. When she'd visited him a couple of weeks ago, he'd assured her she was making good progress. Losing the desire to make everything 'just so' was a positive step, he'd said, an indication that she'd finally 'dropped the stick'. The bad news was that this had allowed the grief she'd suppressed for so long to take its place. The sense of loss she was experiencing was only to be expected. But now that she'd 'sunk to the bottom', she'd be able to float back up to the top and sail away down the river stress-free and unbuttoned, ready to live a happy and relaxed life. God, she hoped he was right.

She watched a squirrel scurry across the grass and disappear into the undergrowth.

It didn't help that she was staying in a cheap B&B Lawrence had organised for her, or that she'd been lumbered with Dodgy Roger – whose building skills hadn't improved over the summer – on three separate jobs. There was no doubt about it, Lawrence was paying her back for suing him. Whatever the reason, London life no longer held the same appeal.

'Miss Hughes asked me to pass on a message.' Charlotte turned to find Freya's assistant standing in the lounge looking apologetic. 'She's unable to continue with the meeting, and will need to reschedule.'

'That's unfortunate. Nothing wrong, I hope?'

'No, madam.' The resignation in her words indicated that running around after her demanding employer was a common occurrence. 'I'll show you out.'

Charlotte packed up her mood boards, cursing the thought of another difficult Tube journey with bulky hand luggage and nothing to show for her efforts. Lawrence wouldn't be happy. Nothing she could do about that.

The rain was coming down harder. With no free hand to hold an umbrella, she accepted the inevitability of getting wet, and headed for the Tube station. The traffic was heavy, with vehicles hurtling past, splashing up water, their emissions an assault on her senses. That was another thing she missed about Cornwall, the fresh air.

The Tube was packed, even though it was barely the beginning of the rush hour. She squeezed into a seat, her large holdall banging against her leg every time someone moved past. The atmosphere was steamy and unpleasant, the combination of wet clothes and warm bodies adding to the rancid odour emanating from the gentleman next to her.

She closed her eyes, hoping to transport her mind back to a happy place. Penmullion in the sunshine. The crash of waves lapping the sandy beach filled with holidaymakers, fishing boats bobbing on the water, her niece and nephew building sandcastles. Barney out surfing on the water, his coal-black hair slicked back, his tanned chest unashamedly on display.

She sighed. Lovely as it was, it wasn't enough to ease the stiffness creeping into her shoulders – something that had started almost as soon as she'd returned to London. Apart from the annoyance of physical pain, it served to remind her of Barney's lovely shoulder massages, his dexterous fingers kneading her flesh, creating warmth, relaxing her muscles as his hands...

She opened her eyes. Thinking about Barney Hubble was not helpful. She'd never settle into London life if she kept allowing her mind to drift backwards.

By the time she'd changed trains at Victoria and navigated her way to South Croydon, it was gone six o'clock. She was tired, wet, and miserable. Rain lashed against her as she walked up the hill towards the B&B. Unlike the hill in Penmullion, it wasn't winding and narrow, taking her past quaint cottages, set against a backdrop of lively seagulls and an impressive historic castle. This hill was lined with rows of bland terraced houses, which masked any kind of view, and littered with SUVs parked nose to tail.

She entered the B&B and made her way up to the single room where she'd been staying for the past month. She recalled the sinking feeling she'd felt on entering Lauren's flat and seeing the tired décor and cramped conditions. Ironically, she'd give anything to be back there now, sleeping on the lumpy daybed, having to use a knife to open the kitchen drawer with no handle. Despite its shabbiness, it had been a place filled with love and happiness, a proper family home. Compared to her current abode, it had been a palace.

She dumped her holdall on the dark-red carpeted floor. There was no window in the room, the electric lighting gave it a dungeon-like quality, as though it was situated underground. The view of a snow-capped mountain, painted on the wall and framed with thick curtains, failed to dupe her into believing the room overlooked a pretty Austrian village.

She undid her suit jacket, only to find the top button already undone. She didn't need her GP to tell her this wasn't a good development. Having finally overcome her compulsive behaviour, she couldn't bear the thought of her anxiety returning. But quite how she was going to keep it at bay when she was already fighting off neck pain, she wasn't sure. Covering herself in a bathrobe, she headed into the hallway, only to find the communal bathroom occupied. She returned to her room, forced to use the toilet crammed into what could only be described as a cupboard. Lawrence had gone out of his way to find the most offensive dwelling possible.

Her phone rang. Talk of the devil. 'Hello, Lawrence.'

'Tell me you secured the deal?'

The days of preamble and niceties had gone. 'The meeting was cut short. Something came up, and the client needed to reschedule.'

'When for?'

'We didn't get a chance to discuss alternative dates.'

'Disappointing, Saunders. We need this job.' Another development was the calling of her by her surname. And to think she'd objected when he used to call her Charlie. Now, she'd prefer it. 'If you're not taking care of the customer, the competitor will.'

She rubbed her forehead, aware of a dull ache around her temples. 'Not much I can do when the client cancels, Lawrence.'

'We miss a hundred per cent of the sales we don't ask for, Saunders. You know that.'

She really didn't need a lecture. His endless sales quotes were painful at the best of times. As he prattled on about 'success only occurring when your dreams get bigger than your excuses', she flopped onto the single bed. She was tired, her headache was getting worse, and she was incredibly, heartbreakingly lonely.

She looked up at the stained ceiling. Why was she so unhappy?

But, deep down, she knew. She no longer wanted to strive towards achieving someone else's dream. She wanted her own dream. Dusty had been right: she hadn't been as happy in her old life as she'd imagined. It'd just been safe, a habit, something she'd worked so hard for that admitting it was stressful and challenging and not always rewarding would feel like failure. When her anger had eventually faded, she realised she'd used her argument with Barney as an excuse to run away. She'd been scared.

But Dusty hadn't been right about everything. She'd said Barney would call her when he returned to London, and he never had.

Chapter 33

Saturday, 15 October

Barney had found himself in some strange situations over the years, but watching Nate trying to coax an eight-stone dog into the inflatable rescue boat was right up there. His mate was currently tugging on Bubba's lead, one leg on the rocks, the other still in the rescue boat, as he tried unsuccessfully to save the animal from drowning. But Bubba wasn't cooperating.

'Get his owner in the boat first,' Tony called, trying to keep the vessel steady as another wave hit, sending a spray of water into the air. The sea was getting choppier now the daylight was fading. 'The dog might follow.'

'I'm not leaving him!' The woman flattened herself against the rocks, her love for Bubba the St Bernard preventing her from cooperating with her rescuers.

'We need to get you both in the boat,' Barney shouted across to her, battling to be heard above the crash of waves. 'The tide is coming in.' Realising that the woman wasn't able to climb into the boat unaided, he jumped onto the rock face and held out his hand. 'Come on, I've got you.'

The woman had lived in Penmullion all her life and was

used to the rapid changes of tide, she'd told them. She'd always been careful not to get cut off, but Bubba had got carried away chasing seagulls, and had disobeyed numerous orders to 'heel' – which was how they'd both ended up getting stranded.

Tony had been right. The moment Mrs Bubba climbed into the boat, her dog followed. He jumped from the rocks, and landed on Nate's midriff, causing his mate to stagger backwards, his arms full of St Bernard.

Barney wrapped the woman in a foil rescue blanket, trying not to laugh at Nate's disgruntled expression.

With owner and dog reunited, Tony manoeuvred the inshore rescue boat away from the rocks, and they headed back to dry land. It was the second successful rescue of the day. The first one had called on Barney's medical skills. The swimmer involved had developed something he now knew as 'post-rescue collapse', when a person suffers shock-like symptoms, and needs oxygen to stem a full-blown panic attack. He was certainly learning on his feet. Thankfully, all the boats came equipped with Entonox, so he'd been able to manage her condition with gas and air until the paramedics arrived.

Barney was loving his new life. It was everything he'd hoped it would be... career-wise, at least. His training had included spending two days at the RNLI college in Poole this week, completing his accredited course. He'd learnt all about the equipment and different types of boats in the fleet. They'd also covered safety regulations, lifeguard skills, and tested his fitness levels. He'd had to swim two hundred metres in less than three minutes, and run two hundred metres across the sand in under forty seconds. Thank God surfing had improved his stamina.

It was almost dark by the time they arrived back at base and drew alongside the jetty. The wind had picked up, making the boat unstable. Barney helped the woman onto solid ground, leaving Nate to handle Bubba – who jumped before Nate was ready and ripped the lead from his mate's hand. An unhappy Nate climbed onto the jetty, rubbing his arm and mouthing obscenities at Barney for laughing.

Yep, being back in Penmullion was definitely good for the soul, even if it hadn't eased the constant ache in his chest.

Despite his best efforts, he still pined for Charlotte. He'd hoped that keeping busy might help eradicate her from his mind, but it hadn't worked. There were too many reminders, like seeing her sister all the time. Lauren was a regular at The Mousehole now she and Nate were a couple, and as much as he liked Lauren, it wasn't helping him to forget Charlotte. But he needed to try. She wasn't here anymore, and he had to find a way to get over her and move on.

He glanced up at Morholt Castle silhouetted against the inky sky, his mind drifting back to the summer. The fun and laughter they'd shared, the intimacy and sense of closeness that had developed between them, his hope for a future together. How the hell was he supposed to get over that? It wasn't like you could just decide to stop loving someone.

He helped Tony secure the boat, and made his way up to the boathouse, leaving Nate to deal with the woman and her dog.

Despite only being back in Penmullion for two weeks, it felt like he'd never been away. Nate and Paul had welcomed him like a long-lost brother, and Dusty had coerced him in to playing Mustafa Kit-Kat in the Christmas pantomime. He was probably taking on too much, especially as he started his new job on Monday, but he figured that keeping busy might help him get over Charlotte. Fat chance of that.

He removed his drysuit, and flicked on the kettle. The noticeboard behind was crammed full of photos depicting various rescues over the years. It filled him with a sense of pride to be a part of that tradition now. His love life might be dead in the water, but at least his career was on the up.

No sooner had he poured boiling water into the three mugs than the alarm went off. His first Saturday on the roster was proving to be a busy one.

Tony and Nate hadn't undressed, so they were ready to go quicker than he was. He tugged his drysuit up over his hips, and followed them down to the jetty. 'What have we got?'

'Reports of a woman in a sailing dinghy being dragged out to sea.' Tony jumped into the rescue boat and started the engine. 'The caller said the woman didn't appear to be wearing appropriate sailing gear, and she didn't look in control of the boat.'

Barney fastened his suit. 'Is she drunk?'

'Who knows.' Tony waited until Barney had secured his helmet. 'Take the lead on this one, Barney. Then we can sign you off. Okay?' Without waiting for a reply, Tony gunned the engine and pulled away.

Barney looked across at Nate. 'Great. My final assessment and I get a joyrider.'

Nate grinned. 'Welcome to the colourful life of an RNLI helmsman.'

It served him right for laughing at Nate's attempts to rescue Bubba the dog.

It was now fully dark, the moon providing the only light as they left the bay and ventured into deeper water. The sea was rough, the waves bouncing under the boat, lifting them up and crashing them back down. It wasn't a nice night for sailing. If the woman had capsized, then she wouldn't last long in the water. Time was critical, they needed to get to her as quickly as possible. He'd learnt that as part of his training. No one wanted to drag a body from the water.

Lights came into view as they neared where the boats were moored alongside the harbour wall. He switched on his flashlight. 'You take the port side,' he shouted to Nate, who gave him a thumbs up.

Both their lights skimmed the water, looking for the stranded boat. Tony slowed the engine as they neared where the vessel was last seen. And then he pointed. 'Straight ahead.'

Barney flashed his light to where Tony had directed. Bingo. A small sailing dinghy came into view. It was just like the one Tony owned. It was tilting violently from side to side, the boom swinging about untethered, the hull low in the water, indicating it was taking on water. Logic dictated that if the woman didn't do something soon, the boat was going to capsize.

A gust of wind caught the mainsail, dragging the boat further out to sea. And then Barney spotted the woman. She was clinging hold of the mast, making no attempt to stabilise the boat. What the hell was she doing?

Tony sounded the horn, which made her jump. The dinghy tilted further.

Barney addressed her through the loudspeaker. 'This is the RNLI. Are you experiencing difficulties, miss? Do you require our assistance?'

Nate's searchlight landed on her, and he nudged Tony. 'I think that's your boat.'

Tony drew closer to the stricken vessel. 'Bloody hell, it is.' He peered closer. 'Is that... my daughter?'

Barney looked again, confusion and shock vying for prime position in his brain.

The woman waved frantically. 'Help me!' she yelled, holding onto the mast. 'I need help!'

Barney nearly fell out of the boat. 'Shit!' He staggered to his feet. 'Charlotte? Is that you?'

And then the boat lurched again, momentum sending her one way and then scrabbling back the other.

What the hell? 'Stay where you are,' he called. 'We're coming to get you.'

Neither his brain nor the boat would move quickly enough. It seemed to take forever to reach her. Tony had to slow the engine so the swell didn't tip the sailboat over. Questions filled his brain. Why was she here? What was she doing? But the only words that left his mouth were, 'I didn't know she could sail?' to which Tony responded, 'She can't!'

Chapter 34

… Earlier that evening

Having made the decision to quit Quality Interiors and permanently relocate to Penmullion, Charlotte hadn't known what kind of reception she'd receive when she'd arrived at Lauren's flat earlier that evening. But she needn't have worried. The moment she stepped over the threshold, bodies had appeared from nowhere, letting off party poppers and yelling, '*Surprise!*' Tears had filled her eyes as they'd hugged her and welcomed her home. They were right. Penmullion was home.

Her dad and Nate hadn't been at the flat to greet her, they were on call, which was how she'd discovered that Barney had moved back to Penmullion and was volunteering for the RNLI. She couldn't believe it. Barney was back in Cornwall? Apparently, he didn't know about her return, either. Her friends and family had kept it a secret, figuring she'd like to surprise him herself. It had been a surreal moment; one her brain was still struggling to compute.

Urged on by her friends and family, she'd run from the flat and headed for the quayside, her mind in overdrive. Would Barney be pleased to see her? Would he forgive her for running away? God, she hoped so. It couldn't have been easy for him to admit he didn't want their 'fling' to end. And how had she reacted? She'd thrown his outpouring of love back in his handsome face. It was up to her to make amends. She needed to do something big, a grand gesture that would show him how she felt... because, despite her continued insistence that he was only a temporary distraction, she was head over in heels in love with him.

It was only when she was almost as the quayside and running out of breath that it occurred to her it would have been easier to drive to the boathouse. The shortest route might be across the bay, but she would have arrived sooner if she'd jumped in her car and taken the coastal road. What an idiot. She was obviously too flustered to think straight.

She could see the RNLI boathouse across the other side of the water. However, running across the beach in the dark would be challenging and exhausting. As would running back up the hill to fetch her car. She needed another mode of transport. Maybe she could catch one of the water taxis?

Buoyed by the idea, she crossed the footbridge, her new-found confidence squashing any nervousness at being suspended over water. Her desire to see Barney overrode any fear of falling in. But her enthusiasm took a brief hit when she realised the water taxis were no longer running. What had she been thinking? It was gone seven o'clock on a dismal October evening. Of course the taxis wouldn't be running.

And then she realised she didn't have her handbag with her. Which meant she had no phone. Stupid woman.

Maybe she could persuade someone with a boat to take her across?

She resumed running down the wooden mooring where all the boats were secured.

Adrenaline, excitement and a tad too much Prosecco meant that when she ran past the sailing boat moored alongside her dad's houseboat, she ground to a halt. A flash of inspiration hit.

The tale of Tristan and Isolde filled her head. The romance of Barney looking out from the RNLI boathouse and for him to see the white sails flapping in the wind, an indication that his love was on board and coming home. It was enough to spur her on. It was the perfect gesture. Romantic... daring... dramatic...

And then common sense prevailed. She was not a sailor, she wasn't wearing a life vest, and getting stuck at sea was far from romantic. It was idiotic. She needed another plan.

But her sudden change of direction toppled her off balance and she lost her footing. There was nothing solid to grab hold of, only air, so when she reached out, gravity took over and she found herself falling. It could have been worse; she could have landed in the sea. As it happened, she fell haphazardly into the boat. Pain shot up her legs as her shins banged against the hull. One shoe pinged off, landing in the water. Great. Now she was lopsided.

But she had more pressing things to worry about, like the instability of the boat. Having never been on a sailing dinghy before, the shock of suddenly rocking from side to side almost sent her overboard. She grabbed hold of the boom to steady herself, which tugged on the rope securing the boat to its mooring. Before she knew what was happening, the boat was drifting away from the dock. She tried to grab hold of the jetty, but it was out of reach.

She needed to do something, and quickly. Trying to steady her nerves, she focused on what her dad had instructed the kids to do when she'd watched him teaching Freddie and Florence to sail. *Use the boom to change direction. The centre-board to balance the boat, and the jib to propel the boat forwards*. She also needed the sails up, otherwise she was going nowhere.

Realising the boat wasn't about to stop rocking anytime soon, she tentatively untied the ropes securing the mainsail and watched as billowing white sheeting caught in the wind, expanding like a giant balloon and shooting her forwards. Oh, God. She was making things worse.

The boat was tilting to one side, water was collecting by her feet, and the boom was swinging about like an untethered... well, an untethered boom. Logic told her that if she didn't do something soon the boat was going to capsize, and there was nothing romantic about drowning.

A gust of wind caught the mainsail, dragging the boat out to sea. This was not good.

A flash of light caught her attention. A woman was standing on the deck of one of the moored boats waving a torch, asking if she was okay. No, she was most definitely not okay.

'Help!' Charlotte called, her voice almost lost in the wind.

The woman disappeared inside her boat. Thankfully, she reappeared moments later with a phone attached to her ear. She was getting help. Excellent.

Exhaustion was now a factor. Charlotte's jeans were damp from water spray, she was cold and losing her grip on the tiller as her hands became sore. It therefore didn't register what kind of help was on its way. It was only when she saw the distinctive orange boat and flashing searchlights skimming the water that she realised she was about to be rescued by the RNLI... and there was a good chance Barney would be on board. Not awkward at all.

The sound of a horn made her jump. The dinghy tilted further to one side. She tried to shift her weight to the other side. Jesus, and she'd thought climbing up a tree house was scary.

And then Barney's voice cut through the night air via a loudspeaker. 'This is the RNLI. Are you experiencing difficulties, miss? Do you require our assistance?' The searchlight landed on her.

Using her free hand, she waved, lopsidedly balancing on one shoe. 'Help me!' she yelled. 'I need help!'

'Shit! ...Charlotte? Is that you?' He sounded surprised. She couldn't think why.

The boat lurched again. She struggled to find her footing, the momentum of the waves sending her one way, then scrabbling back the other.

'Stay where you are,' he called. 'We're coming to get you.'

Despite slowing the engine, the sailboat rocked harder as the rescue boat neared. The front end lifted and then dropped, causing her to stagger backwards and lose her other shoe. She wasn't sure how much longer she could hold on.

And then a sudden swirl of wind whipped the boom from her hand. The next thing she knew it was swinging towards her. If she didn't duck soon...

Too late.

A crack to the head. Blackness. Pain.

When her senses returned, she felt the sting of cold sucking air from her lungs. More pain. A rushing in her ears. An inability to move, to breathe, to scream... it was like being in the weir all over again... her life flashing before her, images flickering like old cine-film, memories of Muddy Sunday, her mother, Lauren, her dad... she couldn't lose them, not again...

And then someone grabbed her by the shoulders, dragging her from the water. Her hips banged against something solid, and she was pulled into the inflatable lifeboat. In amongst the trauma of trying to cough up water, a familiar voice penetrated the noise of the boat engine, the wind, and water filling her ears. 'Charlotte! Can you hear me? Look at me.'

A warm hand touched her cheek. She opened her eyes. All she could see was a white helmet and a mass of blue and yellow. Slowly Barney's face came into focus. 'H... h... hello.'

'It's okay. You're safe.' He wrapped her in a large piece of foil, pushing wet hair from her face. 'I can't believe you're really here. I didn't think I'd ever see you again.'

The boat moved beneath her as they bounced across the water, but she no longer felt concerned. Barney had hold of her. She was safe. 'Sorry... for... for... running... away.' Her teeth were chattering so hard she could barely speak.

He pulled her close, something she guessed wasn't in the RNLI training manual. Not unless they encouraged volunteers to cuddle the people they'd rescued. 'That's okay. I'm sorry I didn't warn you about Glenda.'

'I understand why... why you... didn't.' Her whole body was violently shaking, like a malfunctioning washing machine.

He felt the side of her head, where a lump was forming. 'You might have concussion. How many fingers am I holding up?'

She squinted, trying to focus on his hands. 'Four.' He had lovely hands.

'Good. Can you see me okay? Am I in focus?' He looked at her with such concern, she wanted to stay like that forever, in his arms, being caressed… if she wasn't soaked through to the skin.

She was by no means warm, but her jaw was starting to loosen, allowing her to speak through the chattering of her teeth. 'So, you're… you're a volunteer now? That's… that's good.'

He rubbed her back. 'I also have a new job. I'm a medic with the Cornwall Air Ambulance.' His grin told her this was good news. 'I start on Monday.'

Warmth flooded her insides, a contrast to the chill biting her skin. 'Does that mean you're staying in Pen… Penmullion?'

He nodded. 'How lucky am I? I get to live the dream. Surfing, singing, acting, a career that excites me. It took me a while to get there, but I'm finally where I want to be.'

Even in the darkness, she could see the sparkle in his eyes. 'I admire your determination to live a… a life less ordinary.'

'I have you to thank for that. You encouraged me to try something different.' He held onto her when they bounced over a high wave.

'I'm pleased for you.' Her voice was almost lost against the noise of the engine. 'You've got… everything you wanted.'

'Almost.'

Dare she hope?

As the boathouse came into view, she could see Freddie and Florence standing on the jetty with Lauren, flanked by Sylvia and Dusty. They were huddled together looking concerned: they must have been alerted to her antics out at sea. She guessed she'd given them quite a fright. Herself included. She'd always wondered how people got themselves into such dangerous situations, and now she knew the answer. Pure stupidity.

As her dad drew alongside the jetty, the sound of Barney's

voice brought her back to the present. 'Mind your step,' he said, helping her out of the boat.

Her dad pulled her onto the walkway. 'I don't know whether to hug you or shout at you,' he said. 'What were you thinking?'

'I... I'm sorry. I didn't mean to cause so... so much trouble.' Her teeth were still chattering.

'What on earth made you think you could sail a boat?'

She flinched. 'It just sort of... happened. I was at the quay-side... trying to work out how to... to cross the bay when I saw... your sailing dinghy.'

He looked incredulous. 'And you decided to take it? You could've drowned.'

'I realise that now, but I lost... lost my balance and the next thing I knew I was... drifting out to sea. I'm so... sorry.'

He shook his head. 'Never mind, it's over now. Let's get you inside and warmed up.' He led her down the jetty.

Entering the boathouse, she could see that the welcome party had relocated from Lauren's flat. Food was laid out in the kitchen, and balloons were scattered about the floor.

'Give the poor girl room to breathe,' Sylvia said, bustling past. 'She's probably exhausted. Cup of tea, love?'

Dusty appeared, and offered her a large glass of pink Prosecco, towering over her in red knee-high boots. 'This is a party, Sylvia. The woman needs booze.'

Sylvia gasped. 'She nearly drowned.'

'All the more reason to celebrate.' Dusty pinned Charlotte with a look. 'You stole a boat? A little dramatic, darling, even for you.'

Charlotte started coughing, her lungs still full of seawater. 'Dumb, huh?'

Lauren patted her on the back. 'Let's get you out of these wet clothes. Barney says he has something you can wear.'

Freddie ran over, carrying a squashed jam sandwich. 'Try one of my sandwiches, Auntie Charlie. I made them specially.'

'*Es*pecially.' Lauren rolled her eyes. 'And use a napkin, please, Freddie.'

He ran off to fetch one.

Florence hugged her wet aunt. 'I'm *especially* happy you've come back, Auntie Charlie.' She glanced up at her mother. 'Girls are much smarter than boys.'

'Is that so?' Nate picked her up, making her squeal with delight as he carried her around the boathouse. His eyes drifted to Lauren, and they shared a moment, a look laced with love, lust, and a longing to be alone.

Charlotte smiled. 'No need to ask how things are going with Nate.'

Lauren's cheeks coloured. 'We've been on a few dates. So far so good. He's...'

'Lovely? Besotted? Devoted?'

Lauren laughed. 'All of the above.'

'I'm glad to hear it. Not that I doubted for a moment that he wouldn't be,' she said, following her sister upstairs, so she could remove her clothes, which seemed to have glued themselves to her skin.

Fifteen minutes later, she emerged from the shower stench-free and no longer quite so cold. Her head was sore where the boom had hit, but there was no blood. Wrapping herself in a towel, she came out of the bathroom to find dry clothes waiting for her. 'So, what else have I missed while I've been away?'

Lauren handed her a pair of jogging bottoms. 'Glenda's

been sentenced to community service. It was her first offence, and she didn't use violence, so in the scheme of things, she's considered a small-time player.'

'It didn't stop her making your life miserable, though.' Charlotte accepted the offer of Barney's hoodie.

'I know, but thanks to the Proceeds of Sale Act, she's had to return everything I paid her. I felt bad about accepting the original loan money, so I donated it to the RNLI. I'm using the rest to buy the kids bikes for Christmas.'

'Great idea.' Charlotte couldn't be prouder of her sister, who was positively glowing. Love suited her. 'Has there been any backlash?'

Lauren shook her head. 'Everyone's been really supportive. Glenda's talking about moving away, so that'll make life easier. I can't say I'm sorry.'

'Me neither.' Her sister handed her a pair of RNLI yellow wellies. 'Seriously?'

Lauren laughed. 'Sorry, it's all they had.'

Charlotte didn't need a mirror to tell her she looked a mess. Her hair was a riot of wet curls, she was wearing a man's tracksuit, and now she was waddling about in too-big yellow wellies. A few months ago, she would have had a meltdown. Not now... well, not much.

'Ready to rejoin the party?' Lauren linked her arm through her sister's.

As they descended the stairs, Charlotte spotted her dad's tentative expression. He was chatting to Sylvia, his attention switching to his daughters as they neared. 'Is Dad okay about everything?'

'Totally. Plus, now he and Sylvia are officially a couple, his loyalties have been redirected elsewhere.'

As if sensing he was the topic of conversation, he came over and kissed Charlotte's cheek. 'Feeling better, love? You gave us quite a fright.' He looked a little emotional, causing Sylvia to scuttle over and check he was okay.

Charlotte hugged him. 'Much better, thanks. Sorry again for causing so much trouble.'

'Just don't do anything like that again,' he said, trying to look reprimanding. 'The sea is an unforgiving place. Supposing I'd lost you?' His hug tightened, as he rocked her from side to side, just like he'd done when she was a child. 'You're safe, that's the main thing.' And then he pulled away, his expression turning serious. 'I know this probably isn't the time or place, but... well, I... just wanted to say that I'm sorry too.'

'What on earth for? I was the one who nearly capsized a boat.'

'Not about tonight.' He shook his head. 'For not trying harder to bond with you after your mother died. I was so caught up in my own grief, I failed to notice how you were affected by it. By the time I realised, it was too late. I'd lost you.'

Stunned by this sudden outpouring, she took his hand. 'Oh, Dad. Don't say that.'

'It's true.' For a horrible moment, she thought he was going to cry. 'You were always such a mummy's girl. I failed you.'

A lump lodged itself in her throat. It was true that without their mum to balance out the family dynamics, she'd felt like a third wheel. Lauren and her dad had always been so close; they were a team. But she couldn't let him take all the blame. She'd contributed to the situation.

'Hindsight is a wonderful thing, Dad. Isn't that what they say? For example, I now realise that losing my mother at a young age, and feeling distanced from the rest of my family, left me with a deep-seated craving for love, coupled with an inability to express that love.'

'Bloody hell, have you had therapy?' Lauren looked more amused than shocked.

'No, my GP recommended a book on the subject. When you told me you didn't think I'd dealt with Mum's death properly, I thought I'd better look into it.' She shrugged. 'You're not the only one with issues, Dad.'

'But as the adult, I should've stepped up.' He was looking for forgiveness, she realised.

She gave him a quick hug. 'You weren't well. And even if you hadn't been struggling with depression, I'd still have used building a career to avoid dealing with my own grief. It's how I'm programmed. But I now realise that a successful career, with nothing else in your life, isn't enough. I've avoided any meaningful attachments, using excuse after excuse to resist committing. I blamed you both for moving away and leaving me, but emotionally I'd already left *you*, and I'm sorry for that.'

Lauren wiped away a tear. 'Christ, that was some book you read.'

Charlotte hadn't realised that all three of them were crying until Sylvia blew her nose. 'That's so lovely,' she said, dabbing her eyes with her hanky.

Barney appeared dressed in jeans and a T-shirt. 'I need to steal away the guest of honour. She has a head wound that needs assessing.' He took Charlotte's hand and led her into a small lounge area at the front of the boathouse. 'Christ, your hands are cold.' He sat her down on the sofa. 'Are you okay? That was some stunt you pulled.'

She felt her face flush. 'I was trying to be romantic.'

He raised an eyebrow. 'Romantic?'

The heat in her cheeks intensified. 'I was attempting to recreate the story of Tristan and Isolde.'

The sound of his laughter did little to ease her humiliation.

She shrugged. 'As romantic gestures go, it was pretty flawed, but I was trying to make an impact.'

He smiled. 'Mission accomplished. You know, a phone call would've sufficed. You didn't have to drown yourself.'

'I appreciate that now.'

He held eye contact for a moment, before searching in his bag for a light. 'So, I hear I'm not the only one making big life changes?'

She nodded, glad for a change in topic. 'It took me a while, but I realised I no longer wanted my old life.' At some point during one of Lawrence's ramblings about 'being the energy you want to attract', she'd realised her energies no longer lay with Quality Interiors. She wanted a fresh challenge.

He shone a light in her eyes. 'Look up. So, what do you want instead?'

It was a good question, and one she'd spent a good deal of time deliberating over. 'Well, firstly, I want to design the set for the Isolde Players' forthcoming production of *Aladdin*.' When she'd discovered that Flo had been cast as Wishy-Washy and Freddie as Abu, she'd immediately imagined a magical world filled with exotic jewels and a mystical genie. It was a project she definitely wanted to be involved in. Especially now she knew Barney was in the show.

'Look to the left... now right.' He switched off his light. 'Do you feel nauseous?'

She shook her head. 'I also want to spend more time with

my family, have girlie chats with Lauren about her new relationship with Nate, and improve the situation with my dad.' She'd only been gone a few weeks, but she'd missed them all dreadfully.

He felt her pulse. 'Any dizziness?'

She shook her head.

He crouched down in front of her. 'I'm going to hold my finger in front of you. Touch my finger, and then touch the tip of your nose as quickly as possible. Okay?' When she did as he'd asked, he smiled. 'Perfect.' He had a lovely smile.

'I want to live by the sea, walk along the beach at dusk, and hang out with my new friends. I want to take part in the Morholt Festival, and get more involved in community life.' There were so many things she wanted to do. Feeling energised and excited about the future was apparently another sign that her anxiety was under control. Who knew?

Barney's hands gently moved around her skull, feeling for lumps.

'The big news is that I'm going to start up my own business. I figure there must be a need for interior design in Cornwall. Paul's offered me space at the back of his boutique, to use as an office base, and Lauren's insisting I stay with her until I'm settled.'

His hands moved lower, his nimble fingers checking for injuries. 'Sounds like a plan.'

'It's risky, but as I've discovered, taking a risk often comes with huge reward.' She looked right into his eyes, distracting him from his assessment. 'Thank you for pushing me to be more adventurous. Turns out taking risks is good for me.'

He smiled. 'It's good for me too. I get to reap the rewards.'

'I haven't worked out all the details yet, but I'm happy for things to be a bit messy for a while.'

He raised an eyebrow. 'A bit messy? Wow.' He started laughing.

'Shocking, I know.' She studied his handsome face, the way he smiled at her, the love she could see reflected back in his eyes. 'I realised something else while I was in London. I no longer cared whether you were a doctor or a surfing instructor. Being happy is what matters. And people need to work that one out for themselves.' She placed her hand over his. 'Sorry for being judgemental.'

His smile told her she was forgiven.

Spending the summer in Penmullion had made her happier than she'd ever been in her entire life. There had been no defining moment, it had crept up on her, a gradual softening towards the place and its inhabitants. A reluctant romance that had blossomed into a full-blown love affair. And Barney Hubble had been a big part of that.

She squeezed his hand. 'Sometimes the best things in life are those experiences you never expected to have. And the best relationships are the ones that sweep you off your feet and challenge every view you've ever had.'

His expression turned mushy. 'Is that right?'

She nodded.

'So, what happened to being all buttoned-up and wanting the perfect life?' She liked the teasing tone in his voice. Plus, it was a valid question.

'Well... I've learnt to accept that life isn't perfect. And you know what? That's okay, because neither am I.'

He ran his thumb across her cheek. 'You don't have to be perfect to be amazing.'

‘You know what would be perfect? Being with you.’

He smiled. ‘No argument from me.’

The warmth of his lips touching hers was glorious. It wasn’t an ideal setting for rekindling a romance. She was still shivering like an electrocuted turkey, dressed in baggy joggers, and wearing yellow wellies, but it was still the most beautiful moment of her entire existence. When they fell against the sofa, the kiss deepened, his lips warm and soft and bone-meltingly gorgeous. And he didn’t stop kissing her, even when the doors crashed open and the sound of whistling and laughter filled the room.

Let go, her sister had said.

Do something reckless, her sister had said.

And that’s exactly what she intended to do.